A Fraternal

By

Jacobus Rawley

First published in 2018 by:
(Titania Publishing)

© Copyright 2018
(Titania Publishing)

The right of Jacobus Rawling to be identified as the author of this work has been asserted by him in accordance with the Copyright, Designs and Patents Act 1988.

All Rights Reserved
No reproduction, copy or transmission of this publication may be made without written permission. No paragraph of this publication may be reproduced, copied or transmitted save with the written permission or in accordance with the provisions of the Copyright Act 1956 (as amended).

[ISBN: 9780957442191]

Printed and bound in Great Britain by:
Book Printing UK, Remus House, Coltsfoot Drive, Woodston, Peterborough PE2 9BF

Chapter One

Louisa Belle, or Loubelle, as most people called her, ran a small bakery-cum-coffee shop in the centre of Main Street in Harperville, Kentucky. It was popular with early risers like long-haul truckers or law enforcement officers, who generally stopped by for a coffee or one of her famous home-baked fudge brownies. Loubelle also happened to be the repository of most of the town's secrets, not because she made a point of prying into other folks' business, but because people tended to confide in her and she knew when to keep her mouth shut. A 42-year-old divorcee, she was content to remain single and fancy-free, and her only secret vice was that she had a weakness for young men; she usually picked them between the ages of sixteen and twenty-two, the cusp between boyhood and manhood having an especial appeal for her. Robbie Turnbull had caught her eye the previous year when he was still at Senior High and used to come in with a crowd of classmates after school. She found him totally mesmerising. Apart from his obvious physical beauty, much of his appeal lay in his innocence and apparent incorruptibility. No matter how many smutty jokes were bandied about in his hearing, the innuendo was either completely lost on him or he genuinely had no interest in the topics under discussion. His manners were irreproachable, whereas a lot of the kids who frequented the bakery were loud and foul-mouthed. When he had first sauntered up to the counter to ask her whether it would be possible to place an order for "Twelve brownies, three cherry cokes, and three vanilla floats" the request had been accompanied by a heart-stopping smile.

"I think that might just be possible" she drawled. "How old are you, sugar?"

"Eighteen. How old are you?" he shot back at her.

"Old enough to be your mother, sweetie. Would you like those brownies heated up?"

"If it's no extra trouble" he replied, meeting her gaze with the loveliest pair of blue eyes she'd ever seen.

"No extra trouble at all." At this point he seemed overcome by shyness, and focused his gaze on the coffee machine. Loubelle was amused. "I don't bite. Though on second thoughts, you look good enough to eat. I'm only messing with you, hon" she added, seeing his confusion. When he came in the following week with his friends, his gaze occasionally alighted on her as she went about her business. Finally he came up to the counter and asked her name.

"Loubelle. And yours?"

"Robbie. Robbie Turnbull."

"Are you a mother?"

"No."

"Are you married?"

"Was, but not any more."

"Do you like boys?"

"How did you guess?" She knew she shouldn't be having this kind of conversation with a teenager but wanted to know what he would come out with.

"Well, I'm not, I'm not…" He gestured helplessly.

"You're not what?"

"I'm not in that market." Loubelle threw back her head and laughed.

"What market would that be?" He blushed and made as if to move off, but then got up his courage.

"You've got this reputation for seducing boys, but often the things people say in this town aren't true." He glanced over at his sniggering companions. "So I just wanted to check whether it *was* true, and to let you know that I wouldn't hold it against you. But I'm not really available." Another flash of those blue eyes before they wandered around the room again.

"Well, that's a darned shame because I'd snap you up in a heartbeat if you *were* available." She leaned across the counter. "But you're right. People talk a lot of garbage in this town because they've got nothing better to do. I wouldn't listen to any of it, if I were you."

"You're kind of strange." He gave her a slightly reproachful look as though he knew she shouldn't be talking to him like this.

"Does that bother you?"

"Not really. I'm quite strange too." This conversation was getting more fascinating by the minute.

"Oh? In what way?"

"That's for me to know and you to find out." He smiled mischievously, but wouldn't be drawn. That was the first conversation they had had, but her heart had been irretrievably captured in that first moment. Not in an erotic sense: it was more akin to the excitement of discovering a sex symbol or potential screen icon – what the film producer Roger Vadim must have felt when he came across the fifteen-year-old Brigitte Bardot, or the photographer David Conover felt when he stumbled across the nineteen-year-old Norma Jeane working in a munitions factory. She saw him on and off over the next eighteen months, and they got into the habit of exchanging racy banter over the counter of the bakery, but the next really significant encounter took place when Loubelle was walking down Main Street. Robbie came hurtling down the sidewalk in her direction. He wasn't looking where he was going and cannoned straight into her, as she caught him in her arms.

"Slow down. I must say it's flattering to be so invisible…" began Loubelle in a sarcastic tone, and then she saw that he had been crying. At first she thought something really terrible must have happened, such as a bereavement in the family, he looked so choked up. As he didn't seem capable of speaking she led him over to the bakery and hung a "Closed" sign over the door. Then she sat him down at a table and pulled a paper napkin out of the dispenser. He ignored it and instead used the denim sleeve of his jacket to wipe away his tears, like a typical boy. "No-one's died, have they?" she eventually asked. He shook his head. "Then I'm guessing it must be some kind love trouble." As he said nothing she assumed she'd hit the nail on the head. "If you don't want to tell me, sugar, that's fine. You can stay here as long as you like until you feel like facing the world again. But if you do want to tell me I give you my word that nothing you tell me in confidence will pass my lips."

"You wouldn't understand" he said finally, looking up and meeting her eyes.

"Try me. Believe me, I've been around the block a few times and nothing surprises me any more."

"Yeah, but this is different. I can't tell you this."

"You mean you're too embarrassed to tell me, is that it?" He nodded. "OK. Well, why don't we play the hot and cold guessing game. Now, is it girl trouble?"

"Cold."

"Boy trouble?" Loubelle didn't know what made her say that, but she had an unerring instinct for these things. He hesitated.

"Warm."

"So it's not a boy?"

"Not exactly."

"Well, if it's not a boy or a girl you've got me stumped." She thought about his answer for a minute, then rephrased her question.

"Man trouble?"

"Hot" replied Rob in a low voice.

"Now, why am I not surprised? Men cause most of the trouble in this town. Take my ex-husband. I don't miss that sorry sonofabitch one little bit, I can tell you."

"Didn't you love him?" asked Rob, forgetting his own troubles for a moment.

"For all of two minutes. I was a sweet young thing then, didn't know diddly-squat. But back to you. How can I put this – do you prefer guys to gals?" He hesitated.

"Honey, most of us are attracted to both sexes. Seen *Viva Las Vegas*? Presley or Ann-Margret, take your pick. They're both pretty sexy. I'd jump into bed with either of them." Rob actually laughed.

"You're kind of strange. You're not like most other women."

"Didn't you once tell me you were strange too? So, this man trouble you're having…"

"You're sure you won't tell anybody?"

"Cross my heart and hope to die." Rob took a deep breath.

"All right. I've got this crush on a man, and he's a regular guy, I mean he's straight - and I just saw him talking with this girl he used to go out with a few years ago when they were in high school. Only she got married and he went off to Vietnam. I mean the guy *I like* went to Vietnam, not the one she married. Her husband ran off so she's left on her own now. But I know she's still sweet on him, I mean she's sweet on the guy *I like* not on the husband who ran out on her, so I'm scared they might get back together again. Because that's the kind of guy he is, he takes care of people. And I'm so jealous I could die…." He looked as if he were about to burst into tears again.

"Whoa, slow down. So the guy you like is a soldier?"

"Well, not any more. He came home from the war a few months ago." Loubelle contemplated the boy in front of her. This mystery man was starting to sound suspiciously like his older brother Luke, whom everyone knew had served in Vietnam for two years. Luke was well known in the town, and had been involved with Cindy Foster a few years back. Cindy had married a serial screw-up who'd jerked her around, then left her high and dry with two small children and no alimony payments.

"Maybe he's not involved with her, maybe they were just talking, you know?"

"Maybe, but she's quite attractive. She used to lead the cheerleading team at school." Uh oh, thought Loubelle. Definitely sounded like the Cindy she knew.

"Would her name be Cindy by any chance?" Rob looked at her in astonishment, as if she had psychic powers.

"How did you know?"

"I just put two and two together. It's a small town. Robbie, this man – do I know him?" Rob immediately clammed up. "OK. Let's go back to the hot and cold guessing game. He's someone you've known for quite a while."

"Hot."

"In fact, he's someone you've known all your life." Rob looked increasingly uneasy, and bit down hard on his lower lip.

"He used to do lifeguard duty at the pool summer vacations when he was in high school" continued Loubelle. Rob was starting to look really agitated. "This man is about, oh, I don't know, four or five years older than you?" persisted Loubelle.

"Hot."

"Hmm. I think his name begins with L." Rob got up from the table hastily, and Loubelle caught hold of his sleeve. "Now, don't run off. You've never needed a friend more than you need one right now. You've got a crush on your brother, haven't you?" Rob covered his face with his hands. "Oh, sweetheart. Poor baby. And you've been carrying this secret around inside, trying to deal with it all by yourself." Even though she didn't consider herself to be an especially maternal woman, the maternal instinct kicked in now with a vengeance. She gathered him into her arms and he sobbed on her shoulder, clinging to her like a lost child. Her heart completely melted.

"I love him. I'm absolutely crazy about him."

"Oh my sweet lord. That is bad. I mean, not in a sinful or wicked sense. It's...." She was momentarily lost for words. She had never come across anything like this in her life before.

"A lot of people would say it is. The preacher would. Being a homo is bad enough. Which I'm not, I don't think. But wanting to marry your own brother? That's incest, that's terrible. There must be something really wrong with me. Luke would be disgusted if he knew."

"Now hold on a minute, you don't know that. And just because Cindy still holds a torch for your brother doesn't mean he feels the same way. If he'd wanted to get back together with her he'd have done it by now. Luke sounds like a man who knows his own mind, doesn't he?" Rob nodded, beginning to feel a glimmer of hope. "And he might not be disgusted. If he's the kind of guy you think he is, the kind who takes care of people, then he might surprise you." Rob gazed at her naively. "Now don't look at me like that – like I'm Mama Bear. I don't have all the answers, but between us we're going to come up with a campaign strategy."

"How do you mean?"

"Why, how to get your man and keep him, of course." Although she was in many ways a conventional woman – she religiously watched *Peyton Place*, glued to the TV set three afternoons a week, read *True Confessions* and bawled her eyes out at tear-jerkers like *Gone With The Wind* - she also had a strong rebellious streak. In her teens she had hung out with a leather-jacketed "bad boy" just like the one portrayed in *The Wild One* - the type her disapproving parents had persisted in calling a "juvenile delinquent." Then she had developed a crush on another girl at Girl Scout camp, and in the process she'd discovered a few things about herself. She liked thumbing her nose at custom and tradition, flipping the bird at all those nosy parkers and curtain-twitchers passing judgement on others as if they themselves were lily white and pure as the driven snow. Whited sepulchres, she called them. She knew a few things about people in this town that would set tongues wagging. She knew, for instance, that the Principal of Harperville Junior High travelled to Louisville once a month on "business" – business which entailed picking up strange men in bars. He was just bursting to tell someone, and she just happened to be there when he staggered in one morning punch drunk after an all-nighter. He'd confessed everything to her, how he had to travel some distance so his wife would never find out about his double life. Loubelle had not told a soul; she never betrayed anyone's trust.

In her experience homosexual behaviour was a lot more common than most people imagined. It wasn't even that uncommon in the animal kingdom: she'd seen enough barnyard animals of the same sex humping one another to conclude there was nothing unnatural about it. If something occurred in Nature then it followed that it must be natural. Might as well face facts and stop working yourself into a lather about things which were going to go on happening, whether you approved or not. Incest was also a lot more common than most people imagined. But the two of them combined – homosexuality and incest – now that was a lot more rare and out of the ordinary, abnormal if you like. Rob's confession had really affected her. It wasn't a common tale of sordid lust – men groping each other in the stalls of public toilets – it was a proper romance, complete with passion, heartache, longing, forbidden love. She was an old-fashioned romantic, but not naïve enough to be deterred by the cold facts: Mr. Right just happened to be Rob's brother, his own flesh and blood. After listening to this boy pour out his heart to her, Loubelle had decided she would do everything in her power to help him achieve his dream. Why shouldn't he get his man, and why shouldn't they be happy together? Provided the older brother was willing, of course. That had yet to be ascertained. She had nothing against Cindy Foster, who had once cried on her shoulder, confessing she had made the "biggest mistake of her life" in breaking up with Luke. But all's fair in love and war, Loubelle told herself. Cindy had had her crack at Luke Turnbull years ago and blown it. Tough titty.

"Tell me a bit more about your brother. Do you two ever go out together socially?"

"Hardly ever. When he got back from Vietnam, Dad put him to work out at the sawmill, so he's busy most of the time." Rob explained that the Turnbull ranch had been inherited from their grandfather, who sold off most of the livestock back in the 40s and decided to set up a lumber business. This made sound business sense since the family owned acres of forested mountainside, with an abundance of trees such as oak pine, red maple, and coniferous spruce fir. Luke now did the lion's share of the work, and always seemed to be occupied outdoors doing things like digging post-holes for fencing or felling trees with a chainsaw. He was currently building an extension to the log cabin he had erected on the site of the old bunkhouse, which was situated a few hundred yards behind the main family residence and was where the hired hands used to sleep in the old days when it was a working ranch. The cabin had been constructed using rough-hewn logs just like the traditional prairie homesteads, and Luke had moved into it shortly after returning from Vietnam.

"Do you ever help your brother with any of these jobs?" asked Loubelle curiously. Last week Rob had driven out with his father and brother, ostensibly to learn about the family business, but the latter was too busy concentrating on what he was doing to pay him much attention. Rob had spent most of the time gazing in awe at his brother whilst he loaded and unloaded the trucks, tossing heavy logs and planks about as if they were matchsticks. Eager to be useful, Rob had thrown himself into the work, but after a couple of hours his muscles were aching and his hands were blistered. His father and brother kept telling him to "stand clear" just before a tree came crashing down, and he had soon become bored, eventually retreating to the pickup.

"Dad doesn't like me using the chainsaw because of the kickback. Luke's got better control. He's strong as an ox – I've seen him chop down a huge tree one-handed!"

"Yeah, and I bet he eats mancakes for breakfast. And you know what they say about lumberjacks." Rob frowned slightly. He knew when he was being teased. "Listen, I respect an ox's strength when it comes to hauling lumber. But if we're all to bow down and worship muscle, elephants would be sitting on thrones. Why doesn't your Dad trust you? I bet you could do half these things if you tried."

"He calls me a bubblehead, because I get easily distracted. I climbed up on the roof of the bunkhouse to help Luke the other week, and he wouldn't let me do anything until he'd roped me to the chimney." Loubelle thought it sounded like his father and brother both babied him too much. No wonder his confidence levels were low.

"So when was it you first started to have these feelings for him?" asked Loubelle. "Was it before or after he returned from Vietnam?"

"It's been going on for quite a while" Rob said finally. "Maybe since I was about fourteen or fifteen, but I didn't know what it was then. I think I've always been kind of crazy about him." The morning Luke had left, Rob had hung back whilst his brother said his goodbyes to his parents, because he didn't want Luke to see his eyes brimming with tears and to think that he was some pathetic cry-baby. It had finally sunk in that he was not going to see Luke for a very long time, and he felt desolate, bereft. "What, no hug?" Luke had asked, as Rob stared at the ground wretchedly. But Luke had seemed to know how he was feeling and had pulled him into a close embrace, holding Rob's head against his shirtfront. Another tight squeeze, a valedictory wave, and then he was gone. Rob had moped around for weeks, taking no pleasure in any of his previous pursuits. It was around this time he had started getting into trouble at school and with the law. In his senior year at high school he had become involved in illegal drag racing on a quarter mile dirt drag strip situated out of town, until the Sheriff got wind of what was going on and put a stop to it. Once a car had barrel-rolled just before the finishing line, and the driver had been seriously injured.

The first time Luke phoned home, Rob had been inexplicably tongue-tied, unable to think of anything to say when his mother handed him the receiver, except for dumb questions like "How many people have you shot?"

"Oh, Rob, can't you think of something else to say?" his mother had chided him gently, as he heard Luke's laughter at the end of the line, which had broken the ice.

"Don't hit anyone else on my account, will you" Luke had teased. "Stay out of trouble."

"*You* stay out of trouble" Rob had retorted, with something of his old spirit. "You're the badass gorilla running around the jungle with a machine gun…" He had heard news presenters talk about "guerrilla warfare" on the TV, and imagined a bunch of American GIs swinging from trees in the jungle like Orang-utans.

"Gorilla, huh?" Luke had laughed again with that familiar, deep-throated laugh Rob loved. "Christ, I miss you. Keep on sending me those screwball letters, I love reading them." And then – all too soon - it was time to say goodbye.

"Goodbye, Luke. I love you."

"Right back at you. See you soon, kiddo."

"Mmmm. That is weird " mused Loubelle, interrupting his thoughts. "Because if he'd been away for a while I can see how you might relate to him as a complete stranger. But it sounds like you fell for him when you were seeing him every day – you were even living in the same house then, right?" She had a brother and sister herself but couldn't imagine harbouring those kind of feelings for either of them. Truth be told, it made her feel pukey just thinking about it.

"Yeah, his bedroom was just down the hall. He was yelling out in his sleep most nights, and it would wake everyone up. It was his idea to move out." Hearing his brother shout out one night, Rob had gone into his bedroom and shaken him by the shoulder. He'd been knocked clear across the room, landing against the wall. Luckily, his shoulder had taken the brunt of the impact, and not his head. Luke had woken immediately, and was kneeling by his side, cradling him.

"I'm sorry. Jesus, I'm so sorry. I could have cracked your skull open…" Luke felt him all over to check for broken bones.

"I'm OK" Rob reassured him. They were both holding each other. "I'd rather be hit by you than kissed by anyone else." Luke raised his eyebrows.

"Why are you so sweet to me when I'm such a bastard?"

"You didn't mean to. I guess you thought you were fighting off the enemy."

"Probably. But I'm scared stiff I'm gonna punch my own mother by accident – what if she'd come in here and I'd knocked her out?"

The following morning over breakfast, Luke announced that he would be starting work on the bunkhouse, joking that one casualty of war in the household was enough. They had some fun together demolishing the existing structure, armed with sledgehammers and a crowbar. As Luke had slammed his shoulder into the walls like a human battering ram, Rob had cheered him on, laughing manically.

"Is your brother ever violent or aggressive?"

"He can be. I mean, he was a platoon commander and he killed people when he was over there. But he's never been violent towards me."

"Not ever? He's never bullied you or been mean to you, like big brothers can be?" Rob shook his head.

"No. When we were wrestling or fighting, he never hurt me. Though he could have done, if he'd wanted to."

"Well, that's a relief. I wouldn't want you to get hurt. Flirting can be dangerous with the wrong guy who takes it the wrong way, or believes his masculinity is being threatened. That's why so many men beat up on fags." She took hold of Rob's hands across the table. "Here's what we're going to do. We're going to draw up a plan of action. Can you come over one evening?" He looked slightly wary as if she had proposed to seduce him.

"Relax, hon. Despite what you've heard, I don't molest boys. I'm going to teach you how to seduce Luke and make him fall for you." Now she really had his interest.

"You can do that?"

"I can't give you any absolute guarantees. That sort of depends on what we're dealing with, what kind of guy he is. But we're going to treat this like a military campaign. After all, this is a serious game, the game of love. Your brother is not going to know what's hit him. I don't care how macho and invincible he thinks he is."

"That's Luke all right." Rob smiled. "He's just like Wyatt Earp."

"All men have their weak spots" said Loubelle dismissively. "You just need to know some basic techniques and to build up your confidence. Will you stop looking at me like a scared rabbit! I am not going to tear your clothes off. You've got to trust me."

"OK" said Rob. "I'll come over. I'm not scared of you. I'm quite tough, you know."

"Babe, you had me fooled. How about this Friday night?"

****

"I hope you haven't compromised my reputation, Robbie Turnbull" said Loubelle, as she opened the door and pulled him inside. She ushered him into her apartment, which was strewn with throw rugs, cushions and magazines. There was a stack of *True Confessions* on the coffee table, featuring the most lurid and sensational "true" stories. "Did anyone see you come here?"

"Nope." Rob had arranged to meet some of his friends over at the bowling alley, then made his excuses and slipped out the back exit. "The guys will just think I had a hot date with someone."

"That's what I'm worried about! I can just picture the gossip. Older experienced woman taking advantage of naïve young boy. And you can stop grinning like that. You boys don't have to worry about *your* reputation. When a woman's reputation goes down, the man's reputation goes up, like a damned seesaw. I don't suppose that ever occurred to you?" Rob was far too polite to mention that Loubelle already had a somewhat compromised reputation amongst his male companions, all of whom would love to be in his shoes right now.

"Take a load off, while I fix us something to eat." She shoved him unceremoniously into an armchair.

"Hey!" protested Rob. Loubelle thought he was possibly the most desirable young male to ever cross her threshold. She ran her eyes over him covertly: slim build, average height, narrow-hipped and straight-limbed, thick dark hair with a tendency to curl, clear blue eyes fringed with long dark eyelashes, flawless skin, finely chiselled features with a full sensuous mouth, a taut well-toned body without an ounce of superfluous flesh. He was what girls called a dish - pin-up material – pure perfection encased in jeans and denim jacket, but there was nothing effeminate about him. He was all boy, into boyish pursuits like hunting, fishing, climbing trees, roaming the mountains, fast cars, risk-taking behaviour. But he was not yet conscious of his sex appeal, of the latent power he wielded. When she'd finished teaching this seductive Man Child the stuff he needed to know, he'd be absolute dynamite. No woman or man would be safe in his vicinity.

"Have a look through those magazines. They're mostly trash, but I've marked the relevant stuff." Rob flicked through the magazines idly, grinning at some of the titles:

How to Get Your Man and Leave Him Smitten
Why Must our Love Wait? With so much Wild, Sweet Wanting...
Mr. Right – Searching for the One
I Caught my Brother and Sister in Bed
My Scandalous Little Sister – She's up to no Good!
Teacher's Pet – Hot for the Teacher
High School Horror, Secret Shame

He started to read a story entitled *The Stranger from out of Town*:

"I was a spoilt rich Daddy's girl. I thought I had everything I wanted. But when HE showed up, and strange things – terrible things – started happening around our town, I somehow knew he was responsible. But I couldn't keep away from him. Those snatched stolen kisses had lit something in me, like a burning fire I couldn't extinguish. Daddy hated his guts, said he was no good trash, and that I should keep away from him. But every night I sneaked out my bedroom window, and hurried to our illicit midnight meetings. I just couldn't help myself, I loved him to distraction..."

Rob rather liked this last phrase; it described how he felt about his brother. He smiled up at Loubelle, as she placed a bowl of tortilla chips and salsa dip on the table. "Did you cook those yourself?"

"Those are store-bought, wiseass, straight from a packet. The last thing I need is more slaving over a hot stove when I close up for the evening. I've got a pizza heating in the oven - is that to your satisfaction?"

"Yes, ma'am" Rob suppressed a smile, and helped himself to some chips. "Maybe I should read this one" he suggested, pointing to the article entitled *How to Get Your Man and Leave Him Smitten*, which she had ringed with a red pen.

"Good choice. I've already done some research on seduction techniques, which we'll go through later. OK, let's get down to business." She picked up some sheets of paper, on which she had scribbled notes under various headings. "We'll start with *How to Approach a Man*. What do you do when your brother walks into a room?"

"I guess I just say Hi, unless he's been gone for a long time. When he came back from Vietnam we hugged."

"Well, that is pitiful. You need to be doing more than that. Eye contact is very important. You need to let him know you're interested. The message you want to get across to your brother is that you find him desirable. What is it you want to say to him?" Rob looked embarrassed. "Come on, don't be shy. Pretend to be somebody else, say Liz Taylor in *Cat on a Tin Roof* trying to seduce that self-centred sonofabitch called Brick she's married to. Who incidentally happens to be hung up on his dead buddy. Now look at me the way you would really like to look at your brother, if you had the nerve. Pretend I'm Luke."

"I can't do that" protested Rob "He's think I'm nuts."

"Doesn't matter what he thinks. You're sending a signal to his brain, which he's going to pick up on. What you say with your body is far more powerful than words."

"That's good to know because I'm not much good with words."

"Look, 90 per cent of it is body language, and you've got what really counts – looks, the most amazing eyes. Flaunt those assets of yours, honey. Now give me a lingering look that says *I want to go to bed with you*." Rob composed himself, before picturing his brother walking into a room. It was embarrassing, but he was determined to give this stuff a go.

"Hold it. Hold that for a few more seconds. Don't look away just yet. Now that was powerful. I got that message loud and clear. I'm not saying he's going to leap on you or fall for your charms overnight. It takes time. At this stage, all you're doing is establishing a connection, getting him to notice you in a different way. See what works best, a special smile, a look or a touch." She then told him to go look in a mirror and practice the look so that he could see the effect for himself.

"What if other people in the room see me looking at him like that?"

"Do it when no-one else is around; that way you can get his full attention. Let's move on to the other look – it's called the French technique because the French are really good at this. Look into his eyes deeply. The minute he looks back you look away or lower your eyes and come over all shy. Repeat this a second time, looking at him a little longer. Try it." Rob tried it a few times before Loubelle stopped him.

"You're doing it way too fast. You don't flip your eyes up and away like that – makes you look like some crazy just out of the loony bin." She snorted, feeling a belly laugh coming on. "The best way to learn is to watch the big stars in action – have you seen *To Have and Have Not* with Lauren Bacall and Humphrey Bogart?" Rob shook his head. He hadn't seen half the movies she mentioned. Loubelle seemed to know everything there was to know about Hollywood and screen icons.

"Jeez, you kids live in a cultural vacuum. Bacall is famous for the Look. And it worked because she and Bogie fell in love on the set and got together in real life."

"Yeah, but she's a woman. I bet Bogart wouldn't have fallen for it if another guy tried it on with him. He'd have smacked him in the jaw."

"Maybe. But I don't want you to try that one out until your brother's shown some initial interest. You have to build up to it."

"How?"

"Well, you could try touching him, but don't be too obvious. Brush against his sleeve. His arm or shoulder is a good one." Rob didn't mention that he already did that sometimes, when he could work up the courage. "Touch him casually when you're talking to him. This creates a physical connection between you and communicates on a subconscious level you want to be more than just brothers." Rob listened, absorbing what she said. It all sounded quite thrilling, but scary. "Or you could pick some fluff off his jacket or straighten his tie."

"He hardly ever wears a tie. Is something burning?" he enquired innocently.

"Oh, shoot." Loubelle rushed over to the oven, flung open the door, and started fanning the smoke. "Burnt to a crisp. Honey, I'm sorry – I should have kept an eye on it. What if I fix you a sandwich or something?"

"That's OK" said Rob, taking another handful of chips. "I'm not starving."

"You're such a sweetheart." She tousled his hair. "Where did we get to? Ask him for a light, and lean your elbow on his arm when he lights your cigarette for you. You should watch that scene between Bacall and Bogart." Rob thought she had been watching too many movies. It was OK for a girl to act like that, but Luke would just be puzzled and probably wonder why he couldn't light his own cigarette. "Or hold his hand when you're walking beside him...."

"He'll think I'm a real sissy boy" protested Rob.

"Well, I'm sorry, sweetie, but red-blooded males like girly types. You know that song Marilyn Monroe sings in *Some Like It Hot: I wanna be loved by you, just you. And nobody else but you. Boo-boo-be-doo*. I mean, how does a grown woman get away with acting and sounding like a two-year-old? But you wouldn't believe how many guys drool over that, they just lap it up." Rob scowled.

"I'm not going to do those stupid girly things. I'm a boy!"

"I had noticed, darling. But if your brother just sees you as another guy, nothing's going to happen. You've got to flip that switch in his brain that makes him see you differently. Be mysterious and playful. Be unpredictable, keep him guessing. The point of this is to get his attention, to get him to really notice you. But do NOT throw yourself at him. You don't want to come across as trashy or clingy."

"I'm not trashy or clingy!" Rob defended himself sulkily. He was starting to feel the whole thing was demeaning.

"Don't take it so personally. This article is directed at women who flop down and act like doormats, then wonder why guys walk all over them. You've got to be willing to take a few risks. That means you have to be bold enough to break the rules. Because, let's face it, you've already broken the biggest taboo there is. We're talking incest here…between brothers no less. Most people would find that pretty shocking. If you're serious about taking this further, you can't chicken out now. In fact, I think you should tell him how you feel."

"I can't. I just can't. I'd rather die."

"In that case, we might as well call a halt to this whole thing right here and now." Loubelle gave him a stern look. "Wishing and hoping won't get you anywhere. Fortune favours the bold – ever heard that? If you want something really bad then you have to go out and grab the bull by the horns." She saw that she had his attention, so expanded on the bull metaphor. "Those bullfighters in Spain and Mexico, they don't go into the ring like greenhorns, they've spent years honing their skills. They know what they're doing, otherwise they'd end up badly gored. Now, a lot of the tips and advice in these magazines is pure hogwash so you can ignore most of it, like the stuff about sexy lingerie." Rob looked positively outraged. "Skip all that, ditto for hair and makeup. But how about this one: *How to Kiss Him by Accident*."

"What, my mouth just happens to land on his, and he doesn't notice?" Rob giggled. "That's stupid." Loubelle started to giggle too.

"That is ridiculous" She agreed. "But it says here you're supposed to do it when you're both drunk. If he questions it afterward, just play innocent and say you can't remember what happened the other night you were so loaded."

"Sounds sneaky to me. Besides, Luke isn't that dumb. He never misses a thing."

"OK, forget that one. I agree it's not too subtle. I can't see a classy lady like Bacall doing that. Oh, but how about this: *Wet and bite your lips*. That's a sign of arousal. An experienced guy, and I take it he's a lot more experienced than you in the bedroom department, will pick up on it immediately. Go on, try it. Oh Robbie, that is so seductive!"

"I'm not sure about this stuff" said Rob uneasily. What on earth would Luke think if he did pick up on it? "Am I supposed to do this lip-biting thing at the same time I give him the Look? Which do I do first?" Loubelle started to laugh helplessly.

"I'm sorry for laughing, you're just so innocent. Now let's back up a bit and take it one step at a time. Your idea of combining it with the Look is great. A double whammy, but I think you should probably save that for Phase Two."

"What was Phase One? I've forgotten." Loubelle continued to laugh.

"Phase One is about getting his attention, making him feel special. Let him do most of the talking and just listen. Men love that because they've got egos the size of the Empire State building. Or just admire his biceps or something. Men are so hung up on their physiques it's not true. They're honestly not bothered if they've got a brain the size of a pea. And then while he's droning on about how wonderful he is…"

"You're making him sound like some boring big-headed jock. Luke doesn't talk about himself that much. He hardly ever talks about Vietnam, for instance."

"Well, he dated a cheerleader in high school didn't he? Let's recap: Phase One is where you get him to notice you by giving him lingering looks, smiles, or whatever. Then if you feel that he's responding you move on to Phase Two which is a lot more intense, it's about creating sexual tension."

"But what if he doesn't respond or he gets mad, what then?"

"We'll cross that bridge when we come to it" she told him. "I have full confidence in your ability to charm him. But you need to practice the technique *now* just in case things start to move faster than you expected. In the game of love, things can happen in the blink of an eye." She snapped her fingers. "A girl can end up pregnant before she even knows what's happening."

"No danger of that happening to me" muttered Rob.

"That's where you have a big advantage over a female. You can flirt all you want without having to worry about getting knocked up. When I was ten I asked my friend's big sister how she got pregnant, and she said it was because she walked down a dark alley, so I spent my entire childhood avoiding dark alleys. I wouldn't even ride my bike through one, nossir." Rob grinned. "Now I want you to practice giving me that look you gave me a while ago, and at the same time bite down on your lower lip, sort of chew it. WOW! Robbie, that was sexy as all get out."

"Really?"

"Really. Go over there to the mirror and see for yourself." Rob sauntered over to a mirror hanging on the opposite wall, and practiced a few times until it looked and felt a little more natural. "Well, what do you think?" Rob shrugged.

"I'll have to try it out on him to see if it has any effect."

"I'm pretty darned sure it will have an effect" said Loubelle. "Oh, and while you're over there, would you mind posing in the door-frame?"

"Huh?"

"Don't act dumb, Robbie Turnbull. You've got the most gorgeous body and you can't help but be aware of it. Why do you think girls are always chasing your tail? I've seen the way they look at you. Now, men and women pose in different ways because they're trying to flaunt different assets. Did you see Liz Taylor lounging around in that sexy white satin slip in *Cat on a Hot Tin Roof*, showing off her 22" inch waist and her tits, even if that husband of hers was too busy feeling sorry for himself to notice? Paul Newman can act the most convincing brick wall I've ever seen. And did you see Brigitte Bardot dancing around barefoot in *And God Created Woman* so that every male in the room could appreciate her curves?" Rob was starting to feel depressed.

"How am I supposed to compete with *that*? Seeing as I don't have any curves. And don't want any" he added.

"Do you think Brando was flaunting his curves in *A Streetcar Named Desire*? Of course not" she went on, not waiting for an answer. "He was making the most of his male attributes. Same applies to Jimmy Dean or Elvis. And if you think guys aren't attracted to sexy guys or women aren't attracted to sexy women, then you don't know anything. Someone with *real* sex appeal will appeal to both sexes. Most people swing both ways; it's just that nobody wants to admit up to it. If Luke's a red-blooded male, and you start flirting with him he's not going to know what's hit him. Trust me, most guys respond to certain clear signals, and if you give out those signals you're going to get his attention real fast." It sounded too good to be true. Rob just hoped she was right.

"How should I pose?" Loubelle considered him, head to one side.

"Take off your jacket. Now stretch both arms above your head and grasp hold of the top of the doorframe. Slow and sensual does it. You can use porch rafters, a tree branch at the right height, whatever is handy." As Rob obeyed her instructions Loubelle came up to him and placed a hand on his upper arm. "Good muscle tone. You don't have to have biceps like cannon balls to have an attractive male body. Flaunt your natural assets." Gorgeous abs too, she thought, having caught a glimpse when his T-shirt rode up. "Now sway back and forth ever so slightly on one heel, not so that you're rocking like some retard. It's a very subtle movement to show off your hips and pelvis." She stood back a few paces to get the full effect. "That is a real turn-on, believe me. I'm just about ready to rip your clothes off." Rob blushed. "You can add a little spice to that pose by doing a pelvic thrust. Not a full-on Presley gyration, just a very slight thrust. Wear tight jeans if you're going to do that." Rob released his grip on the doorframe. He was starting to feel too exposed, like a nude model on display.

"And blushing is good. It's another sign of arousal, like biting your lip."

"You can't make yourself blush any more than you can make yourself sneeze" pointed out Rob. "With me, blushing is nothing to do with arousal, it's embarrassment. I wish I could stop it from happening."

"But it's charming, whether you realise it or not. Guys absolutely love it when they can see you're embarrassed or shy because of something they've said or done. Makes them feel powerful. If you find yourself blushing when he's talking to you, don't try to hide it, OK?"

"OK" said Rob uncertainly.

"Back to male poses. The full body one which I just showed you, where you stretch your arms out to the side or above your head, is the most effective. The Head and Shoulders pose draws attention to the upper body. Remember what I said about body language. With guys it's all visual, what they see in front of them. If you were a cowboy you'd stand broadside to a cow or horse, and sling your arms across its back, arms folded. And whoever is standing on the opposite side gets a close-up of your shoulders, upper arms and that face of yours, which is your best asset." She looked around the apartment. "Seeing as we don't have any chest-high props in here, we might have to get creative. Help me stand this couch on its end. OK, now you stand behind it facing me. Rest your elbows on the top, and give me that direct look. Hold it right there." She was starting to feel like she was a film producer with her protégé, but the effect was mesmerising. She suspected he was extremely photogenic, and wished she had a camera to hand.

"So next time Luke is lounging around watching TV I just casually tip the couch on its end, and do my pose?" He grinned at her.

"All right, smartass. It's got to look natural. What I suggest for your prop is the roof of a car – is that your red Chevy convertible you've got parked outside?"

"It's Luke's. He lets me borrow it when I want." And I bet you're one of those boy racers who tops the speed limit every time you get behind the wheel, she thought.

"So you wait for a moment when you're both standing on opposite sides of the car. Then you go for the killer pose, at the same time attracting his attention by…"

"Blowing him a kiss and shouting *Hey, Handsome*"

"I can see you're taking this seriously. Mind if I ask you something personal?" He looked slightly guarded, but shrugged. "Have you ever done it with a female?" His answer was direct and surprising.

"Of course. Did you think I was a virgin?"

"And did you like it?"

"Yeah. What guy doesn't?" Loubelle was astonished.

"Robbie, if that's true, then none of this is making much sense. What you're telling me is that you're basically straight, you've screwed girls, and then all of a sudden you develop this massive crush on your brother?"

"Basically, yeah. I thought I was normal. I dated girls in high school but then something happened to me when Luke got back from Vietnam. I started to fall for him, and it messed me up. I don't know what's normal any more." The maternal instinct kicked in again, and she had to resist a strong urge to take him in her arms and comfort him.

"No wonder you're confused. But sex is different from love. You were never in love with a girl?"

"No. That's how I know this is for real."

"Tell me about some of your dates." Rob cast his mind back. He remembered being chased by some of the girls in his class, who would come to call for him on the front porch. Often he'd make a discreet exit out the back door, much to Luke's amusement. But there had been one or two pretty ones who'd caught his eye. After pursuing one girl, she'd agreed to a date, and things were fine for a while.

"I went out with this girl for a few months. But sometimes she'd blow me off and cancel a date because she said she was washing her hair. That used to bug me. I mean, how long does it take to wash your hair? I hate it when girls do that."

"She was on her period, Robbie. You do know what that is?"

"Of course. We got sex education at school. Girls have periods, boys have wet dreams, and if you get a chancre it means you've got VD..." At the onset of puberty, Rob had become curious about sex and had approached the sixteen-year-old Luke, who was lounging on the porch swing, for further enlightenment.

"We learned about sex today in Human Biology" announced Rob, kicking at Luke's foot with the toe of his sneaker in order to get his attention.

"Yeah? So what?"

"You know when a man gets an erection?"

"A boner? Sure, I know all about it, little brother."

"Well, what causes it to stick out?" Luke took a swig from a bottle of Dr. Pepper, and resumed his leisurely perusal of *Playboy* magazine.

"It's to do with blood flow" said Luke vaguely, who thought his brother was still confused about the mechanics of erection. "The brain sends a signal to your balls so your sperm factory goes into production, and you're all ready for action. And if the girl's ready too, she could have a baby." Rob had found this simplistic explanation unsatisfactory. It didn't answer any of his questions.

"But it can't just be to do with making babies, because Bruce said guys get a hard-on all the time, even when they're asleep. What causes the brain to send a signal?"

"When you see a pussy, you get turned on. Simple." Rob gazed at him. He still didn't quite get it.

"Why?" he persisted. Luke ignored him, and Rob gave him another kick. "Luke, how come it gets hard… "

"-I'll give you hard in a minute" warned Luke. "With my boot up your ass if you don't quit bugging me. Now beat it, I'm trying to concentrate." Rob withdrew his sneaker and turned away, disappointed.

"I guess you don't know the answer yourself, because you're too dumb."

"What, you want a live demonstration or something?" Luke grinned. "Put a dime in the slot and out comes my cock? It just happens naturally when you think about sex."

"I've been thinking about it since we saw that sex education film, and it hasn't happened to me!" Luke laughed.

"Maybe you're abnormal, maybe you'll grow a pair of titties and turn into a girl. You're certainly pretty enough." Rob gave him a sulky look. "Hey, come on. You're too young, that's all. Your body's not ready yet."

Acting on a sudden impulse, Rob had leapt on top of him so that the swing lurched violently. That had galvanised Luke into action. He grabbed hold of Rob and dragged him down onto the yard in front of the porch, where they could wrestle without anyone tripping over them. They rarely wrestled any more since Luke didn't consider his twelve-year old kid brother to be a worthy opponent, and Rob missed the physical intimacy – the way their limbs became entangled and the way Luke bore down on him relentlessly. It excited him and left him breathless, hot and tingling all over. When Luke held him down, he sometimes used to pretend to himself that they were a newly wed couple on their honeymoon. He told no-one about these secret fantasies, and kept them to himself. Later the same day Luke had picked up a peach from a fruit bowl on the dining room sideboard, and beckoned to Rob. He slit it in half with a knife, and placed one half in Rob's hand.

"See that? That's what a pussy feels like. Juicy. And when you slide your dick in it tightens and fits around you like a glove." Rob stared at the peach stupidly, still not getting it.

"I don't feel anyth…" He gasped as Luke suddenly cupped his groin and squeezed gently, before removing his hand. Rob got it, his body thrilling under Luke's casual touch.

"Bet you felt something then, huh? Those films don't tell you shit." Rob would never have dared to touch his brother intimately like that, but Luke considered he was entitled to take such liberties, being older. He had always found Luke sexy, he now reflected, even when he was too young to really know what the word meant. His brother gave off some kind of animal magnetism, and most of Rob's friends agreed that Luke was by far the sexiest guy amongst the seniors. Girls obviously thought so too, because they never told him to get lost or to "drop dead" when he sauntered over to tease them.

"Sounds to me like the sex education left out all the really important stuff" commented Loubelle. "Like how insecure and embarrassed teenagers are over the most silly things. When I was sixteen I was really sweet on this boy. But if I happened to get a spot before a date – just one tiny little zit – I'd lock myself in my bedroom and wouldn't let him see me. Now when a girl has her period she finds it embarrassing, so she'll say she's washing her hair because she doesn't want to spell it out, especially in front of a boy she's really keen on."

"Oh."

"Is that all you can say? Oh?" Rob gazed at her naively.

"Well, how was I supposed to know?"

"Tell me about some more of your dates. This could be very entertaining."

"OK this one is another hair related thing. I went over to pick up this girl and her kid sister comes running out *'She's not ready yet!'* like it's a Thanksgiving turkey in the oven that has to cook some more. So I hang about outside for about twenty minutes, bored shitless, then I decide to take a peek round the back through her bedroom window…" Loubelle was giggling. "She was hooked up to this thing with a long tube attached to – well, it looked like a suitcase. She had a swimming cap on, and she looked really weird, like an alien from outer space." Loubelle shook with laughter.

"Oh Robbie. That was a hair-dryer. They come in little vanity cases. Surely you've seen ladies down at the beauty parlour."

"Well, it made me kinda nervous."

"And that put you off girls?"

"No. It didn't put me off. But I never was interested enough to go out with them for long." Faced with an avalanche of female attention he didn't know how to handle, Rob had eventually come up with a stock response when he was sixteen: "Sorry, but I'm not available." Of course, this only made girls chase after him all the more. It intrigued them. Why was he being so mysterious? Why wasn't he available? Who was he seeing?

"And Luke is your first love?"

"My one and only" said Rob, becoming deadly serious. "He's the only one for me." He looked at the floor. "Will you help me?"

"Yes, but you've got to do your homework. I want you to put into practice what you've learned tonight. We'll meet again next Friday when I expect you to give me a progress report. Then I can see where you're going wrong, what you're doing right. Understood?" He nodded. He had complete faith in her ability, her greater experience and knowledge, and trusted her to know what to do. She was a woman, after all, and women knew about these things.

Loubelle watched from a window as he got into the car and pulled away from the kerb, before zooming off into the night with a screech of tires. Uh-huh, just as I thought. Watch your speed, kid. You don't want to end up in the county morgue. She kicked off her shoes and put her feet up on the coffee table, then lit up a filtered Kool and blew contemplative smoke rings at the ceiling. There was no personal gain to be had from the audacious enterprise she had embarked on, unless it was the satisfaction of bringing a pet project to fruition. Robbie was her project. Their campaign might prove successful, or it might not. In which case he was in for a rough ride if his secret passion ever came to light. She had seen what happened to those of a certain persuasion, who could not control where their inclinations led them. They either ended up in a secure psychiatric facility pumped full of drugs, or as victims of violent crime – lying in a dark alleyway somewhere in a pool of their own blood. This kid really did not deserve what society had in store for those who didn't play by the rules.

Chapter Two

Later that evening, Rob came up to his brother and held out his hand, which Luke took in his own unthinkingly. His warm fingers became entangled in Luke's. "I like you. You're a nice fella."

"Uh, I like you too" returned Luke, caught completely off guard. Rob gave him the sweetest smile ever. It was almost as though he was coming on to him. But then his brother was like that, reflected Luke. He couldn't help flirting with whoever was in his radar. It was the reason people were irresistibly drawn to him. His mother had always said Rob should have been a film star and that he belonged in Hollywood.

"Luke, the Doc said it might help if I wrote down my feelings and my dreams so he could analyse them."

"I guess that wouldn't do any harm" replied Luke vaguely. His brother had recently been referred to a psychiatrist for his violent mood swings, and been prescribed medication which was supposed to control some of the more severe manifestations.

"So I've left you a note under your pillow. I guess you won't want to know me after you've read it. Goodnight." Rob embraced him very warmly, and Luke's arms tightened around him. This was so unexpected he didn't know what to say.

"Don't be absurd" replied Luke. "Of course I'll still want to know you." Back at the bunkhouse, Luke found the note folded underneath his pillow. The handwriting was shaky, and the words had been inked out in places as if Rob had changed his mind several times about what he wanted to say.

Dear Luke,

This is hard so I'll just come out and say it. I don't know how it happened and I wish it hadn't, but I think I'm in love with you. Maybe the doctor will be able to fix it, but I don't think so. I hope you won't feel disgusted when you read this, but it's not my fault and I've tried not to. Nothing is working. If you don't want to speak to me ever again I will understand but....(here two or three sentence had been crossed out) *I can't think of anything else to say except I love you with all my heart. Rob*

When Luke had returned from Vietnam, he and Rob had initially been shy with each other. Then Luke had held out his arms, and Rob had run into them, confessing "I missed you like crazy." As Rob's arms tightened around him, he had felt a surge of affection for his younger brother, and perhaps something a little more illicit as Rob clung to him. Most of the hugs Luke gave or received tended to be quick upper body clinches, but Rob had a habit of pressing his entire body against him and holding the embrace for just a heartbeat too long. Despite himself, Luke had felt himself respond – it was like a jolt of electricity centred around his solar plexus and settling in his groin. It wasn't an unpleasant sensation, just unsettling. He had stood there, squeezing him tight, until Rob finally took a step backwards, then Luke had turned his attention to his parents who were eager to hear of his experiences. He was just as eager to forget them and return to normality, whatever that was.

He had completed two tours of duty in Vietnam, having enlisted in 1965. He had welcomed the punishing physical fitness regime, the advanced weapons training and jungle warfare techniques – all designed to help them survive when they were parachuted into the field from Cobra choppers. Luke was a good fighter, and very strong. He was a quick learner, but not a natural killer so some of the training went against the grain. The rules of engagement were simple. Eliminate the enemy before he eliminates you. Be cold and ruthless. Don't show any sympathy, even if it's a helpless woman bawling her eyes out with a toddler slung over her back. She might have been sent out there to lure you into a booby trap. A wailing child has been purposely placed there to get your sympathy and put you off your guard: ignore it and proceed to your target. Focus on your mission. All this was drilled into them during basic training, as they practised their bayoneting techniques on life-size dummies, dressed like Vietnamese peasants. Luke's instincts towards those he considered to be vulnerable were essentially protective, not predatory: he was capable of great tenderness and compassion but none of these qualities were desired or valued by the army. Where possible they rooted it out. Despite this, the military authorities evidently liked what they saw, and he was rapidly promoted through the ranks, from platoon sergeant to platoon leader. As platoon leader, his responsibilities included planning and supervising tactical operations, maintaining morale and discipline, and doing whatever was necessary to get the mission completed.

In the initial two to three weeks when he had taken command of his squad, Luke was regarded as just another *fanoogie* (fucking new guy) on the army's strict twelve months rotation policy where relatively inexperienced platoon leaders were given sole charge for a period of six months, after which they were likely to be pulled out to command another unit. Although it was intended to reduce the burnout factor, the policy didn't exactly encourage cohesion, when experience in the field and camaraderie was what bonded men to their leaders. Luke's stature and muscular physique gave him a considerable advantage and most of the men respected him. He soon acquired a reputation for toughness, and no-one messed with him. When he issued an order he expected to be obeyed, and came down hard on those who smirked or shirked, but he didn't harass or bully subordinates. He tended to ignore minor infractions, conserving his energy for the more important conflicts. He could handle himself all right and didn't crack under pressure, he didn't get involved in brawls or take unnecessary risks by leading his men on gung-ho power-trips in order to win medals or get his picture in the papers. In short, he was the kind of man the military couldn't wait to get their hands on. He had a great future ahead of him, he was assured, when he was finally given his discharge papers. There were various career paths open to him: he could even apply to Army Special Forces if he chose, acquire expertise in more "extreme" types of warfare. Luke had politely declined the offer. Thanks buddy, but no thanks.

As the war escalated and more draftees started to join the enlisted ranks, a number of men were resentful and discontented. They didn't want to be fighting an increasingly unpopular war, and they sure as hell didn't like being disciplined, especially the ones who most needed it. Incidents of fragging were becoming more common, where rogue elements deliberately killed their superior officers for no other reason than they had been disciplined for dereliction of duty or had their jungle juice confiscated. It was a crime that was easy to conceal and the perpetrator frequently walked away scot-free. Once exploded, a hand grenade left no traceable ballistic evidence, and in a combat situation it could always be deemed an "accident" or blamed on the enemy. No matter how strong you were or handy with your fists it was no protection against a grenade casually tossed into your bunker under cover of darkness. The ever-present threat of fragging further undermined morale, eroding the trust which should exist amongst the men and their leaders, and he was always on the lookout for signs of insubordination or mutiny, watching his men as closely as he watched for the real enemy. After seven months on tour Luke was starting to feel the strain. He was by nature strong, but he'd seen many strong men go under. He rarely relaxed and didn't sleep much. His body was on constant high alert, flooded with adrenaline.

There were also periodic flare-ups due to racial tensions between white and African American soldiers who didn't always work well together. The lack of trust and resentment on both sides could reach flashpoint in seconds. Most of the men were fine with fighting alongside whomever they found themselves with, but some of the white boys south of the Mason-Dixon line were not too happy about it, and made their feelings plain. All it took for a fight to erupt was a muttered comment such as *"Wouldn't trust one of them damn niggers. Knife you in the back as soon as look at you"* which would provoke a resentful *"Wouldn't trust your pale cracker-ass none either, Honky."* One of the black draftees considered it to be a "white man's war" and didn't see why he should be there in the first place, and was given to paranoid mutterings along the lines of *"They just want to kill as many of our black asses as possible 'cos we're expendable, man. That's why they sent us out here."* Which would be met by a taunt from one of the white boys. *"Aw, you're breaking my heart. Boo hoo. Thought y'all would be used to the jungle by now, Sambo."* And so it went on – back and forth – like a game of ping-pong. Luke did not normally intervene in these verbal slanging matches – regarding it as a pointless expenditure of energy – and only stepped in when an argument was in danger of escalating into real violence. After all, they were supposed to be fighting the enemy, and not each other.

Some of the disciplinary issues arose in the field during active combat duty, and he was forced to take action before a situation escalated out of control. One such incident involved a Southerner from Louisiana called Billy, built like brick shithouse, who was prone to outbreaks of violence and had a horror of snakes. They were settling down for the evening after a difficult and tense afternoon hacking their way through dense jungle and swampy terrain when a yellow-banded krait slithered across Billy's sleeping bag. Billy leapt three feet into the air and let out a screech fit to wake the dead. He went after the snake and caught it, then went into a stabbing frenzy. *"Gottcha! That'll teach you, you little motherfucker. Always sneaking up on a fella so he can't get no sleep."* Shortly after that one of the grunts decided it might be entertaining to put a snake in Billy's sleeping bag, only it wasn't a real one, just something fashioned out of some wet socks knotted together. He got the reaction he wanted from Billy, who went totally berserk. Next thing Luke knew Billy was tearing into the prankster, really pounding him into the ground. *"Think that's funny do you?"* PUNCH. *"Is this funny? HowZAT?"* PUNCH. *"I've had it with you, man."* PUNCH. Luke had to haul him off before he did some serious damage. The medic was called over to patch up the other grunt, whilst Luke pulled Billy aside. He never publicly reprimanded a soldier, since this could cause him to lose face in front of his peers, thereby affecting group morale. It was his job to keep his unit tight and cohesive.

"Any more outbreaks like that, and I will thrash the living daylights out of you."

"Huh?" From Billy's point of view the other guy was in the wrong, and he'd just done them all a big favour by killing the snake. He'd eliminated the "enemy" as he'd been trained to do - the enemy, in his eyes, being any cold-blooded reptile that crossed his path.

"I'm not talking about the goddam snake. I'm talking about the assault on a fellow soldier. This guy is not your enemy, we're on the same side, remember? If PFC Rockwell turns out be incapacitated and unfit for active duty due to your actions you're in some serious shit. Consider your position, soldier. With your hollering you've alerted the real enemy to our location, you have endangered the lives of every man in this unit. You've compromised the entire mission. You stupid fuck."

"HE fucking started it! He…"

"I'm aware of that. Shut up when I'm talking to you. I'll deal with Rockwell when the medic's finished patching him up."

"Yessir." Billy made to move off. "But I killed that critter. I did it for the platoon. It coulda bitten any of us."

"You think killing one has made a damn bit of difference? There are thousands of 'em crawling all over the place in case you hadn't noticed. Think you'd be used to the swamp wildlife. From Louisiana aren't you - bayou country?"

"Yeah, but you gotta admit, sir, I got him good, didn't I?" He sneaked a sly look at Luke to ascertain whether he'd retained his sense of humour. The situation was so absurd Luke almost laughed out loud.

"You did." He turned away, concealing a smile. "Kill as many snakes as you want, Private Ballantine" said Luke over his shoulder as he walked off. "But maintain silence at all times." Luke wasn't taking any chances, and had the men set up Claymore mines as perimeter defences, using C-4 explosive rigged to fire when a wire was tripped. Only two days after this incident one of the men had fallen into a booby-trapped pit full of highly venomous snakes during a dawn patrol. They had hauled him out within seconds, but despite their best efforts the anti-venom administered was not sufficient to counteract the neurotoxic and haemotoxic effects on blood cells and human tissue from a dozen different species of snakes. After working on him for a few minutes, during which he never regained consciousness, the medic shook his head. A moment's inattention had cost him his life. This had a bad effect on everyone. Luke had ordered the pit to be fired before they moved off, and they all watched the writhing mass of black shapes turn to ashes. No one played any more pranks like that. It wasn't a joking matter.

Luke read Rob's note twice then folded it up again slowly. He took a deep breath and remained still for a few moments, thinking over the implications of what he had just read. He had been aware for some time that his younger brother looked up to him and admired him, but this was something altogether different. *"I think I'm in love with you."* What exactly did he mean? There wasn't really any ambiguity about the statement. It was a heartfelt confession of love, expressed very simply and directly. What kind of love? Was it sexual? Romantic? Or just the confused rambling of a boy who was possibly mentally disturbed? His next question was how long had Rob felt like this? Those questions would have to remain unanswered for the time being. He wasn't sure what he should do with Rob's love-letter. It was not something he could leave lying around, nor did he want to destroy it. Eventually he made a slit on the inside of his belt with a razor and folded the note and slipped it into the pocket he had just made. Then he lay down on his bed, arms folded beneath his head. He didn't get much sleep that night.

The next morning, Rob refused to leave his room. "He hasn't had any breakfast, and he's shaking like a leaf" said his mother worriedly, in response to Luke's queries. "I think he's having one of his panic attacks." Rob had experienced his first panic attack at school, when the Principal announced that a classmate would not be returning that semester because his older brother had been killed in action in Vietnam. "They shipped him home in a body bag" someone had whispered. Rob had not been sure what a body bag looked like but he imagined it to be something like a zippered sleeping bag containing a corpse. The thought of something happening to his older brother filled him with dread and anxiety. He had started to shake uncontrollably during study period that afternoon. His heart was pounding, and he began to hyperventilate. The female teacher supervising had pulled him out of class and taken him to be examined by the school nurse before calling his parents.

"Maybe I should go talk to him" Luke suggested. His mother put a hand on his arm.

"Better not, Luke. Please don't be hurt by this because I'm sure he doesn't mean it, but he absolutely refuses to leave his room while you're in the house. You boys haven't had a fight or something?" She looked at him anxiously.

"We never fight. You know that." They were interrupted by his father walking into the kitchen.

"Now, Connie, I know he's not well but I don't want you pandering to his moods. I'm taking him in to see the doctor this morning. We're going to knock this thing on the head. Luke, I may need your help, buddy." He turned towards the stairs.

"Joe, you can't use force on him" protested their mother, catching hold of her husband. "It will only frighten him, and upset him further…"

"I'm sorry, hon, but it's not fair on you to have to deal with this alone when Luke and I both have work to do out at the sawmill. That boy needs help and I'm going to make sure he gets it. Luke, come with me."

"Just give me a few minutes with him, will you?" said Luke. His father looked exasperated, but agreed to wait downstairs in the kitchen with his wife. Luke didn't knock on Rob's door in case he bolted it, but walked straight into his bedroom. Rob looked up like a startled deer and backed up against the closet. Luke went over to him and took him in his arms. It was clear to Luke that his mother was right and that his brother was having some kind of panic attack. He was finding it difficult to breathe, his heart was racing, and he was trembling uncontrollably. It took about ten minutes to get him to calm down and for the physiological symptoms to subside, but Luke was infinitely patient: it was like soothing and gentling a panicked colt.

"I'm sorry, Luke…"

"Nothing to be sorry about. It's all right, it's not the end of the world, is it?" His mother knocked on the door. "Yeah, just a minute" replied Luke. He turned back to his brother. "Hey, that was the sweetest Valentine anyone's ever given me, and it's not even Valentine's Day." Rob looked at him wonderingly.

"You're not disgusted?"

"Well, I won't lie, I didn't see that coming" Luke admitted. "If nothing else, it shows you've got good taste." He was making light of the situation in order to put Rob at his ease, and stop him from panicking again. He grinned, then became serious. "Now listen, Mom and Dad want you to see the therapist. He'll probably just give you some pills to get the shaking under control. I'll be right here when you get back, OK? Everything will be fine."

****

"So, how are these, uh, therapy sessions going?" Luke asked, as the waitress set down a coca-cola float for Rob. They were sitting at a table at Henderson's drugstore on Main Street, Luke having just picked his brother up from the clinic he attended on a weekly basis. Rob stirred the vanilla ice cream into the cola and watched it fizz.

"I don't know. He said he thought Mom might be a little over-protective. I told him that was a crock of shit and that she's the best mother in the whole world."

"Time well spent then" commented Luke, lighting up a cigarette.

"The Doc said my problem might be to do with pheromones."

"Say what?"

"You know, those chemical secretions that cause animals to mate. He said that people can fall in love because they get a whiff of your armpits." Luke looked sceptical.

"I was stuck in the Vietnamese jungle for months on end with a bunch of guys who were so rank-smelling they could knock the enemy dead at ten paces, no other weapons required. I didn't fall in love with any of 'em, I can assure you."

"It's meant to be a man woman thing, each sex has their own pheromones. But occasionally the signals get messed up, and men get attracted to men and women get attracted to women. Even women would get into bed with Marilyn Monroe because she gave off this scent that drove everybody wild. And she never wore underwear."

"Is that what the Doc's been telling you? He sounds like some kind of pervert."

"No, Loubelle told me that – she has a thing about Marilyn Monroe. But he got me thinking… there might be something in it. I like the way you smell sometimes, especially when you're all hot and sweaty. It turns me on." Luke darted a hunted look around the room, numbering the potential eavesdroppers. Fortunately the place was half-empty, with a handful of old-timers chewing the fat and young kids flicking through the dirty magazines on the magazine rack.

"I'm not sure that I believe this" said Luke finally. He leaned back against the dividing wall between their booth and the adjacent one, and scrutinised Rob for a moment. "Are you playing some kind of game with me?" Rob shook his head. He wished now he hadn't told Luke how he felt – it was clearly embarrassing him.

"What don't you believe?" asked Rob. "That it could all just be down to biology?"

"No. What I don't believe is that some guy being hot and sweaty turns you on."

"I didn't say *some guy*, I said you. I don't find it sexy in other guys." Luke lowered his voice and leaned forward across the table.

"I'm your *brother* for Chrissake."

"I can't explain it" said Rob miserably. "That's why I'm seeing a shrink." He picked up the sugar dispenser and poured some onto the table, as if he didn't quite know what he was doing. His hand was trembling slightly. Luke took it out of his hand gently. The waitress came up to their table.

"Can I get you anything else?" Rob shook his head.

 "Nothing for me. But he'll have a pheromone milkshake." Her brow furrowed slightly.

"I'm sorry but we don't have those here. We have vanilla, banana, chocolate, strawberry…"

"Ah, he's just messing with you" said Luke "Pay no mind, darlin'. You can refill my coffee, if you'd be so kind." She poured Luke another coffee.

"The Doc also said I was being overshadowed by you" offered Rob "so I couldn't develop properly at my own pace."

"He sounds like a regular Einstein" remarked Luke. "I like the way this joker tries to pin this whole thing on our mother. You and I are not buying that horseshit, so he then tries to drag me into it. In what way am I stopping you from developing?"

"You're a hard act to follow, Mister." Luke had a very commanding physical presence, which tended to have an emasculating effect on other males in close physical proximity. He was the type who always got served first at a crowded bar – bartenders always noticed him – and Rob had seen him dominate social gatherings without having to utter a single word.

"I'm flattered. But you don't need to follow in my footsteps, little brother. You can blaze your own trail. You possess natural assets I don't have."

"What assets?" asked Rob curiously. Luke raised his eyebrows.

"If you don't know I'm not going to tell you" teased Luke "Don't want it going to your head, or you might have me completely at your mercy. Have you never been in love before?" he asked suddenly.

"Once" confessed Rob. "When I did a school project on outlaws and the Wild West I fell in love with Wyatt Earp. He was the toughest frontier Marshall in the West and the last man standing at the gun fight at the OK Corral."

"Sometimes I don't know whether to take you seriously or not, kiddo." Luke signalled for the bill, leaving a tip on the table. "So does this shrink have any other bright ideas?" Rob hesitated. They were standing on the sidewalk outside the drugstore.

"He said that some homos are being treated with something called aversion therapy."

"What the hell's that?"

"They show you pictures of guys with no clothes on, and they make you drink something to make you throw up. Or they give you electric shocks."

"What?" Luke turned to stare at him. "Did I just hear right? The sonofabitch threatened to hook you up to the mains?" Luke started off down the street in the direction of the clinic from which Rob had emerged half an hour ago.

"Luke, if you try anything he'll call the cops and you'll get charged for assault." Rob took hold of his arm nervously. His brother could be quite scary at times. Luke slowed his pace.

"Let me handle this. I'm not stupid – I don't want this business all over town. But I think I'll have a little talk with this guy. I want you to wait outside in the car, OK?"

"Yessir." Rob gave him a mock salute.

Dr. Albert Gottschald was writing up his notes from a series of taped interviews with Rob Turnbull, a half-smoked cigarette burning in the ashtray on his desk.

Subject, aged 20, has trouble distinguishing fantasy from reality, and suffers from severe mood swings. Has been diagnosed with attention deficit disorder and finds it difficult to concentrate for sustained periods of time. Mother fixation. Overprotective parents who will not allow the boy to grow up. Domineering forceful father. Subject hero-worships older brother, aged 25, with whom he claims to be in love.

Albert chewed the cap of his pen thoughtfully. But hero worship was not the same as infatuation. And there was not a lot else he could say about the older brother at this point in time, as he had not had an opportunity to study him at close quarters.

Subject has had intercourse with opposite sex. Claims he is not homosexual and that his brother is the only man he has ever been attracted to. Subject must be mistaken or confused. A perceptual misidentification.

Dr. Gottschald paused again. But what if he was telling the truth? What if this boy genuinely thought he had a crush on his brother, then this would be one of the strangest cases he had ever dealt with. If he were to publish a paper it could establish his reputation. The intercom on his phone buzzed.

"There's a Mr. Luke Turnbull in reception requesting an immediate interview, sir" the receptionist informed him. "He doesn't have an appointment and I told him that you had no available slots this afternoon, but he was most insistent." Albert hesitated. He had been on the point of taking a half hour lunch break before his next consultation, but an informal interview with the subject's brother seemed too good an opportunity to miss. It might afford him valuable insights, and would certainly provide a different perspective. He could spare the man about twenty minutes, he decided.

"Send him in." Albert looked up as a tall, powerfully built man entered the room and extended his hand. Luke clearly took after his father in terms of physical stature. Albert estimated him to be at least six-foot-four, well above average height. At five foot ten, Rob was a respectable height for a young man, but his older brother had a good six inches on him. Both sons were good-looking with the same dark hair and blue eyes as their mother, but Luke had a more pronounced brow ridge - making his eyes seem darker - and a more defined angular jaw line, giving him a more masculine appearance.

"Luke Turnbull." Albert shook his hand cordially. His grip was very strong and firm, as Albert had known it would be.

"Ah yes. I am Dr. Albert Gottschald, and I'm treating your younger brother for a number of emotional and behavioural disorders. Please take a seat, Mr Turnbull. What can I do for you?"

"I'd like you to tell me more about the kind of treatment you're giving him, and what you think might have caused this, uh, difficulty he's having."

"An interesting case. Very interesting. Before we go into that… what do *you* think your brother's difficulty might be?" He deliberately used the same term Luke had used. "What is your understanding of the situation?" Luke looked at him for a moment. He didn't much care for his question being met with another question, but he supposed some basic preliminaries were necessary before they could cut to the chase.

"Anything we discuss in this office is strictly confidential, right?"

"Of course." Albert reassured him.

"OK. Rob thinks he's in love with me. He hasn't told my parents, who have no idea why his moods have been so up and down lately."

"Do you believe that he is in love with you?"

"What I believe doesn't matter. What Rob believes is what counts. Have you ever come across this kind of thing before?"

"I confess that I have not. It is exceedingly rare. Homosexual incest of this nature does not occur between brothers or sisters, or at least it has rarely been documented."

"Rob and I are not an incestuous relationship" said Luke "I'd like to make that perfectly clear."

"How would you describe it?" Luke shrugged.

"He told me he a had a crush on me."

"How do you feel about that?"

"I can live with it. This town probably couldn't live with it, and that includes my old man. My mother would just pretend it's not happening."

"I must say, you're being remarkably casual about the whole affair."

"Casual?"

"Broadminded, I mean. I recently came across a case in a neighbouring county - a seventeen-year-old who had been referred to me by his mother. His father and brother found out about his homosexuality, and he was very badly beaten. He ran away from home and has not been seen since." Luke gritted his teeth.

"Sounds like they're the ones with the problems." Albert eyed him appraisingly.

"My sentiments entirely. You're heterosexual, I assume?" Luke disregarded this question. He was fairly guarded and didn't give much away, Albert noted.

"I'm not here to discuss me. If it hasn't been documented and you've never come across it before, how do you intend to treat it?" Albert went on to explain that the only cases of incest he had come across were between father and daughter, or brother and sister - where the male took advantage of a vulnerable female relative - or where a brother or sister became fixated on a sibling because there was no other outlet for his/her emotions and pent-up desires. Usually it was a clear-cut case of molestation or rape, motivated by lust and not by any romantic feelings. Familiarity tends to breed contempt, or at least indifference, which was why incest occurred so seldom within the intimate confines of family. In the normal course of things people tend to fall in love with a stranger, and not someone seen on a daily basis. Incestuous relationships did, however, occur quite frequently amongst cousins because there was a greater emotional and physical distance. If it weren't for the kinship ties, incest between cousins was no different to ordinary relations between the sexes.

"Yeah, I know all that" said Luke with an impatient gesture. "Rob tells me you discussed something called aversion therapy. What's your take on that?" Dr. Gottschald steepled his fingers and rested his chin on his fingertips.

"Aversion therapy is a *voluntary* course of treatment, which is sometimes recommended for homosexuals who would prefer to be heterosexual."

"What's the point of giving an electric shock to a guy who thinks he's in love with another guy? What does it achieve?"

"Much behaviour is learned, that is to say socially conditioned. Now if we are able associate a certain kind of behaviour, say sexual promiscuity, with something unpleasant, the subject will soon learn to modify his behaviour in order to avoid unpleasant consequences. The classic case was pioneered by Pavlov who used a neural stimulus to trigger a response in dogs, who salivate whenever they see food-"

"My brother is not a dog, nor is he interested in having sex with men." Luke cut him off in mid-flow. "So showing him pictures of naked guys would be a complete waste of time. According to this shit theory, he could be cured by showing him a photo of me, whilst getting him to puke his guts out. That's what you're saying, man, isn't it?" For the first time, Albert felt discomfited. Put like that, it did sound absurd.

"Of course it's highly doubtful he could be conditioned to feel an aversion for his own brother, where there is genuine affection based on strong familial ties. And we would not consider that to be a desirable outcome."

"Then why mention it to the kid in the first place - were you trying to scare him or something?" Albert noted that he had referred to his brother as a "kid." If he had not known there was only a four and half years age difference between them, he would have estimated the age gap as being much greater, with Rob looking no older than sixteen.

"It was mentioned in the context of available treatments, which your brother had enquired about."

"So you can't fix this is what you're saying?"

"It's quite possible we will not be able to "fix" it. It may be a phase he'll grow out of. He may meet a woman some day with whom he falls in love, or another man for that matter, and the situation will resolve itself naturally. But as things stand, being infatuated with your own brother is not socially acceptable and could lead to further psychiatric problems. Your brother is already starting to exhibit classic symptoms of borderline schizophrenia." Albert was on familiar territory now, and proceeded with greater confidence. "Loss of contact with reality is a hallmark of schizophrenia, together with a sense of disconnection from the world. Another symptom is disordered thinking: concentration and focus is difficult."

"What's the treatment you recommend?"

"We use drugs designed to target neurotransmitter function: mood stabilisers like lithium, anti-psychotics such as Thorazine, anti-depressants and tranquillisers."

"What kind of side-effects do they have?" enquired Luke. He leaned back in the chair with his hands clasped behind his head as he scrutinised Albert, trying to get the measure of the man, to get a fix on his character.

"We're not exactly sure at this stage" admitted Albert carefully. He was well aware that some of these drugs could alter the chemistry of the brain, but thought it best not to mention that to Rob's brother.

"I've heard the Thorazine Shuffle is the latest dance craze over at the county asylum. Keeping them in a zombified state must make the job a lot easier for the nurses and doctors. Tell me, Doc" said Luke in a conversational tone "Do you still perform lobotomies? You personally, I mean?" Luke seemed remarkably well informed for a layman. Albert got the impression he was a lot smarter than he at first seemed. He suddenly realised that Luke was interviewing him, and not the other way round. He was checking him out, assessing his responses to Luke's questions.

"We are not living in the Dark Ages" said Albert, adopting what he hoped was a reassuringly avuncular tone. "The procedure is still performed, but only in drastic cases, and has largely fallen out of favour since drugs are far more effective. But it would be totally inappropriate in a case like your brother's."

"Not only would it be inappropriate. Rob has a family who looks out for him, and would not permit – *under any circumstances* – the kind of procedures you've mentioned." Albert stirred uneasily in his seat. Although Luke remained perfectly composed, the underlying menace was palpable. He sensed that Luke would be a dangerous man to cross.

"Can I make it perfectly clear that I personally do not resort to such extreme measures, nor do I consider them to be effective. I am a psychiatrist not a clinical psychologist, and I am seeing your brother on an outpatient basis. He is unlikely to be sectioned unless he proves to be a danger to himself or others. The course of treatment I would prescribe for your brother involves extensive counselling, ongoing individual therapy that will enable him to identify and address gender and relationship issues. Obviously group therapy would not be advisable, given the private nature of the problem. In combination with that I would prescribe sedatives as and when I felt they were necessary for depression, panic attacks and so on to calm him down."

"OK. Carry on, Doc, with your diagnosis, if you've arrived at one."

"Well, I'm afraid these cases are not always easy to diagnose without extensive analysis. But in my professional opinion, he suffers from bipolar disorder. Formerly known as manic-depression, the medical profession regard this as a biological brain condition with a genetic basis, which involves disturbed brain chemistry - in common with schizophrenia, which has very similar symptoms. The disorder usually manifests in late adolescence or early adulthood, the peak age of onset being the mid-twenties. While a stressful event may trigger an episode, often the mood swings are inexplicable, bearing no apparent relation to what is happening in a person's life. The "manic" pole is often associated with outrageous or flamboyant behaviour, characterised by an irritable mood with increased energy, delusions of grandeur, distractibility, impulsiveness, poor judgement, recklessness, questionable sexual behaviour and so on. A person experiencing a manic episode will be highly excitable, on a "high", and in extreme cases delusions or hallucinations can occur. The opposite pole - where the subject will often withdraw socially and be unable to connect with others, is characterised by depression, pessimism, a feeling of hopelessness, worthlessness or inappropriate guilt, problems in concentrating or making decisions, lethargy, recurrent thoughts of suicide or death." Luke listened with interest. Some of it did seem to describe Rob's mercurial moods.

"I once had a client who was struggling with bipolar for twelve years, cycling between mania and depression" continued Dr. Gottschald. "During manic episodes he would be outrageous and pick fights with people; at one point his behaviour led to his arrest on charges of disturbing the peace. During his depressed phases we would see the complete opposite - a lack of interest in previously enjoyable pursuits, the apathy and listlessness which accompanies clinical depression."

"All right. Let's say my brother has this condition. What could have caused it? Is it connected with his feelings towards me?"

"It may have triggered an existing predisposition. Where there is an internal conflict, for instance where a strong societal taboo is being violated - as in your brother's case - the continued suppression of one's true desires can lead to organic disease. The cause of schizophrenia is unknown, but the current medical view is that environmental factors combine with a genetic vulnerability to trigger the disorder: in the case of schizophrenia, taking leave of one's mind is perceived as the only means of escape from the conflict ...the psyche finds the solution in a world of non-reality."

"Rob's not crazy. He knows what's real and what isn't."

"That is your opinion. Your brother's obsession with notorious outlaws such as Jesse and Frank James, Billy the Kid and so on means that he has trouble distinguishing fantasy from reality. He claims to have watched hundreds of Westerns on TV."

"My dad has a thing about Westerns, and we all used to watch them together on TV."

"Your brother tells me that as children you acted out scenes from the lives of outlaws, and that you still sometimes do this - a phase he should have grown out of." Luke shrugged.

"He's kind of young for his age. But I don't see the harm in it."

"Ordinarily no, but your brother is so emotionally involved with this role-play he is losing touch with reality. He is apt to confuse you with Frank James or Wyatt Earp, for instance. These historical characters have become more real to him than his contemporary peer group, and have assumed a significance which may be stunting his emotional development and growth as an individual."

"I don't see that. His teachers couldn't get him interested in class work, so one of them suggested he do a project on something he *was* interested in." During the period Luke was in Vietnam, Rob had found it increasingly difficult to concentrate and flatly refused to do his homework. He started acting up in class, was sassy and gave a lot of lip to teachers, until a female member of staff had taken a personal interest in him and suggested he do a project on the Wild West. "Rob discovered that Frank James was born in 1843, Jesse in 1847. I was born in 1943 and Rob in 1947. Just a coincidence, but he likes to make out we're the James brothers reborn a hundred years later."

"A simple association or coincidence can take on enormous significance in someone whose ability to filter data is impaired. The limbic system of the brain acts as a filter, and many scientists suspect that this area is impaired with schizophrenia. It has been compared to a switchboard operator failing to sort and direct incoming calls. We are all bombarded with a multitude of sensory information on a daily basis, but most people are able to filter out what is unimportant so as to keep from being overwhelmed and going mad. The function of dopamine, for instance, is to enable us to focus and pay attention to events in our environment which could pose an actual danger. However when the brain is flooded with an excess of this chemical, all kinds of things suddenly acquire an importance, and everyday occurrences or meaningless coincidences take on new meaning. The current medical view is that bipolar disorder is a brain disorder involving some kind of neurotransmitter dysfunction."

"Uh, you've lost me there."

"Neurotransmitters are the brain's chemical messengers that enable communication between cells. Both serotonin and dopamine deficiencies are characterised by different kinds of depression: with low serotonin it is the negative variety: suicidal thoughts, sleep problems, agitation, anxiety, anger, and all forms of fear from worry to panic attacks. With low dopamine it is the flat type: the sufferer is tired and can't concentrate, and their vitality is compromised. A deficiency of endorphins results in vulnerability and hypersensitivity …they are emotionally exposed, raw."

"Yeah, he's pretty sensitive" conceded Luke "But we're all wired differently, right?"

"Your brother sees the world in terms of black and white, with no in-betweens. I would not normally breach patient/doctor confidentiality" continued Albert "but since you are a close relative, I am going to tell you something which I think you need to know."

"I'm listening."

"I believe your brother to be a serious suicide risk. Last week he said …" Albert consulted his notes, found what he was looking for, and read aloud: *"The day Luke marries will be the day I die. Everything will go black and the world will come to an end for me."* He looked up. Luke had gone quite pale and was visibly shaken. There was a moment's silence, then Luke fumbled in his pocket for a pack of cigarettes.

"Do you mind if I...?"

"No. Go ahead. I am glad that you are taking this seriously. Your parents told me that as a child Rob was something of a daredevil, and could never resist a dare. In my experience young men who display these character traits – risk-taking, thrill-seeking, impulsive behaviour - will see the act through to its conclusion, with tragic consequences." Luke took a couple of deep drags then said, enunciating clearly "That is not going to happen. But thank you for letting me know that. I keep an eye on him insofar as I'm able, but I can't be there all the time. Please tell me you have some method of treating this."

"The problem with the pharmaceutical approach is that although it recognises that certain neurotransmitters are implicated in schizophrenia and other mental disorders, it is more complicated than just ensuring an adequate supply through drugs. The point to note is that the human brain is an immensely complicated organ. Having a normal level of a given neurotransmitter – by correcting that deficiency through drugs - does not guarantee that the mind/body will receive its benefits: schizophrenia is more likely to be the result of a dysfunction in the complex connections linking different areas of the brain. In any case, attempting to correct neurotransmitter supply or function does not address the root problem of *why* the supply is low or why the neurotransmitters are not working properly." Luke ran a hand through his hair.

"Are you telling me you can't treat this condition, if that's what he has?"

"No, I'm not telling you that. We have had considerable success with a variety of therapies, and it very much depends on the severity of the condition. Often the psyche itself will develop its own coping mechanism to deal with stress or trauma. Stress is, of course, a very subjective thing. A healthy and happy person can tolerate relatively high levels of stress without adverse effects: what may be stressful to an acutely sensitive individual may simply be perceived as challenging or stimulating to another. Multiple Personality Disorder, for instance, is usually triggered by severe trauma: the survivors of concentration camps were able to a survive by operating at one remove from reality, either by pretending it wasn't happening or by creating an imaginative alternative world, complete with fully functioning alter egos, just as in a movie set." Luke snapped to attention, leaning forward in his chair.

"Oh, come on, Doc. First, it's this bipolar thing, then it's schizophrenia, now it's multiple personalities like in that movie *The Three Faces of Eve*. I'm not buying that. I accept that he has problems, and he's going through a rough time right now. I'll do everything I can to help with that, but you're overcomplicating things. You and I both know what the fucking problem is: he's embarrassed by what he feels for me and he doesn't know what to do about it. I'll get him through this, I'll take care of him."

"I wish I were overcomplicating matters, as you put it. But as I have explained, the human brain is a very complex organism, and these mental disorders are often interconnected. As with schizophrenia, the medical consensus is that multiple personality disorder is a coping mechanism to deal with stressful situations. With respect to your brother, I have been able to identify three well-defined personas or *alter egos*: Johnny Angel – clearly homosexual, attractive and flirtatious. Your brother avails himself of this personality to express aspects of his personality he would rather suppress. Johnny Angel is bolder than Rob and gives him the confidence to behave in outrageous ways he would not normally dare to. Your brother also identifies with Jesse James, a strong masculine character who is outside the law and lives by his own rules - an integral facet of his character in that your brother is an inveterate risk-taker just like the outlaw. Finally, we have Billy the Kid, an *alter ego* who appears to combine qualities of Johnny Angel, the beautiful seductive boy, and Jesse James the outlaw.

Interestingly, Billy the Kid was an orphan, who may have been seeking a father figure. This personality enables your brother to explore his own relationship with his father, and to integrate the feminine and the masculine aspects of his personality in one character." Albert had spent some time arriving at his preliminary diagnosis, and was rather pleased with his conclusions.

"It's a fucking *game*, man. He's play-acting, he can switch it off whenever he wants."

"Are you quite sure he is able to switch it off? Alter egos, once created, have a nasty habit of invading the psyche, and assuming temporary control – almost like a case of possession." Dr. Gottschald went on to talk about "breaking down the defences", getting the patient to "open up", "weakening their resistance" and so on. Luke listened with increasing scepticism. The strong autonomous individual – whom he considered himself to be - was focused and alert, lived strategically, and was on his guard at all times. But the doctor seemed to be suggesting that this was a bad thing, an example of "character armouring", and that a man should not put up any resistance or defences.

"Wait a second" said Luke, interrupting. "When a warrior dons armour, he is usually preparing for war, and there is a damn good reason for it. He's not going to go into battle without any weapons." This man had served in Vietnam, Albert recalled, and was speaking as a professional soldier.

"That is armouring in the literal sense of the word, but the subconscious works on a symbolic level. The shield and the sword symbolise the confidence that comes from one's centre. Where someone is in a state of denial, for instance by denying their true inclinations, they often resort to what is called character armouring. However, defensive character traits associated with character armouring not only serve to protect the individual from pain but also severely restrict the capacity for pleasure."

"Perhaps if it's *involuntary*, but you're losing sight of the fact that it is often quite intentional. Wearing armour is a deliberate act. You completely break down a person's defences, he may be left with nothing. These different personalities may be Rob's way of handling things, and you might end up doing a lot more damage if you don't respect what the mind is trying to do. When you capture an enemy and take him prisoner the first thing you do is strip him of his weapons, then you might try to break him if he puts up any resistance. It's a power thing, man, but you don't *need* to establish your power over someone who is sick or vulnerable. They're not your enemy. Unless you're on some kind of power trip" he added. It was starting to appear to Luke that Dr. Gottschald thought the primary purpose of therapy was to undermine a person's natural defences, and to disempower the patient: it also struck him that therapists had a vested interest in keeping people weak or making them weak, and in offering varying degrees of support and sympathy in order to keep them coming back for more, possibly because they felt more comfortable with weak personalities.

"I'm not sure that I agree with your approach or that it's helpful" concluded Luke. For a moment, Dr. Gottschald was taken aback, not by what the man was saying, but because he had not expected such a well-reasoned argument from Luke. If he was honest, he had expected to encounter some stereotypical macho redneck, displaying overt signs of aggression and hostility. What he had not expected was the degree of intelligence or perception Luke had demonstrated. He was smart and quite capable of thinking for himself. At first glance, Rob's older brother was a prime example of an alpha male, the type who likes to take charge and who thought he had every situation under control. His father's outlook was similar and Albert had come across many such types. When he had first emigrated to the United States in the 50s with a wife and two young children, Albert's first impressions were that many Americans were rather naïve in their approach to problem solving. Since then he had been forced to revise his opinion and had discovered that it was a grave error to underestimate Americans. Their forthright manner and directness of speech could be highly misleading to a European, who might mistake this for simple-mindedness. Their colloquial speech was sprinkled with figurative turns of phrase like "plain talking" "shooting straight from the hip", "beating around the bush", "hold your horses" and so on – that were throwbacks to a violent and lawless era when settlers and pioneers had spent months at a time on horseback on the plains and prairies, fending off attacks from Native American Indians, free-roaming gunslingers, and outlaws.

The Americans Albert had come across were for the most part direct descendants of those who had been tough enough and resourceful enough to survive and to adapt to a hostile environment. They were only three or four generations away from the Wild West, and when you scratched the surface you came up against a very tough resilient breed. The state of affairs that had existed up until the end of the last century – the untameable Wild Frontier - was deeply embedded in the American psyche, and their cultural heritage was a source of pride to them. In their minds America would always be the "land of the brave and the free." Most Americans felt they had a god-given right to defend and protect their families and homesteads against armed and dangerous desperadoes. And to a certain degree this mentality still prevailed, especially in the mid-West or Southern states, where the Civil War and the deep divisions and rifts it had thrown up was still fresh in peoples' minds, as though it had happened only yesterday. Many of them still retained a deep-seated suspicion and distrust of officialdom in any form, whether derived from central government or professions such as law or psychiatry.

"I won't take up any more of your time, Doc." Luke rose to his feet and came forward to shake Albert's hand. "A lot of what you said made sense. Some of it didn't. If I've offended you, I'm sorry. Just saying what was on my mind."

"I'm glad you did" returned Albert "And no, you have not offended me in the least."

Rob was asleep in the car, curled up on the front seat. As Luke moved him gently from the driver's seat, the action awoke him.

"You were in there for quite a while. You didn't hit him, did you?" Luke laughed.

"No. He's not such a bad guy. I think you should continue with the sessions." Luke felt that he was dealing with an intelligent man who would do his best to treat his brother, and that Rob was in relatively safe hands. If it didn't work out, the family could always intervene and stop the treatment at any point. There was another consideration. Luke was aware that his parents were working on getting Rob diagnosed as mentally unfit for combat, and this was what the therapy sessions were all about. He was receiving treatment for his panic attacks and sudden mood swings, which were real enough, but the ultimate goal was to keep him out of the firing line. But if Rob so much as suspected he was being "babied" or cosseted he would revolt. He was no coward and was utterly fearless, but it was this recklessness, a complete disregard for his own safety, which would place his life in jeopardy. Those kind of character traits generally ensured you didn't make it home. From what he'd heard the draft wouldn't become compulsory for a year or so, but as an able bodied young man over the age of eighteen Rob would pass the medical board without a hitch. He would be able to cope with the physical challenges but the psychological factors would break him. He was just too sensitive and vulnerable.

"Luke, tell me the truth: do I disgust you?" Rob had one hand over his eyes, half covering his face. Luke swung around to look at him.

"Not at all. If my kid brother happens to be sweet on me, I'm OK with that. Now that I've kind of got used to the idea, it doesn't bother me. Better not shout about it from the rooftops though." As he switched on the ignition, Rob leaned his elbow casually on Luke's shoulder.

"I meant what I said before. I think you're a really a nice guy."

"I try to be" replied Luke. He was rummaging through the trash in the glove compartment, and extracted a crumpled packet of Camels. "I don't usually smoke, but you drive me to it, kiddo. I want you to promise me something."

"Anything, Marshall. My life is in your hands. Don't hang me just yet."

"All right Jesse. Now I'm being serious. If you're ever feeling really down, if things are getting to be too much and I'm not around, you're to go straight to Mom."

"But I can't tell her certain things, like I can with you. She doesn't know about-"

"I know. But I might not always be around when you need me. So when something's bothering you that you can't talk about with her, then I want you to see the doctor. Don't wait for an appointment. Go and see him immediately, or call his office. If you're feeling bad I don't want you to be alone. Do you understand?"

"I'm to come to you first. But if you're not around I'm to go to Mom. And if I can't talk to her about something I'm to go to Dr. Feelgood."

"Correct. Under no circumstances should you remain alone."

"Why don't you just hire a babysitter or handcuff me to the porch railings?"

"And why don't you do as I tell you, huh? Am I usually right about things or not?"

"Whatever you say, Marshall. I promise to obey you in all things." Luke cuffed him playfully.

"Lose the attitude." Rob suddenly smiled at him disarmingly. "Try and act normal, for mom's sake, will you?" said Luke, as they pulled up into the drive.

****

"Hear the one about the hillbilly and the city slicker?" said Luke to Rob. They were lounging around outside in the back yard at the barbecue their mother had arranged. Various family members had been invited including their father's younger brother Jim and his wife Martha, their mother's older sister Edith and her husband Vernon, plus the latter's daughter Pamela and their grandchildren. "The hillbilly says: *I knows a good place we can go. There's dancin', fightin', drinkin' and plenty of screwin'* City slicker says *Sounds great, man. Who else is going to be there?* Hillbilly says *Why, just you and me, boy. Now git your pretty little ass on over here.*" The joke was greeted with guffaws from the males, the women being clustered by a picnic table cooing over a baby who was being held up for inspection and passed around like a Christmas parcel.

"Let's tone it down a little, gentlemen" said Joe. "There are ladies present."

"None within earshot" returned Luke. "What is it with women and babies - they gonna eat that little thing alive or what?" Rob contemplated his brother gravely, wondering why he had told that specific joke. Was he having a dig at "city slicker nancy boys" or was he having a personal dig at Rob? Dirty jokes were common currency when you got a bunch of guys together, but for some reason he felt the joke had been directed at him. Although Luke hadn't looked at Rob when he was telling it, he'd flashed a look at Rob immediately afterwards to gauge his reaction. Rob had laughed like the others (the joke was funny) but felt himself blushing and couldn't meet his brother's gaze. Luke had smiled to himself, as if he had got precisely the reaction he wanted.

A few months ago, Rob had given in to an entirely new and unfamiliar impulse. Some friends of his had been joking about Todd, who had spent most of his childhood in an orphanage. When he came out at the age of sixteen Todd's uncle had offered him accommodation in a beat-up trailer on his property and given him a job in the garage he owned. Not the sharpest knife in the box, Todd nevertheless knew enough about car mechanics to do his job competently. He largely kept himself to himself, and had an obsessive preoccupation with the genitalia of adolescent and teenage boys.

"I mean, can you imagine that big retard slobbering all over you?" said Bruce, who had known Rob since sixth grade. "He can't keep his hands off your pecker. Anyone fool enough to go into the back room with him is fair game. He's well known for it." At the time Rob had not paid much attention to the conversation, but one afternoon he found himself wandering up the road that led to Todd's automobile repair body shop. There didn't seem to be anyone about, and he hovered on the empty forecourt. Spencer, the other mechanic who worked there, must be on a lunch-break. He was about to move off, wondering what on earth had come over him, when Todd emerged from the back office – little more than a glorified broom cupboard.

"Want somethin' boy?" He was a big guy, almost Luke's size, with a prominent gap in his front teeth and a harelip.

"Uh, no I was just...."

"Come on in and have a soda." Todd inserted a dime in the vending machine and offered a coke to Rob, who took it. As he raised the bottle to his mouth he felt Todd's hand cup his crotch through his jeans. He kept it there for a moment, watching Rob's reaction. Seeing that Rob didn't pull away, he gave it a gentle squeeze.

"I bet you do want somethin', dontcha? I can always tell." Rob said nothing but allowed Todd to lead him into the back room, which he locked. Then he leaned back against the desk, clasping Rob to his chest with one hand, whilst he unzipped him with the other and fumbled with his underpants. Rob tried not to listen to the stream of dirty talk that came out of his mouth, as Todd handled him. "What you got down there? You like that? Oh yes, you like it all right." Rob stared unseeingly at the wall as Todd's big calloused hand fondled him intimately and expertly. "That bobby dangler of yours is jumping around like a jack rabbit. Want some more of that?" Rob gasped as Todd brought him to a climax. "Come back again some time soon, y'hear?" Rob zipped himself up and almost ran out of the garage. But he found himself returning two weeks later for more of the same. The dirty talk continued as the marauding hand went about its business, making pointed references to his "bundle of joy", "sugar plums", "red rooster", "spunk gun" and so on. Rob never uttered a word, just allowed the man to do what he wanted.

"Can't get enough, can ya? Just like milking a snake." Afterwards, when he tried to clean himself up with a tissue, Todd said "Let me do that for you." When he felt Rob responding again to his touch he continued "Think I might do you twice, that felt so good." Rob bit into the sleeve of Todd's shirt as Todd brought him off for the second time. He then tried to kiss Rob, who resisted. He almost gagged as Todd thrust his tongue down his mouth, which was accompanied by a wad of saliva. He liked the sex but he didn't want to be kissed by Todd, who soon got the message, and stopped. "You know, I like you best out of all the boys that come here" said Todd, fingering his hair. "Real nice looking, aren'tcha? Gonna stop by again some time soon?" Rob avoided his gaze, and wriggled free from his grasp. As he emerged from the office, to his complete mortification he saw the other mechanic looking at him.

"Hey, I didn't see nothin'" said Spencer, a big grin on his face.

As their uncles took charge of the grill, Luke was prevailed upon to perform his customary party trick: he stood in a strong man's classic pose, biceps flexed, whilst his young nephew and niece swung from his upper arms, one on each side.

"That's enough now, kids" declared Pamela. "You're getting too big for this game."

"No we're not! Uncle Luke doesn't mind." Luke was now tossing them into the air and catching them as they clamoured for more, screaming delightedly.

"My grandkids just adore him" remarked Edith to her younger sister Connie. "Luke will make a fine husband and father one day." Rob looked away moodily. He hated that kind of talk. The thought of his brother being domesticated and surrounded by squalling babies and diapers was intolerable. He wanted Luke to remain just as he was. He walked over to the cooler, pulled out a beer, and handed it to his brother.

"Thank you" replied Luke. Rob leaned against a tree, positioning himself so that he was directly within his brother's line of vision. The weight of his body was suspended from a low-hanging tree branch he'd hooked his elbow over, his other hand dangling provocatively but casually in the area of his crotch. He felt Luke's eyes ranging over him in a lingering fashion, the way men looked at a striptease artist when things started to get interesting. Nice little pose you've got going there, thought Luke. He kept trying to catch Rob's eye, but the latter was studiously avoiding his gaze. About a week ago, Luke had been tipped off by one of the mechanics that Rob had been paying discreet visits to Todd's garage. "Saw your kid brother come out of there the other week looking hot and bothered" said Spence, with a knowing smirk. They were shooting pool down at the pool hall. Luke chalked a cue and broke the rack of balls, wondering how he should handle this information. But he needn't have worried. According to his informant, quite a few boys who couldn't get past first base with a girl went to Todd to get their rocks off. Given his brother's propensities, Luke was not all that surprised to hear what Rob had been up to, but was relieved that Spence did not seem to think this behaviour in any way abnormal, since most of the other boys engaging in similar activities were known to be straight. Rob now flashed him a dazzling smile before releasing his hold on the branch.

"Why do you keep staring at me like that?" enquired Luke, getting straight to the point.

"You're a big guy" replied Rob "Kinda hard to miss." Luke was standing right in front of him, had him backed up against the tree trunk, so that he felt hemmed in.

"All right. You have my full attention."

"Anyhow, if you weren't staring so hard at *me* you wouldn't know I was staring at you" returned Rob. Luke smiled faintly, acknowledging the hit. Rob could be quite smart like that, always ready with a quick fire response.

"I can't win with you, can I?"

"If it's a *physical* contest, then you'd win of course" said Rob. "You always do."

"If it was a *flirting* contest, I think you'd win hands down." Rob said nothing, just gave him another one of those intense looks. Luke laughed. "Just keep on flashing your blue eyes in my direction. You can't help it, can you?"

"You mean like you keep flaunting your biceps?" retorted Rob.

"Listen, any moron can pump iron. Doesn't mean a damn thing."

"It doesn't mean anything to you because you don't have to work at it" said Rob. "Most of the guys who work out in gyms are seven stone weaklings who think if they lift a few weights it makes them macho." An artificially pumped up body without Luke's height and shoulder breadth just looked grotesque. "They look kinda stooopid."

"They spend so much time gazing in the mirror you have to feel sorry for the poor bastards" Luke agreed, with the nonchalant air of one who is fully conscious of his superiority in that department. He now eyed his brother, then said "This picnic's for the older folk, Mom and Dad's crowd. I was thinking of heading up to the creek head to cool off – wanna come?" Clearwater Creek was about a couple of miles up a mountain trail, by a clearing in the woods where a waterfall tumbled into a clear pool. It was their favourite spot when they were kids, where they went for a swim or to just hang out. Luke had built a tree house there when they were younger, and they still kept a coil of rope hidden underneath a boulder.

Luke stopped by the bunkhouse so he could grab his rifle, just in case they came across any black bears. Most had been hunted down but there were still a few roaming at large in the woods. He cracked the rifle open to check it was fully loaded, then headed off up the mountain trail just behind the bunkhouse. It took them about forty minutes to reach their destination, by which time Luke was drenched in perspiration. He had flung off his shirt, under which he wore a white undershirt - the type which didn't do anything much for a Pillsbury doughboy or an undersized wimp, but looked sensational on someone with his brother's impressive physique.

"What's the point of insects?" asked Luke, swatting away a swarm of mosquitoes that were buzzing around him. "The red ants in the jungle used to drive us nuts. How come they don't bother you so much?"

"Maybe they're turned on by your pheromones." Rob lay back down on a big log that Luke had hauled there a few years ago to act as a bench, his feet resting on the ground either side of him. The log was just wide enough to accommodate his body, but not his arms, one of which flopped to the ground. The sunlight filtered through the canopy, dappling the ground with gold medallions, and picking out the golden glints in his hair. His eyes were a clear blue as he gazed up at the tall pines overhead, then shifted his gaze to his brother.

"Feeling frisky?" Frisky was Luke's term for amorous or horny. Rob didn't at first reply. His T-shirt was riding up, exposing his bare midriff. The atmosphere had suddenly become sexually charged. Luke put a leg astride the log, straddling him, then grabbed hold of both his arms, pinioning them behind his head.

"Quit it, you bastard" protested Rob feebly. "I feel like one of those human sacrifices the Aztecs used to go in for." It felt like his heart was pounding a thousand beats a second.

"I'm steadying you" said Luke, tightening his grip "So you don't roll off."

"You're not steadying me, you're-" He gasped as Luke pressed his crotch hard against his and started up a grinding motion. Luke kept up a steady friction, each thrust jolting Rob back against the log. The sensation was intensely pleasurable. He could have asked Luke to stop at any point, but didn't want him to. Butterflies didn't even begin to describe it. It was more like plummeting from the highest point of a roller coaster, when your stomach lurches and goes into freefall. Luke felt himself getting aroused, watching the effect he was having on Rob, who had his eyes half-closed, his rib cage rising and falling beneath his T-shirt. At one point his entire body shuddered, and he nearly cried out. The seam at the crotch of his jeans felt way too tight, with no immediate means of release. Luke was really getting into it now, bearing down on him with increasing pressure. He felt the pressure suddenly ease as Luke sprang to his feet with a hunter's instinct, having heard something lumbering towards them through the underbrush.

"Get up, Rob." Luke had his rifle trained on a point where the sound was coming from, ready to fire in case a bear charged his brother. Probably just a racoon, skunk or a wildcat but it was best to take no chances. Two months ago someone had been badly mauled by a bear, wandering around in the woods like a fool without a gun. Seconds later, Rusty bounded into the clearing, barking joyfully, his tail wagging. Rob sat up slowly, feeling dazed, hot and sticky. Rusty picked up on the exciting new scent immediately, launching himself like a heat-seeking missile straight for Rob's crotch, sniffing and poking his nose right on in there. Luke lowered his rifle and pulled the dog off his brother as their father emerged into the clearing.

"Down boy, easy boy. Settle down now."

"Thought I'd find you boys up here" said Joe, panting with the exertion of the climb. It was a fairly steep hike the last half mile, and at fifty-four he wasn't as fit as he used to be. Jesus, thought Luke, that was a close call. Another few seconds, and he'd have caught them in *flagrante delicto,* as they termed it in the divorce courts. Joe looked curiously at his older son, who was leaning forward at the waist, hands on his knees as if he had some kind of stomach cramp. Better take yourself off somewhere private and do something about that hard-on, brother, before you break your oversized balls, thought Rob. "Been for a swim yet?" enquired Joe. They both looked as though they were burning up. They hadn't been anywhere near the water, he was sure.

"Ah, no, we just got here" said Luke, straightening up and shouldering his rifle. What had just happened back there? He'd dry-humped his kid brother, that's what. It was what sophomores did when they were making out, with both partners fully clothed so the girl didn't get pregnant. Of course one thing led to another and the girl ended up compromised in one way or another, and the boy ended up with a bad case of blue balls. He had engaged in a lot of that activity in his teens and had gone through the motions with Cindy, the nylon of her panty-hose acting like a makeshift condom until it inevitably split. At the drive-in theatre they rarely watched the movie, being otherwise occupied in the back seat. Preliminary foreplay consisted of a game called "Hunt the Popcorn", where Luke tipped a handful of popcorn down her front and then tried to locate the stray kernels, with Cindy giggling and squirming: it was quite amazing where some of the pieces ended up – trapped in her bra and panties or lodged in all kinds of concealed crevices. Most other couples were similarly engaged, which is how drive-ins had earned their immoral reputation as "passion pits."

"I had a dizzy spell back there" said Rob. "I was just resting up for a minute." Luke excused himself and took off down the trail ahead of them, Rusty scampering at his heels. Rob gazed after him.

"Are you feeling OK?" asked his father "Been taking your meds?" Rob scowled.

"I don't NEED to keep on taking those pills. I'm doing OK now."

"I'm glad to hear that, son, really I am. But your mom and I think it's best if you keep up with the program." Rob sighed. When they reached the house, Rob saw Luke's red Chevy Impala disappearing down the track in a cloud of dust. Luke didn't return home that evening, and Rob became increasingly uneasy. Was he seeing Cindy?

Chapter Three

Luke strolled in the following morning after they had all breakfasted. His parents were having coffee on the porch and Rob was sitting on the steps, whittling a piece of wood with his knife.

"Morning, Luke" said his mother "Have you had breakfast yet?"

"Thanks, I'm fine. Just a coffee." Rob didn't bother looking up. He seemed moody and withdrawn. "What are you carving there?" asked Luke.

"Nothing." Luke raised his eyebrows. The other day when their father's unexpected appearance had interrupted their play, Luke had hoped he would disappear again so they could finish what they had started. His father, however, seemed inclined to hang around and speak to his youngest son so Luke had made himself scarce. He had actually found himself getting physically aroused by what they had been doing, and had sought an obvious means of release. A woman called Barbra whom he'd known since high school and was usually glad to see him, lived in a trailer park in one of the poorer sections of town, and Luke had showed up on her doorstep with one thing on his mind: "Feeling lonesome?" He'd taken her in his arms, and she'd welcomed him with her usual flirtatious banter.

"Hi Luke, what a surprise. If you think you're man enough to satisfy me come right on in, sugar."

"If you're woman enough to accommodate me then let's get started." The preliminaries over, Luke had wasted no time in getting down to business. As Luke now leaned across to accept a cup of coffee from their mother, Rob suddenly noticed the telltale signs of makeup and lipstick on his shirtfront. He got up without a word and went indoors, slamming the screen door behind him.

"Robbie!" called his father. "What on earth's got into that boy?" Luke made a move to go after him but Joe signalled to him to remain where he was. "Leave him be, Luke." He turned to his wife. "This is exactly what we were talking about, honey. He needs to keep taking his medication. His moods are all over the place." Connie sighed heavily, then followed her younger son indoors.

Luke was leaning against the wooden porch railing in his shirtsleeves, a cup of coffee in one hand. He turned slightly as his father came up beside him. Joe was aware that his older son had been tomcatting around. He'd been seen paying nocturnal visits to a woman who lived in a trailer park on the south side of town. Like a lot of men who were successful in that department, Luke rarely talked about his dalliances. In Joe's experience, men who were rebuffed by women tended to brag the loudest and longest about their non-existent conquests.

"Luke..." Both of them faced outwards as if seeking some answer in the distant mountain peaks. "You spend quite a lot of time with him. You probably know him better than most people." Luke nodded. He felt that his father was somehow acknowledging his failings as a parent - the fact that whenever his younger son was in distress or trouble he went to Luke instead of his father. It was almost as if Luke had usurped his paternal role. "So what do you think's going on with Rob?" Luke took some time to consider his answer, then finally admitted "It's got me totally beat."

"Aw come on" said Joe impatiently, meaning a feeble response like that doesn't wash with me. "You must have some opinion. He's your brother. All I know is something serious is going on with him, and I don't know if the doctors can fix it." Luke swung round to face him, one elbow resting on the porch railing.

"If I knew, Dad, believe me I'd try to put it right." Joe nodded, waiting for him to continue, but Luke had lapsed into silence again.

"Your mother thinks he's having some kind of nervous breakdown. And I'm inclined to agree. But why is this happening to us? He comes from a loving family."

"Sure" Luke agreed, seeking to reassure him "You and Mom are good parents. Don't beat yourself up about it, Dad. It may all just blow over."

"People break down for a number of reasons or for no reason whatsoever" said their mother, suddenly appearing in the doorway. "He's at the age when…" She hesitated to mention the word schizophrenia, but their brief chat with Dr. Gottschald had raised a number of points: that young people were most susceptible to mental illness in their teens or early twenties, and Rob was only twenty. He was a grown man, but very young for his years. Maybe he was still developing and there were a lot of hormones kicking in. Dr. Gottschald had talked about brain chemistry a lot and how the right medication could regulate imbalances, but when he started mentioning things like dopamine and so on, she had started to feel somewhat out of her depth. She had studied Biology at school and knew the basics, but mental illness had not been on the school curriculum. They had both sat there in his office, Joe's brow increasingly furrowed as he struggled to follow what the man was saying. Eventually Dr. Gottschald had handed them a leaflet.

"Take this and read it. Medication can provide some alleviation, but families need to educate themselves about the condition." None of this was exactly reassuring or what they wanted to hear.

"What could there possibly be to depress him?" went on Joe "He's got a good home here, he's got his whole life ahead of him, he's such a good-looking boy he could have any girl he wanted. Remember how they used to chase after him at him at high school, ringing up all the time. Used to drive your mom crazy. And he was so darned popular at school." Luke rubbed the stubble on his jaw thoughtfully.

"Maybe that's the problem" said his wife slowly. "I had a private chat with the doctor the other day when I went to pick him up." Rob had been loitering outside in the waiting room, kicking at a potted plant. The female receptionist had eyed him, but hadn't intervened. She saw all kinds of odd behaviour from the clients. "I didn't catch all of what he said, but he said popularity can swing both ways. It can lead to an identity crisis." His father laughed, breaking the tension.

"Hell, you're starting to sound like a shrink. You sure are picking up the lingo fast, honey." He and Luke viewed the entire mental health profession and its attendant psychobabble with a certain amount of scepticism. Neither of them took it seriously.

"Well, that was the term he used. People expect a lot of him, and maybe he just can't handle it. When you've got so many people wanting to get close to you, and get a piece of you – like Elvis or Marilyn Monroe - you must get heartily sick of it. Maybe Rob just needs some space" concluded his mother.

"You may be right. Maybe that's all it is. It was a damn sight easier when he was a little boy" reflected Joe ruefully. "I could just buy him a grape Popsicle. Though what in the world's Marilyn Monroe got to do with this?" They both laughed.

"You know what I'm saying. All those big Hollywood stars ... they were like little kids let loose in a candy store. And they lost their way. They ended up not knowing who they were any more." Luke got up.

"I'm going to go check on him." He took the stairs two at a time and knocked on Rob's bedroom door. No answer. "Robbie? Can I come in?"

"Fuck off."

"Come on, Robbie. Let me in." He tried the door handle, and the door opened. His brother was leaning against a far wall glaring at him.

"Leave me alone. Don't touch me, you bastard." Luke went over to him.

"Hey, take it easy." Luke tried to catch hold of him but Rob launched a ferocious attack on him, punching him until Luke caught hold of his fists.

"Get away from me!" yelled Rob with blazing eyes. "I hate you. I cannot STAND you! You're nothing, you bore me to death, you're NOTHING at all!" Luke was at a complete loss as to how to explain his erratic behaviour, but knew his brother well enough to understand that something had upset him on a profound level, and that he was lashing out like a wounded or cornered animal. He therefore did not take offence at any of the insults Rob hurled at him, no matter how hurtful they might be. Their mother appeared at the bedroom door.

"Darling...." she addressed Robbie, who was trembling violently. He pointed at Luke. "Tell HIM to leave! I want him out of here right now."

"Please leave us, Luke" said his mother, giving him a despairing look. Luke gritted his teeth, and left the room quietly. Outside, he stood against the wall on the landing, attempting to collect his thoughts together. He didn't understand where Rob's sudden fit of temper had come from, but he had an idea it was connected with what had occurred the other day. Had he taken unfair advantage of his younger brother, who was confused and clearly very vulnerable? Had he entirely misread the signals Rob was sending out? He tried to recall exactly what had happened between them, and kept coming to the same conclusion. Yesterday, Rob had been openly flirting with him, or so he believed. He didn't think he was imagining it. Luke was a man who mostly operated on an instinctual level. Which was fine if your instincts were sound, but what if they weren't? What if they led you astray and he was barking up the wrong tree? In his experience, if a woman pressed her body up against yours – the way Rob did - she was clearly signalling she wanted you to take her to bed. And Rob's behaviour towards him the other day, and on other occasions, had been quite unmistakeable. But just because Robbie had invited a sexual encounter and Luke had responded in kind, that didn't mean he should have given in to the impulse. That didn't make it right. That was how child molesters justified their actions, claiming the child had been provocative and "led them on". But Rob was no child. He was not under the age of consent, and was not mentally handicapped.

His father was pacing up and down at the bottom of the stairs. He beckoned silently to Luke, who descended slowly. "We need to get him checked into a clinic where they can straighten him out" said Joe. Luke said nothing. There was nothing he could say. "We need to get this problem fixed" went on his father in a low tone. "Your mother can't take much more of this. His therapist says there's a place over in the next county where he could be admitted…"

"What?" cut in Luke, suddenly catching his father's drift. "What are you talking about? He's not crazy, he's just upset that's all."

"Just on a temporary basis, Luke" continued his father "One month, that's all we're talking about. They have one-on-one counselling, group therapy sessions and what not. All that stuff. I know Rob's not crazy, it's just some kind of breakdown. It can probably be fixed with the right treatment. It's not like the old days, where they put people in a straitjacket and threw away the key."

"What does Rob have to say about this? I'll tell you right now, I'm not in favour of having him admitted anywhere without his consent. You try to have my brother sectioned, I'll fight you every step of the way." His father sighed.

"I have to go out now, I've got business to take care of. We'll talk about this later. Sounds like he's quietened down - your mother took him a sedative." After his father had left the house, Luke ascended the stairs again. There was no sound from Rob's room and his mother had not come out. When he knocked gently she whispered "Shhh. He's sleeping." Rob lay across her knees on the bed like a small child, his head in her lap. She was stroking his hair. The sight tore at Luke's heart.

****

Rob looked up as Luke mounted the porch steps. Their parents were in the kitchen fixing themselves postprandial drinks, before taking up their usual seats on the porch swings.

"Hi" murmured Rob. He was wearing a faded grey college sweatshirt that used to belong to Luke, which was too big for him and made him look childlike.

"Hey, how's it going?" returned Luke, a little warily. "Still love me?" By way of answer, Rob came forward to embrace him wordlessly, and Luke held him for a minute.

"I'm sorry I punched you."

"As you can see, I'm still standing."

"You never really talk much about Vietnam" said Rob suddenly, as Luke took a seat on the porch swing. "I tell you personal stuff."

"What's brought this on?"

"Dad was sounding off about the war again." Neither Luke nor his father had much respect for the talking heads and Joint Chiefs of Staff headquartered in the Pentagon, irrespective of their political persuasion. Whether they were Democrat or Republican "they all piss in the same pot", as Luke put it. His father held similar sentiments, maintaining "nothing good ever came out of Washington." Just recently this had been expanded to include the state of California - a hotbed for radicals, bleeding hearts, and "a bunch of fruitcakes and snowflakes" with no conception of what their boys were going through in Vietnam.

"I guess it must be like the Wild West out there" said Rob, as Luke struck a match to light a cigarette.

"Nothing like the Wild West, little brother. You can't ride a horse through a flooded rice paddy. Stick to robbing banks and trying to outrun the law, Jesse."

"What's it really like then?" asked Rob curiously.

"It's a shit-storm" replied Luke shortly. "I don't even know what we're doing out there any more. Join the army and see the world. See some jungle and the inside of a whorehouse, more like." Luke's platoon had been assigned to a task force just outside Saigon in the zone known as *III Corps*, shortly after the Gulf of Tonkin incident when things were heating up. When the boys went out "sightseeing" in their evenings off, heading for the city in convoys of army jeeps and trucks, they had one thing on their minds. The Asian hookers were petite, pretty and fragile-looking: they all wanted American dollars and knew how to make themselves as appealing as possible. Although they tried to look sophisticated and worldly-wise with their eye makeup and provocative skimpy clothing, many of them were scared. They looked so young and delicate: most of the GIs could have snapped them in two easily. The girls pretended they were enjoying what they were doing, but Luke was not fooled. His tastes ran to mature women, in any case, not little girls. A Playboy centrefold was what turned him on – not some tiny gazelle-like creature who barely skimmed his waist and whose nervous smiles said so clearly *You can do whatever you want to me because you've paid but please don't hurt me.* In one brothel he had been faced with a slender young girl with child-like features who gazed up at him expectantly: "OK, Mister? We do it now?" He couldn't bring himself to have sex with her. It made him feel like some kind of monster, a child molester. Downstairs in the bar area, she had been sitting in his lap, giggling and clinging around his neck, whilst he fondled her and stroked her hair. All the guys played with them as though they were children - dandled them on their knees and gave them candy bars, and then they were supposed to fuck them? It just felt wrong. The whole set-up was sick, perverted.

In the end Luke had backed off. He had not laid a finger on the girl but had paid her generously for her "services" so she wouldn't get into trouble with her employers. If you didn't want to visit the brothels then the assumption was you must be a queer, so quite a few of the guys went along with the charade, just as he did. If you didn't want to get a reputation as a fag, you hit the whorehouses. Of course there were a few mean motherfuckers who went on the rampage, and felt they had a licence to do whatever they wanted. Fuelled up on testosterone, adrenaline and cheap alcohol, the officers in charge had a full-time job on their hands reining them in. There was a lot of brutality – on both sides – but the worst excesses took place away from the whorehouses, which were regulated to a certain degree. When they were stationed out in the boonies, far from the cities, other stuff went on. One guy forced a frightened 18-year-old "cherry" to perform fellatio on him, and had laughed about it later as though it were a huge joke. His victim was little more than a kid, straight out of high school, and he hadn't been able to hold his head up afterwards. A lot of that going on down through the ranks. Not that any of them considered themselves to be anything but regular red-blooded heterosexual males. It was fine to pick on someone younger or more vulnerable, and considered perfectly OK to sodomise a fellow soldier so long as you took the dominant position.

"Did you have to kill a lot of them?" asked Rob.

"What do you think? That's whole point of warfare." Rob had always known this was the case, but it felt strange being the brother of a man who had killed other human beings - albeit in the heat of battle. He would have to do the same thing if he was called up. As platoon leader, Luke was somehow supposed to keep a tally of the body count, but that was near impossible in a fire fight where visibility was poor and the primary objective was to hit hard then get out. "The Viet Cong and NVA tend to use guerrilla warfare tactics – not much else you can do in the jungle - so we were sent in to recon and to conduct search and destroy missions. You hunt them down, try to avoid ambushes, get the job done and then get the hell out of there."

It was a war of attrition the enemy conducted by stealth, by means of booby traps: pits containing sharpened *punji* stakes or venomous snakes. They also had access to an extensive network of underground tunnels which served as barracks, munitions dumps, hospitals - like the one known as the "Iron Triangle" a few miles south of Saigon. On one occasion, when they were holed up in a temporary base camp near abandoned farmland, Luke had gone to investigate the sound of shots he heard coming from the direction of a barn. His best sniper in the field, a crack shot called Paterson, was kneeling behind a tree stump. He had lined up his telescopic sights on the silhouettes of some villagers moving around in the next field over, and was casually picking them off like ducks in a rifle range.

"Jesus Christ! What are you doing, man?" Paterson looked up and lowered his rifle.

"Eliminating the enemy. They're not our guys. Easy to tell 'cos they're only about 5'3, ha ha ha."

"Are you insane? We're here to PROTECT these people, not terrorise them. The North Vietnamese and Viet Cong are our enemies, the South Vietnamese are our allies."

"How was I supposed to know" came the reply. "Little dinks all look the fucking same to me. Man, it's hot out here. I don't feel too good." Luke stared at him. Paterson's skin had an unhealthy clammy sheen. He'd been on his feet for over 48 hours with no sleep (it couldn't be helped, as they hadn't been able set up camp in swampland) but there was something else wrong with him. He was going through the motions like a robot, but he just wasn't functioning right. Normally Paterson was one of his most reliable men; he kept his shit together under sustained fire, and his stamina was good. When the others were flagging under the 85-100 pound loads they had to carry in extremely humid conditions with temperatures running as high as 112 degrees Fahrenheit, Paterson would offer to help with some of the weight - shouldering a radio, extra ammo or grenade launchers. Dehydration was the real killer, and there never seemed to be enough water, despite each man carrying ten canteens a day. Luke took his rifle off him and ordered him to get some rest. Paterson moved off unsteadily, swaying like a mad dog with rabies, and Luke got the medic to check him over before he collapsed with exhaustion.

"High as a kite, sir" reported the medic. "Also suffering from severe dehydration and lack of sleep." Luke was aware that stimulants and amphetamines were issued to soldiers for reasons of endurance: to numb the emotions, and to keep them alert during extended periods of combat when they were under hostile fire and got little or no rest. You didn't drink hard liquor or smoke dope when you were out in the field or on patrol, unless you were courting the mother of all hangovers and had a serious death wish. Luke enforced a zero-tolerance policy of drug or alcohol abuse, but had always wondered why drugs were made so easily available to the men. Paterson's over-use of amphetamines had escaped notice because it hadn't affected his aim: he was a dead eye and never missed, even when he was amped out on Dexedrine.

"Can't you give him some downers, something to counteract the effects so he can rest up?" enquired Luke. "He's been on his feet, buzzing like a chainsaw for over 48 hours and he's starting to crack. I can't afford to lose a guy like Paterson. He's one of our toughest. But right now he's lethal." Paterson was reputed to have nerves of steel. He didn't much care who he killed, but he at least drew the line at shooting men on his own side.

"I just gave him a sedative" replied the medic. "Sleeping like a baby." They glanced over in Paterson's direction. He was stretched out on the ground, fast asleep and dead to the world.

On another occasion Luke's unit had been hacking their way through dense jungle for nine hours when a lone VC scout suddenly leapt out of a tree onto Billy's shoulders, brandishing a knife. At first, Luke had just seen a blur out of the corner of his eye, which he had mistaken for a monkey. Drenched in sweat, he had to keep mopping his brow to keep his vision clear. This annoyed the heck out of Billy, who bucked him off and started pounding him with his fists. What kind of crazy fucker leapt out in front of a squad of armed American GIs on a search and destroy mission, Luke couldn't imagine, but he'd more or less signed his own death warrant. Billy was knocking seven shades of shit out of him.

"Ain't no fun when the rabbit's got the gun...."

"All right" said Luke, holding Billy off. "Go kill a snake or something. And get that knife wound seen to." Platoon Sergeant Moreland, his second-in-command, had in the meantime secured the prisoner.

"What do you want to do with him?" asked Moreland. They didn't have an interpreter with them, and hauling his ass back to base for interrogation was more trouble than it was worth. Their orders were to take no prisoners. If they allowed him to live he'd report their whereabouts to his comrades and they'd be surrounded within minutes. There was no knowing how many of the enemy were crawling about in the undergrowth: according to the latest intelligence reports, probably hundreds. Luke hesitated for a fraction of a second, then said "Shoot him." He signalled to Paterson, who took him down with a single shot. They disposed of the body, weighting it down and shoving the corpse into a muddy watercourse, before continuing on their way. Billy had sustained quite a deep ugly-looking gash just above his left shoulder which could have proved fatal if the knife had plunged into the top of his spinal cord, as intended, but he nevertheless insisted on shouldering his rucksack after the medic had bandaged him up. Luke and Paterson relieved him of most of the weight, ignoring his protests. Later, Luke heard one of the cherries voicing disapproval of their earlier action. This guy was constantly bitching and griping about something, and it was starting to piss him off.

"What did you say?"

"What we did back there was wrong. It's the principle of it, sir." Luke looked at him for a moment. He'd seen what the Viet Cong did to captured prisoners – soldiers and civilians alike – bodies so horribly mutilated it turned his stomach.

"We don't torture prisoners" said Luke curtly. "If we need to kill them we do it quickly and cleanly."

"That makes us better, does it?"

"You tell me." He didn't want his men infected with any of this morale busting *We're no better than the enemy* shit. Damned if he was going to risk the life of every man in his unit just to appease the bleeding heart of some Shake 'n' Bake draftee with no experience of jungle warfare. They'd been sent out here to do a job, and Luke's job was to ensure they got the job done as effectively and safely as possible. He turned back to the platoon. "Fall in, gentlemen."

"Ah, just ignore it" advised his sergeant later on when they were having a quiet smoke together. "Some of these new guys don't seem to realise we're in a war. Out here principles are just excess baggage: it ties you up in knots so you end up running around like a goddam headless chicken."

"That's good. A triple metaphor" grinned Luke. "Excess baggage, knots and headless chickens. I'll try and remember that."

The war they were conducting was frustrating to many of the men because it was totally unlike conventional warfare, where you zeroed in on an identifiable target. The enemy was for the most part invisible. Sgt. Moreland had described the insurgents as a "bunch of crazy midgets running around the jungle" who could pop up at any time, from an underground tunnel or an overhanging tree branch. Luke slept with a loaded Colt .45 by his side, and the slightest sound would cause him to spring to his feet, adrenaline pumping. On one occasion he nearly shot one of his own scouts, who woke him out of a light doze to report he'd just located an enemy camp less than three quarters of a mile away.

"Don't ever sneak up on me again like that without warning, soldier" said Luke. "I damn near killed you. How many?"

"About twenty-five, sir."

"You checked for booby traps?"

"Yep. Clean." Despite the fact the men had all had very little sleep Luke roused the platoon. This was the opportunity they had all been waiting for. Twenty minutes later they had crept up on the enemy camp, and Paterson and another guy took up their positions, waiting for the signal to open fire.

"Let 'em have it, boys." Paterson laid down a barrage of covering fire, while Luke led the charge. A mopping up operation afterwards recovered twenty-three VC corpses and only one casualty from their own unit, who would have to be evacuated as soon they could establish radio contact and rendezvous to an extraction point where a chopper could get to them. Wounds could quickly become life threatening in a jungle environment. His first priority was to check their perimeter defences, as the mines were the only thing which stood between them and a retaliatory assault by the enemy, but Moreland was already on the job, working his way methodically down the line.

"Fuckin' A, man. Goddam turkey shoot" commented Paterson. "Gimme some more of that."

"How's the casualty?" Luke asked the medic.

"Comfortable as can be expected, sir. I shot him up with morphine, but we can't get a signal here." Luke made a mental note to dispatch the RTO to the nearest summit at first light with an escort for fire cover, before wandering over to have a few words with the wounded man, who looked up at his approach. Luke recognised him as the new recruit who had objected to his decision to shoot the

VC captive, and dropped to his haunches, forearms resting on his thighs, to speak to him.

"How you doin', buddy? Casey, isn't it?"

"I'm OK, sir. The Doc said my leg's been fractured in several places below the knee and I'll probably need surgery – will I be able to walk again?" Without an X-ray, the medic couldn't be sure how badly his leg was damaged, but providing the tibia wasn't completely shattered, they could do wonders with metal plates and screws.

"Don't see why not. You'll be up and about on one of those civilian protest marches in no time." Casey looked sheepish and Luke grinned, to show he was only teasing.

"I guess this is what happens when you lose your focus" said Casey resignedly, paying lip service to the basic military drill. In a close fire fight there was never any time to stop, to evaluate, or take stock. If you lost your concentration for one second you were dead on the ground. Even when a comrade had taken a direct hit and was screaming for help, you couldn't stop to administer aid or comfort unless you wanted to end up on the ground beside him. You just kept on firing, remained focused on what you were doing, and didn't allow yourself to get distracted. You picked them up afterwards, the casualties, and just hoped they would be OK.

"Could have happened to any of us" said Luke, placing a hand on his shoulder. "Luck of the draw. You did a good job back there. When you've been out here long enough you begin to realise it's best to leave politics to civilians. Soldiers can't afford to get sentimental. We're fighters, and we fight better without that kind of distraction." Casey was trying to concentrate on what Luke was telling him, but his eyelids were beginning to droop as the morphine took effect. "All right, we'll have you medivaced out of here tomorrow and that leg taken care of. Now get some sleep."

Joe appeared at the screen door with a glass of whiskey in his hand, and took a seat on the swing beside Rob so that they were both facing Luke on the opposite side of the porch. Luke was taking up most of the space on the other porch swing, with one arm resting along the back of the seat, his ankle crossed on his other knee. Rob couldn't make out the expression on his face, which was partially obscured by shadow in the deepening twilight.

"Did you have to use napalm?" Rob asked. At home they had all seen horrific photos of napalm victims in *LIFE* and *Time* magazines.

"Not personally. Flamethrowers are not used on the ground so much now with the bombers providing more effective air cover." A single napalm bomb dropped from a B-52 could destroy up to 2500 square yards of bush. In the face of elusive guerrilla forces, bombing systematically destroyed the vegetation cover that sheltered the enemy and camouflaged the *Ho Chi Minh* trail, a network of roads and tracks used by Communist insurgents in the North to supply South Vietnam. "That stuff is terrible" said Luke. "It's got a gelling substance that sticks to anything, like molasses; it's not a pretty way to die." He had once come across a screaming human fireball who'd been hit by a napalm flamethrower. Luke had pumped a round of bullets into him with an M-60 machine gun to put him out of his agony, and kept on going.

Exposure to *Agent Orange*, a highly toxic chemical defoliant designed to eliminate forest as well as the crops that fed the enemy, was another major concern. The U.S. airforce was spraying millions of gallons of the stuff from C-123s. The idea was to deprive the enemy of clean food and water to force them into areas more controlled by American troops. In many ways it had turned into a helicopter war, with the air cavalry laying down the groundwork for the infantry. One of the men had come up to Luke during a rest break to voice his concerns.

"What is it?" asked Luke, absorbed in cleaning his rifle. You wouldn't be issued with another one, so you looked after your weapons. They were mostly issued with M-16s and M4s, which tended to jam in the humidity and heat of the jungle. The ideal rifle was one that strips down in seconds and never jams, and is easy to clean and reassemble, like the AK47 submachine carried by the enemy. In a close fire fight the M16 could always be counted on to jam at the worst possible moment, and many soldiers resorted to the age-old expedient of pissing down the barrel to wash away some of the gunk residue left by burnt powder and high humidity.

"If our boys in the air are spraying this stuff on the ground, and it's toxic to crops, and we're breathing it in…" He left the sentence unfinished, and looked at Luke uneasily. He was only voicing what Luke and others were already thinking.

"We consume U.S. army rations, not local crops, but your concerns are duly noted. We'll be out of here soon" Luke assured him. "In the meantime, I would strongly advise you keep those sentiments to yourself."

"Why are the Americans over there anyhow?" asked Rob.

"We're there to protect the South Vietnamese" said Luke. "North Vietnamese warships attacked an American destroyer, so LBJ ordered retaliatory air strikes. The number of American troops serving in South Vietnam was substantially increased, so we got involved in the whole shebang, and things just escalated. You want the truth? It's the mother of all clusterfucks. And the top brass won't admit up to it." Rob was about to ask Luke something else, when Joe stopped him. "Stop pestering your brother with questions, Robbie. War is not something people care to dwell on, not when you've been in the thick of it." Their father had served in the South Pacific theatre during World War II, and was no more forthcoming than Luke about his experiences.

"Sorry" said Rob to Luke. "I was only wondering, just in case I get called up."

"I think that's doubtful, son" replied his father. Joe had taken out his tobacco pouch and was tamping down the tobacco in the bowl of his briar wood pipe in a leisurely nightly ritual. Then he struck a match – the flare illuminating his face briefly - and Rob caught a whiff of the Virginia tobacco his father smoked. When he was a small boy this was usually the signal for bedtime, and the comforting aroma would send him to sleep. Not if I can help it, thought Luke. When things got really bad he had often thought of his younger brother, and swore to himself that he would do everything in his power to ensure Robbie did not end up in that hellhole. Luke had enlisted of his own accord, but people were already talking about the draft. The worrying thing was that the war showed no signs of ending any time soon. If anything, it was escalating and Robbie was in imminent danger of being drafted. The Communists were gaining ground and the Viet Cong were committing unspeakable atrocities against a defenceless populace. Whilst on active combat duty he had seen sights that shocked him to the core. Rape and mutilations were commonplace and the evil of Communism would just spread from Southeast Asia. It would eventually take over the Western world unless it was stamped out, or so they were told. American troops were needed to restore order. Nixon was set to succeed LBJ in the White House and had made it clear he would not be scaling things down. Quite the reverse.

"Things are hotting up over there" commented Luke. He still had contacts in the military and had been informed by a reliable source that there were plans afoot to invade Cambodia (not yet operational) in order to disrupt North Vietnamese supply lines, and U.S. naval gunboats were patrolling the meandering muddy waters of the Mekong Delta for Communist insurgents. "If the Khmer Rouge take control the people are fucked. It will be total genocide."

"Language, Luke" said his father "Tone it down a little. Your mother will be out in a minute." The ice cubes clinked in his glass. "You know, when I was your age, I used to be able to run up that mountain." He gestured towards the dark shape of the forested mountains looming behind their property.

"But Dad" asked Rob "How did you manage to stop the ice from falling out of your glass?" His father and Luke chuckled, and Luke moved over to make space for his mother, who had just joined them.

"What were you all laughing about just now?" she asked.

"This boy is keeping us entertained" said Joe, tousling Rob's hair affectionately. "I don't know what we're doing to do with you, son."

"How are you getting on with Doctor what's his name?" his mother now asked Rob. "I can never remember these foreign names."

"I call him Dr. Strangelove" said Rob. "I think his plan is world domination."

"Wasn't Peter Sellers marvellous in that film? But darling, you must take this seriously. He has a lot of medical qualifications - we looked into it. He's been to all sorts of prestigious universities, and has written papers, even had books published."

"Yeah, like *Mein Kampf.* Who was that doctor who performed medical experiments on Jews in the concentration camps? Maybe he's an escaped Nazi" said Rob.

"Now sweetheart....I know he must be doing you some good because your moods have been so much better lately. Shall we have a light on out here? It's getting rather dark." Rob could just make out the orange glow at the tip of Luke's cigarette. His mother got up to switch the porch light on.

"That will attract all the moths, Connie" said Joe, puffing on his pipe. "Not to mention the skeeters." He always claimed his pipe tobacco smoke repelled mosquitoes.

"Remember when you boys used to collect lightning bugs in jars?" said their mother. "They made the most wonderful lanterns. What a lovely night with all the stars out. It's like velvet."

"Answer your mother's question, Rob" said Joe. "Tell us what's been going on in these therapy sessions. Does he have you lie down on a couch?" Rob giggled.

"I think he's a married man with kids, Dad." The innuendo was lost on his parents, but Luke smiled. Rob could see his brother clearly now in the light, and the five o'clock shadow that covered his jaw line. He rarely bothered to shave in the evenings.

"Does he put you under?" asked his father.

"Put me under what?"

"Hypnotise you. They usually do it with a watch on a chain."

"Oh, Joe, don't be silly" said Connie "They only do that in the movies and if the patient's been traumatised. And Rob's not suffered any traumas, have you, sweetheart?"

"No, apart from when I got bit by that cottonmouth. It was like being stung by a hundred hornets at once" replied Rob.

"It was a timber rattler" corrected Luke. "You shouldn't have been poking it with a stick." The pain in his thigh had been agonising, but Rob had gamely tried to stand up. Luke had ordered him to stay still, aware that any movement would only cause the deadly venom to circulate more rapidly through his bloodstream. He had picked Rob up in a fire fighter's hold, clamped against his body to keep him immobile, and carried him down the trail as fast as he could without stopping. By the time they were halfway down the mountain the skin around the swelling had turned black, and Rob was losing consciousness. Rob had been fifteen at the time, and Luke nineteen.

"If you hadn't got him to the hospital when you did, Luke, he wouldn't be here with us today" said their father.

"I love you, brother" said Rob. "You must have saved my life oh, at least a million times. Anyhow, Dr. Gottcha says I have some issues I need to work through."

"Issues!" scoffed Joe. "In my day they used to call it problems. I don't have much truck with the notions these fellas come out with. Freud saw everything as a phallic symbol. The statue of liberty, for instance. That would be another phallic symbol even though it's clearly a statue of a woman. What we want to know is, has he identified what the problem is, and can he fix it?"

"I told him what I could, Dad. He asked the most dumb questions, like what was my relationship with my mother."

"What?" exploded Joe "If this guy is trying to put the blame on your mom…I'm spending good money on this…. *quack.*" Luke shook with silent laughter.

"I wish you wouldn't smoke, honey" said Connie to Luke.

"You want me to put it out?"

"No, sweetheart. Just don't take up a habit like that when you're so young and fit, otherwise you might regret it when you're older and can't kick the habit."

"Dad doesn't regret it" pointed out Rob. Joe hawked up a gobbet of phlegm and spat over the side of the porch railing, before striking another match against the heel of his boot to relight his pipe (he rarely used a lighter)

"Joe…" murmured Connie disapprovingly.

"Now come on, Connie. You knew I had some uncouth habits before you married me."

"So what does the doctor think these issues are, Rob?" asked his mother pointedly.

"Oh, I don't know. Just stuff" said Rob evasively. Luke's eyes were boring into his. Maybe it was the half-light or the faint stubble, but Rob thought he looked devastatingly handsome.

"Darling, you know you can tell us anything. You don't have to bottle it up and keep these things inside" said his mother earnestly. "That's often what causes the problem in the first place. Now, if there's something bothering you…" Rob looked at the floorboards, and started to rock the porch seat back and forth with his heel.

"Robbie, quit that" said his father sharply. "I don't need a fairground ride at this time of night." Luke stubbed out his cigarette, and got up.

"Can I get y'all anything else to drink?"

"We-ell" said his mother "I know I shouldn't, but if you could just fix me another Martini? Do you know how to do that, or would you like me to show you?"

"I know how to do it" said Rob quickly, rising to his feet. "I'll go in and help Luke."

"You can get me a refill, son" said Joe, handing his glass to Luke.

In the kitchen, Rob followed his brother into the pantry. They were standing very close to each other. Luke turned to face him, holding him at arm's length.

"Cool it. One of them could walk in any minute."

"I like to live dangerously" said Rob.

"Don't I know it" muttered Luke. His brother was attracted to danger like a moth to a flame. Rob had been dicing with death at a very early age. At the age of nine he perfected what he called the "death dive". He would stand at the top of the highest diving board with his arms clamped rigidly to his sides, and launch himself like a human catapult, surrounded by a flock of children who screamed and gasped. Luke had stood there watching, chewing his lip grimly, fearing for his brother's life. Rob's trick was to fling his arms out in the nick of time before he hit the bottom, but another kid who tried the same stunt had cracked his skull open on the concrete floor. When they went tobogganing in winter Rob picked his slopes with care; he liked ninety-degree angles and always went down headfirst. At zoos he would stick his arm through the lions' cages, withdrawing it just in time while onlookers screamed in horror. He had a habit of wandering off on his own and Luke would be dispatched to look for him. On one occasion Luke found Rob up to his usual tricks, mesmerised by a growling tiger that was prowling up and down restlessly. Rob stuck his fingers through the bars and called out to it in provoking tones. Luke had jerked him back roughly.

"What do you think you're doing?"

"Teasing the cat."

"That's no cat, Rob. Look at his eyes. That tiger's so angry he doesn't want to be stroked, he wants to tear you to pieces."

"I know he's mad. That's why I'm teasing him." This response was typical. Rob had never been able to turn down a dare, and when he was about twelve years old another boy called Randy had dared him to crawl through the big concrete pipe leading to the reservoir. At one o'clock every afternoon the local water authorities flooded the pipes, and the water came barrelling through like Snake River in Colorado. If you got stuck in there you'd drown. It was twelve-thirty and Randy figured there was plenty of time to make it to the other end since Rob had gone through the pipe once before in ten minutes flat. Rob had disappeared down the pipe like a dog after a rabbit before Luke could stop him. He had waited tensely for his brother to emerge from the other end, whilst Randy stood by making unhelpful remarks like "Perhaps a copperhead's got him." Randy never took any risks himself; he got a vicarious thrill from getting Rob to act upon his dares. Luke ran down the length of the pipe banging on it with a rock, until he heard Rob's cries echoing faintly. He had somehow managed to get stuck about a third of the way along the pipe.

"What's the problem, Rob?" he shouted.

"My foot's stuck… I think the shoe-lace got caught."

"Take your shoe off."

"I can't reach it" Rob called back "Not enough room to turn." For the first time in his life, Luke had panicked. It would have been madness for Luke to attempt go after him as he was considerably bigger than the other two boys, and would have got stuck himself, creating a human barrier which his brother couldn't get past.

"Got your knife?" The boys never went anywhere without their knives.

"Yeah, but…"

"Grab your knife, reach down and cut the lace."

"I can't quite reach…."

"Yes you can! Bunch yourself up like a cat. Do it NOW." There was silence for a whole minute, while Luke paced up and down. It was now 12:45pm. Only fifteen minutes before the pipes were flooded. "Robbie, I don't care if you have scrape all the skin off your arm, just DO IT!!" Another minute went by and then "I got it" came the faint but triumphant reply.

"Scoot back the way you came. Backwards not forwards. As fast as you can." Rob had only managed to get a third of the way through the pipe, and although it was more awkward to crawl backwards there wasn't enough time for him to crawl forwards through the remaining two-thirds before water flooded the feeder pipe from another section which joined up to the main pipe. When the soles of Rob's feet appeared five minutes later - one of them missing a sneaker - Luke took hold of his heels and yanked him out. His elbows were skinned raw from shimmying backwards over the rough concrete interior. The boys retreated to the top of a bank from where, several minutes later, they heard the thunderous rumbling sound of the water rushing through the pipe. Another eight minutes or so and Rob would have been drowned.

Luke strode off rapidly towards a nearby creek, the other two boys close on his heels. Rob could tell his brother was furious since he wasn't talking to either of them. Once at the creek, Luke stripped off to his jeans. Then he jumped in, wading out to where the water was deepest.

"I dare you to come in for a swim with me." As Rob started to follow Luke said "Not you. Him" pointing to Randy.

"Are there any water moccasins in there?" asked Randy suspiciously, wondering why Luke wanted him to join him in the creek.

"Nope. Why, you scared of something, little sissy pants?" Randy took off his T-shirt and shoes, then leaped in. As he swam towards the middle of the creek, Luke seized him by the shoulders and ducked him underneath the water, holding him down. He'd recently landed a summer job as a lifeguard at the public swimming pool so he knew exactly how long most people could hold their breath under water. He could hold his own for between 60 – 90 seconds, but most people started panicking after about twenty seconds or so. When Randy started to thrash around Luke allowed him up for air, giving him a couple of seconds to recover, before ducking him again. He repeated this a few times before finally releasing him. "If you *ever* put my brother's life in danger again with one of your stupid dares, I'll hold you under for twice as long." Randy never asked Rob to perform any dares again.

"Some time before Christmas might be nice, boys" came their father's sarcastic voice, in much the same tone as when he told them to "pipe down" when they were younger and playing some boisterous game, or when he complained they sounded "like a herd of buffalo" when they came thundering down the stairs after smelling the aroma of pancakes wafting up from the kitchen.

"Coming right up" called Rob. "Hey, Luke, what do I put in a Martini?"

"Thought you said you knew."

"That was just an excuse to get right up close to your manhood."

"I mean it, Robbie. Get back in the kitchen and fix Mom a Martini before I..."

"Before you give me a good leathering with your belt?" Rob mimicked a brutish character he'd seen on a daytime soap opera, a West Virginia coal-miner who staggered home drunk every night and slapped his wife around: *"Now git in that kitchen, little lady, and fix me an apple pie before I whup your ass. And then I want you to git up them stairs and warm my bed for me"* continued Rob, who had quite a talent for mimicry. Luke laughed as he poured a generous slug of Maker's Mark into his father's glass. Rob took an egg from a carton, cracked it, and dumped the contents into his mother's glass.

"What do you think you're doing? You don't put an egg in a Martini." Luke poured the contents down the sink.

"I've seen her do it!"

"That's a prairie oyster, you fool."

"Shaken not stirred, please" called their mother. Rob put *Mony Mony* by Tommy James and the Shondells on the record player, and started mixing another drink, shaking the contents whilst jiving around the room:

Break 'dis, shake 'dis, Mony, Mony
Shot gun, get it done, come on, honey

Don't stop cookin', it feels so good, yeah
Hey! well don't stop now, hey, come on Mony,
Well come on, Mony
I say yeah, (yeah), yeah, (yeah)
Yeah, (yeah), yeah, (yeah), yeah, (yeah)

"Turn that racket off, boys!" yelled their father, at the same time as Rob dropped the drink onto the floor, shattering the glass into fragments.

"That's enough. I want you out of here." Luke picked Rob up bodily and dumped him back outside on the porch swing.

"Luke, don't get rough with your little brother" said their mother "Just because you're bigger than him."

"He was asking for it. What are the ingredients for a Martini?"

"Oh, I'll come and do it myself." His mother rose from her seat and followed him back into the kitchen, sighing. As she passed Luke, she murmured. "How is he? He's been on a high, what the doctor calls manic, ever since you called your uncle about the cabin." Jim and Martha owned a log cabin in the Appalachians not far from the Cumberland Gap, and Luke had suggested that he and Rob spend a long weekend together hiking through the woods.

"He's been a little hyper" admitted Luke, who was on his knees, attempting to mop up the mess on the floor.

"I think it's very good of you to spend time with your brother, it will do you both a world of good....Oh no!" exclaimed his mother. "Who broke the cabinet door?"

"Luke did" giggled Rob, appearing in the doorway "He's got such a delicate touch." When Luke opened the cabinet door to get the whiskey it had come off in his hand.

"Honey, while you're here, it's time for your medication." Rob scowled as she shook out some pills from two different bottles and handed them to him. He swallowed the pills, and went back out onto the porch, followed by his mother, who joined her husband on the porch swing. Joe put an arm around her.

"Finally got your martini, hon?"

"I always say 'If a job wants doing, do it yourself'" replied his wife. Luke came out a moment later, and leaned his elbows on the wooden porch railing, a whiskey in his hand. Rob was swinging from the porch rafters like a monkey, hand over hand, going from side to side.

"Thought those tranquillisers were meant to calm him down" muttered Joe, re-lighting his pipe. He raised his eyes ceiling-ward in exasperation.

"They take about twenty minutes to kick in" his wife replied. "Would you listen to those crickets. I love that sound. It's so peaceful." After exchanging glances with his parents, Luke hoisted Rob down from his perch and pulled him onto the opposite porch swing beside him. Most people thought he picked Rob up to show off his superior strength, but Luke wondered whether it wasn't just an excuse to hold him in his arms for a couple of minutes: his skin smelled fresh and clean, like soap, or the pine needles of the trees he was always climbing. Rob rarely objected to being manhandled by Luke for much the same reason. The close physical proximity was a secret source of pleasure for both of them.

Connie looked over at her two sons. Luke was sitting lengthways across the porch swing, with one leg stretched across the seat and his other foot on the floor. He had one arm resting along the back of the porch seat, with Rob firmly clasped against his chest, cradling him like he was a child. Or like a man and his sweetheart, thought Connie. If it was a father and child, or husband and wife you wouldn't think anything of it, but they were both grown men. Luke had turned twenty-five last month and Rob was twenty. It was touching that they were so close and never bickered like most siblings do, but on the other hand maybe Joe was right in thinking the relationship between them was a little unhealthy. He had voiced his concerns to her the other night, stating that in his opinion the brothers were "far too close." She watched them for a few more moments. They were conversing together in low tones, Luke bending his head slightly forward to catch his brother's words. It was if the outburst the other week had never occurred, and Rob had completely forgotten whatever it was that had upset him.

It was probably nothing, she told herself. Joe was making a mountain out of a molehill. At the barbecue her older sister Edith had remarked "I think it's so sweet the way your boys are so close. Mine just squabble all the time. I can't even get them to shake hands after they've had a fight." Rob had always been openly affectionate as a child, embracing his parents before he was sent to bed. "Goodnight Daddy, I love you. Goodnight Mama, I love you." She smiled fondly. He was such a precious boy; he would always be her baby. And as for Luke, he had always been a big strapping boy with Joe's wide shoulders, though he now topped his father by a good two inches. He'd been practically a grown man at the age of twelve, and so sure of himself: when Joe had been away for a couple of days to attend a relative's funeral, Luke had shouldered his father's shotgun - which he knew how to use - and looked directly at his mother: "Anyone comes around here bothering you, I'll scare 'em off. You and Rob don't need to worry about a thing." Joe and Luke had both served in the armed forces and Joe could still pack a pretty good punch if he'd a mind to, but there the resemblance ended. Her husband had a quick temper, and had a limited tolerance for men whom he considered to be weaker than himself, whereas Luke had a slower fuse and more patience. He had always been protective towards those who were younger or more vulnerable: that was how he was made. He realised his younger brother was emotionally fragile right now, and was making a point of spending some time with him. And it was perfectly natural for boys to idolise an older brother or another boy who was bigger and stronger. It happened all the time, and they usually grew out of it. Rob was scarcely out of his teens and she was aware that boys matured more slowly than girls. That was it, she decided. Rob was still growing, and needed to be given the space to develop at his own pace. They were both good boys.

She looked at them again. Rob was telling Luke about the time he had been pulled over for drink driving about two years ago when Luke was still in Vietnam. Normally a competent driver, Rob had been a little over the limit and had scraped the fender of a stationary vehicle at a gas station. A law enforcement officer had slapped a pair of cuffs on him and thrown him in the county jail on a DWI charge. Joe had decided to let Rob stew for a couple of days in jail before posting bail.

"I tried to make a deal with him" Rob now said. "I said *'Look, you seem like a nice fella. How about you let me off, and I don't tell your wife about the lipstick on your collar?'* He said he didn't much care for my attitude." Luke and Joe guffawed.

"Trust you to get fresh with an armed state trooper" said Luke. "Those guys don't have much of a sense of humour." Rob mimicked the officer's deadpan demeanour: *"Licence and registration. Step out of the vehicle."*

"I thought they were a little harsh, in the circumstances" Connie said. "No-one was actually hurt. Aren't these matters usually settled by the insurance companies?"

"He was over the limit and driving recklessly" Joe reminded her. "They were quite right in pulling him over. The only reason the officer threw him in jail was because Rob gave him some backchat."

"I tried to get a couple of the guards interested in a game of stud poker" said Rob. "But they kept telling me to shut up, which kinda hurt my feelings." Luke smiled.

"Robbie, did it ever occur to you that it's not in their job description to keep you entertained?" Rob examined a broken fingernail and didn't reply. Luke was kneading his ribcage absently with his blunt fingers, causing his heart to skip a few beats. Like a lot of big men, Luke had a tendency to stroke and fondle anything cute and cuddly which landed in his lap, whether it was a cat or a puppy, or in this case, his kid brother.

"We're going to turn in for the night" said his father eventually, knocking the ashes out of his pipe bowl. "Don't stay up too late, boys, if you plan on making an early start." After their parents had left, Luke pulled Rob closer into his arms, and they stayed in that position for several minutes without speaking. Eventually Luke prised Rob's arms from around his neck gently, before heading off in the dark towards the bunkhouse.

"Goodnight, Robbie. See you in the morning."

Chapter Four

Luke was tossing things into the back of the pickup, a Ford F-100, whilst his mother fussed around with Tupperware containers. "Don't forget to put in your warmest jackets" said Connie "The nights are drawing in. It can be cold up there, and I don't want you to get caught out in it while you're up in the mountains."

"We'll hole up in a cave" said Rob, leaning through the window to embrace his mother. "Besides, Luke knows how to survive anywhere." Their mother exchanged looks with Luke, who acknowledged her silent plea *Look after him* with a reassuring smile. He kissed his mother's cheek. "You and Dad take it easy. See you Monday."

They arrived at the cabin late in the afternoon, and after dumping their things by the door they brought in some more firewood from the stack outside.

"Might need to juice up the generator" said Luke. "I'll check it in a minute." Since the log cabin was off-grid, they relied on a diesel generator for a power supply, which ate up diesel and propane gas. There was an old outhouse with a pit latrine situated at some distance from the cabin, and it wasn't so very long ago that the young cousins had to be accompanied by an adult male with a shotgun: "Don't want to be caught with your pants down, boys, if a bear decides to come sniffing around" Uncle Jim would warn them, whilst standing guard outside. He had installed an indoor toilet three years ago at Aunt Martha's insistence. Uncle Jim was their favourite uncle, and Aunt Martha was their favourite aunt. Uncle Vernon was pleasant enough, but he was a different kind of guy altogether – he taught over at the Community College – whereas their father's younger brother Jim was a Turnbull and liked the same rough-and-tumble games they liked.

"Let's pretend we're hillbillies" suggested Rob. "You can be a mountain man going stir crazy up here in the mountains all by yourself." Luke advanced towards Rob in a shambling gait.

"Well, well, what have we got here….who's this cute young fella, fresh from the city and all decked out like a Christmas cracker…" Rob made a run for it. He got as far as the front stoop before Luke caught up with him and slung him over one shoulder. "Reckon you'll do, boy. You'll do just fine. Think I'll take you back to my love shack where we can get better acquainted…how 'bout it, sugar?"

"Turn me loose, you big dumb-ass" Rob protested, as he pounded Luke's back, laughing. After they'd played out the possibilities of that game without straying too much into dangerous territory, Rob declared he was Billy the Kid, who'd just been captured by a cattle rancher and tied to a tree.

"Give me one reason why I shouldn't shoot you" said Luke *aka* Tunstall.

"I'm just a poor orphan boy. My Daddy ran off before I was born, and my momma died in Silver City. I bin wanderin' about on my lonesome ever since."

"That's a mighty sad tale. Enough to make a fella weep into his pillow. Whilst wandering about on your lonesome you didn't happen to steal any of my cattle, did you, boy?"

"Why, nossir. Well, I mightta stole just one. Or two. A fella has to eat, and I'm on the run from the law."

"By my reckoning you stole forty. Where's them cattle, boy?"

"Uh, I'm real sorry, Mister, but I sold 'em. If I'd known they belonged to *you* I wouldna touched 'em. You look like a nice fella, not the kind of sorry-assed sonofabitch who would shoot a poor orphan boy in cold blood."

"I've a mind to give you a thrashing with this rawhide bullwhip. Tell you what, though, since you got such a cute little face, I'll sleep on it. In the meantime, I'm gonna leave you tied up to this tree so you can meditate on your sins." Rob widened his eyes.

"But what if a bear snuck up on me in the night and I couldn't defend myself? Why not untie me, Mister? You've got my gun."

"Think I'm gonna fall for that one, huh? I heard you busted out of jail no less than three times."

"You surely ain't scared of an unarmed and defenceless boy like me, sir? A big strong man like you." Rob ran his hand up Luke's arm, cupping his bulging biceps. "I never had no Daddy to teach me right from wrong. After Momma died my step-daddy put me in a foster home, and made me earn my own keep…"

"If I hear that orphan sob story one more time I'm gonna start bawling my eyes out. You may be a baby-faced kid but you ain't no tenderfoot. You've already shot and killed thirty men and not yet reached the age of twenty-one. If I untied you I'd have to stand guard all night long, and a man likes to get some shut-eye."

"You could keep me real close" suggested Rob coyly. "Take me into your bed, and share some of your man warmth. If I made a wrong move you'd know about it."

"*Share some of my man warmth?*" Luke started to laugh. Rob was starting to sound more like this Johnny Angel character his doctor had mentioned than the outlaw Billy the Kid. "Don't be in such a hurry to get your cherry busted." Rob blushed and backed off a little, then suddenly switched roles, assuming the more familiar character of Jesse James.

"What are we going to do, Frank? There's a 100-strong posse hard on our trail, I've got a $5000 bounty on my head, and we've been hiding out in this stinking cave for a coon's age. We need money and we need it fast - why don't we rob another bank?"

"You've robbed just about every bank in Missouri, Jesse" replied Luke. "I think we should head down into Kentucky and maybe hook up with some of Bloody Bill Anderson's bushwhackers or Captain Quantrill's Raiders. Just like old times. Too many damned Jayhawkers in these parts for my liking." He paused to toss another two logs on the fire, sending up a shower of orange sparks.

"This is two days later" said Rob. "Frank has just been captured and taken prisoner by your posse. He's holed up in some lock-up somewhere in Dodge City and I'm spitting blood. You're Wyatt Earp, and I've just requested a private parley with you in Rattlesnake Canyon to see if we can cut a deal."

"How come you didn't get caught too?" enquired Luke.

"Not only am I the fastest gun in the West I can ride like the wind. Your gang couldn't keep up with me. Frank's horse took some buckshot and threw him off. Get into character." Luke grabbed hold of him.

"Not so fast, there, Jesse, my boy. I sure hate to have to put a gallows necktie around that neck of yours, but you're gonna swing for this. You just shot two of my men in cold blood."

"My condolences, Marshall. But you'll have to catch me first, big man." He smiled at Luke.

"Ain't gonna do you no good flashing those blue eyes at me" said Luke. "Don't think you can sweet-talk your way out of this one." Robbie took a step closer so that their bodies were practically touching, never taking his eyes off Luke for one moment. Wyatt Earp, the tough Frontier Marshall, was his favourite hero – tough enough, strong enough, and smart enough to track down infamous outlaws like the James brothers, and Luke was perfect in the role.

"I didn't know you cared, Marshall. You like my blue eyes? Uh, is that a six-shooter I feel pressed up against my manhood or are you just pleased to see me?" Luke's lips twitched and he suddenly guffawed. His brother's flirting was outrageous. Rob slithered out of his grasp and Luke gave chase, with Rob dodging behind the back of the couch and aiming an imaginary gun at him. "I'm real sorry, Marshall. You're one heck of a handsome fella but that won't stop me from blasting you out of the saddle. I understand the good folks of Tombstone want you to be their sheriff and I know you're headed that way real soon. You may be the toughest lawman in these parts but you can't be in two places at once. If you don't turn my brother Frank loose, I'm going to ride into Dodge City and tear the place up, then I'm going to rob every bank and freight train from Kansas all the way clear to Tennessee." Luke pulled him right across the top of the couch, before pinning him down with his body weight.

"Don't get fresh with me, son. I'm getting tired of all this backchat. I'm gonna run you out of Dodge if it's the last thing I ever do. But first I'm going to teach you a lesson you won't forget in a hurry." Rob gazed up at him, biting his lower lip. Loubelle's strategy was working beyond his wildest dreams. When she'd told him *"Most people swing both ways, it's just that nobody wants to admit up to it..."* he hadn't believed it could work on a straight man, let alone his own brother.

"Well, Marshall?" Rob challenged him. "I take it you're not gonna string me up after all – perhaps you got other things in mind you want to do to me?"

"A piece of advice, Robbie" said Luke, releasing him. "Don't ever come on to a guy like that, otherwise you might just get more than you bargained for."

"I don't come on to other guys. You're the only one." Rob had by this time manoeuvred himself across Luke's knees, so that he was stretched out flat on his back. "You wouldn't deny a condemned man a last smoke, Marshall?" Luke reached across to the side table and picked up a pack of Marlboros. He had a sudden image of a Zippo Raid, where they would burn down a village occupied by insurgents, igniting huts with a Zippo lighter. The raids were specifically directed at Communist strongholds, where VC guerrilla fighters were terrorizing the local peasantry, but inevitably innocent civilians got caught up in the crossfire. Luke lit a cigarette, took a drag, and placed it in his brother's mouth. "Come on, Marshall. You've been sorely tempted ever since you laid eyes on me. Not many folks get to see Jesse James up this close. I would do just about anything to get my brother out of jail. Anything special I can do for you, sir?" Robbie was blowing smoke-rings, seemingly lost in a trance. The top three buttons of his flies had somehow come unfastened and Luke knew he wasn't responsible for that.

"Thought we laid down some ground rules" said Luke, after a moment's pause. "No below the waist action."

"Those are *your* rules, Marshall." Rob tossed the butt into an ashtray. "I'm an outlaw and I play by my OWN rules." He gazed at Luke through half open eyelids, his long dark eyelashes feathering his cheek, then slowly raised his arms behind his head, stretching languorously. "I bet you can't resist me" went on Rob "If you're a man of the law, the man you claim to be, it shouldn't be too hard.

Why don't we put it to the test? I give you ten minutes at most." Luke rested his forearms along the back of the couch and shifted his mental focus elsewhere, anything to take his mind off the beautiful boy lying across his knees and offering his body. As the minutes ticked by Luke contemplated the oak rafters, and made a mental inventory of the jobs that needed doing when they got back. He needed to erect a 3-rail wooden fence between a line of fence posts he'd sunk the other day. Then he wanted to finish laying down the floor joists for a carpentry workshop he was building as a rear extension to his bunkhouse. Rob raised himself up and kissed the base of Luke's throat, just beneath his Adam's apple. "I think you just passed the test, Mister. You're strong. And I don't just mean *this*." He landed a playful punch on Luke right bicep before getting up and fastening his flies.

In the kitchen, Rob handed Luke a bottle of cold beer from the fridge. Then, instead of grabbing one for himself, he took a swig out of Luke's. "Now that's what I call giving with one hand and taking away with the other" said Luke.

"It's called sharing, brother. Don't you think Jesse would have shared things with Frank? And Doc Holliday would have done anything for Wyatt Earp."

"Did any of those guys actually run into each other?" enquired Luke.

"Yeah, Billy the Kid once had dinner with Jesse James, and he also gambled with Wyatt Earp's best buddy, Doc Holliday, and beat him. Wyatt didn't drink" added Rob. "He preferred ice-cream."

"Steered clear of the old rotgut, huh? Smart guy" commented Luke. "A lot easier to win a gunfight against a bunch of cowboys who are so liquored up they can't shoot straight. How about some music" he suggested, his eye alighting on a record player gathering dust in a corner. Rob thumbed through a stack of singles, occasionally snickering. "Jim Reeves. *Welcome To My World. The Last Waltz* by Engelbert Humperdink, *Release Me* by Humperdink again..." They both laughed.

"Sounds more like Aunt Martha's taste than Dale's" smiled Luke. "What else have they got?"

"Country and Western. Johnny Cash. That'd be Uncle Jim. Oh wait, here's some other stuff that might be better. *Woolly Bully* by Sam the Sham and the Pharaohs, *Wild Thing* by The Troggs, *Light My Fire* by Jim Morrison...hey, did you know that Janis Joplin knocked him out cold at the *Whiskey A Go Go* Club on Sunset Strip? He was coming on to her and she wasn't interested. After that, he was absolutely crazy about her."

"Morrison probably deserved it" commented Luke. "He's that weird dude who performs on stage with a snake down his leather pants, right? I always had him pegged as a sissy boy. I prefer Hendrix. That cat can really play the guitar."

"*Light My Fire* is about getting it on" said Rob, as he selected half a dozen singles and slid them onto the central spindle.

"Half the stuff in the hit parade is about getting it on. C'mere and I'll show you some moves." Rob placed his hands on Luke's shoulders tentatively. "Now jump up on me" directed Luke. "Come on, it's all right, I've got you." Rob jumped up onto him, wrapping his legs around his mid section. Luke bent him backwards, supporting the small of his back with his right forearm, and started to swing him around. "Hold on tight."

Here she come down, say Mony Mony
Well, shoot 'em down, turn around come home, honey
Hey, she gimme love an' I feel all right now...

I say yeah, (yeah), yeah, (yeah)
Yeah, (yeah), yeah, (yeah), yeah
Break 'dis, shake 'dis, Mony, Mony
Shot gun, get it done, come on, honey

Don't stop cookin', it feels so good, yeah
Hey! well don't stop now, hey, come on Mony,
Well come on, Mony
I say yeah, (yeah), yeah, (yeah)
Yeah, (yeah), yeah, (yeah), yeah, (yeah)

As Luke placed his hands beneath Rob's butt and lifted him up a little in order to consolidate his position, Rob suddenly sprang free from Luke's grasp and landed back down on the floor.

"What's the matter?"

"I'm not doing that girl thing any more." It felt too much like the "stand-and-carry" position, where a man with a sufficiently strong back and shoulders is able to fuck a woman whilst supporting her weight in his arms. He had seen Luke carry Cindy Foster around like this at someone's pool party when Luke was about eighteen. Although Luke had been in his swimming trunks and Cindy in her bikini, it was pretty obvious to onlookers what was going on between them.

"All right" said Luke. "Let's try something else." He swung Rob away from him in a Rock 'n Roll dance move, then yanked him forward again, slamming his pelvis against Rob's so hard it made him gasp. I'm going to get you for that, thought Rob, as the next single dropped onto the stack. Just wait, you bastard.

Wild thing, you make my heart sing (Bump and GRIND)
You make everything groovy, wild thing
Wild thing, I think you move me
But I wanna know for sure (GRIND)

Luke's style of dancing – if you could call it dancing – was fast and exciting, if somewhat rough. "I knew you were a hard man, Marshall" said Rob. "But this kind of hard is beyond belief." Luke's eyes bored into his. The next single *Do You Love Me?* by the Contours, dropped onto the turntable and the needle moved across the vinyl, finding its groove.

Do you love me? (I can really move)
Do you love me? (I'm in the groove)
Now do you love me?
(Do you love me now that I can dance?)
Watch me, now
(Work, work) ah, work it out baby
(Work, work) well, I'm gonna drive you crazy
(Work, work) ah, just a little bit of soul, now?

Now I can mash potatoes (I can mash potatoes)
I can do the twist (I can do the twist)
*Tell me, baby, do you like it like **this**?*

Rob had insinuated his right thigh between Luke's. He hooked an elbow around Luke's neck to steady himself, and then suddenly brought his knee up to his groin, working it into his crotch.

Tell me, tell me
*Tell me, baby, do you like it like **this**?*

"Whoa. Little prick tease" murmured Luke. "Would you care, or would you *dare* to try that again?"

"Did it turn you on?" asked Rob. Johnny Angel was back with a vengeance. Luke laughed and caught a handful of Rob's hair in his fist.

"Wanna play catch-up?" He was referring to their afternoon up by Clearwater Creek - resuming where they'd left off. Before Rob could answer, they were interrupted in their revels by an insistent knocking at the door. Rob looked at Luke, wondering who it could be at this time of night. Luke grabbed his shotgun and flung open the front door, flipping the outside light switch on. Two men stood there, silhouetted in the doorframe. They'd been out hunting elk, they explained, but didn't appear to have much to show for it and had been looking in all the wrong places.

"We saw the lights from the cabin, heard the music and all..." said one of them.

"So you thought you'd come on over and gatecrash a private party" said Luke. "What do you want, gentlemen?" His tone wasn't too friendly.

"Uh, it's cold out there, you got a nice fire going, and some bottles of beer would go down real nice" suggested the other hopefully. "Thought there might be some kind of party going on."

"Like I said, this is a private party" repeated Luke unhelpfully. He stepped outside, closing the door behind him.

"Say, if you've got a chick in there or something we didn't mean to interrupt your private business." At this point Rob came strolling out onto the front porch, cool as a cucumber, and clad only in his white T-shirt and jeans. He stationed himself against one of the wooden porch uprights, widening his eyes innocently. "What's going on, fellas?" Thanks, little brother, thought Luke. That's just fine and dandy. Adonis himself takes centre stage. The men eyed them both speculatively. A man and a beautiful boy, alone in a cabin. Probably thought they were a couple of fags.

"Who's that?" asked one of them, gesturing in Rob's direction. "Acquaintance of yours?"

"This here's my brother" replied Luke. "I keep my acquaintances tied up in the barn." It was a corny line plagiarised from some Western. He thought the original line might have been "This here's my buddy...." but it only served to confuse the two men, who looked back and forth between them.

"This is Dale's cabin" said one of them finally. "He said, uh, we could use it from time to time."

"Dale's our cousin, as it happens" said Luke. "As you can see, it's occupied right now." One of them clapped a hand to his forehead.

"You've gotta be Joe Turnbull's boys. You're the one who went out to 'Nam. Pleased to meet you, buddy." He held out his hand to Luke, who shook it, but didn't offer any other comment. "So you gonna let us in or not?"

"Not. Thought I'd made that clear."

"Maybe let them have a beer or something, Luke" suggested Rob in a conciliatory tone. Luke gave him a glance and shrugged as if to say *"Go get some then. I'm keeping an eye on these dudes."* Rob returned a moment later with some drinks and the tension eased somewhat, as they lounged on the front stoop shooting the breeze.

"What were the Vietnamese chicks like?" asked one of them.

"Girls are girls" said Luke laconically.

"Didn't you go out with Cindy Foster? I hear tell she's on her own now. You hear anything from her these days?" Luke shrugged again. He didn't care to discuss his former girlfriends with these two. And he very much doubted Cindy would give either of them the time of day. Rob got the impression he didn't like them much. Luke was being cordial enough on the surface, but was watching their every move. Any funny business and he'd be on them like a shot.

"No need to be quite so unfriendly. I call that downright mean, not inviting us in."

"My brother's not mean at all" said Rob, moving to stand beside Luke. "He killed a bunch of bad guys when he was over there. But apart from that" He favoured them with one of his dazzling smiles "he's a heck of a nice guy." After sizing up Luke again, they evidently thought better of pursuing whatever it was they were in pursuit of, and made themselves scarce. Luke kicked the door shut behind him, locked it, and drew the curtains.

"Let's dance some more" said Rob "A slow dance this time – no more fast stuff."

"All right" said Luke, gesturing towards the stack of singles. "So long as it's not *The Last Waltz*...." Rob picked *Crazy* by Patsy Cline and *Smoke Gets In Your Eyes* by The Platters, Luke amused at what he considered to be a "girlie" choice. "You like that smoochy, romantic stuff, huh?"

"Sometimes" admitted Rob. He liked it when he was slow-dancing with the man he loved. Luke sensed a change of mood in his brother. Robbie could switch quite suddenly like that. One minute he was acting outrageously, subject to wild enthusiasms, and the next he was withdrawn or quiet.

"Who are you now?" asked Luke, holding him closer. Rob had his arms clasped around Luke's neck, cheek on his shoulder "Billy the Kid, Jesse James, or Johnny Angel?"

"I'm me, Robbie" said Rob. He'd had his excitement for the night, and wanted a little tenderness. Luke gave it to him.

****

The next morning Rob was in a playful mood again. He was attempting to tussle with Luke, who was stripped to the waist and shaving in front of a foggy mirror. A line of black hair like a marching column of ants led from his navel all the way down to the hard-to-ignore bulge somewhere beneath his belt.

"Cut it out, will you. I've got a razor in my hand."

"You think you could wrestle me to the ground, muscleman?"

"I doubt that would take very long" replied Luke. Rob grabbed hold of his belt buckle and tugged at it. Luke took hold of Rob's hand, curled it into a fist and very slowly crushed it in his.

"Ow. That hurt."

"Curiosity killed the cat. Lay off my equipment."

"I've already seen you in the shower" countered Rob provocatively. Luke continued shaving.

"Hope it gave you a thrill."

"Very impressive, Mister." Luke made a move as if to come after him.

"Get outta here. Go see if there's anything in the cupboards we can eat for breakfast."

"Yessir." Rob reported back a few moments later. "Nothing except popcorn." The previous night they'd polished off everything their mother had packed in Tupperware. Luke put away his razor and shrugged himself into a tight-fitting black T-shirt, which emphasised his well-defined muscles and powerful shoulders.

"We'll take a ride into town, pick up some supplies, and catch up with Dale if he's around. Put on a jacket or something. It's cold out there." Luke put on his tan buckskin hunter's jacket, and tossed Rob's sheepskin-lined denim one to him.

Luke drove the pickup down the rutted track and turned off onto the back route into town for some breakfast at *Donna's Deluxe Dinette*. They used the payphone to make a call to Dale, who said to hang on and that he'd be right over. Rob slid into the red vinyl booth opposite his brother, as the waitress skipped up to their table to take their orders.

"What can I get you boys? We got pancakes, waffles, ham and eggs, sausage and eggs…" Luke ordered sausage and eggs for both of them, and a pot of coffee. Whilst they were waiting for their order **Patsy Cline crooned** *I Fall to Pieces* on the jukebox, and ten minutes later **Dale swung open the door, accompanied by a cold blast of wind.**

"Hey, little cuz" said Luke, catching him up in a bear hug. Dale wasn't little, being six foot tall, but he was younger and Luke regarded him as almost a second little brother.

"Hey, cuz" said Rob, smiling at him. He and Dale were about the same age and had always got on pretty well. His cousin had sometimes joined them in their childhood cowboy games up in the woods, when they visited with their parents. He and Luke were usually the James brothers, and Dale was Billy the Kid.

"Hey, guys. Everything OK up at the cabin? Looks like there might be snow."

"Sure. We appreciate you letting us stay there" said Luke. "A couple of dudes showed up last night who said they'd been out hunting elk, whitetail or whatever but these guys couldn't take down a bear taking a nap at a distance of twenty paces. They said you loaned them the cabin from time to time."

"Well, they were lying. No-one's been in there since last fall, and I haven't got any arrangement with anyone except you guys. They give you any bother?"

"Nope. Scared 'em off. But I think they were expecting to find something else. Beaver-hunting was their game, I would say." Dale became serious.

"We've had some trouble around here just lately. A woman was attacked near the trail some weeks ago, and another girl was damn near raped. She and her boyfriend were staying at one of the other cabins. He left her for about fifteen minutes to get some more firewood, and two guys came out of the woods and jumped her. Boyfriend came back just in time. They gave a description to the sheriff – you think they're the same ones?"

"Could be" said Luke. "Thanks, darlin'" The waitress set down some plates on the table and poured them some coffee.

"Mind if I join you guys for breakfast?" Without waiting for an answer, Dale proceeded to attack a stack of waffles he had drenched in maple syrup.

"They must have been local because they knew who our dad was and they knew it was your cabin" supplied Rob. "Luke didn't like the looks of them from the get go. How did you know they were up to no good?" he asked his brother.

"I've got an instinct for that kind of trouble. Can smell it a mile off" replied Luke, who had come across similar incidents in

Vietnam. Whilst passing through some rice fields, Luke had overheard one of the grunts - a big tattooed meathead called Dorsey - mutter something about snatching a girl. Luke had kept a close eye on him, but later that afternoon when he was busy checking through their kit, one of the other men had come up to him.

"Sir, Dorsey's got hold of a girl, and won't let go of her." Luke grabbed Sgt. Moreland, and they both set off at a run. When they got to the scene, they saw a young Vietnamese girl struggling to get free and sobbing. Dorsey had picked her up off the ground and tucked her underneath one arm like a bedroll, whilst simultaneously slapping her around the face with his other hand to shut her up.

"Shut up, will ya, I ain't gonna hurt ya-" The sight of two more big men racing in her direction only served to terrify her further, and she was by this time hysterical.

"Put the girl DOWN!" Dorsey dropped her to the ground seconds before Luke and Moreland slammed into him, and the girl took off – heading towards a cluster of huts in the distance. Dorsey was strong-armed back to camp, before being taken to one side.

"Hold him down" said Luke. He and the sarge were compelled to act as Enforcers whenever discipline was required. Moreland held Dorsey in an arm lock while Luke roughed him up.

"We follow orders in this army, soldier, not instincts. Otherwise we're no better than animals. You feel the need to shoot your wad, go to a brothel. The local female population is strictly off-limits. If I ever catch you fooling with a girl again, not only will I see you court-martialled, I'll twist your fucking balls off." For added emphasis, Luke grabbed hold of the guy's balls and gave them a vicious twist. Dorsey let out a bloodcurdling yell, sounding like he'd got his dick caught in a wringer. Some of the other men, who'd been surreptitiously watching the proceedings from a distance, turned back to their main preoccupation, which was shovelling food down their necks as fast as possible. The unit frequently had little more than five minutes to grab something to eat before they were on the move again, and they knew better than to interfere when the platoon leader and sergeant were administering discipline, or "tough love."

"And that's just a taster. Got the message?"

"All right, all right. I was just fooling with her. Wasn't gonna hurt her none." He bent double as Luke landed a punch in his solar plexus. One more stunt like that, and Luke would have him transferred to another outfit. He didn't want some doofus like Dorsey in his squad, a maverick rotten apple infecting the rest. What Dorsey regarded as "fooling around" was major trauma for a woman, and they didn't need that kind of trouble. The villagers were hostile enough as it was, and they didn't trust American GIs any more than they trusted VC guerrilla fighters. Every time a soldier broke out it gave them all a bad name, and made their missions that much more difficult to accomplish.

They had orders to search every village they encountered for enemy insurgents, and Luke therefore had no choice but to round up the inhabitants of the village to which the girl had fled, whilst his men searched the huts. Dorsey was almost immediately surrounded by a swarm of small boys who darted around him with miniature penknives, then streaked off before he could retaliate. Increasingly maddened, Dorsey had borne it for as long as he was able, then he'd finally grabbed hold of two of the nearest and cracked their heads together.

"Knock it off, Dorsey" said Luke sharply. "They're just kids." Dorsey looked outraged.

"I'm supposed to just stand here like a human pin cushion and take it?"

"You stand there and take it" Luke told him. "Big tough guy, aren't you?" He scanned the knot of huddled villagers, in an attempt to identify a parental figure or someone who wielded some authority over the kids. They all looked frightened. Luke did not think for one moment that these people posed a threat, they were simply defenceless peasants caught up in a war they did not comprehend and had not asked for. There was absolutely no need for his men, who were fully armed, to throw their weight around. Eventually a woman stepped forward and spoke to one of the boys (his mother, Luke assumed) which had the desired effect, and the boys backed off. Luke asked if anyone spoke English, and when an elderly man responded in the affirmative he said "Please accept our apologies for the earlier incident with the female. It won't happen again." He also gave them to understand in no uncertain terms that if they didn't rein in their kids there might be consequences. The man nodded before relaying this message to the others. Dorsey punched the air, and Luke turned to him.

"What did you expect, man? That was somebody's sister, somebody's daughter you tried to assault. Actions have consequences." Having found no trace of the enemy, the platoon had then moved off with all the usual gripes – in this instance that the military authorities hadn't seen fit to provide them with an APC to carry them through flooded rice paddies and irrigation dykes without getting their feet wet.

"Luke…" Rob was touching him, lightly stroking the hairs on his muscled forearm, which was laid out on the Formica tabletop. Dale was at the counter settling the bill and chatting with an older woman, probably the owner.

"Sorry, I was a million miles away just there." Rob smiled at him and silently mouthed *I love you.* On the jukebox Patsy Cline was still singing mournfully about a discarded mistress.

I've got your picture
That you gave to me
And it's signed with love
Just like it used to be
The only thing different
The only thing new
I've got your picture
She's got you…

At home Rob had an old photo of his brother in battle fatigues, leaning against a utility truck or "quarter-ton", and cradling an M-60 machine gun. He was looking directly into the camera, but his eyes had a far off glaze, like those of travellers who have returned from distant parts of the globe. Rob treasured that photo which had been taped to the inside door of his high-school locker, and now took pride of place in his bedroom. He had another favourite snapshot, taken in the arrivals lounge of the airport concourse when they had all gone to meet Luke after he had completed his last tour of Vietnam. Luke was in his khakis, standing between their parents with his arms around them. Rob had taken that photo himself, after requesting they all smile for the camera. Luke tended to smile with his eyes rather than his mouth, and the effect was very sexy. It was around the time Rob was starting to realise he might be attracted to men, and the sight of his strong handsome brother, someone he had always known and admired but who was in many ways a stranger, had stirred something in him. And then Luke had caught him up in his arms for a bear hug, lifting him off the ground and practically squeezing the life out of him. He had felt strangely excited all afternoon as Luke exchanged small talk with his parents. At one point, Luke had turned to him. "So how have things been with *you*, little brother. Missed me?" Wordlessly, Rob had handed him a thick leather wristband he had purchased for him from a Native American Indian crafts store.

"*Thank* you" replied Luke, placing the emphasis on the first syllable. "Is that for me?" He had smiled at Rob, before putting it in his pocket. "Sweet of you. I'm sure I'll find a use for it."

"You didn't even look at the engraving on the back" Rob had protested. As a matter of fact Luke had glimpsed the inscription *Love from Rob XXX* etched onto a small metal plate like a dog tag, but had thought it advisable not to advertise this in front of his parents, who might wonder about the three kisses.

"Boys, you can't leave without tasting some of my homemade pecan pie." The woman Dale had been conversing with came over to their table carrying a pie dish.

"I couldn't eat another thing" protested Rob, who didn't have as large an appetite as his brother. "I guess you must be Deluxe Donna of the Delicious Dinette or would that be Delicious Donna of the Deluxe Dinette."

"You guess right, sugar. Dale, you never told me you had such gorgeous cousins."

"That's why I keep them so well-hidden. Wouldn't want them showing their faces around here too often, otherwise the rest of us guys wouldn't stand a chance."

"Honey, can I tempt you?" Donna offered Luke a slice, which he accepted.

"Never tasted better" affirmed Luke. "Maybe you could wrap up the rest of that pie so we could take it with us."

"Knew you wouldn't be able to resist. Be right back."

"I always thought I was something special" said Dale "Until I found out Donna flirts with all her customers, even the female ones."

"I just can't help it" retorted Donna over her shoulder in a lazy Southern drawl. "You know what they say. Northerners are uptight, and Southerners are sexy." She returned a few moments later with the pie wrapped up in greaseproof paper, and handed it to Luke, who reached for his wallet. She swatted his hand away.

"Compliments of the house." She trailed her fingers through Rob's hair. "Come back real soon." Dale and Luke laughed.

"Women ALWAYS have to do that" said Dale, with mock exasperation, turning to Luke. "Can't keep their hands off him. What's he got that we haven't got?" Rob shrugged and smiled as if to say *How would I know?*

"Aw, now would you look at that. He's blushing" said Donna. "Ain't that about the sweetest thing you ever saw?" Rob dipped his gaze, and looked around the room helplessly.

"Guess we'd better make a move" said Luke, rising from the table "before this kid has the whole town chasing his tail." As they went out through the door, they heard Donna exclaim to a female patron who was wearing a Western-style fringed mini skirt and cowboy boots "Darlin' where did you get that cute outfit? Why, if I wasn't a happily married woman, you might just have me batting for the other side." Luke and Dale laughed again.

"Don't you just love her?" Dale said he had to take care of some business and they parted company at the hardware store.

Chapter Five

Luke drove south towards the Cumberland Gap, the scene of many fierce engagements between Unionist and Confederate forces during the Civil War, and where - a visitor information board informed them - the borders of three states (Kentucky, Tennessee and Virginia) converged: the Cumberland Gap had once served as a gateway through the Appalachian mountain range and been used by Native American Indians before the 200-mile trail known as the "Wilderness Road" was blazed and made accessible to pioneers and settlers by frontiersmen like Daniel Boone.

They set off to do some backcountry hiking through miles of trails through the forested mountains, occasionally stopping at elevated lookout points to admire the views. Luke had often dreamed of the Blue Ridge Mountains whilst he'd been away: the spectacular colour of the leaves in fall, and of hiking through crisp virgin snow with Rob by his side, and the afternoon entirely lived up to his expectations. It was one of those perfect days with nothing to mar their enjoyment – beautiful scenery, good company. At about 3pm he called a halt, as snowflakes started to feather the air. "Looks like Dale was right" commented Luke. "We'll take a shortcut back. It could come down heavy." Although it was only October and snow was unusual at this time of year, deep snowdrifts could obscure the trails and it might prove difficult to retrace their steps. Although they were both pretty good at finding their way around, they were hiking through less familiar terrain: the woods extended for miles and people had been known to become lost in the mountains for days.

"What shortcut should we take?" asked Rob, glancing around him for something as obvious as the Yellow Brick Road.

"Damned if I know" grinned Luke. "Down as opposed to up. Come on, let's get going." They picked up their pace. At one point they had to negotiate a steep overhang, a rocky cliff face with stunted trees and bushes clinging to its flank. "Should be able to swing ourselves down hand over hand" said Luke, peering over the edge and making a rapid assessment. "Otherwise it means going up the mountain again and the long way round."

"Or we could go back the way we came" suggested Rob.

"There won't be much of a trail left in half an hour's time, Robbie, if it carries on like this" said Luke. It had begun to snow quite heavily. "And I estimate that would take us about four hours. This way we should get down in less than an hour. Test your weight first before grabbing hold of anything. If it holds my weight it will hold yours. Just follow me." He tossed his rucksack to the bottom of the overhang, then started down. Rob followed him, keeping his eyes on his brother. About two-thirds of the way down, about twelve feet from the ground, the rock face became sheer with nothing much in the way of handholds except moss.

"OK, I'm going to jump and roll" Luke called up to him. "Stay where you are until I tell you." He landed on the ground safely and looked up at his brother. "You know how to do a parachute landing fall? Keep your knees slightly bent and roll sideways as soon as you hit the ground. Hey, I'm just kidding. I'll catch you." Luke caught him in his arms a second later, the impact rocking him a little.

"But I wanted to do the parachute thing" protested Rob.

"If you were heavier or the drop was steeper I would have insisted on it" Luke told him. They were soon able to see the Government Pike beneath them, as they slithered their way down the rest of the mountain, emerging onto the highway at a point several miles from where they had started. They hitched a ride back with a trucker.

"Been out huntin' boys?"

"Nah, just sunbathing."

"Nice day for it." The radio was playing *Tobacco Road* by the Nashville Teens:

I was born in a bunk
Mama died and my daddy got drunk
Left me here to die alone
In the middle of Tobacco Road...

Grew up in rusty shack
All I had was hangin' on my back
Only you know how I loathe
This place called Tobacco Road

"Love that song." He turned up the volume.

But it's home, the only life I ever known
Only you know how I loathe
Tobacco Road...

The trucker dropped them off where Luke had parked their Ford pickup. "Here you go, boys. I got about a hundred miles to go before I'm home, then you know what I'm gonna do?"

"Guess it depends on what – or who - you got waiting for you at home" said Luke, jumping down from the front seat.

"You guessed right. Got me a woman who'll be pleased to see me. Even if she ain't, I'll still be pleased to see *her*, know what I mean?"

"Think I do" replied Luke. "Thanks for the ride, man." Further down the road he swung into a Texaco station to fuel up, dispatching Rob to Stuckey's convenience store for some groceries. By the time Rob returned, Luke had picked up a couple of propane tanks for the cabin generator and loaded them onto the flatbed. "All right, Robbie? Let's get this show on the road. It's coming down some now." Luke threw the truck into gear and edged back out onto the highway, which was now covered by a thin layer of snow.

The lights went out minutes after they'd arrived back at the log cabin, and they were left without power. Luke used his lighter to locate the flashlight, then went outside to hook up the fuel tanks to the generator, cussing aloud as he crashed into something. The lights came back on a couple of minutes later, and Rob heard Luke stamping the snow off his boots on the porch before he reappeared, rubbing his forehead.

"What did you hit, big man?" asked Rob, laughing.

"No idea. Whatever it was, it was sharp and pointed. Say, aren't you that cute little fella I tied up in the back room? How'd you get loose, boy?" Rob backed up against the kitchen table as Luke advanced on him. "About as bashful as a baby doe meeting up with a big old bull moose, aintcha?"

"I don't care for that hillbilly game any more."

"Don't be scared, pretty boy. Most mountain men are as innocent as newborn babes" remarked Luke, reverting to his normal self. "I've never come across any six-fingered banjo-pickers. It's those bastards from the cities you want to watch out for." He disappeared into the living room to get a fire going, leaving Rob to unpack the groceries they'd purchased. In the food mart Rob had raced up and down the aisles, tossing whatever looked easy and convenient into the cart.

"Hmmm" said Luke, reappearing a few moments later and peering dubiously at the contents of the skillet. Rob had tipped in a packet of ground beef and was stirring it around with a spatula. "That looks...interesting." He came up behind Rob and slipped a hand beneath his shirt, exploring the smooth flesh with his fingers, before squeezing his rib cage.

"Um, Luke, are you trying to bust a couple of my ribs?" Rob put up a token protest, his heart fluttering like a bird trapped in a cage, as Luke tightened his grip. "Now I know what it's like to be hugged by a grizzly bear."

"Who are you calling a grizzly?" growled Luke in a passable imitation of a bear. As Luke removed his hand, Rob could still feel the weight of it, burning into his skin. "What exactly are you meant to be cooking?" enquired Luke with exaggerated politeness.

"I don't know" confessed Rob. He had seen his mother fry ground beef before making a meat loaf, but that seemed too complicated and took far too long in the oven, so he planned to just fry it all up in a pan. Luke was still standing right behind him, his heavy forearms resting on Rob's shoulders, causing him to lose all concentration. Luke eventually moved off to rummage through the box of groceries set out on the table, and produced a can of Sloppy Joes.

"Here, shove this in. I'm sure it'll be fine." They sat at the kitchen table facing each other as they dined on their makeshift dinner, which Luke said put him in mind of army C-rations. "Just like old times."

"Luke, you can be so complimentary."

"Am I complaining? Ask any GI what the highlight of his day is and he'll tell you it's chow time. Man, we'd eat anything." Rob thumped him. "Any of delicious Donna's deluxe pecan pie left?"

"You ate it all when we out hiking" Rob reminded him. "But I got some blueberry Pop-Tarts for breakfast."

"Another interesting choice" said Luke "Seeing as there isn't a toaster in the cabin." He smiled at Rob, who returned his smile.

"I wasn't to know. And anyway, I've never been food-shopping before." Luke picked up a Pop-Tart and took an experimental bite. The raw pastry tasted floury, like an uncooked pie. "But we could cook them on the stove" suggested Rob.

"Sure" conceded Luke. "Wanna play that pan-flipping game Mom hates so much?" They took turns with the frying pan, flipping them up in the air like pancakes.

"If it hits the ceiling you're out" said Rob, after one of Luke's Pop-Tarts just missed a rafter.

"If it misses the pan you're out" said Luke, as one of Rob's flips nearly ended up on the floor. "And if one lands on my *head* someone is going to be in some serious shit…" Rob giggled. Most of the Pop-Tarts ended up as a soggy mess in the trashcan. After clearing up in the kitchen, they moved into the living room and settled down to watch some TV. The evening's entertainment featured a World War II drama called *Twelve O' Clock High* with Gregory Peck as the male lead in charge of a bomber squadron, followed by *Track of the Cat* starring Robert Mitchum in his usual tough-guy role on the trail of a black panther in deep snow and arctic conditions. The black and white picture was so fuzzy they could hardly make out anything on the screen. Rob fiddled with the aerial, jiggling the antenna up and down in every possible direction in an attempt to capture a signal, whilst Luke lounged on the couch, his boots up on the coffee table.

"Hold it right there" said Luke. "I think we've got ourselves a picture." Rob sank down on the couch, half reclining, and hooked his knee over Luke's. After glancing at him, Luke slung an arm around his shoulder. Last night, the rascal had sneaked into his bed, complaining that his bedroom was like an icebox. The temperature had dropped overnight, and Rob had woken up shivering. After a cursory investigation Luke had discovered a draught coming through a gap where the window catch had broken. The cabin only had two bedrooms, and when their two families had vacationed here in former years, the three cousins had slept on the livingroom floor in sleeping bags whilst the adults occupied the bedrooms.

"Do you think we'll be snowed in tomorrow?" asked Rob, hoping there would be a blizzard so he could spend more time alone with his brother.

"We can shovel our way out if necessary" replied Luke. "Though if I'd thought on I should probably have left the pickup at the bottom of the track. They'll grit the main roads."

"How come you're always so warm?" Rob marvelled, running his hand over the corded sinews and muscles along the inside of Luke's bare forearm. His brother rarely felt the cold. When other people were bundled up in fleece-lined jackets and woollen caps he was quite comfortable in his shirtsleeves.

"Muscle produces more heat since it increases the basal metabolic rate" Luke informed him, something he had learned during basic training.

"Which greatly adds to your sex appeal during the winter months" said Rob.

"There is that" agreed Luke "Though of course it can have a repellent effect in the summer. Folks keep their distance." The room had warmed up considerably with the woodstove going, and Rob was conscious of a deep contentment. He would have been perfectly happy to spend the rest of his life in a small log cabin like the one they were in now, providing he could be with Luke. He had no desire to socialise with other people, and liked being curled up on the couch close to his brother.

"So, how have you been feeling?" Luke asked him during a commercial break. Without telling their parents, they had decided on an experiment: Rob would stop taking his medication completely for the three days they were away.

"Fine" said Rob "but I don't think anyone really understands me, not even the Doc."

"Sometimes the best people are misunderstood" said Luke. "Maybe Dr. Strangelove belongs to an inferior species, and you're just too damned complicated for him to figure out. How's a worm going to understand how a human brain operates? Einstein's parents didn't understand him either. You know what he said to them when his baby sister was born - *But where are its wheels?*" Rob smiled at him.

"I don't think I'm much like Einstein."

"No" agreed Luke all too readily, which earned him a playful dig in the ribs. When Rob had been in Junior High, Luke had come across his younger brother frowning with frustration as he struggled with elementary algebra. Their parents had imposed a strict rule forbidding TV until he'd completed his homework.

"Want me to show you the formula?" Luke wrote it down for him and they worked through the exercises together, Luke leaning over his shoulder.

"But isn't that cheating?" Rob asked. "I couldn't have done it without your help." Luke winked at him.

"Who's to know? Your maths teacher should have given you the magic formula: once you know that you can solve any quadratic equation." They were just in time for *Bonanza*, and the family settled down to watch the Cartwrights grapple with the latest moral predicament to grip the *Ponderosa* ranch.

"When was it you started having these panic attacks?" Luke now asked him. Rob explained about the classmate whose brother had been killed in Vietnam, and how every time the doorbell rang he'd been filled with terror and dread in case it was the mail delivery van with a body bag.

"I somehow don't think they would have delivered me to my parents' doorstep in a pretty parcel tied up with ribbons and a bow" said Luke sardonically. "I'd have ended up in a metal drawer at the morgue, just like the other poor bastards who bought the farm." Seeing Rob's stricken face, he pulled him close in a hug. "Hey, it never happened." Luke had been permitted one R&R leave during his first hitch in a restricted number of destinations like Sydney, Bangkok, Manila, Singapore, Tokyo, and Hawaii. His first choice had been Hawaii but there had been a long waiting list owing to the fact it was on familiar American soil, so he had ended up in Bangkok, where he had managed to come down with a bad case of cerebral malaria that laid him up in hospital for three days. When the family had been due to meet up with Luke in Hawaii and he got routed to Bangkok instead, it had been a bitter blow for Rob who had been looking forward to seeing his brother, literally counting the days.

Once Luke had stepped off the plane and taxied into the city he was faced with yet more bars and whorehouses, constant noise and traffic - the assumption being that all American GIs wanted to do was drink themselves into a stupor and fuck everything that moved. He wasn't stupid enough to do either, and had availed himself of some of the recreational facilities of the R&R centre. Although he didn't miss the Vietnamese jungle, he did miss the banter and easy camaraderie of the men in his platoon. It was amazing how attached you could become to a bunch of guys whom you had spent every waking moment with for the past few months: the unit had served as a substitute mobile family, and being suddenly dumped in a foreign city and left to his own devices merely added to his general malaise. He felt adrift, cut loose from his familiar moorings. On his first night he had wandered about the city, trying to avoid the ubiquitous pimps and other lowlifes, and had eventually ended up in a bar recommended by the hotel manager as being GI-friendly. A knot of soldiers from some other company he didn't recognise were lounging at the opposite end of the bar, drinking and chatting amongst themselves. Although he could have used some convivial company, Luke wasn't the type to barge in on an established social clique without being invited. He'd only been in the bar for about five minutes before he was accosted by a little queer wearing women's eye makeup, giving him the appearance of a startled racoon.

"Can I buy you a drink?"

"No thanks" muttered Luke, staring straight ahead. He was quite capable of buying his own drinks and had no intention of giving this character any encouragement.

"I suppose you're going to ignore me like all the others." The man, who was easily twice if not three times his age, extended a hand. "I'm Raymond." Luke felt obliged to shake his hand, not wishing to appear impolite. The handshake was as limp and boneless as he had expected. He wondered idly what the reason was for the limpness: was it some kind of code for identifying one queer to another, like a Masonic handshake, or did it just betoken general submissiveness? "Usually I can tell if a soldier wants to beat the shit out of me" continued Raymond in a world-weary tone "But you don't strike me as being the sort. Otherwise you wouldn't have shaken my hand. Believe me, I do appreciate it." Luke eyed him, wondering why he chose to frequent such places if this was the kind of hostile treatment he was accustomed to. "I've been beaten up three times. The second occasion was the worst – I've only just recovered from the bruises - and I swore to myself I'd never venture out again at night, but one gets so bored staring at four walls."

"You don't say" replied Luke automatically. The guy was not exactly a bundle of laughs, and the conversation was bringing him down. He was bored shitless. Hell of a way for a guy to have to spend his few days leave before returning to the combat zone, thought Luke morosely. Thanks, Uncle Sam.

"Are you an officer?" asked Raymond, determined to pursue the conversation. "A sergeant perhaps?" he persisted as Luke didn't immediately answer.

"What difference does it make?" returned Luke, without volunteering any information.

"Oh, none at all, I assure you. I was just curious. You seem very sure of yourself, so I assume you hold some position of authority. You don't come across as a complete ignoramus – unlike that noisy rabble over there - and yet you don't speak like one of the officer class either. I would say you're far too young to have progressed into the upper echelons...." As he babbled on in this speculative vein, Luke was very much aware that Raymond was invading his personal space, pressing up close against him. The last thing he needed was some fag crawling up his arms. He moved away slightly.

"Look" he said finally "If you want to talk to me, that's fine. But I don't want you leaning into me like that. What's the matter with you, can't you stand up straight?" Raymond apologised profusely.

"Actually, you're making me feel quite giddy…" He placed a hand on Luke's shoulder, as if to steady himself. His touch was feather-light, like a girl's. I'll make you feel giddy all right in a minute, thought Luke, if you don't keep your hands to yourself. "I'm so sorry if I've offended you" added Raymond quickly, seeing Luke's exasperation "But I do find you very attractive…" Jesus Christ. Luke turned away, catching the eye of one of the soldiers, who had come up the bar to order another round of drinks and overheard this exchange. He said something to the other men, who broke out into loud guffaws. One of them began to imitate Raymond's breathy voice, uttering in a thin falsetto "Oh, you make me feel quite giddy…Drill me, sergeant. Give it to me. Harder, harder." His companions laughed uproariously. Luke had already made up his mind to quit the premises as soon as he'd finished his drink, when Raymond addressed the group of soldiers, who were sniggering quite openly.

"Please don't put words in my mouth, dear boy. I would never come out with anything so crude. I consider you to be nothing more than a bunch of hooligans and thugs. The man I am currently conversing with happens to be a gentleman - a cut above the usual riffraff who come in here."

"Hey, is that Maybelline around your eyes or did someone give you a black eye?" asked the one who'd been mimicking Raymond.

"Precisely the type of puerile observation one would expect from an ephebe" returned Raymond imperturbably.

"Say what? Hey, what did he just call me?" The soldier looked around at the others, seeking enlightenment. Luke shrugged, as if to say *How the fuck should I know?*

"Please don't distress yourself, dear boy. In ancient Greece an ephebe was a young man undergoing military training" replied Raymond.

"You're a regular Oscar Wilde, aren't you" muttered the soldier. "I'd button that lip of yours, if I were you."

"Or you'll do it for me, I suppose? What a charming expression - it so perfectly matches your gruff voice and fierce demeanour. Do you see how they menace me?" Raymond asked Luke. This was a rhetorical question and he didn't really expect an answer. "That's all I'm fit for, you see, to be constantly menaced and threatened. I'm not even allowed to speak. But I am sincerely flattered by the compliment. Oscar Wilde was enormously intelligent, courageous, and much misunderstood. Nice shoulders, by the way" he murmured, gazing up admiringly at Luke, who was towering over him. Luke was not used to being looked at with such naked desire by another man, and it was making him feel uncomfortable.

"Oooh, what nice broad shoulders you have" mimicked the joker who'd spoken before in a high whispery falsetto. "What a nice big cock you've got. All the better to fuck me with…" He thrust his pelvis suggestively in Raymond's direction. "Like some of that, huh?"

"Knock it off, guys" said Luke in a bored tone. Raymond turned on the soldier who was making fun of him.

"Such a blatant display of your virility is quite unnecessary – I have no doubt whatsoever of your prowess in that department. I am sure either of you could knock me senseless, or to use the vernacular, *coldcock* me…" He paused as their laughter momentarily drowned him out, before continuing "Yes, you might well laugh. I am more than happy to be able to provide you all with some entertainment. After all, a soldier's life must be such a dull one. I suppose you're all so busy playing with your rifles and machine guns you haven't much time to cultivate your minds-"

"-Busy *playing* with our rifles and machines guns?" interrupted one of the men in a belligerent tone. "Well, that's one way of putting it. We're busy fighting a war in case you hadn't noticed, buddy."

"Very brave of you, I'm sure. But you're off duty now, aren't you? Can't you at least be civil?" Emboldened by Luke's presence, and clearly delighted to be the centre of attention – even if he was an object of ridicule - Raymond continued to bait them whilst subtly flirting at the same time, throwing them off balance. Which wasn't too smart, thought Luke. Like butting your head against a brick wall, and hoping the hard surface might eventually yield to something a little softer. He'd have done far better to ignore the provocation. "If, however, you are able to tear yourself away from your manly pursuits, I would highly recommend Joseph Heller's *Catch-22*, a satirical novel about the army set during World War II, which you might find vaguely amusing."

"He's in here every night, looking to pick up some poor unsuspecting mug" said one of the soldiers, addressing the latter remark to Luke over Raymond's head. "We were about to warn you, buddy, but he made a beeline for you soon as you walked in. Care to join us?" Luke felt trapped, in the sense of being emotionally blackmailed. If he were to join the other guys, which he would most certainly have done if Raymond had not been present, it would look as though he were just another prejudiced bigot, which he wasn't. What consenting adults did behind closed doors was strictly their business, as far as he was concerned. To abandon someone who had engaged him in conversation, simply in order to score a cheap point - that he wasn't "one of them" - would be callous and insensitive. Luke did not feel the need to make that point at Raymond's expense. Although he had not initiated the conversation, there was no need to be gratuitously cruel to someone who was so desperate for companionship he was prepared to risk bodily injury and put up with any amount of verbal abuse. On the other hand, Luke did not relish the prospect of getting involved in a fist fight if the other guys decided to get rough with Raymond and work him over, though he realised he would have little choice as he couldn't stand around and watch whilst someone so utterly defenceless was beaten to a pulp. He remained where he was.

"Ah, thanks, but I'll be heading off soon anyway" said Luke noncommittally to the man who'd invited him to join them. Raymond had in the meantime edged closer to him again, which was seriously starting to bug him. He swivelled around with his back against the bar and his elbows on the rail, so as to preclude the possibility of Raymond trying to climb onto his knee.

"I could bring the book with me if you're going to be here again tomorrow night. Or if you're at a loose end, I know this wonderful little restaurant. My treat, of course…" Raymond looked at Luke hopefully. He kept miring himself in deeper shit with every sentence he uttered.

"I won't be there, pal, so don't waste your time. Just to make things perfectly clear, Raymond" enunciated Luke, tossing his cigarette butt away. "And I'll say this just once…"

"You actually said my name. How thrilling. And in that deep, husky voice too…"

"Whatever it is you're looking for" continued Luke, annoyed at being interrupted "I'm not interested. You've got the wrong guy. Do I need to spell it out?"

"Oh, but on the contrary, you're *exactly* what I'm looking for. The entire package." Luke stood up, and tossed a few dollar bills on the counter. "Oh, I can see I've offended you. You're not going?"

"I'm leaving now. And you would be well advised to get the hell out of here before you get yourself into serious trouble." Raymond looked heartbroken.

"You're leaving? Must you? I was so enjoying your company."

"Kissy kissy. Bye bye" said one of the soldiers to Raymond mockingly. Raymond turned on him.

"You see what you've done? You've driven him off with your coarse lewd behaviour. The only man in here worth speaking to…" Raymond dipped his fingers into his glass then flicked his drink in the man's direction. The soldier stepped up to him and eyeballed him.

"Did you just flick your drink at me, you little pansy faggot?"

"Hey, keep your shirt on, pal" muttered Luke to the soldier, sensing an imminent confrontation. "Simmer down." Raymond moved closer to Luke as if Luke were his protector, his knight in shining armour, before launching into another tirade.

"Although virility is traditionally associated with strength and force, the Roman definition of *virilitas* also embodied the virtues of self-restraint and control. The strong man who is capable of violence but refrains from brutality is truly manly. Whereas a man who becomes aggressive at the slightest provocation and who gives way to his baser impulses, was said to have compromised his virility, and was regarded by the ancients as being contemptible, lacking discipline. You might want to bear that in mind the next time you are tempted to a public exhibition of your gladiatorial skills." Luke eyed him appraisingly. He had guts all right. And he certainly had a way with words. But, boy, was this guy ever asking for it. He just didn't know when to shut up, and kept pushing his luck.

"You belong in the booby-hatch, that's for sure" returned the soldier, flexing his fists. He locked eyes with Luke, who stared him down. *You want to butt heads with someone? Try me.* He didn't say it aloud, but the other guy got the message. Luke felt quite confident in taking him on if it came to that, whilst soberly reflecting on the inadvisability of doing so. The military police would come down on them like a ton of bricks. If Luke was caught brawling in a bar, defending the honour of some ageing queen who'd tried to pick him up, they would automatically assume he had been engaging in the kind of sexual activity the authorities frowned on. No-one would believe that he was an innocent party trying to keep the peace. They'd have thrown the book at him.

"What do you want to waste your time talking to that little fairy for, man? Boy, has he got the hots for you. And he's not going to leave you alone until-"

"What the hell" said Luke impatiently. "Have a nice night, fellas. You too, Raymondo." As he exited the bar, Raymond ran after him and caught up with him.

"Do you think I could prevail upon your good nature and chivalry to escort me to the end of the street?" Luke turned around.

"What?"

"This isn't a pickup line, I assure you. I'm actually quite scared." He looked over his shoulder nervously. "As soon as you disappear from sight I know those ruffians will come after me. It's just sport to them." Luke looked at him, not knowing whether to take him seriously or not. "Please, if I could just accompany you to the next intersection. Then I can sort of fade into the crowd – would you mind so very much?"

"All right" said Luke, relenting. "But then you go your way, and I'll go mine."

"Whatever you say, sergeant."

"I'm not a sergeant" said Luke. "I'm an Infantry Platoon Commander."

"How thrilling. I'm yours to command. Whatever you are, I think you're absolutely adorable." Christ, thought Luke. He'd be glad to shake this one off his tail. When they eventually reached a busy junction where people were milling about, Luke turned to face him. "There's no-one after you, as far as I can see. You should be fine now."

"I'm enormously grateful for your protection." He gazed at Luke wistfully. "I suppose I'll never see you again?"

"Probably not. I'm due to fly out to rejoin my unit on Friday."

"You will be careful on the battlefield, won't you, with all those bullets whizzing about. I shall pray for your safety every night. And remember to wear your helmet at all times." Luke grinned despite himself. The sheer absurdity of this womanish character earnestly offering him advice on how to stay safe in a combat zone struck him as being faintly comical.

"I'll do that." He searched for something to say before they parted, something sympathetic or less harsh. "I don't get it. Are you a glutton for punishment or something? Why don't you go to some other bar where you won't get hurt and you might actually meet some, uh..."

"Meet other queers like me, you mean?" Luke shrugged.

"I guess that's what I mean. Yes." Raymond sighed theatrically.

"Queens don't interest me. It's my curse and my misfortune that I am attracted to masculine men, superb physical specimens like yourself who on the whole despise invertebrates like me."

"You're not so bad. It took balls to stand your ground back there. Maybe work on that limp handshake a little?" suggested Luke teasingly. Raymond smiled.

"You somehow manage to be direct without being offensive. It's a rare quality." Raymond came up close to him and attempted to embrace him, but Luke held him off firmly with an arm.

"Thanks for recommending the book. Goodnight, Raymond." He strode off rapidly into the night without looking back. The following morning he'd woken up in his cheap hotel room with the shakes, aching all over and scarcely able to walk, before staggering to the nearest medical centre. After scolding him for not taking his army-issued malaria tablets, the doctor who treated him informed he had been on the point of slipping into a coma, and they'd caught it just in time.

"Crazy to think I went through all that shit out in Vietnam" said Luke to Rob "and then this tiny little skeeter comes along and damn near kills me! The little fuckers have got something called a proboscis, and they suck your blood through it like they're sipping from a straw."

"I love you" said Rob. "I don't care if you've killed people. I'll always stick by you. You're a good guy."

"Love you too, mushhead. What if I wasn't a good guy? Supposing I were a bad guy, would you still stick by me?"

"Yes" said Rob unhesitatingly. "Brothers are forever. Like Frank and Jesse. I'd stick by you no matter what."

"Aw shucks" said Luke, in imitation of the TV character Opie Taylor. "I'm gonna start bawling any minute." He was touched by Rob's declaration of loyalty, unsure what he had done to deserve such unwavering and uncritical devotion. He glanced down at his hands. Those same capable workmanlike hands with which he had built his cabin, had also been the instruments of murder: they could wield a chainsaw to cut down trees or a machine gun to mow down men with equal proficiency. Most of the skirmishes in Vietnam had been conducted with firearms but whenever the opportunity for hand-to-hand combat arose most of the men welcomed it. American soldiers had a natural advantage when pitted against the smaller, physically weaker, and malnourished enemy forces: they were bigger and stronger, and enjoyed a regular supply of U.S army rations. On one occasion when his M-16 had jammed at a crucial moment, Luke had seconds in which to bring his opponent to the ground before facing certain death with an AK-47 levelled at his head. As his enemy counterpart, an NVA regular, paused to reload Luke had dived for the man's feet, bringing him down in a flying tackle. He'd been a linebacker on the school's football team in Senior High, and killer tackles were his specialty. And then they were both locked in a death struggle, which could only have one outcome. Greater muscle mass and bone density counted when you were grappling with a foe with your bare hands, and Luke had easily overpowered him. *You're not going to come out of this alive, little fella, so the sooner you stop struggling the quicker and easier it'll be,* he remembered thinking quite calmly and dispassionately, as he forcibly applied pressure to the carotid artery with the balls of his thumbs and throttled him to death. Yes, he recognised those hands alright: they belonged to him, just as the acts he had committed in the heat of battle were an irrefragable part of him. *And if thy right hand offends thee cut it off...*but Luke was not given to gratuitous soul-searching or self-laceration - just one of the ways war had of messing with your head. He didn't think he was a "good guy", but neither did he think he was a hard-hearted bastard either. He was just himself.

"Who do you think has the most chest hair, Bob Mitchum or Gregory Peck?" asked Rob, mesmerised by the close-up view afforded by Luke's open shirt, the top two buttons of which were undone; a tuft of curly dark hairs straggled out from beneath his white undershirt.

"I wouldn't know. Can't say it's a topic I've given much thought to. You like that, do you?" Rob considered.

"I don't like it when it covers the guy's chest like a rug. Tom Jones and Sean Connery might as well be apes. But yours is just the way I like it." He made it sound like a well-done steak. Luke laughed.

"What's so funny?" Rob asked him.

"You are. How did I wind up with such a kooky little brother? I was just thinking about a night out in this GI bar in Bangkok. I can't believe we almost came to blows over some fag. He kept goading these guys, who were about ready to pile into him, but I think he was enjoying all the attention - like he thought he was the belle of the ball or something." Rob was immediately intrigued.

"Was he hitting on you?" Luke smiled.

"What do you think?"

"What did he look like?" asked Rob.

"Oh, he was a pretty boy all right" fibbed Luke, who couldn't resist teasing his brother. "A regular beauregard. I think he wanted to sit on my knee."

"He had some nerve, coming on to you like that" declared Rob heatedly, already hating the unknown boy who had tried to seduce his brother. Had Luke found him attractive? He felt so hot with jealousy he could have killed him. Luke was shaking with laughter. "Not jealous, by any chance?"

"Not in the least. He sounds like some sleazy rent boy" said Rob in disgust, who was still seething with jealousy at the idea of some strange boy making a pass at his brother. "Not worth fighting over. I hope you didn't speak to him. How old was he? Was he my age?" Rob was becoming increasingly agitated.

"Hey, I was just messing with you" said Luke soothingly, stroking the hair that curled around the nape of Rob's neck. "He was about as ancient as an Egyptian mummy. Pretty damned smart though, but nobody wanted to talk to him. I felt sorry for him."

"Oh." Rob felt foolish, now that the threat had receded. "I guess he must have been pretty lonely" he added artlessly, much to Luke's amusement. "It's a shame he had no-one to talk to. What's beauregard mean?"

"Well, there was this guy in my unit called Beauregard Thompson who told us his name meant *beautiful face* in French." Rob turned his attention back to the TV screen where an impossibly handsome Gregory Peck strode around the airbase barking orders to his demoralised squadron of fighter pilots. "First I've ever heard of a General flying bombing missions as lead pilot" remarked Luke sceptically, as Gregory Peck strapped himself into the cockpit. "But I guess they do things differently in Hollywood."

"He's so sexy I just can't take my eyes off him" said Rob provocatively.

"Pretty good at switching horses midstream, aren't you? Guess me and Bob have been thrown over."

"I still love Robert Mitchum. Luke, what do I smell like?" asked Rob suddenly. He had woken up early that morning and propped himself on his elbow to gaze at the parts of his brother's body that were visible above the sheets, fascinated by the powerful muscles of his shoulders bunching and flexing as he shifted in his sleep. Luke had been muttering something, the garbled words emerging as a low deep rumble from his chest. And then his voice had become suddenly louder and more emphatic: *When I order you to do something....* before the words tapered off and became unintelligible again. He was probably dreaming he was still in the army, bossing people about as usual. Rob had trailed his fingers through Luke's chest hair, planting a row of kisses all the way to his armpit. This had roused Luke, who sat up against the pillow protesting, "Well, good morning! Sneaking up on a fella like that when he's asleep..." Rob had murmured something about pheromones in a muffled voice. "Pheromones my ass" Luke had growled good-naturedly as he'd reached across Rob for his watch on the nightstand, his bare upper torso covering him for a few heart-stopping seconds. "I wish Dr. Feelgood had never mentioned the damned things. Is this your latest fixation?"

"Christ. Your hair smells of Palmolive shampoo, OK?" Luke now replied in answer to his question.

"But what does the rest of me smell like to you?" If Luke's bodily scent could drive him wild, Rob wondered whether it worked two ways: would the scent of his own skin have any discernible effect on his brother? Luke rolled up the cuff of Rob's sleeve, and gripped the inside of his wrist where the pulse was in order to breathe in the scent of his skin.

"Uh, like toasted marshmallow" he said finally, somewhat surprised. "Hmmm. That's kinda nice." Rob smiled, and a dimple appeared in his cheek. Pretty baby, thought Luke. When Rob was about four he was so cute Luke had been unable to resist cuddling him, when no-one else was around to see. Luke had been twice his size, and he felt big and clumsy in comparison to this perfectly formed angelic little creature. He would pick up his baby brother and carry his precious bundle off to the porch swing where he could fondle him, marvelling at the tiny hands curled into fists, the eyelids as delicate as rose petals. Occasionally Rob would protest if Luke squeezed him too hard, and try to wriggle free. At other times, he was content to sit in Luke's lap, gazing up at him solemnly with huge eyes, and sucking his thumb. Luke would pluck the thumb from his mouth, which popped out with a satisfying plop like a cork from a bottle, and Rob would promptly put it back in. Every time he put his thumb back in his mouth Luke would pull it out until Rob protested audibly: "Don't, Luke!" Then Luke would poke his soft little belly with one of his fingers. Rob didn't care for this new game very much, and after a few experimental prods he would attempt to clamber out of his lap. Luke would hold him tighter, preventing his escape. Bewildered, Rob's lower lip would begin to quiver and his eyes would fill with tears. He wept on Luke's shoulder, his muffled sobs sounding like little hiccups. Luke was immediately contrite and would comfort him, stroking his silky curls and crooning: "I'm sorry, pretty baby. I didn't mean to make you cry, little angel." The tears would stop, and Rob would nestle in his arms uncomplainingly, submitting to his caresses. He was used to being petted and fussed over by grown-ups, and his older brother was so much bigger he must have seemed like just another grown-up.

"Why are you looking at me like that?" asked Rob. Luke's eyes were ranging over him speculatively.

"In what way am I looking at you?"

"Like you might be a homo or something." Luke laughed.

"Well, that's rich, coming from you. I was just thinking how cute you are."

"I'm not!" Luke caressed his cheek.

"You most certainly are. Besides, cuteness is in the eye of the beholder. If we get holed up here, guess who's gonna get eaten first?" teased Luke.

"Shut up. Numbnuts."

"Mine are rarely numb, I can assure you." Rob blushed at the inappropriate thoughts that popped into his head. He'd snatched a fleeting rear view glimpse of his brother in the shower that morning before Luke had turned his head and caught him staring openly. Rob had clapped his hands in front of his eyes, stammering "I didn't see anything much, Luke. Honest." Nothing much except a stupendous pair of cannonballs dangling between his thighs. He could still recall the lines from *Julius Caesar* which had made them all snigger in English class:

Why, man, he doth bestride the narrow world
Like a Colossus; and we petty men
Walk under his huge legs, and peep about

Luke had laughed at his embarrassed reaction, before wrapping a towel around his waist. "What's the matter, you want to spend some adult time with me?"

"Have you seen that James Bond film *Thunderball*?" Rob now asked mischievously.

"You mean the one where the bad guys wanted to hold Nato to ransom by hijacking an atomic bomb?" enquired Luke, who was on his third beer. "Sure, they had movie theatres for the guys on R&R so we could catch up on the latest films."

"Yeah, but in the film they were trying to hijack *two* atomic bombs, not one. So when Tom Jones sung the title song it should really have been..."

"Right. Which wouldn't have got past the censor" returned Luke, who had noticed the crimson colour spreading across his brother's cheeks. "How fast can you make some popcorn?"

"Five minutes?"

"In that case, I'm putting you back on KP duty."

"Coming right up, sir." Rob saluted him smartly. "Private Turnbull reporting for duty." His brother had a rather endearing tendency to lapse into military speak. A clearing in the woods which had been demarcated for tree-felling was the "strike zone" and the terminus of the old logging road where the trucks were parked - to which Rob was frequently banished by their father when he proved too much of a distraction - was base camp or the "DMZ" (demilitarised zone)

Luke glanced over his shoulder at the sounds of loud popping coming from the kitchen area. "What's going on in there? Sounds like a freakin' war zone." When he went to investigate he found Rob wading knee-deep in the stuff.

"When I took the lid off it kinda got out of control." Luke ducked as a hot kernel nearly got him in the eye. Rob started to laugh and so did Luke. They were soon scooping up handfuls of popcorn and chucking it at each other. By the time they returned to the couch with a big bowl heaped with popcorn they had managed to salvage, they had missed about fifteen minutes of the movie. Luke pulled Rob onto his lap, and Rob settled into his favourite position, leaning back against his brother's chest with Luke's arms firmly clasping him.

About an hour later Rob was nodding off on his shoulder, relaxed by the warmth of the fire and probably tired out by their long hike. The World War II drama had finished some time ago, and Rob had lost interest in the second film as soon as his hero had suffered a fatal fall into an icy crevasse whilst tracking the elusive cat. The previous night he had cried out in his sleep: *"Frank! Coyotes...getting closer. Can you hear them?"* His eyes had been shut, his breathing deep and rhythmic. He was obviously having one of those nightmares where he was the outlaw Jesse James on the run: sometimes he was being chased by a posse of men, this time he was being menaced by coyotes as he and his brother slept out in the open in wild country.

"It's alright, I've got my gun" Luke had said softly into his ear, leaning over him as Rob shifted uneasily in his sleep. "The coyotes can't get you while I'm keeping guard. I'll shoot their heads off if they come any closer. Go back to sleep, Jesse." Rob mumbled something, his words tailing off, and Luke smoothed the hair back from his forehead, the gentle action waking him.

"Luke?" Rob's eyes had blinked open. "I was dreaming about coyotes...."

"Yeah, I know" replied Luke "No need to worry. I'm armed and more dangerous than they are. Go back to sleep, little brother."

"But that's more or less what Frank just told me...how did you know? Were you in the dream too?"

"I heard you talking in your sleep" Luke had replied. Rob had grasped hold of his hand and kept hold of it until his fingers relaxed their grip and became limp, as he'd drifted back off to sleep. Luke now idly wondered whether it was possible for a person who was fully awake to conduct a meaningful conversation with someone who was dreaming. Had he somehow managed to get through to his sleeping brother, his words of reassurance penetrating Rob's subconscious?

"Time to hit the sack" said Luke. Rob's eyelids were flickering and he didn't reply. When he was sleepy he was as tractable and compliant as a small child. Luke scooped him up in his arms, shouldering open the door of the bedroom, and deposited him on the bed. He stood silhouetted in the doorframe for an instant, blocking out the light, before shutting the door softly behind him.

Outside, he paused to light a cigarette, leaning against the wooden porch railing. The earlier snow flurries had stopped, and only a thin layer had settled on the ground. Overhead the stars were swarming in the night skies, and it was quiet and peaceful - the only sounds being the creaking and rustling of trees stirring in the breeze and the call of some nocturnal creature, probably a screech owl. One day he'd build himself a cabin retreat just like this one, in a secluded location high up in the mountains. Since returning from Vietnam he had become more anti-social, less able to tolerate people for any length of time. He didn't have a regular girlfriend, though he'd been briefly tempted by a couple of married women he'd seen around at the country club. His parents had dragged him along to a formal suit and tie affair one evening in an attempt to get him to mingle with "civilised society." Luke was by far the youngest man there, and had made heroic efforts to engage in polite conversation with an assortment of couples, steering clear of four-letter expletives and topics that might prove too shocking. He really couldn't blame some of the females for champing at the bit, once he saw what they were yoked up to – for the most part pompous and paunch-ridden windbags who loved the sound of their own voices. He'd found himself exchanging inanities with one such couple, the female half of whom was about twenty years younger than her husband, with an enticing cleavage on display.

"Denise Randall." She smiled at Luke, extending her hand. "I'm sure you've seen me working up a sweat on the club's tennis courts" (letting him know just where to find her, if he was so inclined) She'd actually winked at him whilst her spouse was pontificating about "our fine young upstanding men serving in

Vietnam", murmuring in Luke's ear *"An upstanding prick hath no conscience."* Luke had caught the allusion - the original proverb being something they used to bandy about in the army - and had returned her wink when hubby was looking the other way.

"So, what do you think of Nixon's chances?" Randall had asked him, clapping him on the back in a hearty patronising manner. "Think he'll do a better job than LBJ?"

"Both grade A assholes, as far as I'm concerned" Luke had replied. And hubby was in for a right royal cuckolding if he didn't quit with the backslapping routine. One day Luke might just happen on by the tennis courts where he knew Denise practised her forehand stroke. They'd go for a little stroll in the adjacent woodlot and find an out-of-the-way spot where he could sample the delights on offer. She was clearly attracted to him, but Luke figured if he wanted that kind of action Barbra was always available. She didn't have a husband in tow; she was well stacked and pretty hot in the sack, which suited him fine for now. At least two women with a pulse had made a play for him that evening, and he had briefly considered the pros and cons, before deciding a quick roll in the hay wasn't worth the potential aggravation. If their husbands found out or if one of the wives decided to get clingy there would be all kinds of repercussions, which would only cause his parents embarrassment. He had once overheard his father remark to his mother that the reason he worked his oldest son so hard was because "Luke has a healthy libido and needs to keep extra busy, otherwise we'll have a string of unwanted pregnancies on our hands."

In the army there had been plenty of opportunities for getting laid whenever they were in spitting distance of a whorehouse, and that's what the men mostly spent their army pay on – screwing and drinking - until the top brass had the bright idea of cutting out the middlemen by bringing the hookers directly to the soldiers, transporting them by jeep to purpose-built barracks or "boom-boom parlours." This solved a lot of disciplinary problems connected with soldiers going on the rampage in red-light districts, with fights breaking out in bars and strip joints. It was also a lot cheaper for the men. More bangs for your bucks, so to speak. Luke was sometimes called upon to act as an unofficial bouncer, hauling rowdy soldiers back to base before they were picked up by the authorities and slung into jail - effectively doing the job of the military police, who had their hands full dealing with disturbances elsewhere. On one occasion he'd been caught up in a noisy altercation between U.S. soldiers and the Vietnamese owner of a strip joint. The men were annoyed because they couldn't get their hands on the girls unless they spent a small fortune on the watered-down piss they tried to pass off as beer. It was the usual set-up: an attractive girl had been posted on the door to lure the guys in with promises of "plenty nice girls, plenty nice cold beer." Once they were inside they discovered that the girls were off-limits, and the price of alcohol was extortionate, most of the club-owners being racketeers with underworld connections. The owner had turned on Luke, who had arrived at the bar in the absence of any uniformed MP patrols, and started screaming hysterically at him.

"You pay! You pay for damage!" Luke was already in a filthy temper, ready to tear a strip off any of his men who were involved, whilst at the same time recognising that many of their grievances were genuine.

"You can tell this asswipe" said Luke to the interpreter at his side "that if he thinks the U.S. government is going to compensate him for any damage he claims our lot have done, he's sadly mistaken." He had scant sympathy for any of these unsavoury characters, being wise to all their little scams. They pimped out local girls, robbing them of most of their earnings and threatening them with violence if they didn't perform. They had even been known to rough them up, alleging American GIs were responsible and then claiming compensation from the U.S. army. They were raking in massive profits at the expense of American soldiers, most of whom would rather their dollars went directly to the girls who actually earned the money, instead of into the pockets of these parasitical sleazebags.

"Yeah, you tell him, sir" cut in a soldier who'd been listening to the exchange, the others having been loaded into two waiting jeeps outside. "Pay for *what*, you fucking little gook?" He stuck up a middle finger in an obscene gesture at the bar owner, who continued to harangue Luke in Vietnamese.

"Shut up!" snapped Luke. "I thought I told you to leave the premises. NOW." The soldier hurriedly left the bar. Luke was becoming more pissed off by the minute, as the owner kept jabbing his forefinger dangerously close to his chest. He turned back to his interpreter.

"You can also tell him that if he doesn't get the fuck out of my face and quit squawking like a goddam parrot, he'll get my fist rammed down his throat."

"Shall I phrase that more diplomatically, sir?" His interpreter grinned at him.

"Phrase it however you like" replied Luke, turning on his heel. The bar-owner suddenly dropped all his aggressive bluster, having just realised he'd lost a profitable source of income. A couple of soldiers who were loitering outside scrambled into the back of the lead jeep as Luke slammed the tailgate shut and jumped into the front seat. The driver didn't need to be told to floor it: they were sitting ducks, and the longer they remained stationary the greater the danger. He accelerated, burning rubber as they sped off through the streets at top speed, scattering any foot traffic in their path. "Roll" said Luke to the driver, who slewed the jeep back and forth in a zigzag motion to foil any hidden snipers who might feel tempted to take a pot shot at them.

But casual sex was not the same thing as companionship, reflected Luke, his thoughts returning to the present. He didn't consider he had much in common with the people he used to hang out with prior to enlisting, and was bored by their inconsequential chatter and facile observations about the war. He wasn't inclined to talk about his experiences – unless it was with other ex-soldiers, of whom there were none in his immediate social circle. The preoccupations of most of his peer group struck him as being infantile. He felt years older than them, as though he'd matured mentally and emotionally, and they hadn't progressed much beyond eighth grade. They seemed like naïve children with very little experience of life beyond high school: some of them had never even ventured as far as Dixie Highway or the Ohio River. Consequently Luke spent increasing amounts of time either on his own or working alongside his father at the sawmill, frequently putting in a ten-hour shift. After the rigours of war, the company of his brother - now his closest companion - was exactly what he needed. He had treasured the letters he had received from Rob when he was away on active duty, with their numerous misspellings and heartfelt outpourings: they had never failed to lift his mood and make him smile.

"Today I got into a fight at school. Some jerk was saying that our soldiers in Vietnam were baby murderers, and I hit him so hard I broke his nose. Served that sonofabich right. He was balling his eyes out..."

"Guess what, I got an A+ for my project! Miss Radcliff over at the librery helped me some, and corected my spelling. I think you and me are just like Frank and Jesse James, I hope you got the enemy whipt. Don't let them sneek up on you..."

"Dear Luke, no matter what you do, I will always be your loyal and allegant brother. Even if you come back without a leg..." Now there's a cheering thought. Luke had smiled and shook his head as he read the letter. Thanks, little brother. *"The principle makes us*

swear allegance to the flag every morning but its you I really swear to ..."

"I dont go into the woods so much now, only to walk Rusty – its not any fun without you. But I've got some new cowboy games we can play when you get back. You can be Wyatt Earp. From the old photos Miss Radcliff show'd me he was a handsome sonofagun..."

He always signed off affectionately with *"Your loving brother, Robbie"* followed by a row of kisses. Luke particularly liked the reference to the sonofabitch who was "balling his eyes out." A contortionist skull-fucker, no less. Glad you hit him hard, little brother. He was also amused by Rob's confession that he was pledging allegiance to his brother every morning instead of to the flag, like a true patriot. Luke chuckled softly to himself as he stubbed out his cigarette. He picked up his shotgun to do a routine perimeter check, and then stopped himself. You don't need to do a perimeter check. You're not in the Vietnamese jungle any more, pal. You're no longer surrounded by invisible enemies out to kill you. Everything's fine, copacetic. At least it was in this part of the world. But elsewhere on the planet war still raged, and life was absolute hell for those caught up in it, civilians and soldiers alike. He considered himself to be one of the lucky ones. He had emerged from the war with his limbs intact and a sound body and mind, whereas many of them didn't. When Luke had returned home after two years in Vietnam, it had taken him months to adjust and adapt to civilian life again. Initially he was jumpy and suffered from insomnia. The slightest noise – a door or window opening, or footsteps close to his bed - had him on his feet in a state of high alertness, ready to do battle. Gradually he had acclimatised himself back to civilian life, and Rob had helped enormously with his warmth and affection. Rob included him in all his activities and interests, listened to whatever he had to say, laughed at his jokes, and gave him a thousand hugs.

Some veterans who had seen years of service never really did adapt. They became drug addicts and ended up in jail or mental facilities, or homeless on the streets. Trained in the art of warfare, used up and spat out by the army when they were no longer needed, and with no daily structure or purpose to their lives, they were dangerous to be around. What didn't help matters was that when they stepped off the "freedom birds" onto the tarmac, they were faced with demonstrations and marches, full of long-haired protesters shouting *"Down with the war. Scum. Murdering bastards."* They were not the conquering heroes they were led to believe they were, they were the bad guys, despised by an increasingly radicalised anti-war movement. It bothered Luke. He was under no illusions about his fellow soldiers, who were certainly no angels, but they had done what had been asked of them, they had made sacrifices no civilian was ever asked to make, they had all been to hell and back again and this was the reception they were given. No welcoming committee. Like most sane people he wanted the war to end, but it didn't make much sense to take it out on the poor suckers who'd been sent out there, helicoptered into some of the most hostile terrain they were ever likely to encounter, and then just left to get on with it. These pampered college students knew jackshit about what was going on over there. The war was just another convenient peg to hang their discontent on.

Luke lingered outside for a while longer so as to give his brother a chance to drift off to sleep, before retiring himself. The temperature seemed quite mild and he didn't think the snow would stick, but he managed to lay his hands on a couple of shovels – one from the lean-to which housed the generator, and the other from underneath a tarpaulin in the flatbed of their Ford pickup. Whilst fumbling around in the darkness he almost managed to whack himself in the forehead again with an up-ended hoe, the same one he must have stepped on earlier. He stood the shovels beside the door in readiness, just in case the weather should take a turn for the worse during the night.

Chapter Six

The next morning dawned bright and sunny. The pristine layer of snow covering the ground the previous night was patchy, and had mostly thawed to slush. Rob scraped up some snow and threw a few snowballs in Luke's direction half-heartedly.

"A feeble effort. Very feeble" commented Luke. He picked up a handful of snow and came towards Rob with it. Rob covered his face protectively, but Luke stuffed the snow down the front of his shirt, making him gasp at the sudden shock. "That should cool you down, son."

"Bastard." They bagged up their garbage and put it in the back of the truck to discourage vermin, then Luke went back inside to fix the window in the other smaller bedroom that had remained unoccupied during their stay.

"That ought to do it" said Luke, reappearing ten minutes later with a hammer protruding from his pocket. He locked the door behind him. "Looks like a forced entry to me – I'll mention it to Uncle Jim." As he swung himself into the driver's seat, Rob noticed a tiny abrasion near his top lip where he'd cut himself shaving. On impulse, he leaned across and kissed it. "Hey" said Luke, eyeing his brother before starting up the engine.

Half an hour later they were on the main route, heading homeward. Rob felt unexpectedly deflated. Would things go back to normal when they got back, with Luke reverting to type: the slightly mocking, patronising older brother who teased and humoured the kid brother he didn't take seriously? Although they had only been away for three days they had achieved a closeness and intimacy he would never have thought possible only a few months ago. He had loved sleeping in the same bed with Luke and waking up beside him. It was almost like being a married couple. He thought the heavy weight of depression bearing down on him was connected with a sad dream he'd had last night. He'd dreamed he was Jesse James, pleading with his older brother to stay with him. Frank had had a bellyful of being a fugitive with a price on his head – never out of the saddle and his trigger hand never far from his gun holster – and wanted to settle down, farm some land and raise a family: *"But I left home at sixteen to be with you. I've followed you my whole life. You can't leave me now, Frank, after all we've been through together..."* The dream had been so vivid his cheeks were wet with tears when Luke had woken him gently.

"It's me, Luke. Wake up, Robbie."

"I dreamed Frank didn't want me around any more, said I was too much trouble...there were a hundred men chasing us who wanted me dead, and you rode off and left me."

"Hush now, it was just a dream." Luke had held him, comforting him.

"And then someone snuck up behind me, shot me in the back and killed me...."

"You'd hardly be talking to me if you'd been shot and killed. Think about it. And if I were Frank James and you had a hundred-strong posse after you, you must know I wouldn't have left you in a fix like that." Luke's words had a calming effect, and soon afterwards he'd fallen back to sleep.

"You alright?" Luke now asked, sensing the change in Rob's mood. His brother had been rather subdued and quiet all morning.

"It's hard for me to be happy sometimes" Rob tried to explain.

"Why is that?" asked Luke gently, wondering if this was a symptom of the bipolar disorder Dr. Gottschald had talked about. Rob didn't reply, but gave him such a sweet sad smile that it tore at Luke's heart. "What can I do to make it better?"

"I don't know if you can do anything except just.... be there. Don't go off to war again." And don't ever get married, he thought.

"Hey, I'm not going anywhere" said Luke. "Heard the one about the Indian chief and his little boy?"

"No" said Rob artlessly, resting a hand on his shoulder. "Tell me."

"All right. The kid says 'Dad, how did we get our names?' So the chief says 'Well, son, we named you all after what we saw immediately after you were born. When your older brother was born I stepped out of the tepee one morning and saw *Running Water*. When your sister was born I saw a *Shining Cloud*. But why are you asking me this, *Two Fucking Cowboys?*'" Rob laughed despite himself. "Nice to know someone appreciates my jokes, no matter how corny they are" said Luke, pleased to have put a smile back on Rob's face and lifted his mood.

"You're much nicer since you came back from Vietnam. More considerate." Luke gave him a quizzical look. "I mean, you were nice before, but I thought you might have turned into one of those mean badasses, always beating up on people."

"I guess that happens to some guys" said Luke. "but I saw enough violence and brutality when I was out there. With me, it taught me to value my family and my home. The thought that I might not make it back made me appreciate those things a lot more. You especially" he added.

"I'm one of 'those things' you appreciate?" teased Rob.

"You know what I mean." They were silent for a moment, then Luke said "There were times I felt enough was enough, but most of us just toughed it out. You're never alone in the army. The other guys become your second family, sorry-assed bastards that they were." He smiled in fond recollection. "You know, you and I are very fortunate to be born in this part of the world. We've got a good life here. The families I came across live in a state of terror. They didn't know what was going to happen to them from one day to the next. I'm not just talking about Vietnam; war is going on all over the planet as we speak. No-one should ever take peace and safety for granted."

"Did you think about any of that stuff when you were fighting?" Rob wanted to know.

"Hardly ever" admitted Luke. "You can't afford to, you just keep going. Do you think about it when a dentist is drilling into a tooth too close to the nerve? I had a machete in my hand half the time with sweat pouring down my face: where there were no trails we had to hack our way through the jungle." Luke had a ridged scar near the base of his right thumb where the machete, slick with sweat, had slipped and sliced through a tendon. "The only time I'd ever enlist again is if this country was under serious threat of invasion, like Europe was in the Second World War. I'd fight to defend what we've got, the life we had growing up. The fun things we used to do, like trick-or-treating…" he glanced over at Rob. "The kids over there don't get to do any of that. They don't need to spook themselves out at Halloween when they're seeing people blown up in front of their eyes. But enough of this gloomy talk." Rob was silent, thinking of all the good times he and Luke had enjoyed together when they were kids: they had camped out in the woods at night, toasting marshmallows speared on twigs; they had rummaged around at the municipal dump for the inner tubes of truck tyres in order to surf the fast-flowing waters of turbulent creeks, ensconced in their rubber donuts. At Halloween a parent would drop them off in a residential area, where they raced up and down the darkened streets knocking on doors, returning at the end of the evening with pillowcases laden with candy bars and other goodies.

"You were Frankenstein, remember?" said Rob.

"Huh? Oh, you mean that mask I wore one Halloween." Luke chuckled. "You were about eight, and I thought I was too old for trick-or-treating, but Mom and Dad wouldn't let you go out on your own without me." Rob remembered that Luke hadn't been too happy about having to baby-sit his younger brother, and had got his revenge by scaring all the other kids out of their wits, some of whom had gone home in tears. When he and Luke had rung the doorbell of a woman they didn't like much because she was always screaming at them for cycling over a tiny corner of her unfenced front lawn, Luke had leaned forward in his mask and said in a deep voice *"Show us your tits, lady"* before Rob could open his mouth to say *"Trick or treat."* They had both run off in fits of laughter, as she'd slammed the door in their face.

"We ended up at this spooky graveyard" said Rob. The cemetery had a reputation for being haunted, and Rob had persuaded Luke to take a detour from the residential streets so they could hunt up some ghosts.

"Nothing spooky about it" said Luke, smiling. "Shaking like a leaf by the end of the evening, weren't you?" Luke had been leaning up against a tombstone unconcernedly, whilst Rob flitted about the graveyard in his *Casper the Friendly Ghost* costume. "You gonna be out there all night?" Luke had called, growing impatient. "Only spook I see so far is you, little brother." Rob's costume – which was basically a white sheet with cut-out eyeholes - had become snagged by something in the dark, probably a tree branch, but he'd thought a bony hand was clawing him. He'd come hurtling across the uneven ground, straight into Luke's arms. Luke was at the awkward age when he was embarrassed about overt displays of affection, and had shoved him off.

"I saw something move, Luke. And I heard whispering right behind me."

"Just a breeze, little scaredy-cat" scoffed Luke, as Rob clutched at his sleeve. Luke had continued to pour scorn on his fears, laughing somewhat callously.

"Let's go now, Luke" urged Rob, who was genuinely frightened of anything supernatural. When the entire family had watched *The Haunting of Hill House* on TV one night, Rob had thought it was the scariest film he'd ever seen, especially the part where the female lead reaches across in the dark to hold the hand of her companion in the bed beside her, only to realise with a start that her friend was fast asleep. *Whose hand have I been holding?*

"Nope, I think we'll go take a look. You were the one who wanted to come. If there's any dead folks wandering about I'll make 'em crawl right back into their graves." Luke had not been able to resist startling Rob by creeping up behind him, or jumping out at him unexpectedly. The Frankenstein mask had not helped.

"I was pretty mean to you back then" said Luke, breaking in on his thoughts. "Put it down to adolescent hormones."

"I didn't mind" said Rob. "I always had fun when I was with you." When he was small they had shared a wooden sled - handcrafted by Luke and far superior to the flimsy plastic models sold in stores - Rob's arms wrapped tight around his brother's waist. Luke would dig a heel in the snow and glance over his shoulder before he kicked off: "Hold on tight now" before plunging headlong down snowy slopes.

"Yeah, we had some fun times" agreed Luke. "And we'll have plenty more. Now that you're all grown up" he drawled, leaning towards Rob "Aren't you?"

"Yes. More grown up than you think." retorted Rob.

"Sure, if you say so" smiled Luke. "We'll do this again some time, OK? Go camping in the spring, maybe do some kayaking and whitewater rafting. Just you and me."

"Do you really mean it, or are you just being kind because you think I'm a nutcase?" Luke considered.

"Well…I seriously doubt I could find more interesting company bouncing off the walls of a padded cell. Of course I mean it" added Luke, ruffling his hair affectionately. "A little dippy, perhaps, but I love you. You're my favourite fruit loop." Rob gave him a shy smile.

****

"Oh, I almost forgot Cindy phoned this afternoon" said their mother to Luke, as they sat down to supper that evening. "She wanted to know if you'd help her move some furniture. She and the kids are moving into another house, and she'd appreciate some help with the heavy stuff."

"OK, sure. I'll give her a call later" replied Luke casually. Rob stared at his plate. He felt physically sick. Cindy was obviously trying to get back together with Luke, and this was a ploy to get him to come around. No doubt once he'd moved her stuff she'd be waiting for him in the bedroom. When Luke had been away in Vietnam, Cindy hadn't bothered what she looked like. Rob had seen her trundling a shopping cart through Kroger's in Bermuda shorts and flip-flops, with her hair in rollers. But as soon as Luke was back she'd started to look pretty again, with her long blonde hair tumbling about her shoulders – wearing mini-skirts and attracting wolf-whistles, although she was now a young mom. Just when things were going really well – he and Luke had never been closer – something like this had to happen and spoil things. Why couldn't she just leave Luke alone? He had a vivid memory of stumbling across his brother and Cindy in a secluded spot in the woods when he was thirteen. Luke had been on top of her, thrusting vigorously, and Cindy was making these gasping noises, saying his name over and over again. Rob had backed off, feeling nauseous. They weren't aware of his presence. At the time he had no idea why it should have affected him so much, since couples were always making out – in parked cars, at private parties, at the drive-in movie theatre. He knew it was perfectly normal and that most people did it, but Rob had unexpectedly found himself in tears.

Luke had eventually noticed that Rob had become very withdrawn, and seemed to be avoiding him. "What's up, Rob?" he had asked, confronting him. Rob had tried to push past him, but Luke had held him in place firmly. "Come on, don't give me the silent treatment." Rob couldn't speak. How was he to explain to his brother that he was jealous of his girlfriend? He didn't have the words to articulate what he was feeling. In a clumsy attempt to restore his good humour, Luke had startled tickling him beneath the ribs and under his arms, a strategy that usually worked since Rob was extremely ticklish. This had soon become unbearable, and Rob threw his arms around Luke in a plea to get him to stop. "Nope. Not until you tell me….alright, alright." Luke had stopped, seeing his obvious distress.

"Has someone been picking on you at school?" Luke had demanded. "Point me in his direction, and I'll kick his ass from here to kingdom come."

"No, it's just that we never do things together any more" Rob had finally confessed in the face of Luke's persistence. "You're always with *her*." He couldn't even bring himself to mention Cindy's name.

"Who? You mean Cindy? But what do you expect, we're going steady." As far as Rob was concerned this admission had only made things worse. If it had been a casual relationship, lasting only a few weeks, he wouldn't have minded so much. But it had been going on for months now, and he couldn't avoid running into the two of them together: Luke either had his arm around her as they strolled down the street, or she was sitting on his knee on the porch swing. Luke had stared at him with a mixture of astonishment and tenderness. "You're such a kid, aren't you" he'd said. "When you get older you'll be doing the same thing."

"No, I won't. It's disgusting!" Luke had chuckled.

"How do you think you were born? You know about the birds and bees, right?" Rob felt wretched. His brother just didn't get it: it wasn't the fact that he was screwing a girl that had upset Rob. It was that he felt Luke had been irrevocably taken from him. He wanted the old Luke back, not this one who fooled around with girls and was no longer available to him. He wanted his brother back.

"Is she going to have your baby?" Rob had demanded resentfully. Luke threw back his head and roared with laughter.

"I hope not. Ever heard of a rubber?" As Rob didn't reply but continued to throw him sulky looks, Luke caught him up in a tight hug. "Tell you what, we'll go fishing on the lake on Sunday. Just you and me, OK?" Luke had kept his promise and they had spent a magical day together, but it hadn't really changed things. He was still spending most of his time with Cindy, and Rob had been left out in the cold. And now it seemed as though history was repeating itself, with Luke's earlier promise to go camping: *"We'll do this again some time, OK? A camping trip – just you and me."* Had things really changed that much between them, or was Luke just being kind because his younger brother was going through a rough patch, in much the same way a parent placates a small child with an ice cream? If Luke were to get back together with Cindy, Rob really didn't think he could stand it. He just couldn't go through all that anguish and torment again. All the old feelings of abandonment and betrayal now threatened to re-surface and overwhelm him. He felt himself spiralling down into a black vortex of despair and clenched his fists underneath the table, in an effort to keep them from shaking.

"Aren't you eating anything, darling?" his mother asked him.

"Not hungry." He tried to regulate his breathing as he'd been told to do when he was hyperventilating and could feel a panic attack coming on.

"Robbie, have you taken your medicat-" began his mother.

"NO!" shouted Robbie. "I'm tired of swallowing pills. Like they do anything. Like they help." He banged his knife down on his plate.

"Rob, do not use that tone with your mother" admonished his father, somewhat sharply. "Apologise to her right now."

"It's all right, Joe" said his mother. "He didn't mean anything." Rob got up from the table and put his arms around his mother's neck.

"I love you, Mama. I didn't mean to shout at *you*."

"That's all right, precious" she said soothingly, stroking his hair. "Why don't you try and eat something? It might make you feel better."

"Mama, I was just wondering…"

"Yes? What is it, sweetheart?" Rob indicated Luke as if he were some stranger or interloper who'd wandered into their dining room.

"Was it very painful giving birth to a brick wall?" His parents exchanged glances with Luke, who leaned back in his chair and contemplated his brother, hands clasped behind his head. Rob returned to his seat and pointed at Luke with his fork. "What is that thing over there, anyway? Some kind of degenerate life-form from outer space?" The tension was building in the room, and Rob was going to break out any minute. His parents generally relied on Luke to physically restrain him, as he had been known to smash things and cause considerable damage.

"I'm going to bed now" said Rob suddenly, rising from the table. He put his hand to his head. "Got a headache." This usually signalled the onset of a deep depression, which could last for days. On his way out he picked up a glass of water and chucked its contents over Luke, who didn't move a muscle.

"Goodnight, Robbie" said Luke gravely, looking at him. Rob ignored him completely, as if he didn't exist, and left the room. His mother followed him.

"Do you see what I mean?" said Joe quietly to Luke when they were alone. "This is what we have to contend with. These moods just suddenly descend on him out of nowhere, and there's no reasoning with him. He becomes hostile and rude. That boy needs help. And I don't know whether that doctor is helping him or not. Luke, say something." He looked at Luke, as if seeking an answer from him.

"Let's go outside for a smoke" suggested Luke. Both men retired to the porch, Joe with his pipe, and Luke with a cigarette. Despite his outward composure, Luke was in fact profoundly troubled by what he had just witnessed. Maybe it had not been such a good idea after all to leave off Rob's medication for a few days. Less than half an hour ago his brother had seemed on top of the world when his mother had asked them whether they had had a nice time: "Yeah, we had a great time!" he had enthused. "And Luke and I are going to go camping in the spring, go whitewater rafting …" Being an adrenaline junkie, this was the type of exhilarating white-knuckle sport Rob loved.

"That sounds a little dangerous, darling. People have been known to drown" his mother had demurred.

"Luke is a strong swimmer" Joe reminded his wife. "He was a lifeguard for two summers over at Cherokee Park. I'm sure they'll be just fine." And then, with no warning, Rob had gone off the deep end and started hurling insults at Luke - having lost his appetite completely - and complaining of a headache. If Rob was capable of such abrupt transitions of mood, maybe Dr. Gottcha was partially correct in his diagnosis: that his brother had schizoid tendencies. Luke had little or no experience of mental illness, if this was what they were dealing with. All he knew was he hated seeing that wounded and bruised look in his brother's eyes, and being powerless to combat such an intangible adversary.

"I could do with a whiskey right now" muttered Joe.

"Yeah, me too" said Luke, his thoughts still churning. "But go easy on the hard liquor, Dad. We don't need you keeling over with another heart attack." Their father had been admitted to the county hospital last fall with a mild heart attack or myocardial infarction, as they'd termed it, and had been told to slow down and lay off the whiskey nightcaps, which advice he had mostly ignored.

"Medicinal, Luke. Purely medicinal." Luke went inside and returned with a couple of tumblers of bourbon.

****

Rob was lying supine on the floor in Loubelle's apartment, propped up on his elbows. He had been prescribed anti-depressants, which Dr. Gottschald had assured him would lift his depression, but the chief reason his mood was more positive was because Luke had returned home shortly after helping Cindy to move house, which meant he had not spent the night with her: maybe Loubelle was right in thinking he did not reciprocate her feelings. Though of course he could have fucked her after hauling her furniture up three flights of stairs. Wham bam, thank you Ma'am. There was no telling with Luke, but Rob put that thought resolutely out of his head. He's not interested in her, he told himself. After all, she had called him and not the other way round. She was doing all the running, and Luke was just lending a helping hand because that was the kind of guy he was. Women leaned on him all the time.

If the break-up with Cindy four years ago had affected him, Luke hadn't shown it. Rob had heard him on the phone one afternoon, lounging against the newel post at the foot of the stairs. He guessed Cindy must have been giving him a hard time or was upset about something, because Luke's responses mostly consisted of reassuring one-liners such as "Sure thing, baby doll", "That's fine, honey", and so on. Then as Cindy had apparently become increasingly frustrated by his casual laid-back attitude, Luke had varied his responses a little: "Hey, now. You're putting words in my mouth", "Come on. Getting yourself all worked up about nothing", "Huh? What's the big rush?", "Is that right? So what is it you want, honey?" followed by a lengthy pause during which Luke had listened to what she had to say, before commenting in a more ominous tone: "Fine. That's the way you want to play it, girl." Then he'd hung up, cool as anything. Not a flicker of emotion or a word to anyone that he'd just broken up with his steady girlfriend of three years, who was absolutely nuts about him. Rob knew this for certain because he also happened to be nuts about Luke, and recognised the signs. He had an idea the argument had arisen because Cindy was pestering him to get married, though Luke was barely twenty-one at the time. He was glad his brother had the sense not to tie himself down, and had vaguely wondered whether Cindy might be pregnant. That might explain why she was in such a rush to get hitched, but Rob didn't think his brother was the sort to leave a girl in the lurch if she'd got herself in the family way. After all, it would have been Luke's baby. When he'd heard Cindy had got engaged to someone else, Rob had breathed an enormous sigh of relief that she was finally out of the picture.

He was already regretting the hurtful things he had said to Luke, who had pulled him aside earlier in the day. "Look, if I've said or done anything to hurt you I'm sorry. But I need to know what, so I can put it right." Rob had been standing in the hallway, on his way to keep an appointment with Loubelle.

"You haven't done anything" Rob had murmured. "It's me." He felt that he had been mean to his brother when Luke had been unfailingly kind and patient with him. It was true that Luke was a terrible tease, but his teasing was more in the way of good-natured ribbing, a form of affection, and never malicious. And he had never once retaliated, despite being on the receiving end of several vicious punches. Initially this had offended Rob's pride because it implied Luke was treating him like a girl: *A real man never ever hits a woman* their father and their Uncle Jim had drilled into them when they were younger. *Even if she's a wildcat. You might have to hold her off, but you never hit her.* Rumours had reached them of a man in town who beat up his wife on a regular basis, and Joe and Jim had spat on the ground to signal their disgust at such contemptible behaviour. *A real man always behaves like a true gentleman.* This was the ethos they had grown up with, the code of behaviour the men in their family honoured. Luke had never got into fights with boys smaller than himself when he was growing up, regarding such scraps as beneath him.

"What's going on, Rob?" Luke had slapped his palms on the wall either side of Rob's head, effectively imprisoning him. He was a hard man to ignore when he wanted answers. Rob wavered. If he stayed a moment longer in Luke's presence he would lose his resolve. Whenever he was standing close to his brother he felt helplessly attracted to him.

"I didn't mean those things I said to you." Rob was trying, unsuccessfully, to duck beneath Luke's rigid forearms. "I'm sorry I called you a brick wall."

"That was the deadliest insult anyone's ever hurled at me" replied Luke, utterly deadpan. Rob tried a different tack. Maybe it was time for what Loubelle called "the Look." He placed his hands on Luke's shoulders, and gazed at him from underneath his eyelashes.

"Don't be so *hard-on* me, Sheriff. If you find me that irresistible I'm sure we could come to some other private arrangement." Luke had shook with silent laughter as their mother appeared in the doorway, and Rob had taken the opportunity to make his escape.

His parents were completely mystified by his burgeoning friendship with a woman old enough to be his mother, which he had not been able to keep secret in such a small town. His mother was worried that a 46-year-old divorcee might be "corrupting" her boy, whilst his father had merely chuckled and winked complicitly at Luke.

"About time. An experienced older woman is the best thing for him; she'll teach him a thing or two, eh Luke?" Confronted by his parents, Rob had hotly denied that there was anything going on between them. "We're just FRIENDS that's all. I'm platonic and unavailable. She's my best friend in this town." Luke had believed him, but was still somewhat baffled. He eventually concluded that Loubelle acted as some kind of agony aunt to whom his younger brother could confide his troubles. Rob had always been a Mama's boy, and with respect to the opposite sex he felt more comfortable with older maternal types rather than girls his own age. The Deputy Head of the high school, a Miss Grant, had the reputation of being a battleaxe because of her stern no-nonsense manner, but somehow Rob had managed to get her on side when he had been hauled before the Principal for punching a teacher. Rob claimed the man had assaulted him first, slamming him against a locker for answering back and being a "smart aleck", and that he had only acted in self-defence. As there were no witnesses to the alleged incident, which had occurred after class, Rob ran the risk of expulsion. Miss Grant had sat him down in her office, saying "You're a smart boy. You've got everything going for you. Why are you acting like this?" Rob had replied "You're a nice lady and I'm an outlaw, but you don't need to worry about me" then impulsively kissed her on the cheek. She had been utterly and unexpectedly charmed, and had pleaded his case with the Principal, citing Rob's anxiety about his older brother who was then serving in Vietnam. When he'd got off with a light suspension – thanks to Miss Grant's eloquent intervention - his standing amongst his classmates had soared: he was thereafter known as the boy who had "melted the Dragon's heart."

"Sounds like you're doing just fine" said Loubelle, after Rob had given her a full progress report. "Either that, or this brother of yours has the patience of a saint. Ready for Phase Three?"

"Lay it on me."

"So far you've been massaging his ego, making him feel like Superman. But all gods have feet of clay. I'm sure he has plenty of faults you're not aware of."

"No, he doesn't. Luke's really nice, he…"

"Shut up and listen. I'm willing to concede he's nicer than your average guy, your average guy being a pile of steaming horse manure.... well, I don't want to infect you with my cynicism so we'll leave it at that. The problem here is he holds all the cards. He snaps his fingers and you come running, am I right?"

"That makes me sound like some puppy dog yapping at his heels. It's not like that."

"Well, I can't comment because I haven't been able to observe the two of you at close quarters. Don't suppose you could bring him into the bakery one afternoon, and I can watch you both-"

"-No! That would be too embarrassing, and he might catch on."

"All right. Forget that idea. You've already signalled your interest in him and he's responding. That's a good sign. Now you need to show disinterest."

"Show no interest at all?" Rob was thoroughly confused. "But if I ignore him, it might hurt his feelings. Or he might get pissed at me." What if Luke reacted in the same way as when he'd broke up with Cindy? *Fine. That's the way you want to play it, girl.* Whatever she'd said to annoy him (probably threatened to go out with some other guy) it was Cindy who'd suffered the fallout and not Luke, who'd got on with his life.

"Never mind his feelings. You're the one who's suffering here, not him. He doesn't sound like the sort who's going to weep into his pillow if you ignore him from time to time. He's a big tough soldier, for heaven's sake. I'm sure he can handle it." Rob was silent. He wasn't very happy about the direction this was taking. He was so accustomed to accommodating his brother that the idea of ignoring him seemed almost sacrilegious. "Either ignore him or back off" continued Loubelle. "I'd offer you a drink, hon, but I don't want you behind the wheel if you're tight. You don't mind if I indulge?" Without waiting for an answer she fixed herself a gin and tonic, and handed him a cold Pepsi.

"How does he react if someone defies him?" asked Loubelle curiously.

"I don't know" confessed Rob. Luke had occasionally been known to lock horns with other males, but on these occasions he always emerged as the victor. When they were growing up, other boys had soon learned that the outcome of any fight with Luke was a foregone conclusion. He invariably won so there wasn't much point. Loubelle put her hands on her hips and faced him.

"I bet you've never said no to him, have you? Be honest."

"Uh, well…"

"All right, you've answered my question. Guys like him who've been in the armed forces, especially if they've held positions of authority, expect everyone to snap to attention when they walk into a room. Yessir, nossir, three bags full sir. The army spoils them; they get to expect the same treatment from everyone. And if they don't get the respect they think they're entitled to, they can turn into monsters in the blink of an eye, wife-beaters even …"

"Stop it. That's not Luke you're describing. You haven't met him." Rob sounded genuinely distressed at the portrait she had drawn, which bore no relation to the caring brother he knew.

"I'm sorry, sweetie, I'm sure he's a really nice guy. You wouldn't love him like you do if he wasn't. Let's read some more *True Confessions*. How about this one?" She picked up a magazine and read aloud: *"His love put me through hell but I couldn't give him up – a slave to his caresses.* Lordamercy, who writes this stuff?" Rob started to laugh. "God Almighty, listen to this: *Watch his pants get tighter as he gets a hard-on..."* Loubelle collapsed in a fit of laughter, which set Rob off. They were both laughing so hard they were rolling about on the floor. "Are you sure you wouldn't like to watch his pants get-" Rob threw a cushion at her.

"Get outta here."

"Sweet Jesus, this stuff is so awful, it's killing me. I can't take any more!" gasped Loubelle. She rolled up the magazine and threw it across the room.

"You're the one who buys those stupid magazines" pointed out Rob, with a grin.

"I know" wailed Loubelle. "What is wrong with me?"

"You're a degenerate" suggested Rob.

"You could be right. But believe me, you and I aren't half as degenerate as some of the folks in this town" said Loubelle darkly.

"Who?" asked Rob, his curiosity piqued.

"Don't expect me to mention names, but there's this fine upstanding citizen who likes getting his bare ass whipped by his secretary." The citizen in question was an attorney by the name of Darlington who lived alone with his wheelchair-bound mother. The secretary was Candace Sloane, who had gone to school with Loubelle and often came into the bakery for a quick bite of lunch, and to grumble about her boss.

"He gets me running around after him ...to the drugstore for Tylenol if he gets an itsy bitsy headache, for coffee and doughnuts while he's yapping on the phone to clients, shopping at Kroger's for his mother who's so skinny she looks like a goddamn toothpick on wheels...Then I'm expected to stay late in the office typing up legal documents he dumps on my desk at the very last minute when we're ready to close up for the night. I'm supposed to do all this *extra* stuff on the measly pay I get…"

"Ask him for a raise" said Loubelle briskly, who was sick and tired of listening to all this bellyaching. "Ten per cent. And if he doesn't agree tell him you're quitting." Candace looked shocked.

"Are you kidding me? That tightwad wouldn't buy flowers for his own mother's funeral, he'd go pick some daisies from the roadside and wrap them up in toilet paper."

"Just do it, honey" said Loubelle. "Either do something about it or shut up." A few weeks went by and Loubelle couldn't help noticing that Candace seemed flush with money, splashing out on new furniture for her crummy duplex apartment, a brand new stereo and TV set, and new outfits from the most expensive store in town. "OK, what's going on?" asked Loubelle finally. "And don't lie to me because I always find out the truth." After inviting Candace back to her apartment one evening, Loubelle had poured a bottle of wine down her throat without compunction, and got her to divulge the details of the new "accommodation" she had reached with her employer. Following Loubelle's advice, Candace had asked Darlington for a raise, expecting to be fired on the spot. He'd raised his head from his paperwork and looked at her with a gleam in his eye she'd never seen before.

"You're pretty ballsy, aren't you? I never noticed before. You know, I kind of like that in a woman. If you want a raise, I've got a proposition for you."

"I thought he was going to ask me to do something really disgusting like suck his dick, and I was all ready to skedaddle on out of there. I'm no cheap motel hooker, I don't need the lousy job that bad. You know what he wanted me to do?" Without waiting for an answer, Candace continued "Every Friday night the little shit shows up at my apartment as meek and mild as can be: *'May I come in, Ma'am?'* I kick his ass into the bedroom and tell him – correction, I *order* him – to strip. He's so excited he can't get his pants off fast enough. *'Please Ma'am'* he goes *'I've been a bad boy. I need to be punished.'* You bet your bottom dollar I'm gonna punish you, you sorry sonofabitch, I think to myself. Then he lays face down on the bed and I whip his lily-white ass with a paddle until he's yowling and caterwauling like a cat tied to a hot stove. Whenever I stop he begs for more: *'Beat me harder, harder. Chastise me, Candace.'* I say *'Did you just forget to call me Ma'am? Uh oh, buddy are you in for it now..."*

"You mean to say he's paying you that much you can afford to buy all this stuff only six weeks after he raised your salary..." interrupted Loubelle, somewhat sceptically.

"Well, here's the doozy, wait for it. I get a BONUS every time he opens his mouth without my permission, every time he forgets to call me Ma'am. If he so much as goes to the bathroom to take a leak without my permission, or if he messes up my bedspread with his spunk, not only do I get a big fat bonus but I get to whip his ass even harder." Candace tossed back her head and laughed uproariously. "Some days his behind is so sore he can barely sit at his desk. I think he was actually wearing a diaper last week. Mind you, he still treats me like shit in the office Monday through Thursday, but come Friday night the shoe's on the other foot, *I'm* in charge, *I'm* the boss lady. And that kinky bastard just loves it, can't get enough of it." Loubelle now related all of this to Rob, careful not to mention any real names. Rob started to laugh. Soon they were both doubled over again, in stitches. Loubelle handed him a handkerchief.

"Here, stuff this in your mouth. I'm going to be sick if I laugh any more, but I haven't had such fun since those slumber parties I used to go to." Rob had always been curious about the pyjama parties where teenage girls would congregate at one another's houses to have sleepovers.

"What did you get up to at slumber parties?" he asked.

"Oh, just girl stuff. The reason it was fun was because no boys were allowed."

"I thought you painted each other's toenails and talked about boys" said Rob.

"Boys think the whole world revolves around them. We might occasionally talk about cute boys, but a lot of the time we told each other spooky stories about ghosts and things that go bump in the night. Or we played spin the bottle. *Strip Poker*, or *Truth or Dare*. You get to know a lot about people that way. And we'd have pillow fights, which could get quite rough. Once we locked a girl in the basement, and left her there for two hours in the cold and darkness."

"Why?"

"It was my idea. She was a crybaby and a tittle-tattle. The other girls were all scared to death of me, and I just loved it." Rob looked at her. Loubelle rather fascinated him. "OK, let's get back to business. Phase Three is more difficult because you need to make it look like he's the one pursuing you. He must think he seduced you, and not the other way round. Let him be the victor, the conqueror. Masculine men love that."

"But he's basically straight so he probably wouldn't want to seduce me."

"Don't be so sure about that. What did I tell you about how most people swing both ways? You're going to drive him crazy."

"How?"

"Use your charm, your physical attributes, everything we talked about. Have you done a full-body pose yet?"

"Yeah, a couple."

"And how did he respond, if at all?" Rob hesitated. He was reluctant to tell her about what had occurred between them, when Luke had straddled him on the log. It was the most exciting thing that had ever happened to him but it was private, and he didn't want to talk about it.

"Come on, don't be shy. I don't need a blow-by-blow account, but I need to know if this strategy is working or not."

"It's working" said Rob, but wouldn't be drawn further. Instead he told her about when he had gone in pursuit of Luke and found him at the top pasture, stringing barbed wire between some fence posts. Seeing his approach, Luke had stopped what he was doing and looked at him questioningly. "Um, do you have a light?" Rob had asked him.

"You came all the way over here to ask me for a light?" Meaning Rob could easily have found one in the house. "Do you actually have a cigarette that needs lighting?" Luke had then enquired, with a smile. Rob rarely smoked and had forgotten to bring a pack along with him.

"I nearly died with embarrassment" Rob now confessed to Loubelle, blushing at the memory. "I asked him for a light when I didn't even have a cigarette on me. I meant to give him the Look first, then do the touching thing on his arm. But somehow I got them mixed up in the wrong order, and then I couldn't give him the Look because I couldn't look him in the eye." Loubelle started to giggle again.

"Oh Robbie, you're priceless. You poor baby. But you've got to concentrate more on what you're doing, rehearse your moves instead of going off half-cocked and diving right on in there." She considered for a moment. "I hate to say it, but I think that on the mental level he's going to outsmart you every step of the way. We're going to have to rely on your physical charms, because that's obviously working. You're starting to get under his skin."

"I hate being in love" Rob declared passionately. "I hate everything about it! Whoever invented love should be stood up in front of a firing squad and shot." The agonies of jealousy he went through whenever Luke was seeing a woman, the tears he'd shed in private, the constant heartache and yearning for something he knew he could never have, all just served to convince him that being in love was an exquisite form of torture.

Loubelle was beginning to wonder whether Luke was a serial heartbreaker. It wasn't that he was callous or heartless. Far from it. From what she had heard he was considerate and treated women pretty well, but he always kept something of himself in reserve: no-one knew where they stood with him. Cindy Foster had once confided that the only reason she broke up with Luke was to try and get him to marry her, but the strategy had backfired. Luke had gone off to Vietnam and she had ended up marrying someone on the rebound. After dispensing some brisk advice to Cindy shortly after Luke had returned home "Honey, I would advise that you give that guy a wide berth. You're wasting your time with him" Cindy had stopped coming by the bakery for coffee and sympathy. Of course the situation had changed radically since Loubelle had met his younger brother Rob, and learned of his secret passion. Had Cindy showed up again asking for her advice Loubelle would have discouraged her even further: she figured that if Luke had really wanted to get together with Cindy again there was absolutely nothing stopping him. He clearly had no interest in doing so. A person had to take sides, and Loubelle was not one for sitting on the fence. She had come down firmly in favour of Rob.

"I don't want him to see me as just someone to fool around with, like his plaything. I want a proper relationship with him" said Rob. Luke had told him he thought he was "cute", and that he was his "favourite fruit loop", whatever that meant.

"Yeah, I can see where this is heading" said Loubelle thoughtfully. "When it comes to sex, if a guy is feeling horny he doesn't much care where he puts his dick..."

"He didn't! I wouldn't let him do *that*" said Rob, who was very sensitive on the subject of sodomy.

"You know what I'm saying. Men have been known to do it with sheep if there are no women around. And what goes on in prisons..." Rob frowned, and ran a hand through his hair.

"I don't want to talk about this any more." He looked agitated.

"What's the matter?" She put her arm around him. "Are you OK?" He nodded. "Men aren't big on romance on a first pass – that comes later. The physical always comes first, before you can engage their brains. That's why when a very pretty girl walks into a room they all swarm around her, and other females don't get a look-in, no matter whether they have nicer personalities or a lot more to offer." Rob was amazed how much Loubelle seemed to know about men. He didn't think her knowledge came from trashy magazines like *True Confessions* and he was determined to absorb everything she could teach him.

"Tease him" continued Loubelle. "Not all the time, but occasionally take him down a peg or two. Phase Three involves reversing what you've been doing so far. You don't want him to get too complacent or to take you for granted. So I want you to play hard to get but not too hard, just enough to challenge him. Don't make it too easy for him." She picked up the issue with the article entitled *How to Get Your Man and Leave Him Smitten* that she had originally earmarked for their study: *Dress attractively when you're out so he can see other men admiring you. This will make him realise how lucky he is to be with you."*

"That's no good because there are no other men standing around admiring me" said Rob. "And what does dress attractively mean?"

"Ignore that. If you're good looking it doesn't much matter what you wear. Whereas …I don't want to sound cruel, but you can spend a thousand dollars on an outfit and it won't do a damn thing for you if you're butt-ugly or well past your prime. You ever seen these old ladies in sparkly dresses that cost a small fortune, flashing their diamond necklaces on their wrinkly chicken necks?" Rob laughed despite himself. He'd seen the type down at the country club his parents belonged to. "Exactly. Mutton dressed as lamb. Well, I'm sorry, honey, but if a cute young sixteen-year-old walks in wearing nothing but a dime store rag who are the men going to look at? The tasty young lamb or the well-preserved tough old mutton? The mutton might as well just scoot back into its icebox. But you don't need to worry. All you have to do is swivel your hips on the dance floor."

"Luke doesn't dance much."

"Too klutzy, huh, like most big guys" commented Loubelle.

"So how do I get him to take me seriously?"

"You make him jealous. You might not have any male admirers at the moment, but we can easily fix that. Just a question of showing you off in the right quarters."

"How do you mean?"

"I happen to know this guy who works over at the Levi store who likes other guys. I could set you up for a date with him. See how your brother reacts to that!" Rob looked unsure.

"But wouldn't that just be using him? Because I wouldn't want to date him for real, you know. Or do anything. I'm not available."

"You mean he might get frustrated if he took a real shine to you. Well, we're only talking about one date, and you need never see him again. Are you up for it?" She thought it highly likely Rick would fall for Rob's charms – that was the whole point of the exercise – but there was no need to let Rob know that, or he would back out. As he hesitated, Loubelle smiled encouragingly "Fortune favours the bold. Have I been right so far?"

"OK" said Rob finally. "How do I meet him?"

"Don't worry" She smiled. "I'll arrange everything." Loubelle picked up the phone and dialled a number. "Hi, Ricky. Loubelle here. Uh-huh. Uh-huh. Listen, I've got this young fella here with me, a real stunner, and he's just dying to see the local sights..." *See the local sights?* What did she mean? When she hung up, Rob looked desperate.

"What have you just got me into?"

"Relax. There's this cruise joint outta town somewhere, which few folks know about. Rick's safe, I know him" she added, seeing his unease He hasn't got the balls to lay a finger on anyone on a first date. All you have to do is show up, have a few drinks, a dance. Just enjoy yourself. I've fixed you up for next Friday night. But make sure that brother of yours knows you're seeing a man, OK?"

Chapter Seven

When Rob walked into Dr. Gottschald's office he took one look at the stranger sitting in the doctor's chair and walked right out again.

"Where's Dr. Strangelove?" he demanded of the receptionist.

"Excuse me?" The receptionist and the new assistant typist both looked up.

"Dr. Gottcha, the usual guy who sees me."

"Oh, he's away on vacation. He arranged for a locum to stand in for him – weren't you informed? Dr. Carter is very well qualified...."

"-I'm not seeing him! I don't like substitute shrinks any more than I like substitute teachers. And you can tell him that."

"You want me to tell Dr. Carter..."

"No! I want you to tell Dr. Gottcha when he gets back from sunning himself in Florida that Jesse James said he can go to hell."

"Actually, he's on a ski-ing trip in Colorado. But I'll be sure to tell him" replied the receptionist.

"That's Rob Turnbull" she giggled as soon as Rob had exited the office. "The one who punched out a teacher and is into fast cars, who Sandy's always drooling over. He's a dish, don't you think, even if he is a little screwy? I wouldn't mind a date with him."

"Mmmm. Drop dead gorgeous" agreed the typist, who was fairly new. "He's the type who'll probably die young, likes James Dean. You can always tell."

The following week Rob was back in the office, facing Dr. Gottschald across his desk. He resembled some gunslinger from the Wild West, and was wearing a low-slung leather belt and cowboy boots. He was an extraordinarily good-looking young man, Albert reflected, not for the first time. It was hardly surprising the girls in the office were half in love with him. He had clearly inherited his looks from his mother, who was a good twelve years younger than her husband and a natural beauty with dark hair and blue eyes.

"I understand you were a little upset that I wasn't here last week" said Albert, as Rob lounged in a chair, his boots up on the table.

"Who says I was upset? I don't mind that you took a vacation, Doc. What I don't LIKE is that you put this dummy in your place, a lousy SUBSTITUTE, and you think I wouldn't be able to tell the difference?"

"Dr. Carter is perfectly competent and experienced. Why should you object to him? Have you become especially attached to me?"

"Dream on. I'm not ATTACHED to you. I just don't like change. I like things to stay the same."

"This may be something we need to talk about further. However, today we're going to explore the topic of monsters in the closet."

"How old do you think I am? I'm not scared of monsters in the closet!" Rob looked at him with such an expression of disgust, that Albert sat up and paid attention.

"I'm sure you're not" said Albert in a placatory tone. "But it's a well-attested fact that most small children go through a phase when they're frightened of bogeymen, monsters in the closet, what have you. It's perfectly normal. What I want to discuss with you today is anything that might have frightened you when you were very young – let's say four years old – can you remember back that far?" Rob looked at him suspiciously: he suspected some kind of trap. The doctor was probably trying to trip him up. It wouldn't be the first time.

"OK" he said finally. "When I was very little I sometimes thought I heard whispering coming from the closet. I thought there might be somebody in there who'd jump out if I opened the door. A man with a pumpkin's head."

"A pumpkin's head?"

"Yeah, you know, like those Halloween pumpkins. Sharp teeth, and a wicked grin."

"Did you tell your parents about being frightened?"

"No. I told my brother."

"How did he react? Did he taunt you for being a baby – anything like that?"

"No" said Rob angrily. "Luke said he'd go after them and that I didn't need to worry." The eight-year-old Luke had flung open the closet door, brandishing his homemade wooden sword, and declared in a loud voice that if there were any monsters in there he'd kill them all. Now we're finally getting somewhere, thought Albert. From a very early age, Rob's older brother had acted as his protector. Albert felt that an important precedent had been set. He would come back to the closet theme once Rob felt more comfortable talking about things that had frightened him.

"Tell me about other things Luke did to make you admire him when you were children" said Albert. "Before the onset of puberty." His brother was a topic Rob never tired of, so it wasn't difficult to get him to open up.

"There were these two dogs fighting in the street. Well, it was more like one dog chewing out another one, who was much smaller. The little one was so badly bitten that if someone didn't separate them it was going to die. The big dog was growling and no-one wanted to go near it, because it was well known for attacking people. Everyone said it should have been put down: it belonged to this really mean guy who normally kept it chained up in his back yard, but some kid set it loose when he was out." Luke had picked up the smaller dog by the scruff of the neck and placed it on top of a wall out of harm's way, before warning off the bigger one: *"Go pick on some dog your own size. Go on now, git!"*

"It didn't bite him or anything" said Rob. "It just whimpered, then slunk off with its tail between its legs."

"How old was Luke at the time?"

"About eleven or so." Albert thought he detected a recurring pattern of behaviour here, which helped to explain why Rob was so in awe of his older brother. Of course, there was nothing out of the ordinary in the story Rob had just related.

"Because you were so small at the time - about six or seven, yes?" Rob nodded. "You viewed this as an instance of your brother's invincibility. However, as you are probably aware, dogs - like many animals - can smell fear. Because Luke felt no fear, he wasn't attacked. Nothing miraculous about it."

"Yeah, well how come he never felt any fear when there wasn't a single grownup in the neighbourhood who'd go near that dog? I know why the dog didn't bite him, but what I'm telling you is that Luke has never been scared of anything."

"That is your perception" said Albert.

"It's most peoples' perception, not just mine. All the kids admired him and wanted to be like him." Luke was clearly one of those people who possessed a natural air of authority, thought Albert, which had doubtless served him very well in the military. Being bigger and stronger than your peers counted for a lot with growing boys, conferring innate advantages that tended to follow their possessors throughout life.

"Alright, but they didn't all fall in love with him, did they?"

"I guess not" conceded Rob. "Congratulations, Doc. You just got me to admit I'm abnormal. Tell me something I don't already know. That's why I'm here isn't it?" Albert got him to relate a few further childhood incidents. There was the time when an older boy called Rudy Nelson had started bashing him against the wall in front of the drugstore after Rob had provoked him by chucking water balloons at him. Luke had been busy flicking through the girlie mags in the magazine rack, studying the breasts of naked or scantily clad women with undisguised interest, until one of his pals alerted him to what was going on. Luke had strolled outside onto the sidewalk, coldly enquiring of Rudy just what the hell did he think he was doing?

"Why don't you mind your own business, Turnbull? I can do whatever I damn well want." At fourteen, Rudy was a year older than Luke and pretty cocksure.

"If I was a snail" said Luke "I might find you intimidating." Rob, who was nine at the time, couldn't help noticing that Rudy didn't seem nearly so sure of himself when Luke challenged him to a fight. Of course Luke had won the fight, and Rob had never been bothered again. They had also had several run-ins with a pair of brothers known as the Ballard Boys, whose chief amusement was to tie a piece of string around a bird's neck and slowly strangle it to death. They were known to fight dirty, packing their snowballs with stones and small shards of glass, and every so often their Daddy thrashed them out back with a hosepipe. On one occasion when he and Luke had rode by on their bikes, the boys had tied a cluster of tin cans to a cat's tail. Unable to understand where the fearful clanging noise was coming from, the terrified cat was whirling around and around in panicked circles, chasing its own tail. The brothers were roaring with laughter. Luke had taken out the Buck knife he kept sheathed in his belt and cut the string tied to its tail, ignoring the hissing, snarling creature that clawed and scratched at his arms before making its getaway. Then he'd acted all friendly and invited the brothers to join him in the woods for some "target practice."

"I generally tie my baby brother to a tree" Luke told them. "And then I hit the target with a knife. Like William Tell and the apple, you know that story?" Sure, they knew that story all right – they'd heard it in grade school – and were eager to participate.

"You ever miss and hit him with the knife?" the older of the two asked, as Luke securely tied Rob to a tree.

"Nah" said Luke, winking at Rob. "I'm much too good for that." After about five minutes of this game, during which time the knife thudded against the tree trunk above his head at regular intervals, Luke suggested that Rory, the older of the two brothers, follow his lead.

"Why don't we tie your baby brother to a tree too so you can get in some practice?" Cody was reluctant to play. "Maybe he won't be such a scaredy-cat if he sees you go first" said Luke to Rory. "Not scared, are you?"

"Who, me? No, I ain't scared of nothin'" Rory allowed himself to be tied to a tree, and Luke practised throwing his knife for a while, never missing his target, a big cross he'd carved into the bark above Rory's head. Then he turned to Cody. "See? It's OK, I'm not gonna hurt you. Wanna try now?" Seeing that his older brother had remained unharmed and lulled into a false sense of security, Cody agreed to play the game.

"Hey, you better untie me first" said Rory to Luke, as his younger brother was tied to another tree. Luke ignored this request, smiling to himself as he untied Rob.

"Now we're gonna see some REAL target practice." The next ten minutes must have been hair-raising for the two Ballard boys, as Luke's self-proclaimed targets got ever closer to their tightly bound squirming bodies. Each time he called out a new target such as "Two inches above his right shoulder", "Let's see if I can hit that little cross I cut in the bark next to his left ear" they flinched and squeezed their eyes shut, bawling like a couple of hog-tied calves about to be branded.

"Hold still now so you don't get hurt" said Luke to Rory. "I'm aiming this one right between your legs. Here it comes." The knife whizzed through the air, its point skewering the tree bark between his outspread legs. "I'm pretty damned good, wouldn't you say?" Luke asked Rob, who had been watching the game from a distance, his eyes never leaving his brother.

Albert listened to these childhood anecdotes with a mixture of amusement and professional interest. He was now pretty sure he had pinpointed an established pattern, a solid foundation upon which Rob's idolisation of his brother had its beginnings. His task now was to probe a little further and ascertain whether this foundation was quite as solid as it seemed.

"Tell me" said Albert "Did your brother ever bully you when you were small?"

"No."

"Often our memory is highly selective and can play tricks on us. Sometimes there are things we choose not to remember. Let me give you an example: I recently dealt with a case of domestic abuse, where the wife was routinely abused by her husband-"

"-What's this got to do with me?" cut in Rob. "I feel sorry for the lady, but she needs to get the hell away from him."

"Please hear me out. This woman, who is not unintelligent, refused to hear a word against her husband. Do you know why?"

"Because she had a screw loose? Is that why she was seeing a shrink?"

"She was deeply in love with him. No matter what he did to her, she refused to accept that he had any faults. She thought the fault lay with her. Even when confronted with the evidence of bruises all over her body, she thought her husband was some kind of hero who could do no wrong…" Rob got up from his seat and walked over to Albert.

"You're a piece of work, you know that? You're lucky I don't knock your fucking head off right now."

"Sit down, please, Rob" said Albert composedly. Rob smiled and picked up a paperweight from his desk, a souvenir from a ski resort in the Rocky Mountains, weighing it in his hand.

"You really don't think I'd attack you, do you? I was just admiring this – reminds me of a snow globe I once had as a kid." Rob put the paperweight down, and resumed his seat.

"I used the previous example to illustrate a well-known psychological phenomenon: if a person doesn't want to believe something, or if the truth is something they find too disturbing to face up to, they blot it out completely and fool themselves it never happened. Or they may invent an alternative scenario: in this case the woman had managed to convince herself that her husband was no wife-beater, that he was in fact John Wayne."

"My dad likes John Wayne" remarked Rob conversationally. "Watches all his movies, especially the Westerns."

"I believe you have a great admiration for the legendary lawman, Wyatt Earp."

"He was one hell of a guy" said Rob, staring hard at Albert. "Pretty handy with his fists as well as a gun, because he was so strong. No-one ever got the better of him in a fight."

"So, do you think Luke is a bit like Wyatt Earp?" asked Albert delicately.

"Yeah, Luke's a one-punch guy, can lay anyone out with one punch." He recalled an incident when Luke was about seventeen and some jock who resented the fact that Cindy Foster had showed a decided preference for his brother, had insulted them both. Luke had walked up to him and patted him on the shoulder: "Well, now, this is kind of interesting" (he was always kind to someone who was about to get a pounding) "Care to repeat that?" Then WHAM. Knocked him to the floor with a solid roundhouse right. Naturally, Luke got the girl and the other guy bit the dust. Just like in the Westerns.

"Wyatt Earp wasn't always on the side of the law, though" said Albert. "He was involved in some questionable, not to say crooked, business enterprises: gambling, prostitution and so on. Sometimes the beatings he dished out were quite brutal."

"So? Those guys probably got what they deserved."

"Although he had a reputation as a tough frontier Marshall, he became an outlaw himself eventually, killing men indiscriminately if they crossed him" continued Albert.

"Not indiscriminately, in REVENGE. Some of those cowboys he went after murdered one of his brothers in cold blood, man. Ambushed him when Wyatt wasn't around. What did you expect him to do?" Rob looked at him defiantly. "Anyone harmed my brother Frank, I'd kill him too." Frank, he'd said. This was getting interesting. Ever since Rob had walked into his office, Albert had been aware of a subtle change in his comportment. His voice had dropped a register, becoming deeper and lower, and his manner was hostile and menacing. He was more masculine somehow, more sure of his ground. Albert tried a different tack.

"Rob, I find it hard to believe that Luke never once bullied you. It is quite normal for an older brother to tease or torment his younger siblings from time to time. In fact it would be abnormal if he didn't. Such behaviour doesn't signify psychopathic character traits, so there's no need to get overly defensive. I'm not necessarily talking about *physical* bullying, but exerting his dominance over you. Did he ever force you to do something you didn't want to do?"

"Such as?"

"You tell me." Albert waited patiently, while Rob's eyes roamed the room in a bored insolent fashion, as if the conversation no longer held any interest for him.

"You're boring as cow shit. You keep harping on and on about the same things. OK, I'll tell you something that might get your juices going. Only because I feel sorry for you, man. It's to do with that "monsters in the closet" thing. I was about five, and he put me in the closet and locked it."

"That was rather cruel of him, don't you think?" Rob hesitated.

"He did it so I could see there was nothing in there to be scared of. And he didn't leave me in there for very long. He came to rescue me when he heard me crying."

"Do you see what I'm getting at here, Rob? You persist in viewing Luke as your saviour, never as your persecutor. He may have rescued you, but we mustn't lose sight of the fact he was the one who put you in there in the first place. What if there are further instances buried deep in your memory, instances where Luke was not such a kind, caring brother, the hero you think he is. What if your memory has decided to select only the "good" things to remember, and conveniently forgotten the bad things…"

"There ARE no bad things. You're full of horseshit, man." Rob leapt to his feet. "And if Luke gets to hear that you've been implying he's some kind of child abuser, I wouldn't want to be in your shoes."

"I hope that wasn't a threat" said Albert, looking up.

"If it was, Doc, I'd advise you to take it very seriously" said Rob in a low dangerous voice, leaning over him and fixing him with a very hard look. For a moment, Albert was actually intimidated. It was as though he were dealing with the outlaw Jesse James, and not Rob Turnbull. Rob stormed out of the office, fisting the door on his way out.

Something had got him really rattled, thought Albert. He was reminded of his first impressions when moving to this part of the world. With a lot of these people, the veneer of civilisation was very thin. Scratch the surface and you came up against something atavistic and primitive - born of a shared cultural heritage - rearing its ugly head. He would have liked to further investigate the Turnbull family history, going back a couple of generations (he believed they had been cattle ranchers) but such an undertaking was probably beyond his current remit. Although Kentucky had officially declared its neutrality at the start of the Civil War, it also supported secession from the Union, and soldiers served in both Confederate and Union forces. A few years later, federal laws were passed which awarded ownership of land to certain families for bravery and distinguished military service during the war, and the Turnbulls had probably been amongst those to benefit. Albert suspected that many of those whose homesteads were in the more remote mountainous areas had simply shot anything that moved, being deeply suspicious of outsiders, and if the preponderance of dead bodies favoured one side more than the other this was a mere accident of fate. He rewound the tape recorder back to the start, so that he could listen again to the clearly audible change in Rob's tone of voice as he switched between different *personas*, then he inserted a cassette tape from a previous session that had taken place three weeks ago, and pressed the PLAY button.

"Let's talk about Johnny Angel" suggested Albert. Rob's *alter ego* Jesse James had at first been reluctant.

"What do you want to talk about that little pansy for?" he had snapped. "He's no better than a whore, man. Puts out for any guy with a six-shooter."

"Is that really the case?" Albert had thought fit to challenge this rather unflattering assessment of Johnny Angel's character. "He's a good-looking boy, so he can afford to be choosy. I very much doubt he'd make himself available to just any man."

"Yeah" agreed Rob slowly. "He's young and beautiful. He never grows old."

"I understand Johnny Angel is very taken with your brother" insisted Albert. "He seems quite determined to seduce him."

"Luke….mmm, yeah, he's so sexy, such a gorgeous hunk." At this point, Rob's entire demeanour had changed, and the expression in his eyes had become dreamy, as though he had gone into a temporary trance. The defiant outlaw Jesse James had faded from the picture completely. *"I want him. And I'm going to have him."* Rob's voice sounded clear and childish on the tape recorder. Albert turned up the volume a little. "We were meant to be together."

"So how do you go about seducing a heterosexual he-man such as Luke, Johnny?" enquired Albert delicately.

"Well…. I just run my hands up and down over his arms and shoulders, which are like, out of this world. And then I get his attention by…." Rob giggled coyly. "Come on, he's a man and he's got a cock. It's not that difficult."

"Do you think he finds you desirable, Johnny?"

"I know he does."

"How do you know?"

"He lets me know, in all kinds of little ways. All I have to do is smile or touch him, and he gets hot under the collar. Do you think I'm beautiful? Everyone tells me I am."

"Why do you find Luke so attractive, Johnny?"

"Because he's big and strong and brave. I like strong men." Rob's voice was softer, more childlike, and the tension had left his body completely - his movements languid and his expression dreamy. It was really quite extraordinary, thought Albert, as he listened with growing excitement.

"Why?"

"Because a strong guy can protect me" said Rob.

"But why do you need protecting?" Albert asked.

"Because there are bad guys out there! Some of them are mean. Not nice. Not nice at all" said Rob emphatically, shaking his head. He had looked like a small child as he shook his head, a bullied child who is too young to understand the warped motives of his tormentor.

"So Luke is one of the good guys?"

"Of course! He takes care of me, he won't ever let anyone hurt me." Albert listened carefully. It was starting to sound like a classic case of abuse. Had Rob been subjected to some traumatic experience that might have triggered a dissociative personality disorder? If so, who had been the abuser and when had the abuse occurred - in childhood, or more recently?

"Who do you think is really in control, you or Luke?" Rob had widened his eyes ingenuously.

"Why, Luke of course. What a dumb question. He's the Boss. How could a bubblehead like me possibly be in charge? I don't know anything. I'm just a pretty boy." When Albert had initially interviewed Connie Turnbull, she had remarked that Rob had been a "pretty child with the face of a cherub", and that as the boys were growing up he had come to view his older brother as his natural protector. According to the mother, there had never been any of the rivalry or competition that normally occurs between brothers. Their relationship seemed to have been more of an attraction between opposites, like the conventional male-female polarity: it was clear to Albert that Rob was drawn to Luke's straightforward masculinity and strength, and although he could only hazard a guess at Luke's feelings, he was probably drawn to Rob's androgynous beauty and childlike qualities.

If he were only permitted to capture these sessions on film, a case such as this could really make his name. But the legal position was very clear. Rob had not been sectioned; he was a free agent, able to come and go as he pleased. Any breach of the therapist-patient contract would leave him wide open to lawsuits, possibly even physical violence. Joe and Luke Turnbull were not the kind of men you would wish to antagonise, not unless you were courting serious trouble. Was it remotely possible, he asked himself, that Luke himself was the abuser, and that his younger brother had suppressed any disturbing memories by re-inventing his tormentor as his champion, the hero who chases away the "bad guys", the bogeymen hiding in the closet? The one-sided portrait of Luke that Rob had drawn, that of Mr. Wonderful who could do no wrong, sounded suspect to his highly trained ears: it didn't ring true. Before reaching a definitive diagnosis, it might be advisable to consult with another psychoanalyst. He felt he could do with some professional advice from someone with more clinical experience in the field of psychosexual development and family dynamics. Albert switched off the tape recorder, before dialling the number of an associate who had published two notable papers on incest-related syndromes, which had been well received in the medical press and which Albert had read with interest.

Chapter Eight

Rob looked up as Luke entered his bedroom. Whilst clearing out the trash littering the interior of his car - candy wrappers and empty cigarette packs – Luke had come across a gay pornographic magazine stuffed down the side of the back seat which had certainly never been there before. He had flicked through the magazine idly, his glance alighting on a piece of fiction entitled *My Cowboy Adventure* and soon got the general idea: cowboys fucking each other like jackrabbits, most of the action taking place out on the open range; outlaws or "bad boys" who'd been taken prisoner by a tough law-enforcer or vigilante equally hell-bent on dispensing his own brand of rough justice, which chiefly consisted of stripping the boy buck-naked and having his wicked way with him. A complete travesty of the real Wild West. Most of it was badly written trash with submissive-dominant themes and S&M overtones.

"Where the hell did you get this? Not down the local drugstore, that's for sure."

"Some guy I met gave it to me. I was going to give it back to him-"

"-Burn it. If anyone were to see this..." Meaning their parents. Luke left the sentence unfinished. "You realise you can be busted for the possession of obscene material?"

"I don't see how it differs from those centrefolds in *Penthouse* you used to look at when you were at school. Don't try and deny it. I saw them underneath your bed." Luke paused for a second, mentally picturing the split beaver shots which left nothing to the imagination.

"I don't make the laws. Obscenity is defined as deviant behaviour. Besides, I never read those magazines. I just used to look at the pictures."

"That makes it better, does it?" Luke grinned despite himself.

"No, I guess not. The point is, none of it's real. If you do it with real live women you soon realise they don't sit around with their legs open waiting for some guy to stick it to them. They've got better things to do. Matter of fact, I'll let you in on a secret: most chicks don't even like sex that much. You have to sweet-talk them into it most of the time. And as for this garbage" He tossed the magazine aside. "Real cowboys didn't act like this. Outlaws like Jesse and Frank James were hardened killers who robbed banks or freight trains for a living. Try coming on to one of those guys and they'd shoot you dead without thinking twice about it. I don't want to rain on your parade, kiddo, but this stuff is just fantasy. Pretty third-rate fantasy at that."

"You know something, Mr. Hotshot?"

"I'm listening."

"Well, apart from being the most boring man in the universe...." Rob struggled to remember the term Loubelle had used to describe the town hypocrites, and then it came to him. "You're a white sepulchre."

"A what?"

"A hypocrite." Luke cocked an eyebrow. If Rob was hoping to get a rise out of his brother he was disappointed. "Because of what you did to me on the log." Rob looked at him accusingly. Luke refrained from pointing out that his brother had not put up much resistance at the time. They were standing very close to each other. "Anyone would think" continued Rob provocatively "that you have unnatural tendencies." Luke didn't reply but merely looked him over. Just keep right on pushing those buttons, boy. "How do you sleep at night?" asked Rob.

"I struggle sometimes" replied Luke "when I dwell on my many character defects." He held up five fingers and started ticking them off: "I'm a complete NOTHING, a brick wall, the most boring man in the universe, a degenerate life-form from outer space, and a hypocrite. There's no hope for me at all." He smiled, to show that he wasn't offended. "Though I'm a little puzzled by that last accusation - I assume you meant whited sepulchre?"

"Um, yeah. Maybe" murmured Rob, distracted by Luke's muscular forearms. He was dressed casually in khakis and a safari shirt, almost identical to his army issue dress uniform, with his sleeves rolled up to the elbow (he found cuffs too constricting) On the rare occasions Luke was obliged to wear a tie, it always ended up loosened around his collar. Rob had once seen him in a formal tuxedo on his way to pick up Cindy for the Senior Prom and thought he looked pretty amazing.

"You can burn that stupid magazine if you want" he said to Luke. "I don't care. For your information, I'm NOT into that stuff." Until very recently he had had absolutely no idea there was a cowboy subculture amongst gay men. When Loubelle had introduced him to Rick she had left them alone for a few minutes, and Rick had casually asked Rob what he was "into". Rob had replied innocently that he liked Westerns, and Rick had slipped him a rolled-up magazine: "You'll love this then. Plenty of cowboy action in this issue."

"What are you into then?"

"I'm into you. Only you. You don't get it, do you?" Rob bolted from the room and Luke stared after him.

"Robbie...." Luke shook his head, and later disposed of the magazine by tossing it onto a pile of garbage out back, which had been gradually accumulating until he had the opportunity to light a bonfire. Rob kept out of his way over the next two days and Luke threw himself into hard manual labour, riding out with his father in the pickup to the sawmill most mornings. Joe had recently taken a large order for some freshly milled lumber, which kept them both busy.

****

Left to his own devices, Rob decided to bike over to Miss Radcliff's place as he'd promised to rake the leaves piling up on her lawn before the weather got too frosty. The banana seat and butterfly handlebars felt a little awkward at first - he hadn't ridden his *Stingray* since he was in Junior High - but it was fun freewheeling down the steep hill towards his old school. He felt like a kid again when he used to ride with his feet on the handlebars. *Look, Ma, no hands.* Miss Radcliff's house was a few blocks from the school, and handily situated on the same street as the public library, where she still worked as Head Librarian. As he coasted past Harperville Junior High, he passed a cheerleading tryout. The girls were practising their dance moves behind the chain link fence, twirling their batons, and kicking high in their short skirts and white Majorette boots to the strains of Martha Reeves and the Vandellas:

Jimmy Mack Jimmy,
Oh, Jimmy Mack when are you comin' back
My arms are missing you,
My lips feel the same way too...

The sight brought back bittersweet memories. Years ago, when Luke was in Senior school and making quite an impact as their best linebacker on the football team, Cindy Foster would coach the cheerleading squad with the same ferocious concentration. The girls weren't above showing off before an appreciative audience, drawn in by the alluring spectacle of fit young female bodies and well-toned limbs as the team went through their well-rehearsed routines. Cindy would shout out instructions as the girls leapt into the air scissoring their legs, doing her best to ignore the wolf whistles from the sidelines.

"Go away! I wish you guys would just drop dead. We're professional *athletes*, in case you hadn't noticed..."

"Oh yeah, we noticed alright" was the enthusiastic male response. Most people knew they were serious athletes, as you needed stamina and discipline to perform some of the acrobatic feats they were capable of. Securing a place on the cheerleading squad was a coveted position, and few made the grade, so it was hardly surprising Cindy had taken her position as squad leader very seriously. In the days leading up to a big interscholastic ballgame she had the team practising after school for hours on end, often until the light fell (in bad weather they all trooped off to the gymnasium and barred the doors so the boys were forced to climb up to the windows to peer in from outside)

On one occasion when Luke had just happened to be passing by with Rob, they had paused to watch. Luke had pretended to go down when one of them swiped at him with her pom-pom, and staggered about clutching his head, earning a baleful glare from Cindy: "Hey, I come in peace, girls. Don't hit me with your pom-poms. Oh, man, that really hurt." Inevitably some of the girls started to giggle, distracted by his antics, though Cindy was not amused. Eventually she had marched right up to Luke, arms akimbo on hips.

"What do you think you're doing? If you don't leave *right now*, there will be consequences." That had amused him. At seventeen he was a fully-grown man and towered over Cindy, who was by no means short.

"What kind of consequences?" enquired Luke with a grin, his eyes raking her from head to toe. She was a good-looking girl and knew it. As the bases and mid-bases formed a two–high human pyramid, Cindy (who was also their top flyer) climbed nimbly onto their shoulders and stood on its apex, looking down at Luke from her lofty perch.

"That's for me to know and you to find out!" She leaped back down to the ground, landing gracefully in front of them. Luke threw her an admiring glance.

"Well, you've got me interested now. I hope you're not planning on whacking me over the head with that candy cane." Cindy was casually and expertly twirling her baton. "You girls want me in good shape for the big game, right? I was kind of hoping you'd be cheering me on."

"I'm warning you, Luke Turnbull. My team doesn't need any distractions right now. I mean it!" Luke was trying to maintain a straight face.

"I'm sure you do, honey. What are you doing Saturday night?" It was obvious to Rob even then, as he'd watched them face up to each other, that they were attracted to each other. Two weeks later they were an item, and Rob's adolescent world had fallen apart.

****

Luke sauntered up to the house Friday evening after finishing work, and encountered Rob loitering at the bottom of the porch steps. The latter had on a pair of form-fitting black Levis with a black shirt and leather vest, and a red bandanna loosely knotted around his throat. All he needed was a gun-belt and holster to complete the effect.

"Handy pair of can openers you got there" said Luke, eyeing the spurs on his boots. "Where you off to, cowboy?"

"I'm going into town" said Rob. After Loubelle had introduced him to Rick, they had arranged to meet outside the drugstore at 7:30 pm the next Friday night, from where they would go on to "Lennie's Bar" in Rick's car. Rob had never heard of the place, but he assumed it was where guys like Rick met to socialise with each other.

"You're under a driving ban" Luke reminded him. Whilst on medication, Rob was not supposed to use heavy machinery or drive. "Want me to drive you?"

"Nope" replied Rob. "Might stay out all night anyway." He waited for this remark to sink in.

"Is that so?" said Luke, after a pause. "Do you need a ride?" he repeated.

"Oh, don't trouble yourself" said Rob unconcernedly. "Shorty's giving me a lift into town." Shorty was the son of a neighbouring farmer – the runt of the litter - who spent most of his time chasing girls who weren't interested or pelting rabbits and squirrels with a BB gun.

"You hanging out with Shorty now?" asked Luke in some surprise.

"No. I'm not that desperate. Gotta get going."

"Hey" said Luke, catching him by the elbow. Rob shook him off.

"It's none of your damned business, but for your information I met somebody. Somebody who appreciates me, even if you don't." Luke tried to catch hold of him again but Rob spun out of his grasp.

"A guy, you mean?"

"His name's Rick. He's taking me to this bar he knows over on the West side-"

"-Right. Got it." Luke cut him off abruptly, as if he was totally uninterested and didn't care to hear any more. "Have fun, little brother." He turned on his heel and strode off, walking rapidly. Seconds later he heard the honking of a horn at the end of the track but didn't turn around. He was stunned, like someone had just sucker punched him in the gut. It didn't occur to him that Rob wanted to make him jealous and had succeeded beyond his wildest expectations. This had been sprung on him out of the blue. He had had absolutely no idea Rob was seeing somebody, or that he even had any desire to do so. The last time they had spent time alone together in Dale's cabin Rob had told him he loved him, and Luke had no reason to doubt him. His brother wore his heart on his sleeve. Of course the relationship between them couldn't go anywhere. They were brothers. But he had underestimated Rob, as usual. His brother had evidently given the matter some thought, and within the space of a few weeks – without telling Luke - had decided to look elsewhere, and had found someone who could return his affection, give him what he craved. It was an inevitable progression of what had been going on all summer, and Luke had allowed himself to be blindsided. Why hadn't he seen it coming? With his looks and his charm, Rob could pull anyone he wanted, male or female. They had swarmed around him like bees to a honey pot ever since high school.

"Luke…" His mother called after him. Luke scarcely heard her – there was some kind of mist in front of his eyes, blurring his vision. He shook his head and blinked rapidly. "Would you be an absolute darling, and fix this screen door for me? It's loose." Luke grabbed hold of the door to examine it, and it came off in his hand.

"Sorry" he muttered. His mother giggled.

"I said fix it, not rip it off its hinges. You don't know your own strength." Luke spent the next twenty minutes repairing the door, re-drilling holes and replacing the screws.

"Good to go" he said finally. His mother handed him a glass of iced tea.

"Are you all right, hon?"

"Sure." He downed the contents and handed the empty glass back to her.

"You seem tense. You haven't had a fight with Rob or anything? What were you two talking about out there?" she asked curiously.

"Nothing much. Asked him if he wanted a ride into town that's all, but he hitched a lift with Shorty."

"Why don't you do the same? Hook up with some of your buddies. Your father has you working too hard. Just because you're as strong as an ox doesn't mean you don't need a break like everyone else. I worry about you sometimes." Luke smiled at her.

"I'm just fine." She came up to him and placed her hands on his shoulders.

"Luke, about Rob. You know what's he's like. His moods are all over the place. We can't get him to take his medication and your father and I are at a complete loss. We just don't know what is going on with him. Most of the time, he's just the sweetest son you could ever hope for. But when he has one of these episodes he goes wild. When you were out in Vietnam he went through this phase when he was a hell-raiser. But he looks up to you. You're the only one who can get through to him."

"Not always" said Luke soberly, recollecting what had just passed between them.

"If you could just keep an eye on him, I'd feel better. I worry what he might do." Luke dropped a kiss on the top of her head.

"I'll keep an eye on him, see that he doesn't get into any trouble." His mother sighed.

"I don't know what I'd do without you. You're the dependable one. I love that boy so much."

"I know. We all do. I'm going to grab a quick shower then I'll head into town." He hadn't yet had a chance to change out of his grimy work clothes when he'd run into Rob. "But I may have to keep my distance. I somehow don't think Rob will appreciate me baby-sitting him."

Fifteen minutes later, Luke was headed down the dusty track that led to their property. He'd taken the convertible as his father tended to use the pickup. Once he'd turned off the dirt track and hit the blacktop he floored the gas. He'd wasted enough time messing with the screen door, and he needed to find out where this place was. He was pretty sure it must be some hangout for queers, but he didn't know of any. Harperville was not the kind of town that accommodated men who liked men so it was unlikely to be anywhere on Main Street. Probably someone's private barn with a makeshift bar rigged up in a corner, like the Prohibition era speak-easies. He could be driving all over hell's acre before he found the damned place. Ah, now wait a minute, Rob had mentioned the West side. Luke thought he could probably find it if he cruised around. He hung a left at the corner of Main and Freemont, passing darkened storefronts, and followed the road out of town where the residences became sparser and more spaced out. If it was an illicit watering hole the owner had to be careful. The cops raided these places periodically, and he'd heard some of the patrons got badly roughed up. It was not that Luke had anything against gays, but there was no question in his mind that it was a dangerous and promiscuous lifestyle. He did not want that lifestyle for Rob, for the simple reason that he felt his younger brother was at risk and very vulnerable. He was perfectly aware that most serious cases of molestation were perpetrated by heterosexual males and not homosexuals, who generally kept a low profile, but did Rob really know what he was getting into? There were some sick bastards out there, queer bashers who hung around these joints, scenting easy prey. And they could pretty much do what they wanted with impunity, because the types who frequented these places were hardly going to go running to the cops. One victim had ended up in traction at the general hospital with multiple fractures: some local boys had really gone to town on him. Rick the Prick or whoever the hell he was, could be some sicko who had targeted Rob and picked him up, intent on having some sport before beating the shit out of him. Luke's jaw tightened and his forearms went rigid against the steering wheel as his muscles tensed. On the radio Little Richard was singing about Lucille:

Lucille, you won't do your daddy's will...
Well, I woke up this morning
Lucille was not in sight
Asked my friends about her, but all their lips was tight
Lucille, you won't do your daddy's will...

Luke switched off the radio so he could listen out for anything that might provide a clue as to the bar's whereabouts, and slowed to a cruising speed. After a couple of miles he spotted some light seeping through the boarded up windows of a barn situated down a track. Most folk didn't keep their barns boarded up. No reason to, there was nothing to hide. He could hear faint sounds of music emanating from the barn and that decided him. This had to be it. The place was discreet but accessible enough to attract a select clientele who knew what they were looking for. Luke killed the engine, then got out and walked up to the barn. The door was also boarded up, and he was about to pound on it with his fist but thought better of it: such a show of aggression would most likely scare them off. Instead he rapped sharply with his knuckles. A moment later the bolt slid back and a guy encased in leather from head to foot peered out. Luke would have laughed outright if he wasn't so riled up. The doorman was wary, being extra cautious.

"Have we met?"

"Nope" replied Luke. "But the night is still young. There's always time. Gonna let me in, buddy, or what?" The doorman looked him up and down, and evidently liked what he saw.

"Uh, sure thing, Handsome. Come on in and join the party." Piece of cake, thought Luke, as he shouldered his way to the bar. It was crowded, with bodies tightly packed together jostling for elbow space. There was no air conditioning, and with no open windows the room was suffocatingly hot. It smelt of male sweat and stale beer. Someone copped a feel of his thigh as he approached the bar, murmuring to his companion "Seen what just walked in? Hardcore muscleman packing eight inches or more. Just my type." Luke scarcely noticed him. He was scanning the room rapidly, looking for Rob, but could see no signs of him. Frustrated, Luke looked harder, squinting through the haze of cigarette smoke. There was a press of men in a far corner, jiving to the jukebox on a tiny dance floor. Luke started to make his way over in that direction, but was momentarily distracted by some skinny dude at the bar with his leg in a cast, propped up with a crutch.

"Hey, can I buy you a beer? A whiskey? What's your poison, man?" Luke declined the offer, and made a move to go but the guy tried to detain him. "Hey, where are you going? You've only just got here." He placed a hand on Luke's arm. Luke knocked it off. "Don't be like that, man. Playing hard to get. I'm just out for a good time." He fingered Luke's biceps lovingly, like he was a piece of meat. Luke flashed him a warning look. "I'm not a cripple, I just broke my leg-"

"-I'll break the other one if you don't quit mauling me." He wouldn't have hit someone on crutches, but the other guy didn't know that and immediately backed off, an injured look in his eyes. At that moment a gap opened up on the dance floor and Luke caught a glimpse of Rob lounging on a barstool, surrounded by a cluster of admirers who were feasting their eyes on him. He looked a little drunk, and was in animated conversation with another man who kept trying to put his arm around him. Rick the Prick, no doubt. Rob was ducking and weaving, as though trying to avoid the other man's embrace without causing offence. He glanced up and spotted Luke. His eyes widened as he started to say something, but didn't get much further than "Luke…"

"Who are you?" enquired Rick the Prick, placing a proprietary arm across Rob's shoulder, like he owned him. This was accompanied by a self-satisfied smirk, as if to say *I've scored the best-looking guy in the room. Hands off,* which only served to infuriate Luke, who pushed Rob aside to keep him out of harm's way. "Hey, next time you shove my boyfriend like that-" began Rick. Luke smashed a fist into him with such force it knocked him to the ground. Rob was taken aback, shocked at the level of violence. Luke had a slow fuse and hardly ever lost his cool, but there was no knowing what he might do next. He was powerfully built and could do a lot of damage if he chose. Rick made no attempt to retaliate, not wishing to be further humiliated in front of his peers, but confined himself to muttering "Jeez, what exactly is your *problem*, man?"

"My problem is you right now. Get up when I'm talking to you." Rick rose slowly to his feet, wincing. Rob was trying to apologise for Luke's seemingly uncalled-for aggression to a dumbfounded Rick, which angered Luke even further.

"He didn't mean it" Rob was saying to Rick "He's my brother, he…" Lost for words, he looked up into Luke's eyes wonderingly. Luke took hold of Rob by the collar, and hustled him out of the bar. Outside, Rob said "Luke, where are we going? You're not mad at me, are you?" Rob looked like he was on the verge of tears, and Luke's anger dissipated, evaporated as suddenly as it had appeared.

"No" said Luke. "No" he repeated as Rob grasped hold of his arm for reassurance. They got into the car, and Luke gunned the engine. A couple of men were hanging about outside, gawking.

"What was all *that* about?" Rob heard one of them mutter to his companion.

"Just some roughneck throwing his weight around" returned the other dismissively.

"Say what?" Luke half-rose from his seat, and made a move as if to come after him. Rob stifled a laugh. He knew his brother was just kidding around, wanting to frighten them a little. The pair hastily retreated indoors, slamming the door behind them.

"Who was the leather Daddio on the door?" enquired Luke with a chuckle. "In the Halloween costume."

"I think that was the bouncer" Rob informed him.

"Had me quaking in my boots, man." Luke let out a low wolf-whistle. "Emma Peel looks a damned sight more appealing in that get-up, in my humble opinion." When they had travelled a few miles down the road, Luke pulled into a lay-by, and cut the engine.

He turned to look at Rob. "Look, I'm sorry I took a swing at your *boyfriend*" He enunciated the word with sarcasm.

"He's not my boyfriend" countered Rob quickly, completely forgetting Loubelle's advice, which was to make his brother jealous by pretending to be keen on Rick. "I've only seen him once. But I don't think he deserved *that*."

"Probably not" conceded Luke, his good humour restored. "Aw, maybe I'll take him a bunch of flowers or something." Rob fingered the knuckles of Luke's right fist, which was resting along the top of the seat.

"I wouldn't want to be on the receiving end of that."

"You never will be" replied Luke. "I could have hit him a lot harder, if I'd wanted. Given him a Russian handshake."

"What's that?"

"When you grab a guy's balls in a death grip and then give 'em a nice little twist. *Allow me to introduce myself...*"

"Luke, you can be so charming."

"Of course a Redneck handshake's a lot friendlier. You might like that one."

"Tell me, Mister."

"When you meet a girl you like, instead of shaking her hand you grab her down below, a nice friendly little squeeze. *Pleased to meet you, honey....*not something I would do on a first acquaintance" added Luke, who was not normally disrespectful to the opposite sex. "Just giving you the definition." Rob kept his gaze averted.

"You're not still mad at me, though?"

"I'm not mad at you" said Luke, becoming serious. "But I don't know what's going on with you. You flirt with me, you tease me, you charm me, and then you're not speaking to me. You've hardly spoken a word to me over the past few days. All of a sudden you won't even give me the time of day. You blow hot and cold, and I cannot stand it. I cannot STAND it." He chopped the steering wheel with the side of his hand for emphasis. Rob threw his arms around his neck.

"I'm so sorry, Luke. I didn't mean to make you jealous. But I wanted to get back at you."

"For what? What did I do?"

"I don't like being used. Like I'm just *foreplay* or something before you go off and screw some woman. I thought I meant something to you. I know you're seeing Cindy again, and the thought of you getting married makes me so depressed I want to die."

"What are you talking about? I'm not going to marry Cindy. She happens to be a nice woman who made the mistake of marrying some deadbeat, and I feel sorry for her is all. We haven't dated since high school. That was years ago." Cindy had led the cheerleading team at high school - athletic, popular and beautiful, the all-American golden girl. A real stunner, and every boy in his class had wanted to make out with her. Of all the boys, she had chosen him, and they had dated for three and a half years. After graduation she got hitched up to some layabout from out of state who had fathered two children on her and then ran off, leaving her to pick up the pieces. She was still a nice-looking woman, and there were plenty of men who would be happy to marry her, but she'd lost her self-confidence. Luke had run into her a few times over the past year, and although he still had feelings for her, he did not allow himself to get involved. Everyone knew she was on the lookout for a husband, someone dependable she could rely on to provide for her and her kids. She'd cried on his shoulder, convinced she was "damaged goods" and that no-one would want her. He knew she still had a thing for him, but he wasn't about to lead her on by resuming where they'd left off years ago. She had already been badly let down by a sorry excuse for a man in whom she had placed her trust, and Luke was not the type to trifle with a woman's feelings. Rob looked confused.

"But I know you were with a woman that night you didn't come back. When we were up by the creek that afternoon, right after the barbecue. You were out all night and then you came in with lipstick and makeup all over your shirt. It was so OBVIOUS and I'm not some dummy."

"I was with Barb. Times when you just want to rock the trailer, get down and dirty, and score a home run. Know what I mean?" Rob had a fleeting image of them coupling, Luke going at it like a jackhammer and Barbra just as bad, clawing his back and clutching him between her thighs. "Think I don't know what you and Todd used to get up to at the garage, huh?" continued Luke. "He still stripping down those engines?" Rob was mortified, and didn't know where to look. Luke started to laugh. "Me, if I'm feeling horny I'd rather roll around in the sheets with a woman than let some slack-jawed grease monkey get his paws on my tackle. I mean, for fuck's sake." Luke laughed harder than ever, as Rob rained blows on him. "Whoa …know what a hillbilly handshake is?"

"No, and I don't want to." Although Luke could be deadly serious when he needed to be, that wasn't often and Rob wished that he would stop kidding around and be serious, just for once. "OK then, tell me."

"Ask your frisky pal down at the garage. All very platonic, I'm sure" he added teasingly. Luke let him get in a few more punches then caught hold of his flailing fists. "I prefer it when you're hugging me, really I do. And you do mean something to me, more than you'll ever know."

"I'm sorry I said those mean things to you" murmured Rob.

"Quite all right. That was some shellacking you gave me, but I'm sure I deserved it."

"How did you manage to find Lennie's Bar?" asked Rob curiously.

"Saw some cars parked out back, and the barn was all boarded up. Go figure."

"Why did you come after me?"

"I didn't like the idea of some guy mauling you like you were ...I don't know, pretty boy jailbait." Robbie bit his lower lip and started to say something. He was clinging to Luke's arm as if he was teetering on the edge of a precipice, and about to topple into the abyss. His eyes were squeezed tight shut and he was trying not to cry.

"What is it, Rob?" asked Luke suddenly.

"I can't tell you."

"I'm sincerely sorry for anything I did to upset you."

"It's not that...." Rob's voice broke. He appeared to be in real distress.

"What? Did I do something wrong?" Rob shook his head.

"I.... something happened when I was pulled over for drink driving a couple of years back. You know I was in jail for two nights before Dad bailed me out?" Luke listened carefully. His brother was trying to tell him something important. Rob covered his eyes with his hands. "I haven't told anyone." Luke leaned forward in order to catch what his brother was trying to articulate between sobs. Then it all came out. Luke's careless remark about "jailbait" had brought all the memories flooding back. The attempted assault by his cellmate, an older hardened con who should have been locked up in the state federal penitentiary, but had been placed in the local county jail pending transfer.

"We can do this real nice or we can do it not so nice. You can suck it, or I can rip your candy ass wide open. Which is it to be, pretty boy?" His eyes had been cold and hard. There was no real desire there, no tenderness, just pure carnal lust. Rob's instinct was to fight back. No way was he going to suck this guy's cock, and no way was he going to allow himself to be butt-fucked. He had fought back with everything he had, punching and kicking ferociously, whilst his tormentor twisted his arm behind his back, forcing him down onto the lower bunk and pressing his head into the mattress so that he could hardly breathe. Panicked and completely powerless (the guy was a lot bigger and stronger, almost twice his size) Rob suddenly allowed his body to go limp, pretending to submit.

"Attaboy. That's more like it. Like trying to tame a wild mustang. Hold still there, little honey. Hell, you might even get to like it." As soon as he relaxed his grip, Rob seized his opportunity, and bit into his forearm as hard as he could. His head was wrenched back and he was smacked in the jaw. As his mouth filled with the iron taste of blood one of the fatass prison guards finally decided to show up, taking his sweet time, and acting as if he had no idea what had been going down on his watch. *"What's going on in here?"* Like he gave a shit. Or maybe the bastards got off on seeing teenagers being violated, watching it all like some porn movie from a remote CCTV camera. Maybe the prison guards took pity on him, or maybe they respected him for having put up such a fight. Rob

didn't know. All he knew was that he was swiftly transferred to another holding cell, and his father showed up the next morning to bail him out. His father was told nothing about what had happened, only that there had been an "incident" and Rob was not about to enlighten him. Until now he hadn't told a living soul about what had happened to him. The experience was still too raw. As he now confessed all this to his brother, haltingly, Luke held him very close, remembering how Rob had made up some entertaining story about trying to get the guards to play stud poker with him.

"Why didn't you tell me?" said Luke finally when Rob had calmed down, pummelling his tears away with his fists the way a small child does.

"I didn't want you to know. I thought you'd despise me."

"Despise *you*?" Rob felt Luke tense up. "If I ever run into that low-life I'll put him in the emergency ward. He won't be able to walk by the time I've finished with him."

"I'm OK" said Rob shakily. "He never got to…. to do what he wanted."

"C'mere." Luke caught him up in a tight embrace again. "Anyone ever tries anything like that again, I promise you I'll take care of it."

"But you weren't there and I couldn't…" Rob took a deep shuddering breath.

"I know" said Luke soothingly, thumbing away a tear. "It's all right. I understand." What on earth had their father been thinking of when he'd left him in the county lock-up? Didn't he know that a young guy as good-looking as his kid brother was bound to attract the wrong sort of attention?

Luke was used to being in control of any situation he found himself in. Nothing really fazed him that much, and he felt he could handle most things. Vietnam was no walk in the park, but he hadn't cracked under pressure. Just occasionally, though, a situation arose which challenged his worldview or undermined his self-belief. The situation in which he now found himself was one of those occasions. During their weekend vacation in the Appalachians they had become incredibly intimate in a short space of time, sleeping in the same bed together, with Rob encircled in his arms when they watched TV in the evenings. Once they had returned home, Luke had found himself missing the physical intimacy. Somehow Rob had gotten under his skin. His bed had seemed strangely empty, and although his brother was only a few hundred yards away in his parents' house, it had taken a while to adjust to his own solitary company again. The words of a song by the Kinks *You Really Got Me* floated into his head:

Yeah, you really got me now
You got me so I don't know what I'm doin' now
Oh yeah, you really got me now
You got me so I can't sleep at night
You really got me, You really got me…

He was starting to feel physical arousal for his own brother. And in his world – the world he had grown up in – things like that just didn't happen. It was unheard-of, almost unthinkable. He would have to figure this thing out. The whole thing was preposterous. Two brothers could not have that kind of relationship with each other, not the way Rob envisaged it. And as for the flirting and the sex games, things were starting to get out of hand: their fascination with each other was fast snowballing into something more unmanageable and dangerous.

Luke sometimes found himself fantasising about Rob. Ever since that afternoon up by Clearwater Creek he would get hot thinking about what they had done, and the sensations it had produced in him. When Rob had looked up at him the other week in that flirtatious, playful manner *Don't be so hard-on me, Sheriff*, Luke had felt his balls tighten and a familiar stirring in his loins. Whenever his brother came on to him like that it did something to him. He wasn't sure what, but he was hooked. As a straight man he liked intercourse with a woman. After all, that was what his cock was for, and he liked doing it whenever the opportunity arose. He was not at all turned on by the idea of anal intercourse with another man. Sticking his dick in some guy's butthole? No thanks. Same with blow jobs. Once again, no thanks, buddy. Get some other mug to suck your stick of candy rock. But there was more than one way to skin a cat. Sex didn't have to involve penetration to be enjoyable. Rob was entirely mistaken about Luke using him for "foreplay." In the seconds before his old man had showed up, they had been really getting into it and Rob had cried out - had he climaxed? Luke thought he probably had. His brother was amazingly responsive; it was as though his entire body was an erogenous zone. Wherever Luke happened to touch him - whether he fingered his throat, stroked the inside of his elbow, grazed a nipple with his thumb - Rob's response was immediate. It might just be a blush, a dreamy expression in his eyes, a sharp intake of breath, a racing pulse, but it always signified *I love what you're doing. Keep on doing it.*

"I want to marry you" murmured Rob. He looked slightly disoriented, as though he'd had too much to drink.

"Don't be absurd. You know that's not possible." Luke disentangled himself gently from Rob. "Why don't you stretch out for a while in the back seat?" Rob obediently climbed onto the back seat, but as soon as Luke moved off from the roadside, he leaned forward and laid his cheek on Luke's shoulder with his arms clasped around his neck - as though drowsing – his breath warm.

Half an hour later Luke pulled up outside their parents' house, leaving the engine idling. His parents must have gone to bed as the lights were out. Rob had by this time woken up and seemed confused about where he had just been: "Rick? I don't know him." He was becoming emotional and incoherent, asking "Why is it absurd?" half crying, half arguing with his brother. Luke took a swift decision to take him straight back to the bunkhouse, in order to keep an eye on him. As Rob stumbled on the top step of the stoop, Luke caught him.

"What I recommend" said Luke, steering him towards the bathroom with one hand between his shoulder blades "is cold water." Holding him firmly in place with one arm, he turned on the cold water faucet and started sluicing him down, whilst Rob spluttered and protested. This soon had the desired effect, as Rob began to sober up fast.

"Luke, are you trying to wash me? I can do that myself...." He started to giggle as Luke continued to douse him with cold water.

"No shit. You just about kissed the floor back there. One more ducking and I think we're through here." He held Rob's head under the faucet for a couple of seconds then turned it off. "You know what your problem is?"

"Yes" replied Rob promptly, blinking and swiping the wet hair out of his eyes. "A big brother who's a bastard and pushes me around."

"A big brother who looks out for you" corrected Luke. "And if you don't do something about that *attitude*, and show just a little more *gratitude*...." He leaned in towards Rob teasingly, then became serious. "The way I see it, here's the problem: you ask for the impossible, and when you can't have it you think it's the end of the world, that life isn't worth living. That line of thinking will get you nowhere fast. Like a little kid asking for the moon. Am I right?"

"Yeah, but...Luke, please don't hit me with that washcloth."

"So a parent with any sense buys the kid a balloon instead" continued Luke, grabbing a towel off the rail, and vigorously towelling him dry in the same way he did with Rusty after he'd been rolling around in mud.

"So you're gonna buy me a balloon?"

"No, I'm telling you to settle for what you *can* have. I can't marry you, and I don't intend to listen to this nonsense all night long. But I'm right here whenever you need me, and I'm not going anywhere. How's that sound?"

"Um, it sounds good. Just so long as you don't...."

"There you go again, getting yourself into a tailspin over hypothetical situations - that I'd come back from Vietnam in a body bag, or that I'm about to run off and get married. You need to lighten up a little" said Luke, taking hold of his shoulders. "Everything's gonna be just fine. Trust me." Rob gazed at him. His brother had a way of putting things in perspective, bringing him down to earth again. Luke didn't entertain notions of the ridiculous or the absurd; he just got on with the practical business of living.

"I trust you more than anyone in the world. I wish I could be more like you."

"I love you just the way you are. Now, are you sleeping with me or on the couch?"

"With you" said Rob quickly.

Chapter Nine

Rob rubbed the sleep from his eyes and half sat up. He thought he could hear Luke talking to someone at the front door in a low voice, and then the voices stopped. He made a dive for the bathroom as he heard his brother moving around in the next room, and gazed at his reflection in the mirror. There was only one toothbrush standing in a plastic cup, and he didn't think Luke would mind if he borrowed it: after all, they were brothers.

What had happened last night? He had a vague recollection of being at the bar with Rick, where he'd felt ill at ease and out of his depth, surrounded by a bunch of weird guys ogling each other. Rick had been nice to him, but Rob wasn't attracted to him in the least: he wasn't sexy or exciting, not in the way Luke was. Rick had been plying him with drinks all evening, and Rob had been knocking them back like nobody's business, hoping that if he got drunk it would make the time go faster. He was beginning to wish he'd never come in the first place. It was not as if he could confide in Rick, who just wouldn't have understood how he felt about Luke. Although Rick also happened to have an older brother, they were barely on speaking terms. At one point, when Rob had been forced to squeeze past a gauntlet of men on his way to the john – something he'd been dreading – this horny guy had started rubbing up against him. Another creep had actually squeezed his butt, really goosing him, and Rob had been incensed. What gave him the right to do that? There was only one man he ever wanted touching him, and that was Luke. He felt that the sex act should mean something, otherwise you might as well be a bunch of barnyard animals rutting in the dirt. The whole experience had been profoundly disillusioning and Rob was on the point of telling Rick that he wanted to go home when, as if by magic, Luke had suddenly materialised in front of him. After knocking Rick to the floor - rather unfairly, Rob had thought - he had then driven Rob home. Rob didn't remember too much after that apart from Luke nearly drowning him in the washbasin after they got back to the bunkhouse.

Rob threw some water on his face and brushed his teeth, then ran a comb through his hair, before joining his brother in the small kitchen. Luke acknowledged his presence with a slight lift of his eyebrows. He was leaning back against the kitchen counter with a coffee in his hand. "Who was that you were talking to just now?" asked Rob.

"That was Dad checking you got home alright. I told him you'd had a few too many last night and were crashed out on the couch" replied Luke, letting him know that this was the official story if his parents quizzed him.

"I hope I didn't make too much of a fool of myself last night" said Rob sheepishly.

"Not at all. You just stayed too long at the ball, Cinderella."

"I loved your impression of Prince Charming" returned Rob, giggling. "But you need to work on your manners. You were about as subtle as a killer shark." Luke smiled and gestured for Rob to sit down at the table.

"Take a seat." Luke lit up a Camel and contemplated Rob, who stared at him expectantly. "So, how do you like it? Hot and fast, or slow and sweet?" Rob caught his breath, as his heart rate speeded up.

"What? Um, I don't know what…" Luke laughed at his confusion.

"How do you like your eggs?"

"Not sweet, that's for sure." He could have sworn Luke was deliberately trying to embarrass him. Or get him all flustered so he couldn't think straight. For some reason, he seemed to get a kick out of seeing Rob blush. "I like them fast and scrambled."

"How do you like your coffee?"

"Hot and sometimes sweet."

"And how do you like being kissed?" Rob's stomach flipped over like a pancake.

"All of the above. Hot and fast, slow and sweet. Sweet and fast. Hot and slow ..." Luke put down his coffee cup and leaned over him.

"And how do you like being fuck-" Rob jabbed an elbow into Luke's rock-solid abs, as he felt the heat radiate through his cheeks. His brother was just kidding around, as usual, but the bastard must have known the effect he was having on him. Sometimes he only had to hear Luke's voice or to catch a glimpse of him from a distance, for his heart to skip a beat. Luke could be unbelievably sexy at times, like when he'd caught Rob staring at him in the shower: *What's the matter? You want to spend some adult time with me?* He was probably joking, but Rob could never be sure. He knew Luke hadn't touched him in bed last night – at least, not sexually, because he would have felt that, for sure. He would have *known*, not matter how drunk he'd been. Luke let out a guffaw, sounding like their father when he was really tickled by something. "I'm sorry. You look like a scared rabbit. Couldn't resist."

"Why do you say stuff like that to embarrass me?" asked Rob. Luke shrugged, and smiled. He liked seeing Rob blush, found it rather charming, in fact. He recalled an incident when Rob was in his teens and being constantly pressured by his classmates to participate in their extracurricular activities. One afternoon Luke had answered the telephone and taken a call for his brother.

"Judy and one of her pals are on the phone. She says there's a drive-in movie they'd like to see. Think you got yourself a double date, little brother." Rob had grimaced.

"It's not my thing. That crowd don't even bother watching the movie. I'm no backseat banger!" He had picked up quite a few vulgar slang terms over the past year and knew, for instance, that "popping a cherry" had something to do with a girl losing her virginity. Luke had come towards him with a big smile on his face.

"You know what a backseat banger is, do you?"

"It means making out in the back seat, dummy! Everyone does it." Luke had just laughed. Rob had been slightly offended by Luke's evident amusement.

"What's it mean then?"

"Bend over, pretty boy, and I'll show you." Rob had flushed deeply and given him a slightly reproachful look, the type a small child gives an adult who is teasing him, not quite sure whether he likes it or not.

"I'm going to tell my shrink all about you" Rob now threatened. "About how traumatic my childhood was, being related to you…"

"You do that. In the meantime, here's some more trauma for you: you can drop to the ground and give me fifty."

"No, Luke, please" implored Rob, laughing. "Have mercy. I'm still feeling hung over." He could manage about thirty push-ups on a good day, whereas he'd seen Luke do a hundred one-handed push-ups, supporting his entire body weight on one arm. He wondered what Loubelle would have to say about that. Probably some sarcastic rejoinder like *Does your brother bench-press trees for a workout?*

"All right. I might let you off this time." Luke ran a hand through Rob's hair caressingly, and Rob realised in that moment that something had changed between them. Luke had been touching him quite a lot lately and he obviously cared, otherwise he wouldn't have gone to such trouble to locate Lennie's bar and to come after him. He also suspected that Luke's chronic teasing was a clumsy attempt to cover up his true feelings of tenderness. When he had half woken in the middle of the night, tousled and flushed with sleep, Luke had reached for him, finding him irresistible. Rob had simply wanted to be held, and Luke had obliged, murmuring endearments like *little darling, sweet angel* and so on. Surely Rob hadn't dreamed that?

"When was the last time you had something to eat?" enquired Luke, opening the fridge door. The fridge was empty apart from a few breakfast items, since he tended to dine with the rest of the family most evenings over at the main house.

"Dunno. Lunchtime yesterday, I think." Rob looked around the rustic interior of the cabin, which was sparsely furnished, plain and unadorned – just like its owner. What furniture there was had been mostly hand-carved by Luke with a chainsaw.

"It's a little bare in here" commented Luke, echoing his thoughts. "But next time you visit, it should be cosier. I'm picking up a woodstove this evening after work, and you can help me install it tomorrow if you like. If you feed the flue pipe to me through the chimney from inside, I can haul it up from the roof."

"Okay" Rob agreed. He loved helping Luke, and he had visions of winter evenings spent by the fireside – just the two of them. Five minutes later Luke placed a dish in front of Rob, and sat down opposite him. Rob forked the fluffy omelette into his mouth appreciatively. He hadn't realised how hungry he was. The centre contained melted cheese and onion, and was very tasty.

"I didn't know you could cook" said Rob in some surprise.

"Yeah, I'm pretty good." admitted Luke. "I can do scrambled eggs, omelette, fried eggs...."

"Can you do anything more adventurous?" asked Rob. "You know, like something with eggs in it?"

"Sure. Poached egg, soft-boiled egg... You name it, brother. I'm not just a fighter, I'm a gourmet chef."

"Wow. I can toast pop tarts, but that doesn't even come close to your talent. Have you ever tried anything more exotic, eggs for instance?" Luke thought for a minute.

"Scrambled eggs in a hot helmet. That's one of my specialties. You take a helmet and strip out the webbing, then heat it up over a fire, crack some eggs into it and stir with a stick..."

"Jeez. I am so impressed." Rob flashed his blue eyes in Luke's direction. *I can tease as well as you, brother.* "You're as bad as Dad. He can barbecue steaks and that's about it."

"Yeah, he's the man alright." Luke grinned, remembering the time Joe had managed to rustle up some cornbread for the boys when their mother was laid up with flu. He'd poured some yellow mixture into a cake tin and shoved it in the oven, and the end result had been surprisingly good.

"I can do Pop-Tarts and ...Frosties!"

"Pouring cereal out of a box doesn't qualify as cooking. I can think of something you're good at, though" added Luke.

"What?"

"You're pretty good at distracting me" replied Luke softly. "Not many people can do that." Rob felt his heart flutter again and lowered his gaze, focussing intently on Luke's shirt front. As he took the last mouthful of omelette, the fork nearly missed his mouth. "Feeling better, cowboy?" asked Luke, as Rob pushed aside his empty plate.

"Yes. What's so amusing?" Luke indicated the spurs on his boots.

"Where the hell did you get those things?"

"At the same store where I got my boots" replied Rob. He'd thought he'd better make an effort for his date with Rick, and had used the cash he'd earned mowing lawns and raking leaves to purchase some new cowboy boots. The store assistant – a girl he'd been to school with called Judy - had persuaded him that the spurs were really cool. "It was a *spur* of the moment thing" he quipped. Luke pulled Rob to his feet and caught him up in an embrace.

"Glad I got you out of that bar when I did. Those dudes would have eaten you alive." Luke released him, and bent down to lace up his steel-capped logger work boots. "Listen, I've gotta shove off in a minute." As if on cue, they heard their father honking the horn of the pick-up, impatient to be off to the sawmill. Rob was reminded that his brother now had a full-time job since returning from Vietnam. It was understood that he would eventually step into their father's shoes, and although Joe employed two other men to help out, he relied on Luke heavily. The plan was to make Luke a partner in the business, but for now he drew a weekly wage as recompense for his labour. Rob thought his father had a pretty good deal as his brother put in as much work as two men combined – felling trees and transporting the lumber down the logging tracks.

"So, um, are you coming over tonight?" asked Rob. "They're showing this Western on TV called *Hour of the Gun* with James Garner as Wyatt Earp." Luke didn't have a television in his cabin.

"Is that when he goes after Ike Clanton's gang?" replied Luke. "Sure."

"Don't forget your lunch." Rob handed him a Tupperware box lying on the table, and Luke smiled his thanks. Rob wondered whether he was remembering an earlier occasion when Luke had forgotten to pick up the sandwiches their mother had made, and Rob had driven out to the sawmill in the Chevy.

"Do you know where my brother is?" he asked one of the guys, who pointed him in the direction of the woods, from where he could hear the loud buzzing of a chainsaw. Luke had been working in his white undershirt, having divested himself of his plaid flannel shirt, and Rob tried not to stare at his rippling muscles and solid biceps but couldn't help himself. Prior to felling a tree, Luke would stand with his feet firmly planted apart, then pull the chainsaw starter cord with an unconscious pelvic thrust that Rob found incredibly sexy. Luke had looked up at Rob's approach, raising the visor of his safety helmet.

"You came out all this way to give me my lunch? Sweet of you, but I wasn't about to starve. There's a roadhouse a coupla miles from here where the guys grab a bite to eat." Rob had felt foolish, especially as the eyes of the other two men were on him. They weren't about to say anything in front of the boss's youngest son, but he could hazard a guess at what they must be thinking. Chasing after his brother like some lovesick puppy. Rob had felt shy and awkward around the other men, who were virtual strangers to him, and stood very close to his brother. "Stand clear, Rob" said Luke, pulling him to one side. "This baby's about to come down any minute now." After the tree had come crashing down, Luke had slung an arm around him, turning to the others: "I think I must have the sweetest little brother in the entire county. Or maybe the entire State" he added, giving Rob's shoulders an affectionate squeeze. They had all laughed and Rob had been so embarrassed he'd wanted the ground to swallow him up.

"You alright?" Luke now asked him. Rob nodded. Luke trailed his thumb down Rob's cheek and over his mouth. He hesitated for a second as Rob brushed his lips against the ball of his thumb. "Robbie…." Luke looked as though he were about to kiss him, then evidently thought better of it. He grabbed his hunter's jacket off the peg by the door. "Catch you later, sweet thing."

****

Luke was damping down the smouldering embers of a big bonfire he'd lit earlier, before driving into town to get the Chevy serviced. They'd had a spell of dry weather, and the conditions were ideal for a bonfire – the leaves as crisp and crunchy as curled-up cornflakes.

"I want to make sure nothing catches fire before you and Rob disappear" said Connie anxiously, hovering nearby. "There's a fresh breeze blowing in this direction." Luke trained a hosepipe on the ashes to allay her fears. Earlier on when the fire had been roaring, Rob had been performing some kind of tribal war dance, whooping and yipping like a young Indian brave, which had alarmed their mother: "He's much too close to the flames. If he were to stumble and fall…."

"Ah, don't worry." Luke had patted her shoulder. "If he's in any danger of being barbecued, I'll turn him over to make sure he cooks evenly." Connie had smiled uncertainly. She didn't always get Luke's sardonic sense of humour, but trusted him to keep his younger brother safe. The family had all had a terrible scare a few years ago when Rob had been bitten by a rattlesnake when he was fifteen. Joe was out at the sawmill, and she had seen Luke emerge from the mountain trail behind the bunkhouse, his semi-conscious brother slung across his shoulders. By the time she had rushed outside, Luke had already laid him out in the backseat of his car and was heading for the track. He had held open the front passenger door for her: "Rattler got him" said Luke tersely, barely giving her time to jump in before speeding off. Rob's breathing was constricted and his pulse very rapid: they both knew how serious this was, and Luke had been tight-lipped on the journey to the ER.

Hours later, after the immediate danger had passed and Rob was sitting up in a hospital bed recovering from his ordeal, Luke had rebuked him gently: "What the hell were you thinking of? Stay away from those damn things! They can strike faster than a whiplash."

"I was just trying to get it to move off with a branch…Ouch!" Luke's intervention had been deliberately timed to distract his brother from a hypodermic needle being wielded by a nurse, who was waiting for her opportunity to jab him with it. Rob had blinked a few times in quick succession (he didn't like needles) and Luke had put a protective arm around him. At this point Joe had come crashing into the critical care unit: "Where's my boy? Where's my boy?" Sighting Rob, who was gazing innocently at the anxious faces congregated around his bedside, he had then turned to Luke. "Luke, I swear to God, I don't want him wandering around those mountains unless you're with him…"

"Don't worry, Dad" joked Luke. "Soon as we get him home, I'm going to harness him up to some toddler reins. Kid's gonna love it." Connie had observed that, like many men, her oldest son had a tendency to use humour to mask his more tender emotions. Luke was not what you would call a fluffy sentimental type, so she had been somewhat surprised to find him cuddling Rob when she had returned to the ward after stepping outside earlier to place a call to Joe. Although Rob's vital signs had been restored to normal function, the hospital staff had wanted to keep him in overnight for observation and further monitoring. Rob had never spent a night away from the family on his own, and had looked somewhat forlorn when visiting hours were over and they all got up to leave. When Luke had volunteered to stay and keep him company, Joe had made a deprecating noise in his throat, muttering "He's fifteen, he's not a baby" but Luke had insisted on sleeping in a chair by his bedside. In her experience most siblings tended to grow apart as they became older and developed different interests, but her sons seemed closer than ever. Just lately, they had been inseparable. She looked after them as the car disappeared down the track, Rob riding shotgun, with his elbow resting on Luke's shoulder.

Outside the auto repair shop and garage Rob hung back, suddenly bashful, much to Luke's amusement: "It's all right, I won't let that horndog get his hands on your lunchbox." On the forecourt a Ford Mustang was jacked up on the ramps for suspension work, and Todd was peering at the engine of another vehicle – its hood propped open – whilst a radio was blaring out *Hang on Sloopy*. He wiped the axel grease from his hands with a rag, before coming over to speak to Luke. Rob was standing off to the side, his back to them, attempting to keep a low profile. He inserted a quarter into the vending machine.

"She started right up and then went dead after fifteen minutes" said Luke to Todd. "Towed her back to the house and let her sit for a while. Fired right back up, but shut off again after three minutes."

"Yeah, I'll check the ignition system" said Todd. "Put her over there and I'll be with you in a coupla minutes." Then he spotted

Rob loitering in a corner, still trying to look inconspicuous. "Hey now, how ya doin' lil' buddy? Ain't seen you around here in ages." Todd lumbered over to him as Rob swigged from a bottle of Pepsi. "Whatcha bin doin' with yourself, hey?" His eyes were roaming all over Rob's body, but he didn't dare make a move in Luke's presence. He reached out to touch Rob's hair, then quickly withdrew his hand when he saw Luke watching him. "Guess I'll catch you later. Any time you wanna drop by...." Rob was too embarrassed to meet Todd's eye, and took a couple of steps closer to Luke. The back office – where they had conducted their private business – was forever associated in his mind with furtive fumblings and the smell of Todd's sweat.

"I think this young fella's been redlining the engine...he's a devil behind the wheel" said Luke, placing a hand on Rob's collar. "We'll check in with you again about three o'clock. That OK?"

"Sure, yeah" said Todd vaguely, turning to watch as Rob raised his arm over his head in a graceful arc to toss the empty bottle in a trashcan. He usually told customers off for doing that because the bottles were supposed to be put back in the rack to be returned, but he hadn't seen the boy for months and he didn't want to scare him off. The other boys were typical acne-ridden adolescents but this one was special: so beautiful, so perfect. He was just itching to get his hands on that warm throbbing package inside his jeans. He wanted that boy so bad he was practically salivating.

"We've just had a request come in from one of our listeners over in Floyd County, Kentucky – a Miss Cheryl Baker from Sandbrook Senior High" announced the DJ over the radio. "You're listening to WNAS broadcasting from southern Indiana."

My boy lollipop
You make my heart go giddy-op
You are sweet as candy
You are my sugar dandy

I love you, I love you, I love you so
But I want you to know
I need you, I need you, I need you so
And I'll never let you go

You set the world on fire
You are my one desire...

Spencer looked up from what he was doing, wrench in hand, and caught Luke's eye. He started to snigger as the object of Todd's desire fled the garage. The other mechanics who worked there were well aware of Todd's proclivities, and accustomed to seeing boys emerge from his office in a dishevelled state, sometimes with their flies still undone.

"Tell me something" said Rob to Luke, as they walked into town. "How come you laid into Rick that night, but you're not bothered by Todd?"

"He's harmless enough, probably been doing it with boys in the orphanage since he was six years old, and doesn't know any different. But he's no kiddie molester. If he was, he'd be run out of town by a lynch mob. Far as I know, he's never forced himself on anyone, and he doesn't ride boys bareback" added Luke, with a sidelong glance at Rob.

"How do you know all this stuff?" Rob was blushing furiously.

"Loose lips" replied Luke carelessly. Spence, a former classmate who hadn't amounted to much, was always running off at the mouth, bashing Luke's ear with salacious small town gossip whether he wanted to hear about it or not. Mostly he didn't. "It's a hot topic down at the pool hall, who's doing it with who, alleged swinging parties… Todd's famous for his hillbilly handshakes."

"You didn't answer my question. Why did you hit Rick?" Luke was not given to gratuitous violence, and it was totally out of character for him to punch out a guy for no reason other than he had taken an instant dislike to him. Rick had done nothing to deserve such an assault, Luke reflected, and it was evident he had done nothing to harm Rob. They were out on a first date, just chatting, and Luke had over-reacted. He had pushed his brother firmly aside to keep him out of harm's way, but Rick had interpreted this as an act of aggression: from his standpoint he probably thought he was protecting Rob from some interloper who'd muscled in on their private tête-à-tête. If Luke was honest with himself he knew perfectly well why he had reacted the way he did. Seeing his brother with this man, who was clearly smitten with Rob, had sent him into an unthinking rage. This prick was stomping on his territory and he didn't like it. It was Rick's cavalier use of the term "my boyfriend" that had done it. The sudden surge of jealousy had seared him like a hot branding iron. Seeing his brother as an object of desire for other men had aroused feelings he had been suppressing for some time. He didn't want some other man touching Rob intimately, or comforting him when he was distressed.

"Maybe I was jealous" said Luke, in a rare moment of candour. "Only reason he hasn't laid a finger on you yet is because he never got the opportunity. He wants to, though, that's pretty obvious."

"Were you really jealous of Rick?" Luke didn't reply, but laid an arm across his shoulder and kept it there. Ever since the night Rob had opened up to him about the attempted assault in jail, Luke had been very protective and tender towards him. "You are coming to my birthday party next week, aren't you?" asked Rob. His parents had hired the hall at the back of the bowling alley, where the owner had recently installed a mechanical bull so patrons could show off their bronco-busting skills.

"I wasn't sure that the most boring man in the universe would be welcome" teased Luke.

"Sorry, I didn't mean what I said." Rob's immediate instinct was to apologise for all the insults he'd hurled at Luke over the past few weeks, but Loubelle had stressed that he must strongly resist this urge if Phase Three was to be successful.

"That's all right. I even bore myself sometimes. Nothing new under the sun, right?"

"You're not boring at all. And I want you to come. Be there or be square!" Luke laughed.

"I'll be there. Though I sincerely hope I'm not in for another soaking" he added.

As they reached the main thoroughfare Candace Sloane emerged from Darlington's office clutching a large manila envelope – heading for the county courthouse - and Rob turned his head to look at her. With her frosted pink lipstick, heavily made-up panda eyes and blonde beehive, she was starting to resemble Dusty Springfield more and more with each passing day. It hadn't taken Rob long to work out who the secretary was who performed extracurricular activities for her boss, since Loubelle had accidentally let slip she typed up legal documents.

"Hey, Good-looking" said Candace, who must have seen him eyeing her. "What you got cooking?"

"A fine morning, Ma'am" returned Rob in the polite tones his father used, causing Luke to glance at him in surprise since his brother rarely gave women the once-over. Rob never ceased to amaze him. He had a string of adoring older women all over town - including Miss Radcliffe, the head librarian, Miss Grant, the deputy head of Sandbrook Senior High, not to mention Loubelle – all of whom mothered him with a vengeance. And now it looked as though Candace was set to be his latest conquest.

"Gonna mow her lawn too?" enquired Luke. Miss Grant and Miss Radcliffe got him to mow their lawns during the summer months and rake their leaves during the fall, in return for which Rob received lashings of iced lemonade and a surfeit of maternal advice. Rob shook his head, laughing helplessly.

"She doesn't have a lawn. She lives in an apartment, like Loubelle." Luke wondered how he knew this fact.

"What's so funny? You like her or something?" persisted Luke, with a smile. Rob was still shaking with laughter, as if he knew something Luke didn't know.

"No, I don't even know her. The people in this town kill me." Luke raised his eyebrows, but didn't pursue the topic. As they passed the doors of the First National Bank on the corner of Court Street and Main, he looked around with an air of indecision.

"Do you think you could amuse yourself for half an hour or so?" he asked Rob. "Take a quick tour around the planet in your spaceship?"

"Sure, Mister" replied Rob uncertainly. For some reason, Luke didn't want him hanging around. It would be more than he could endure if his brother was intending to meet up with Cindy Foster or some other woman.

"You just reminded me" said Luke. "I'd like to get you something for your birthday."

"Oh" breathed Rob, overcome with relief. "You don't have to get me anything."

"Yes I do, it's your twenty-first. But damned if I know what. I'm useless when it comes to shopping for gifts." Rob had spent virtually every cent he earned mowing lawns last summer on Luke, presenting him with an expensive buckskin suede jacket – the type cowboys wore - and Luke had been touched by his generosity. They stood facing each other on the sidewalk. "Uh, could you help me out here?"

"You could give me your class ring" suggested Rob. Luke's graduation ring had been gathering dust in a chest of drawers in his old bedroom. Luke laughed.

"Now why would you want that?" When a boy gave a girl his class ring to wear it meant much the same as giving her his varsity jacket – that they were going steady, dating each other exclusively. "You're welcome to it, though I doubt it would fit you." He took Rob's smaller hand in his, examining the size of his fingers. "You want my varsity jacket too?" asked Luke, who was aware of the significance of his request. Overcome with shyness, Rob hastily summoned Johnny Angel to his aid.

"You wouldn't like me to wear some other guy's ring, would you?" He flashed Luke his most enchanting smile, and Luke's eyes lingered on his mouth – his very kissable mouth – for a moment. Rob looked away for a second, biting down on his lip hard. Utterly disarmed, Luke fought down an urge to caress him.

"Get outta here. Beat it. Scram." As soon as Rob had disappeared around the corner, Luke carried on walking, past Ben Franklin's Five and Dime, past Henderson's drugstore and Woolworth's, then turned into Hardiman's jewellery store.

A block away Rob seated himself on a counter stool at the bakery, waiting for Loubelle to turn around. She was busy arranging some fudge brownies on a plate, before putting them in the glass display.

"Hi, Gorgeous" she said, catching sight of him. "What are you doing here?"

"Just dropped in to say Hi." Rob smiled at her. He was slightly flushed and had the starry-eyed look of someone who was very much in love. "And to invite you to my twenty-first birthday party."

"Are your parents going to be there and all?"

"Well, yeah, but..."

"It's sweet of you to invite me, but I'm going to pass on this one. In their eyes, I'm the town *femme fatale*, the vamp who's got her hooks into their darling boy. And your friends are all going to be there, kids half my age." Rob looked disappointed.

"But I like you better than all of them" he protested.

"You're an absolute doll. But I'd just be a fish out of water, sweetie. You make sure you have a good time, and we'll keep our friendship special, OK?" Rob nodded slowly. "Now, don't run off because I want the low-down on what really happened at Lennie's Bar Friday night. Rick told me your brother went on the rampage and tore the place up." Loubelle had listened to Rick's version of events with a certain amount of scepticism. Despite his formidable physique, Luke did not have a reputation as a bruiser who went around attacking people for no reason. Rob was laughing.

"That wasn't what happened. But he did go after Rick. Luke was mad as hell." Rob gave her an account of what had occurred, as Loubelle listened, wide-eyed.

"Jeez, I'd hate to be on his shitlist. Rick's scared to death of him." Rob giggled. Actually he'd thought Luke had been magnificent, like Wyatt Earp: it had been like when the proverbial gunslinger pushes open the swing saloon doors, and a deathly hush descends on the assembled company. When he'd had shown up at the bar, Rob had been frightened – not that Luke would physically hurt him – but of what he might do to someone else. He was aware that his brother was capable of extreme violence and could be quite ruthless when the occasion called for it, but Rob had rarely witnessed it first-hand. When Luke had advanced on Rick at Lennie's Bar, his eyes had suddenly narrowed as if zeroing in on a target. Rob knew that look. It meant one of two things, and could either be a sign of aggression - a hunter sighting his prey - or a sign of attraction. Either way it signified engagement or strong interest. He must have had the same look when he'd gone after the enemy in Vietnam.

"Sounds like the green-eyed monster finally got him" said Loubelle, smiling. "Play your cards right, and I think it's safe to say you've got your man." Loubelle had interpreted Luke's violent reaction as jealousy, and a sure sign that their campaign strategy was working, but Rob was not so sure. Luke was an alpha male and fiercely territorial – the type of guy who wouldn't cede an inch to the enemy, which was why he made such a good soldier. If there was one thing guaranteed to get him going it was the sight of anyone messing with Rob. As the eldest, Luke believed he was fully entitled to tease or boss his baby brother about as much as he wanted - that was his "prerogative" - but woe betide anyone else who took similar liberties. When Rob was only nine and the fourteen-year-old Rudy Nelson, who was twice his size, had laid into him Luke had been furious - though you'd have to know him pretty well to recognise the telltale signs: a barely discernible twitch, an inadvertent tightening of his jaw muscles. He'd punched Rudy very hard, and Rudy's nose had kind of exploded: he'd screamed obscenities at Luke, windmilling his arms ineffectually, and Luke had punched him about four more times in quick succession. Rudy lay sprawled on the sidewalk, and Luke had stood over him with a faint air of triumph.

"Listen, I've got to go in a minute. I'm meeting him downtown." Rob leaned over the counter and kissed her on the cheek. Loubelle gave him a smouldering look.

"If you don't get out of here, I'm going to have to pull you right across the counter and ravish you on the spot." Rob laughed and swivelled around on the stool, doing a 360 spin, before turning to face her again.

"You have such a dangerous reputation I believe you'd do it. And I know plenty of guys who'd love it. But you know my heart belongs to another. OK, OK I'm going." Loubelle had also foreseen a little problem Rob did not seem aware of. As she had anticipated, Rick had fallen for Rob big time, and the fact that he had a protective older brother only served to fuel his infatuation. It made Rob seem even more desirable in his eyes, like royalty or some unattainable rock star surrounded by bodyguards. Oh well, thought Loubelle. Now she'd let the genie out of the bottle, she would just have to let Nature take its course.

Chapter Ten

Rob sat astride the mechanical bull and gripped the handhold with his dominant hand, using his thigh muscles to consolidate his seat. The mistake many novice riders made was to allow their upper body to tense up and become rigid, but Rob remained loose and relaxed from the waist up, letting the bull ride him. When the bull's head plunged and its back reared up he leaned back to counter the momentum, his heels pointed inward in a spurring lick. With his free hand he twirled a Stetson over his head, which looked cool, but was actually a deliberate balancing manoeuvre. Every time the bull bucked and reared, slewed from left to right, or gyrated in circles, Rob shifted his pelvic weight accordingly. Every now and then he allowed himself to float so that you could see daylight between rider and saddle, drawing gasps from the onlookers who thought he'd been bucked off. Then he would soft-land back down in the saddle with a roguish smile, to demonstrate he was in complete control. At no time did he grab leather with his free hand, which would have caused him to be disqualified.

"Atta boy. Ride 'em, cowboy!" shouted Joe.

"That boy must have been a bronco buster in some previous life" commented Vernon. "He's a natural." The idea was to stay on for a full minute without falling off. Most riders could only manage about 20-30 seconds. Rob beat the record at ninety seconds, attracting cheers and a huge applause, and was crowned undisputed rodeo champion of the evening.

"It's in the blood" said Joe. "A couple of generations ago both my boys would have been brought up on a horse. Rob's Granddaddy could rope a full-grown steer before he was twelve."

"Congratulations" said Luke, clapping Rob on the back. "You knocked 'em dead. And many happy returns."

"Thanks, brother. Is that a hickey I see on your neck?" The other night Rob had walked right up to him where he was splitting logs for firewood. As Luke paused for a moment, lodging the axe head in a tree stump, Rob had sunk his teeth into his brother's throat. Taken by surprise, Luke had just stood there, allowing it. "I couldn't resist" Rob had murmured. "Your pheromones are driving me wild."

"You strike me as being seriously deranged, boy" Luke had muttered, when he'd recovered his composure. Rob was capable of whipsawing between different personalities with bewildering speed, and Luke was never quite sure what facet of his brother's character was uppermost at any given moment.

"To whom do I have the honour of speaking tonight?" Luke now enquired.

"Jesse of course. You saw how I rode that bronco. And Frank, aren't you pleased to see me?" Rob had placed his hands on Luke's shoulders and was looking at him with shining eyes. "You just got sprung from the calaboose in Dodge city. I had to shoot up the whole town to get you out."

"I can't tell you how pleased I am to see you, little brother." Luke smiled into his eyes. "Only I'm not Frank, I'm Luke – you know that, right?"

"Sure." Rob returned his smile. "You're better looking than Frank was." Luke had arrived separately in his own car half an hour later than the rest of the family, and when Rob had seen him come through the door he had got a serious case of butterflies.

"Why, thank you. You're not so bad yourself. What can I get you to drink?" Luke asked him.

"A Tequila slammer...Oh, shit, look who's headed in our direction." Luke glanced over his shoulder and saw Rick the Prick leave the bar area.

"What's Lover Boy doing here? Did you invite him?"

"Nossir. Ran into him downtown the other day. He was trying to get me to go out on another date with him. The guy's like a flea on a hound dog, I can't seem to shake him off."

"Hi, Robbie" said Rick. "That was quite an impressive performance back there..." He suddenly noticed Luke and went pale. "Oh hi. You're Rob's big brother. Or should I say, Rob's bodyguard, ha ha." He laughed nervously.

"Well, this is an unexpected pleasure" drawled Luke, with that slow smile Rob recognised. His brother derived some kind of private entertainment in playing cat-and-mouse games with people who found him intimidating. "Sorry about that little misunderstanding a couple of weeks ago" said Luke, lighting a cigarette. "Hope you don't hold it against me."

"No no, of course not!" Rick seemed eager to put it behind him. "You were just being protective of your brother. And I can certainly relate to that" he added quickly. Rob turned away to stifle a laugh.

"I'll leave you two to catch up" continued Luke. "Be right back." Luke returned a few minutes later with some drinks. He handed his brother a Tequila slammer, and handed Rick a beer. Might as well be civil to him. You almost had to feel sorry for the guy. He obviously had the hots for Rob - had it really bad, otherwise he wouldn't have risked another encounter with Luke.

"You seem different somehow" said Rick, addressing Luke. "More civil -" He had been about to say "civilised" but checked himself. "Politer."

"He can be quite polite when he wants" said Rob, who had downed his Tequila slammer in one shot. "But it's not necessarily a good sign. James Bond is extremely polite when he's at his deadliest. You like Sean Connery?"

"Not really my type" replied Rick, his eyes fixed on Rob.

"Good physique though. Bet he's well hung" added Rob mischievously, with a glance at Luke.

"I'll leave you two gentlemen to pursue this conversation in private" said Luke. "I'm right here if you need me" he said in an undertone to Rob, before backing off and stationing himself against a nearby pillar. Rob had his elbows propped on the back of a chair, his pelvis thrust out slightly – a provocative pose hardly calculated to dampen Rick's ardour, thought Luke. His brother was one good-looking dude, he thought, meeting his gaze. *Not quite sure what you're trying to tell me with your eyes, brother. You want me to hang around? Or do you just want me to admire your body?*

After a while Luke wandered off to speak to some mutual acquaintances he and Rob both knew from Senior High. Although they were a few years younger, Luke knew them all pretty well from summer jobs lifeguarding at the public swimming pool. He had rarely been called upon to rescue anyone from drowning, but was frequently required to step in when the boys were tormenting the girls by unhooking their bikini brassieres. Luke obligingly came to the rescue, cutting through the water like a shark as the perpetrators made a hasty getaway - always arriving just in time to get an eyeful of exposed female flesh. He had regarded this as one of the perks of the job.

A local band composed of some boys from Sandbrook Senior High had been hired for the occasion, and were belting out a variety of numbers in response to shouted requests from the dance floor, before launching into *Louie Louie*:

A fine little girl, she wait for me,
Me catch the ship across the sea.
I sailed the ship all alone,
I never think how I'll make it home.

Louie Louie
Oh no, me gotta go.
Louie Louie
Oh baby, me gotta go.

"I think it's totally pathetic" Judy was saying. "I mean, you'd think the FBI would have better things to do …" They were discussing the fact that the FBI had launched an investigation into the alleged obscenity of the lyrics *Louie Louie*, after receiving a number of complaints from concerned parents. The investigation had dragged on inconclusively because the lyrics proved to be indecipherable. "I've listened to it hundreds of times with the volume right up, and I can't hear anything dirty. What do you think, Luke?" she asked. "And get that brother of yours to come over here and socialise!! It's his birthday and we want to talk to him."

"Try playing it at 33 RPM instead of 45 RPM" offered Luke "Then you get something more like:

A fine little girl, she waits for me;
she gets her kicks on top of me.

Each night I take her out all alone;
she ain't the kind I lay at home

Judy furrowed her brow with concentration, listening hard, as the band played:

Three nights and days I sail the sea
Think of girl constantly
On that ship I dream she's there
I smell the rose in her hair

"Once you slow it down you can hear the alternative version" said Bruce, a former classmate of Rob's. He took up the refrain:

Louie, Louie
Grab her way down low
Louie, Louie
Grab her way down low

Tonight at ten, I lay her again,
Fuck you girl, oh, all the way
And on that chair, I lay her there;
I felt my boner in her hair…

"You guys are so gross!" screamed Judy, feigning outrage. "You're making it up. It doesn't make any difference *what* speed you play it at." The males amongst the party laughed.

"Don't know why the FBI picked on that one though" continued Luke "*Mony Mony* is just as bad. *Shot gun, get it done, come on, honey* – what do you think he's talking about?" Judy swatted him with her purse.

"Oh cut it out, will you. You guys only have one thing on your minds."

Mention of the song had brought to mind an afternoon in Vietnam when Luke's platoon were enjoying a 48-hour breather in a demilitarised zone, enclosed in a one-acre compound surrounded by barbed wire and perimeter guards. They had created their own little slice of Disneyland, complete with hot dog and concession stands where they could spend their army pay. The men were letting off steam by riotous stomping to *Woolly Bully*.

"I could never figure out what that meant" said Luke to Sgt. Moreland. "*Matty told Hatty about a thing she saw. Had two big horns and a woolly jaw...*I mean, what the fuck's that about?" The sergeant laughed.

"I think to pull the wool means to, ah, get it on. Heard about the latest box of tricks to come out of the War Office?" He was referring to psychological warfare operations where helicopters and patrol gun-boats mounted with loudspeakers were broadcasting heavy metal and hard rock to targeted zones, the idea being to deny sleep to the enemy, and to impair their ability to communicate between units. "Blast the enemy with loud rock music."

"Problem with that is we don't get any fucking sleep either" said Luke as Moreland handed him a hotdog with mustard. About an hour ago they'd all witnessed a Huey "slick" transport helicopter explode in a ball of flames after being hit by enemy ground fire. There had been a moment's silence after the chopper crashed on a distant hilltop, before someone turned up the volume of the loudspeakers - not out of callousness, but because no-one really wanted to dwell on such sights. Most of them sought oblivion in alcohol and loud music. Next up was *House of the Rising Sun*:

There is a house in New Orleans
They call the Rising Sun
And it's been the ruin of many a poor boy
And God I know I'm one...

Oh mother tell your children
Not to do what I have done
Spend your lives in sin and misery
In the House of the Rising Sun

Paterson and another guy were having an arm-wrestling match, attended by the usual braggadocio and locker room taunts, with onlookers laying bets on the winner.

"Hate to wreck your arm, sugar" Paterson told the other guy "but a little Pantywaist like you couldn't fight his way out of a paper bag."

"That so?" countered his opponent. "You may be handy with a rifle, but you couldn't drive a nail through soft butter." Dorsey stopped by to place five bucks on Paterson, and popped a bicep the size of a grapefruit.

"See that? Any of you little girls want to take me on?"

"Aw, now that wouldn't be right" replied Paterson without looking up. "Like taking candy from a baby."

"Can you lend me thirty bucks?" Dorsey asked Rockwell somewhat desperately, as they were getting ready to hit the red light district in Saigon.

"Hell no. You blew all your pay on whores that's your problem, man. I can maybe loan you ten. If you're that horny, maybe you should go pick up one of those little pansies who run after soldiers. Probably buy you drinks all night then let you ream his ass for free."

"I might consider it" said Dorsey "Only I'm kinda choosy where I put my dick." This statement provoked a volley of sceptical hoots, Dorsey's reputation as a cocksman having preceded him. "Tell you what, Rockie boy. I ever get that desperate, next time you come out the shower all sweet-smelling and fresh as a daisy, I'm gonna come up right behind you-" Rockwell flipped him the bird.

"Ah, go screw yourself."

"Hey, look what just arrived" said someone else. "No need to go into town to shoot off your spunk gun, boys." Local hookers were being convoyed in by jeep, to the accompaniment of catcalls and wolf whistles, then escorted to boom-boom parlours. Once the girls had settled in behind their curtained love cubicles, soldiers who wanted some horizontal recreation were welcome to pay them a visit.

"Boom boom time" announced Dorsey, who'd just won his bet and managed to borrow some dollars. "Gonna go see my girlfriend." Dorsey reckoned one of the hookers had the hots for him: this girl didn't holler and scream when he touched her, unlike the one he'd tried to snatch in the rice paddy. Dream on, thought Luke. The likelihood of any of these girls having fallen for Dorsey's dubious charms was on a par with Brigitte Bardot riding up naked on a white horse and offering them all free blowjobs. "Might even buy that little beauty a bracelet" said Dorsey. He didn't often get female attention (they mostly ran a mile when they saw him coming) "Hey, they selling any of that tiger soup?" Some of the men had heard that tiger penis had an amazing effect on one's sexual prowess, and were keen to get their hands on some.

"You saying you got no lead in your pencil?" asked someone else. Dorsey swiped him playfully. He was in a good mood because his little honey had blown him a kiss when she jumped down from the jeep in her skimpy dress and high heels, before mouthing "See you later, Alligator" – an American phrase she had picked up and used to good effect.

"Did you see that?" Dorsey asked excitedly "I told you, man, she likes me, can't get enough of me." Dorsey and his new sweetheart, who was a lot smarter than he would ever be, had already had three assignations and she clearly had him wrapped around her little finger. The men in Luke's outfit never ceased to surprise him. He had Dorsey pegged as a serious danger to women, especially after that incident when he had tried to make off with a Vietnamese girl. There was no doubt in his mind that he and the sarge had got there just in time to prevent a rape. Dorsey was the type of guy who was dumb enough to think that because his attentions were welcome in a brothel, they would be welcomed by any female who crossed his path. Billy was another unpredictable one. Despite his terror of snakes, he had been the first to reach down and haul out the soldier who had fallen into the viper pit, dangling headfirst over the pit whilst Luke and two other men held his legs securely. He'd been pretty choked up when the man didn't pull through, and afterwards Luke had gone over to him to offer a few consolatory words, and to thank him for his heroic efforts.

"You did everything you could" Luke told him. "He didn't know what was going on. He was totally out of it, man."

"I couldn't leave him down there, sir" Billy had replied. "I just had to get him out."

Dorsey had cleaned himself up in the shower block and was checking himself out in a mirror to see whether he had suddenly grown more handsome overnight, whilst the other guys were cracking up.

"Yeah, I'd say she's real gone on you" said Sgt. Moreland to Dorsey, who was grinning from ear to ear. "Be sure and treat her nice now."

"Second that emotion" returned Luke, with a smile. Sgt. Moreland was the closest he had to a best buddy during his time in Vietnam.

Two weeks into his first tour of duty they had stumbled across the concealed entrance to an underground tunnel, whilst making a detour to avoid stepping on an army of red ants. As platoon leader, Luke had been on the point of entering first, advancing with a flashlight and a side arm, when Moreland put a hand on his arm, detaining him.

"Strongly advise that you desist, sir. You don't know what's down there." At the time Luke was relatively inexperienced, whilst his sergeant was a seasoned NCO who'd been in the field for longer and was aware that the enemy had a nasty habit of leaving little surprises when they abandoned a tunnel, such as a bundle of king cobras and green pit vipers, or a landmine. "Even if there's a cache of weapons in there, it's not worth it" said Moreland. "Trust me." Then before Luke could argue the point, he'd tossed a hand grenade down the opening, thereby preventing Luke from entering. "Sorry, sir. Acting in your best interests." The sergeant had probably saved his life. Moreland was his right-hand man and always had his back. They shared similar values and the same sense of humour. Guys like Billy and Dorsey – big, strong and stupid - were the raw material the U. S. army loved to mould and turn into perfect killing machines. And guys like Luke and Moreland - big, strong and not quite so stupid – were the types selected to be in charge of them.

Earlier, an argument had broken out in the latrine when a soldier had suddenly shoved another soldier who he thought was getting too friendly: "Hey, whaddya keep making those fag eyes at me for? You wanna get fucked up the wazoo? A ride on my flagpole would kill you."

"Don't flatter yourself" retorted the one who'd been shoved. "No-one's making fag eyes at you, man. You're imagining it." Luke had in the meantime strolled in to see what was going on, and leaned up against the wall, arms folded. His physical presence was usually enough to prevent the men from coming to blows. The first soldier, who was becoming increasingly truculent, gave the other one a poke in the chest.

"This guy's been fucking with my head." He looked around the room, wild-eyed. "Anyone else see what's going on here? Am I the only one who sees it?"

"He's tripping out, sir" volunteered the soldier who'd been shoved. "Paranoid as hell."

"Tell me something I don't already know" replied Luke who was heartily sick of dope dealers and the clandestine drug trade. Weed was one thing, which helped some of them to mellow out, but a few of the guys had been experimenting with heroin or "skag" as well as LSD. The resulting paranoia and delusional behaviour was seriously hampering their ability to function as soldiers. It was also seriously hampering his ability to maintain discipline and order, as he couldn't in all conscience come down hard on someone who was scarcely aware of what was going on around him. Luke went up to him and examined his dilated pupils. The soldier glared at him suspiciously.

"Who the hell are you? Get out of my face, man. You're in on this, too. I KNOW exactly what's going on here." He took a swing at Luke, who blocked it with his arm.

"Carry on like that, pal, and you might end up in the LBJ ranch pounding the walls of a five foot by seven metal box" remarked Luke in a conversational tone. "You like the sound of that?" It was an empty threat, since only dangerous felons and maximum security prisoners were housed in these containers at the notorious Long Binh Jail, which had replaced the former military stockade in Saigon. Normally, just the mention of a stint in the LBJ was enough to calm frayed tempers, but the fact that the soldier did not react to his threat and didn't even recognise him as his platoon commander, confirmed the original verdict. To hell with it, thought

Luke. There was no reasoning with a man under the influence of a hallucinogenic drug until the effects wore off and he crash-landed. "All right. Keep out of his way and don't respond to anything he says" Luke advised the soldier who'd just been shoved. "Wouldn't want to find yourself riding that flagpole, would you?" He started to laugh, seeing the funny side of it, and the others began to laugh too. "If our friend here does anything you think I need to know about – such as attempted homicide - you know where to find me. Otherwise don't bother me" he added, before walking off.

Over on the other side of the compound Billy was whirling a dead Burmese python around his head like a lasso, bashing its head against the concrete wall of the barracks.

"If Bayou Boy stays out here any longer he'll soon be howling at the moon" chuckled Moreland.

"Like your new tie, Billy" quipped someone, as Billy swung it around a few more times for good measure. He was actually conducting a conversation with the lifeless snake.

"Like *that*, do you? Gottcha, you little fucker. Think I don't know about the serpent in the Garden of Eden, huh? You're the most evil critter on the planet."

"Think you killed that thing some time ago, Ballantine" said Luke, lighting up a cigarette. "Give it a rest, man." Billy had eventually been invalided out on grounds of temporary insanity, when he'd been caught screaming at the top of his lungs "I want OUTTA here. I've had it up to here with this fucking country, little slit-eyed gooks and vermin crawling all over the damn place. Shoot me if you want. I want OUT of this shithole."

At that point one of the girls came tearing out of the barracks, pursued by a GI called Private Bulmer: "Hey, come back here! What's your problem, bitch? You don't want to do it with me because I'm black? ..." Luke and Sgt. Moreland both looked up, as the sobbing girl headed straight in their direction. She sandwiched herself in between Luke and Moreland, with whom she evidently felt safe.

"I no want to! I no like!"

"She's a whore, she can't say no to me. ..." Bulmer complained indignantly to Luke.

"Go find yourself another girl" said Luke sharply. "Plenty of others to choose from."

"I want this one" he insisted. "I've paid for it. She has to fuck me..."

"You'll get your money back. Now I'll say this one more time, soldier. Find another girl who's willing." Bulmer backed off, muttering angrily. Luke turned back to the girl, unsure what to do. He had never come across a situation like this before, where a hooker refused point-blank to sleep with a GI who'd paid upfront for her services. He figured she must be new to the job, and inexperienced. Bulmer had clearly been drinking, and had possibly been a little rough with her. Or it could be that he'd hit the nail on the head, and she didn't want to sleep with a black guy. Some of the Asian hookers would only go with white men, and made their racial preferences quite plain, which naturally caused resentment.

"Maybe this is her first time" suggested Moreland in an undertone. "We could put her in the back of the jeep, and she can stay there until it's time for the others to go."

"I stay here with you, yes?" appealed the girl, looking up from one to the other. She was barefoot, and in her panic must have fled without thinking to put on her shoes. Most of the girls also carried a little shoulder bag containing their makeup and condoms.

"Uh sure, honey, that's fine" said Luke awkwardly.

"Not tell?" She was clearly anxious about it getting back to her employers.

"Not tell" Luke promised. He lifted her up into the back of the M-715, catching a faint whiff of perfume as her bare limbs brushed against his arm. She was as light as a feather. "You want an ice cream?" Sgt. Moreland obligingly went off to one of the concession stands and returned with a vanilla ice cream cone, which he handed to the girl. She clutched it tightly in one hand with tears streaming down her face and mingling with the ice cream.

"Hey, that's no way to eat an ice-cream" teased Moreland gently, leaning across the tailgate to peer at her face, which was partially hidden behind the curtain of dark hair. "Ah well, if you can't beat 'em join 'em." He went over to join the other men in their roughhousing and horseplay. Some of them were playing a rambunctious game which resembled "pass the parcel" - the parcel being one of the smaller guys, rumoured to be a fag, who was being tossed from one man to another like a rag doll. He was taking it pretty well, considering: "Hey fellas, not so rough. You're messing up my hair." There was no actual evidence he was homosexual, and he cleverly managed to deflect any real aggression with a constant stream of wisecracks.

Luke hoisted himself onto the hood of the jeep and leaned back against the front screen – elbows folded behind his head - letting the music wash over him as he contemplated the pyrotechnic displays taking place overhead. War was terrible, but the night skies were insanely beautiful, streaked with vivid orange and black, like a tiger's pelt. A fragment of poetry, learned by rote in high school light-years ago, floated into his head:

Tyger Tyger, burning bright

In the forests of the night;
What immortal hand or eye,
Could frame thy fearful symmetry?

There had in fact been numerous tiger sightings by U.S. soldiers, the attacks having increased due to the frequency with which bodies were left unburied. Mercifully, Luke's platoon had not encountered any big cats, which were mostly to be found in the highlands and mountainous areas, from where it was reported several marines had been dragged away in the night. One nervous new recruit fresh from basic training had come up to Luke asking if the reports were true.

"The reports you've heard are perfectly true" Luke affirmed. "Tigers have also been known to swim through mangrove swamps. Though you're far more likely to encounter tiger leeches" he added. He was half teasing, but also putting the young soldier on notice not to get complacent or to drop his guard for one moment. It was the best advice he could give to anyone newly arrived in Vietnam.

"Who's that weirdo Rob's talking to?" asked Bruce, interrupting his reverie. Rick had got hold of Rob's arm, and they appeared to be having some kind of altercation.

"Just some gatecrasher" said Luke "I'll go check it out." As he approached his brother, he could hear Rick whining "Yeah, OK I get it, you're involved with someone! How come I've never seen him with you? And if you're so *involved* how come he's not here tonight? Just who is this mystery man?"

"Let's just call him Wyatt Earp" said Rob. "Don't get heavy, man." He sighed.

"Don't you think I have a *right* to know-" began Rick.

"-You have no rights whatsoever, where my brother is concerned" remarked Luke, placing a hand on Rob's shoulder. "All right, Rob?"

"Jeez, can't a guy even have a conversation with you without your personal bodyguard muscling in. I mean, this is just *ridiculous...*"

"My mystery man has a pressing engagement at Tombstone" said Rob, leaning against Luke. "And since he's requested the pleasure of my company, I may have to leave at a moment's notice."

"Oh, I get it" said Rick with a touch of bitterness. "You've just been leading me on, haven't you?" Rob felt a little guilty. Perhaps he had led Rick on unintentionally. He had welcomed Rick's friendly overtures the night of their first date, his emotions still raw from his earlier bruising encounter with Luke, who had cut him off in mid-speech with a caustic "Have fun, little brother" before striding off. Rob had felt choked, sensing his brother was genuinely angry and that he had perhaps gone too far this time. But there was no turning back, and he would have to go through with the date.

"I don't believe we've been properly introduced" said Luke to Rick. "Allow me to introduce myself…" Rob shook his head vehemently at Luke. Not a Russian handshake, Luke, please. Then Luke suddenly smiled, winking at Rob. He was just kidding around, Rob realised. *Get rid of him* he silently implored Luke. "I think it's time you left, buddy" continued Luke, placing a hand on Rick's collar. Rick didn't look too happy about it, but had no choice in the matter as Luke escorted him to the door. Outside, Rick tried to quiz him about Rob's "mystery man."

"Do you know this guy Rob's involved with?" As Luke remained silent, he persisted "Look, I know this is a private party and I had no business turning up, but I thought he *liked* me, man. I thought he was unattached. That was whole point of our date…"

"-You're wasting your time" Luke cut him off. Rick was starting to be a serious pain in the ass. Having ascertained he was relatively harmless did not make Luke any more kindly disposed towards him. "I can assure you, my brother has no interest in you" he added brutally, not sparing his feelings. This was true. If Rob had any feelings whatsoever for Rick he wouldn't have tamely suffered Luke to escort him from the premises without a protest. "Am I making myself clear?" Rick took one look at Luke's steely implacable gaze, and beat a judicious retreat. He felt like cornered prey, ensnared in the rifle sights of a practised hunter. For some reason Rob appeared to be completely in thrall to his older brother, and Rick wasn't about to tangle with this guy. He knew queens who assiduously pumped iron and acted tough, like puffed-up banty roosters, but it was mostly posturing. Rob's brother was the real deal. He'd served in Vietnam, and wouldn't think twice about flattening anyone who stood in his path, squashing them like bugs. And his message couldn't have been clearer: his younger brother was strictly off limits. Just his luck, thought Rick dejectedly. Whenever he came across someone really gorgeous, like Rob, he was either straight or already taken. Or in this case, as closely guarded as the gold at Fort Knox.

Rob had rejoined his pals at the bar by the time Luke returned. His hand brushed against Luke's lightly as he murmured "Thank you."

"My pleasure" replied Luke. Judy was running her fingers through Rob's hair "You're such a dreamboat, you know that? Where have you been all my life?"

"Nowhere" smiled Rob shyly, ducking from another caress. "Just hanging out."

"I don't get it" said Bruce to Judy. "You never hit on *me* like that. He's just a pretty face. There's nothing going on in there."

"Oh right. And you're the brain of the century" returned Judy.

"Remember how old Taylor was always banging on about the Greeks at school? He was right about one thing: if you want to impress a girl you either have to be an Adonis or a Hercules" remarked Bruce, with a sidelong glance at Luke's heroic proportions. "You know who Adonis was?" he asked Rob.

"He was that dude who fell in a pool of water because he couldn't stop looking at his own reflection."

"That was Narcissus" corrected Bruce, with a smirk.

"Yeah, whatever. Taylor said Hercules had this thing about another guy called Patrick" said Rob, leaning his body slightly back against Luke, who was standing close behind him.

"That was Achilles not Hercules." Bruce's smirk became wider. "Achilles loved Patroclus."

"Whatever" snapped Rob.

"See, what did I tell you?" said Bruce to Judy. "I rest my case. Nothing going on in there. Just a pretty face, that's all. I'm surprised he didn't flunk everything on the syllabus." Rob drew his fine dark brows together in a slight frown.

"Just because he's not an expert on Greek mythology doesn't mean he's dumb" said Luke, coming to his brother's rescue. Rob had experienced problems with concentration and focus as a teenager, diagnosed as attention deficit disorder, which the other kids didn't know about. "Ignorance is not the same thing as stupidity."

"What's the difference?" asked Bruce.

"You can be ignorant of the annual Russian output of coal, but still be pretty smart" replied Luke, steadying Rob, who was a little tight. He had been brushing against Luke all evening, in an inconspicuous sort of way.

"That shut you up, didn't it?" said Judy to Bruce. "Smartass. I think we can guess what *you* were up to last night, Luke." He was wearing an open-necked blue shirt and she had just spotted the purplish bruise on his throat.

"Yeah, that looks really bad" agreed Rob, who had turned around so that he was facing his brother, ostensibly to inspect the hickey, but really so that he could gaze into Luke's eyes without attracting attention. Luke returned his gaze steadily. Rob turned back to the others. "I think Luke must have a secret admirer. Do you know what they called him in the army? *Thunderballs*." Luke chucked him under the chin.

"Keep it up, sweet brother of mine, and you'll be singing *It's My Party and I'll Cry if I Want To* before the night's over."

"Guys like Luke always have some chick hanging around their necks" said Bruce dismissively before returning to his theme. "Adonis was the Greek god of beauty" he informed Rob. "Guess what I got you for your birthday? A compact so you can powder your nose in the Little Girl's Room." Luke flashed him a warning look, but Rob did not appear to require his intervention. He now slid his back alongside the bar, so that he was right up against Bruce.

"I didn't know you cared, Brucie. How long has this been going on? Honey, I had no idea. You really think I'm that beautiful?" Rob moved even closer to Bruce, and leancd forward in order to look him full in the face and gauge his reaction.

"No! Get off-"

"But you just said it in front of all these witnesses. You called me Adonis and he's the Greek god of beauty. Y'all heard him, didn't you?" Judy giggled. "I'm real sorry, Brucie, but I'm already spoken for. I'm with Hercules." He pointed at Luke. "But hey, why don't you call me sometime?" Luke laughed at Bruce's discomfiture. Once again he had underestimated his brother, who had managed to turn the situation to his advantage so that Bruce ended up looking foolish, whilst Rob appeared more desirable and sought-after than ever. Rob suddenly looked up at Luke and flashed him one of his special smiles: it was like having a powerful 1000-watt beam of light focussed and concentrated on him, and then it was gone, as swiftly as it had appeared.

Luke had always been aware that Rob possessed the kind of charisma that knocks flies off walls, but until recently he had imagined himself to be immune to that charm. Just lately, however, he had found himself increasingly drawn to his brother, intrigued by his complex character. He knew very little about schizophrenia, apart from the common perception that it involved a "split personality." As far as he could tell, the split appeared to be between his shy sensitive kid brother – who was frequently tongue-tied and blushed at the drop of a hat - and this character Johnny Angel, who seemed more in control – someone who knew exactly what he wanted and how to go about getting it. Try as he might, Luke could not reconcile the two distinct personalities. But he was gradually becoming familiar with the latter's *modus operandi*: he would flash Luke a seductive smile, accompanied by a slight flickering of his eyes – nothing so obvious or effeminate as fluttering his eyelashes – but with the hint of a challenge in them: *Do you find me irresistible? Do you want me?* The disquieting truth was that Luke actually found it quite sexy. Johnny Angel's flirting took the same direction as that of a girl, leading up to and anticipating some kind of physical resolution. With that line of attack Luke was wholly familiar: he'd had enough experience with women to know what that was about.

But whenever Rob appealed to him with that beseeching "little boy lost" look, Luke felt his defences crumbling. Ever since they were children he had been susceptible to his brother's vulnerability; he had never been able to resist that childlike helplessness: *I seem to have got myself into a terrible mess, Luke, and I honestly don't know how it happened, but will you take care of it?* It got him every time - connected with his essential nature on a much deeper level than a merely physical appeal ever could. Rob was the chink in his armour, his Achilles heel. Luke wasn't sure when he first became aware that his brother was coming on to him, but he dated it back to a family barbecue earlier on in the summer. Rob had been dangling from a tree branch with one arm and rocking on his heels, whilst staring challengingly at Luke. *Am I turning you on?* Later, when they were alone up in the woods, Rob had stretched out on the log like a sacrificial offering, his T-shirt rucked up over his navel in a classic "Fuck me" pose. Or that's how it had seemed to Luke, who was on him in a trice. He had no idea where the sudden urge had come from - he only knew he was feeling horny as hell and that he had a massive hard-on. Before he'd even stopped to consider what he was doing he had mounted his brother in time-honoured fashion, according to the old English proverb about standing pricks....

But had that really been his brother egging him on, or had it been some other *persona*, whose provocative behaviour was guaranteed to get him going? Yeah, that's highly convenient, you randy bastard. Blame it on this Johnny Angel character, who probably didn't even exist except in Dr. Strangelove's imagination. A piss-poor excuse if ever I heard one, Luke berated himself sternly. You should have left the kid alone. And then about a week ago, Rob had come up to him and offered to wash the convertible. Luke was on the front stoop of his cabin, absorbed in sharpening the teeth of his chainsaw, which was clamped securely between the jaws of a vice.

He employed a smooth even stroke with a file, occasionally looking up to smile at his brother, who was dancing around to the music coming from a transistor radio. Unlike Luke, who tended to be somewhat clumsy whenever he could be enticed onto the dance floor, Rob was a natural mover. Definitely worth watching. Luke put down the file and sauntered up to the Chevy, leaning his elbows across the opposite side of the hardtop roof so they were facing each other.

"Looking good" he said, glancing over the gleaming bodywork of the car. "Is the entertainment extra?"

"All part of the service, sir." Rob finished hosing off the fenders then took a bow. "Sorry about redlining your engine, Mister."

"Don't worry about it. Watch your revs in future, though, kiddo" Luke replied automatically, before pausing to absorb the *double entendre*, which he might have missed if it weren't for the disarming smile which had accompanied Rob's apology.

"Alright, you got me. Don't you *dare*" warned Luke as Rob aimed the hosepipe at him, realising too late he had just raised a red flag. Rob soaked him liberally before sprinting off as Luke chased him across the yard, eventually cornering him by the oak tree from which they had hung a plank swing when they were younger. Seconds later they were tussling on the ground, and Rob was begging for mercy.

"Is Mama's precious little boy feeling scared? Who you gonna run to? Ain't nobody home, just you and me, baby" taunted Luke, in the menacing tone he used when they were a lot younger and he was required to baby-sit Rob when their parents were out. They hadn't played this type of wrestling game for years – not since they were kids. "Say uncle" persisted Luke, grinding him into the grass.

"No." Luke nudged Rob's thighs apart with his knee, applying more pressure.

"Luke, don't. That hurts."

"Asking for it, weren't you?" returned Luke. "You've gotta learn some day. Actions have consequences." He had a sudden incongruous flashback of the last time he'd had another male pinned to the ground beneath him in the Vietnamese jungle: he'd snuffed out his opponent's life, strangling him to death. Rob was gnawing at his thumb, and his breathing had become fast and shallow. He had stopped struggling, but refused to say the word for surrender. "All you've got to do is say uncle, and I'll let you go." Then he'd hooked his legs around Luke's waist so that their crotches were pressed up close and tight in the drill position, with Rob wriggling around underneath him, bucking with his hips. Luke felt himself responding - or at least his cock was responding. That little prick-tease AKA Johnny Angel was redlining his engine all right. What would have happened if they hadn't both been fully clothed and out in the open? That old army joke came to mind. *Hey buddy, if you're in a tight spot you can count on me to cover your ass.* Rob had clasped his arms around Luke's neck, pulling him down closer, so that there was no mistaking what he was after. By no stretch of the imagination were they just "wrestling". Luke had eventually rolled off him and walked off, but not before Rob had called out after him, with a note of triumph "You didn't make me say uncle." Only because I didn't want to hurt you, angel face, thought Luke.

He tried to remember what Rob's doctor had said about some of the symptoms of bipolar disorder: impulsiveness, recklessness, and "questionable" sexual behaviour. That business with Todd, for instance. Luke wasn't unduly concerned about these little sessions – which had in any case stopped months ago – since his brother wasn't the only one who allowed Todd to give him a hand job. Luke grinned as he had a sudden vision of a queue of teenage boys waiting their turn, like in a conveyor belt. Probably it was all just down to sexual frustration. Rob had the same urges as most males but didn't have a normal outlet for his pent-up desires, since he didn't go with girls. It was Todd's behaviour that struck Luke as being questionable – what did he get out of it? Though what the guy got up to in his rundown trailer was anybody's guess. This town was a like a goddamn freak show: few of the residents were in a position to point a finger at anyone else. At the country club, supposedly a bastion of respectability, Mrs. Randall had thrust her tits in his face and given him the eye, right under her husband's nose. Well-shaped and voluptuous tits, if his memory served, Luke having been afforded a good view from the vantage point of his much greater height. At that point his mother had come up and placed a hand on his arm, gently but firmly steering him away from Mrs. Randall. This had amused him, as he'd probably had more women during his two tours of Vietnam than he'd had hot dinners: did his mother actually think he was some kind of innocent who needed protecting?

In fact if you sat down and analysed it – as shrinks are paid to do – most peoples' sexual behaviour was questionable. Including his own, like when Luke had pretended to be some deranged sex-starved backwoodsman chasing his little brother around the kitchen up at Dale's cabin. It had just been a game of course, but where had that come from? Then later on the same evening Rob had been lying across his knees, his flies half unfastened, challenging Luke to resist him. Which he had, thank Christ. What troubled him about the way Rob sometimes acted was not only did it appear to be totally out of character – as if some other personality had temporarily taken possession of his psyche – but the prospect that one day he might just come across a guy without Luke's scruples who'd give it to him good and hard. Like that whoreson motherfucker who'd tried to rape him in the county jail. And Rob probably wouldn't like it very much. His brother had been quite adamant that he was not "into other guys." He didn't want casual promiscuous sex with other males, all he wanted was a monogamous relationship with Luke. Not that wanting a relationship with your own brother was normal. It obviously wasn't. The more Luke thought about it the more he kept going around in circles. Dr. Gottcha had said that multiple personality disorder was the mind's coping strategy to deal with stressful situations. Was Rob a schizophrenic? Or were the signs of mental instability just the inevitable result of trying to repress his true inclinations?

"Hi, Robbie. Happy birthday" said a girl called Sandy, who had been standing on the perimeter of their circle. "Judy and me were just wondering when you were going to ask one of us to dance?"

"Hi. You and Judy want to dance…" Rob shrugged unconcernedly. "Well, you know, it's cool for girls to dance with each other." Sandy gave an exasperated sigh, and Judy took hold of her arm.

"Come on, Sandy, let's go talk to someone else. Boys aren't interested in dancing. They just want to make out."

"Fine, but don't expect me to do all the running" Luke heard Sandy say indignantly to Judy as they marched off together, arm in arm. "I've already demeaned myself enough. What does a girl have to do to get Robbie Turnbull to notice her?" Luke laughed to himself and said to Rob "Hey, why don't you dance with that girl? She's quite cute." Rob gave him a smouldering look but said nothing.

"I know what your problem is" said Bruce suddenly to Rob.

"Yeah? And I know what yours is. But like I said, Brucie baby, I'm already spoken for." Bruce ignored this.

"You're banging her, aren't you?" Rob looked at him.

"Who?"

"You know who. Loubelle. She must be really hot stuff. So what's it like, does she-"

"-Shut your filthy trap. Did it ever occur to you I might find her conversation more interesting than yours?"

"No, that never occurred to me. What did occur to me is that you're into older women. That explains a lot. Mama's boy with an Oedipus complex. Hey, do you think I could get some of that action? Think Loubelle might be interested in giving me some French lessons?" Rob laughed.

"Seriously doubt it, jerkoff. And for the final time, I am NOT banging her, not that it's any of your business." He gave Bruce a shove.

"Come on, Johnny Angel" said Luke, slinging an arm around his shoulder. "I think Mom and Dad and the others want to see you."

"Why is it people always get hung up on people who are hung up on *other* people?" Rob asked him, once they were out of earshot "And everyone ends up frustrated as hell." Luke looked at Rob inquiringly.

"Meaning?"

"Girls always want to dance with some guy who only wants to dance with some other guy who happens to be straight ..."

"You referring to anyone in particular?"

"Just the sexiest guy in the entire galaxy."

"That's quite a step up from being the most boring man in the universe. I'm flattered." Rob smiled at him.

"Don't let it go to your head. The galaxy is only a small part of the universe, and it's just possible there might be another guy out there who's even sexier than you."

"You're the one with the charm" replied Luke. "I'm just the hired muscle."

"And there's always some other jerk hanging around" continued Rob, warming to his theme "who gets pissed off because the girls don't notice him. Because they're too busy noticing the guy who's hung up on …" He sighed.

"Yeah, I think I get the picture" said Luke, laughing.

"Well, *you* might think it's funny – from a galactic perspective – but I think it's screwed up. Like a dog chasing its tail."

"Speaking from a purely galactic perspective, I would agree with you there" said Luke. "The world is a pretty screwed up place."

"Here comes the Birthday Boy" exclaimed their mother, as though Rob was only about five years old. Everyone fussed around him, the women in particular, asking him whether he had a girlfriend and whether he had any career plans.

"I've got plenty of girlfriends" replied Rob, which was true enough. He was forever fending off female attention. "Haven't really thought much about what I want to do yet. A rodeo rider maybe, or a stock car racing driver."

"No you won't if I have anything to do with it" said his mother. "I won't have you ending up like poor Mrs. Robson's boy." Mrs. Robson's sixteen-year-old son had crashed his motorbike, wrapping it around a tree, and had been killed instantly. His grieving mother had not emerged from the house for an entire year.

"I might become a monk or a hermit then. Like that saint who perched on top of a pillar in the desert for forty years."

"I told you this kid was strange" said Luke to the assembled company. "I somehow don't think you're cut out to be a monk, though" he added in an undertone to Rob, who had his knee pressed tight against Luke's hard muscled thigh underneath the table. The sexual tension between them was palpable. At one point, Luke turned to look at him and Rob dropped his gaze.

"Special request for *Tobacco Road* coming right up" announced the bandleader, clearing his throat over the mike. "Happy birthday, Robbie!"

"Just one dance" coaxed Rob, trying to entice Luke onto the dance floor, with Luke steadily resisting his blandishments.

"All right, you win" said Luke eventually, thinking some energetic exertion might calm him down. He allowed Rob to pull him onto the dance floor, where they attempted their own unique version of a Texas two-step swing, with Luke steering.

"I think the idea is you're supposed to take two steps backward the same time I take two steps forward" said Luke to Rob, who had his left arm resting on Luke's right shoulder. "Otherwise, I'm going to bulldoze straight into you, sugar." Since neither of them knew the correct moves they clowned around on the dance floor, much to the amusement of a crowd of spectators.

Bring dynamite and a crane
Blow it up, start over again...

But it's home, the only life I've ever known
I despise you 'cos you're filthy
But I love you 'cos you're home...

"Couldn't the band play something quieter like *What a Wonderful World* or *Blueberry Hill* instead of that awful *Tobacco Road*?" suggested Edith, covering her ears.

"Come on, Edie, it'll soon be '68" Joe reminded his sister-in-law. "We might like Louis Armstrong or Fats Domino, but the younger generation don't care for that stuff. And if Rob wants to let off some steam, I guess we should let him. It's his birthday."

"Let's liven this joint up" said Rob mischievously, as Luke swung him in close again.

"You asked for it" replied Luke, taking hold of his brother's wrist and swinging him around and around. Rob felt like he was on some diabolical merry-go-round with Luke supplying the centrifugal force.

"Don't be so rough, Luke!" exclaimed Connie, as Rob fell against a table and a tray of drinks went flying. He staggered dizzily to his feet, laughing manically in much the same way as when he'd cheated death on the now defunct drag strip, and cannoned straight into Luke's arms. Sandy and Judy were watching from the sidelines with bemused expressions, arms folded across their chests, as the brothers became rowdier and less restrained.

"Lively enough for you?" Luke asked Rob, who was feeling light-headed and giddy from his crazy carousel ride.

"Guess who'll be picking up the tab" sighed Joe resignedly. "I know it's his birthday and all, but why can't he just have a normal dance with some girl his own age?"

"He's getting over-excited again" observed his wife, her eyes on her youngest son. "We ought to stop them, honey, before they do some real damage."

"Luke should really know better" muttered Joe. "Boys! That's enough, boys!"

"I'm going to ride the bull" announced Sandy suddenly, after staring moodily at Rob and Luke. "Why should they have all the fun?"

"Don't be an idiot" protested Judy, trying to stop her. "You'll just make a fool of yourself." Sandy marched off and mounted the mechanical bull in her mini skirt and knee-high patent leather boots, ignoring the unwritten rule that bronco busting was strictly for the boys.

"Go, baby!" shouted a male onlooker encouragingly. "Any time you wanna ride me, I'm up for it." Sandy was bucked off within seconds and sent sprawling to the floor. Luke and Rob rushed over to offer their assistance, whilst Bruce grinned broadly as he caught a glimpse of her cotton underwear: "Now that's the kind of entertainment I like." Sandy was tugging at her skirt in a futile attempt to protect her modesty.

"You alright?" said Rob to Sandy, as Luke lifted her to her feet. She turned on him.

"Drop dead, Robbie Turnbull."

"Huh? What did I do?" Luke laughed at Rob's confusion.

"Hey, what about his birthday bumps?" shouted Bruce." Come on, Luke, let's do the honours. You grab his arms, I'll get his feet."

"I think we might let him off this time" said Luke, resisting the impulse to brush away a lock of damp hair that had fallen across Rob's temple.

"Oh, no. You don't get out of it *that* easily" persisted Bruce, who was trying to drag him away from Luke. Not for the first time Luke wondered why Rob tolerated Bruce. They'd hung out together on and off since sixth grade, but it was more a question of Bruce hanging around Rob rather than the reverse, in the hope that some of the glamour surrounding Rob would rub off on him.

"Cage me" said Rob to Luke suddenly. This was a private code they used when Rob wanted his brother to shield him from unpleasant situations or annoying people who were pestering him. Luke came up behind him and locked Rob in his muscular arms. He understood that whenever Rob made this request it was because he felt threatened and wanted to keep the world at bay. Or, in this instance, because he was simply weary of all the unwelcome attention.

"Leave him be" said Luke to Bruce, who shrugged and turned away, defeated by the marked closeness between the two brothers – an intimacy he vaguely envied. The Turnbulls were noted for their clannishness, forming a charmed circle few outsiders were able to penetrate. Rob and Luke returned to the table where their relatives were seated. As Rob reached for another Tequila slammer, Luke moved it out of his grasp. "Think you've have had enough of those. You look like you're still in orbit." Rob's gaze was slightly unfocussed, and his behaviour was becoming increasingly impulsive. Luke wouldn't put it past him to fling his arms around his brother and declare his love in front of everyone.

"No, I haven't." Rob reached across Luke for the glass, and they engaged in a playful tussle for a minute – with Rob attempting to retrieve his drink and Luke equally obdurate in withholding it from him.

"Luke, don't be such a spoilsport" exclaimed their Aunt Edith. "After all, it *is* his birthday." Luke refrained from pointing out that his brother had been prescribed anti-depressants which didn't mix well with alcohol, since this was private business which didn't concern anyone outside the immediate family. After a while Rob tired of this game, since Luke was clearly not going to allow him to have another alcoholic drink. He was far more likely to give him a dressing-down in that soldierly tone he used whenever he thought his younger brother's behaviour was a little wild and needed reining in. Rob had only seen Luke drunk once before - at a *Welcome Home* party held at the exact same venue – a few days after he returned from Vietnam. He generally stopped after three or four beers, but on this occasion people had been buying him drinks all night long and Luke was visibly inebriated, though still capable of functioning on his feet. Rob and Bruce had been standing to one side, doubled over with mirth, whilst Luke fumblingly inserted the wrong change into the cigarette vending machine – wondering why it failed to dispense a pack – before making a second attempt with similar results.

"Sonofabitch. Goddamn machine's not working" swore Luke, seizing it with both hands and shaking it roughly.

"Would you like me to try?" offered Bruce. "Brute force won't solve the problem."

"Wanna bet?" countered Luke, bringing his knee up with such force it loosened the wall brackets. He then ripped the machine off the wall, before pocketing a pack of Marlboros. Rob and Bruce followed him around the room to see what he would do next, giggling helplessly at his antics. After crashing into a startled couple on the dance floor "Sorry, folks, I thought you were a coupla scarecrow decoys put there to fool me..." (at least that's what they thought he'd muttered) Luke ended up sprawled across a leather banquette, fending off all comers with one arm, and fell into a light doze. Bruce had then dared Rob to leap on top of Luke as a prank. Rob was the only person in the room who would have dared to take such liberties, and had dive-bombed his brother, landing on top of him. Luke half sat up, then flipped Rob over in a lightning swift manoeuvre akin to a crocodile's death roll, before going through the motions of humping him: "Pleased to meet you too, Lucille." He later claimed he'd known it was Rob who jumped him, and that he was just playing along to give them both a scare.

"Luke…" Rob had his elbow on Luke's shoulder and was fingering his collar. Luke looked at him questioningly. "Can I spend the night with you?"

"Not advisable."

"Why? You let me stay with you when we got back from Lennie's Bar that night." On the night in question, their father had appeared early the following morning and knocked on the door, wanting to know if Rob was with his brother since he wasn't in his bedroom.

"He's fine. He had one too many last night and we didn't want to disturb you" Luke had said, before adding "He's still sleeping it off" to forestall any further questions. His father had appeared to accept this explanation, but Luke had felt uncomfortable about the subterfuge. He was normally forthright in his dealings with others. There was only one bedroom in his cabin, and Rob had not slept on the couch as he had implied, but had shared his bed.

"If you don't know the answer to that – tonight of all nights - then you've obviously had too much to drink" Luke now replied, gently removing Rob's fingers from his collar. Rob turned away, blinking back tears. Luke glanced at him then excused himself, saying he was going outside for some fresh air. At the door he turned slightly and held up five fingers. Rob gazed after him, biting his lip, and after about five minutes got up from the table to follow his brother outside.

"You know, I think Rob would follow Luke to the ends of the earth" observed Connie to her husband, who didn't reply. "He's hardly spoken a word to any of the guests who've been specially invited to celebrate his birthday. If he doesn't come back in soon I'm going to have to apologise for his behaviour."

Joe watched Rob leave, his thoughts in a turmoil. He had an idea something funny was going on between his two boys, some kind of monkey business – for want of a better term - and he didn't like it. It didn't feel right. What on earth was so important that they had to leave the party, ignoring all the other guests, in order to talk in private? As if they didn't spend enough time together. Only the other week Luke had stayed over to watch some Western about Wyatt Earp. Connie and Joe had settled themselves on the couch, and Rob had perched on the arm of Luke's armchair, attempting to squeeze himself into a space beside his brother. As he was about to tip himself into Luke's lap, Luke had put out a restraining arm: "*Pas ce soir, Josephine.*" Rob had ended up sitting on the floor, leaning back against Luke's legs, prompting Joe to observe "That can't be comfortable, Rob. Why don't you sit in a chair like the rest of us? You're not a child any more."

"I *am* comfortable" Rob had insisted. "Luke doesn't mind, do you?" Luke had shrugged noncommittally as Rob settled himself between his brother's knees. Rusty had also stationed himself at Luke's feet, his tail thumping the floor rhythmically. Following the gunfight at the OK Corral, Earp was arrested for murder and decided to go after the gang who had killed his younger brother, becoming an outlaw himself.

"Adios, amigo" said Luke, as Earp shot and killed one of Ike Clanton's gang, whom he'd tracked all the way to Mexico. Rob had become quite carried away with the action unfolding on the screen, yelling "Get him, Wyatt! Kill him!" Rusty had started barking simultaneously, picking up on Rob's excitement, and Luke had put a hand on his collar to quieten him down.

"Looks like I've got two dogs" Luke had joked. "Which one do I pat first?" That was Luke all over - easy come easy go – a joke for every occasion. "One's straining at the leash, and the other's going stir crazy. Down, boy." And then he'd leaned forward, massaging his brother's shoulders. "Think I'd better give this one a bone." Rob had dissolved into laughter, covering his face with his hands. Connie hadn't noticed anything, but Joe was sure Luke had meant something else, Rob's blushes being a dead giveaway. And then about a couple of weeks ago Rob had gone into town to see some pals of his, according to Connie, and Luke had gone after him in the Chevy. They had returned together later that evening, but Rob had spent the night with Luke. Ordinarily Joe would have thought nothing of it, if it weren't for the fact that the door of the bunkhouse had been locked when he walked up the following morning. Luke never locked the front door. There was absolutely no reason to, unless he didn't want someone barging in on them. Luke had stood in the doorway, effectively blocking his entry. The more he thought about it the uneasier he became.

Earlier in the evening Rob had been agitated and restless until Luke had eventually showed up, half an hour late. Rob had looked starstruck, as if Captain Marvel or Superman had decided to drop by. He really should have grown out of all this boyish hero worship by now, thought Joe, frowning. He had watched them exchange several intense stares and lingering looks during the course of the evening – it was almost as if they were flirting with each other – and Luke didn't appear to be doing much to discourage his younger brother's adulation. Before Rob had followed his brother outside, Joe had seen him ask Luke something with an expression of such earnestness that it had caught Joe's attention. Luke's reply had evidently distressed him, and he had become quiet and withdrawn. Few people in the room were aware of Rob's fragile mental state, but Luke of all people should have known better.

Luke was in a corner of the parking lot out back, one knee cocked, the heel of his boot resting against the wall. He looked up as Rob approached him.

"Hey there, young fella."

"Hello" said Rob shyly.

"Come here" said Luke, as his brother stood there hesitantly for a moment. Rob went up to him and took hold of Luke's strong wrists.

"Thanks for getting rid of Rick earlier. It was never meant to go anywhere…what are you laughing at?"

"I wouldn't like to be in his shoes" said Luke. "You set up this guy for the sole purpose of making me jealous – have I got that right?" Rob nodded, realising too late that he was doing everything wrong. According to Loubelle's plan he was supposed to pretend he was interested in Rick in order to drive Luke wild with jealousy, but he couldn't seem to stop himself from blurting out his true feelings to his brother. "And then he's supposed to just fade into the background. Did it occur to you he might develop feelings for you?"

"No. That wasn't supposed to happen."

"Perhaps you underestimate your charm." Rob pressed the palms of his hands against Luke's, their fingers interlocked, a little game he liked to play. Then Luke did a very unexpected thing. He raised one of Rob's hands to his lips and kissed it. Rob gazed at him wonderingly.

"Why did you do that?"

"I don't know" confessed Luke. He had simply obeyed an impulse. Sometimes Rob would hold out a hand to him as if he were a young crown prince, exacting loyalty from a liege lord or favourite knight. The only time Luke ever took another man's hand in his was to shake it when introducing himself, or to give a triumphant high five. "I'm glad you're here because I want to have a talk with you" Luke now said. That sounded ominous. Rob was filled with a sense of foreboding and suddenly felt very afraid. When Luke said he wanted "a little talk" with someone, the other guy generally came off worse. It was like when Jesse James invited someone who had double-crossed him to go for "a ride" with him. The other guy never came back. Was Luke going to tell him that the relationship couldn't go anywhere, and that it was over between them? Everything will go black and the world will come to an end. Please don't send me into the darkness, Luke, he silently entreated. He squeezed his eyes tight shut and bowed his head, as if awaiting an executioner's blow. His hand, which remained clasped in Luke's, trembled.

"Robbie...look at me." Luke waited until he looked up, then said "Would you like to come out with me on a date?" Rob opened his mouth to say something, but seemed quite lost for words. "It occurred to me" continued Luke, seeing his confusion "that one day some guy is going to ask you out. Rick the Prick has already tried his luck and got nowhere, and since I gather you like me a lot better...I thought I'd lay claim to you first."

"Luke..." Rob's eyes deepened into a more intense blue as he looked into his brother's, the mirror image of his own. "I already belong to you." Luke pulled him into his arms and kissed him. Rob closed his eyes. It was a warm lingering kiss, producing that plunging sensation in the pit of his stomach, as though he were freefalling without a parachute or anything to ground him. It was at that point that Joe walked out onto the parking lot and saw them in a shadowy corner, partially obscured behind a commercial Dumpster. At first all he could make out was Luke kissing someone as Rob's back was to him, then as he took a step forwards he saw his two sons in a passionate embrace. There was no mistaking it for anything other than what it was. It was the kind of kiss that lovers exchange, like the famous beach scene where Burt Lancaster and Deborah Kerr roll around in the surf in *From Here To Eternity*. They were so absorbed in each other they were not aware of his presence. Joe stood stock still in a state of shock. He couldn't believe what he was seeing. And then he rushed forward in a rage and yanked them apart roughly.

"Rob, come here!" Rob clung tightly to Luke for protection, burying his face in Luke's jacket. He couldn't face his father. Luke met Joe's eyes levelly. Then he bent his head and murmured to Rob "I'll take care of this. Go inside. Now." Rob was caught between his brother and father, who ironically were both working towards the same end, to prise him away from Luke. Eventually, Rob came to his senses and fled the scene. Joe turned his attention to his older son.

"You! Do NOT EVER touch my son again." Luke sucked in his breath sharply, but said nothing. "I want you to leave, I want you to move out. I don't want you hanging around my boy." He spoke as if Luke was a complete stranger to him, as if Luke was not also his son, his firstborn, the one who was most like him and in whom he had always taken such paternal pride. And then he turned on his heel and walked off without breaking stride. Luke stood there for a moment, reeling, and slowly put a hand to his forehead as if in great pain. Then he walked towards the Chevy, got in the driver's seat, and drove out of the parking lot. Rob came hurtling out the building a moment later, his parents in pursuit. When he saw the tail-lights of Luke's car disappearing around the bend, he sank to the ground on his knees, sobbing in despair.

Chapter Eleven

Loubelle rolled up the shutters of the bakery humming *"Morning has broken like the first morning..."* as the sun's feeble rays gathered strength, dispelling the darkness. Going to be another bright crisp November day, she observed, although it felt distinctly wintry outside. It would soon be December, time to string up her Christmas decorations and put a tree in the window. She switched on the coffee machine, still humming softly to herself. Her first customers of the day didn't usually arrive before 7:30am so she had plenty of time to warm some muffins in the oven. Five minutes later, Luke Turnbull walked in and slid his six-foot-four frame into a corner seat.

"Why, good morning, Luke" said Loubelle, surprised to see him. He rarely came into the bakery, and certainly never at this hour. As she walked towards his table to take his order, she noticed he looked dishevelled and unshaven.

"Louisa Belle." He acknowledged her presence with a nod. He always pronounced her name in full – the only person in town who did - with that slight Southern drawl of his. His voice was gravelly and deep, sounding a little hoarse.

"You look pretty rough. Been tomcatting around all night?" She realised her mistake as soon as she had spoken. He had a bleak look in his eyes, as though he'd just lost someone dear to him.

"An all-nighter at the Drive-In will do that to a fella. *Night of the Zombies, The Day the Aliens Landed* and I don't know what else. I kind of lost track at about 3am." He was attempting to make a joke of it, but she could see he was in no joking mood. She drew up a chair opposite him and leaned forward earnestly.

"What's the matter, hon? Something's wrong, isn't it?" He looked at her.

"Do you think I could get a coffee?"

"Sure. I've got some banana walnut loaf heating up in the oven. You look like you could use some breakfast." Luke cracked a faint smile.

"You don't happen to have a kissing cousin over in Bell County called Donna, by any chance? Donna's Deluxe Dinette?"

"I know that woman! She's adorable. Wait there. I'll be right back with your coffee." She returned a couple of minutes later with a coffee pot and a plate of banana loaf, which she set before him. "If you want to be left alone, just tell me to scoot."

"You're not bothering me at all." Luke wolfed down the banana loaf and poured himself a coffee. He was like a lot of her male patrons who ate uncomplainingly whatever was put before them, and usually left a generous tip.

"Is it Robbie?" asked Loubelle, unable to help herself. "Is he OK? I am so fond of that boy." Luke looked at her, deliberating as to whether to confide in her.

"You've been a good friend to him" he said slowly. "He thinks very highly of you."

"Not as highly as he thinks of YOU." She paused. "Luke, I know what's been going on. He told me everything, and I would never betray his confidence. I wouldn't breathe a word of this to anyone." Luke nodded gravely.

"I know. If you had, I wouldn't be sitting here." He took out a packet of Winstons and offered her one.

"Thanks, hon, but I'm trying to give up that evil habit."

"My old man found out last night" said Luke suddenly, deciding to trust her. "He saw us."

"Oh Lordy" Loubelle raised her eyes to the ceiling. "I bet Joe practically had a heart attack, and you two…but Luke, wait a minute. Do you mean to tell me that you and Robbie are an *item*? I always thought you were straight!" Luke laughed.

"Last time I looked, yes. I'm the same man I always was. Well, maybe not." He amended his statement to reflect the seismic shift that had occurred: it felt as though the world had tilted on its axis. "Something has changed between us. Don't ask me how it happened because I couldn't tell you. We weren't doing anything much. It was just a kiss, but…ah…" Luke grimaced at the memory of his father's reaction.

"That poor boy must be out of his mind! Where is he? And why are you here, all by yourself?"

"My old man kicked me out. Told me to leave and not come back" said Luke simply. He had always had a good relationship with his father, and Joe's words had deeply wounded him. Despite that, he bore no ill feeling or resentment towards his father. What he had witnessed last night must have come as a terrible shock, enough to unhinge any parent.

"What? But that's just awful. I can't believe it." As the doorbell tinkled, Loubelle looked around. "Do you mind if I just go and serve that customer? I'll be right back. Don't move."

"I'm not going anywhere." Loubelle was back within minutes.

"Luke, what are you going to do?" Don't you go breaking that boy's heart like you broke Cindy's, she thought. You are his entire world.

"Haven't thought that far ahead." Luke considered his position. "Two horrible clichés have just occurred to me. Face the music, or get the hell out of Dodge."

"If you left town, it would kill Robbie. You do realise that?" Luke nodded soberly. If his father thought he was going to just walk away without a word to his mother or brother, he had another think coming. He rose to his feet.

"I'm going to head over there now…"

"And take the bull by the horns? Another horrible cliché." Luke smiled at her.

"I can see why Rob likes you." He peeled off a $5 dollar bill. "Keep the change."

"Don't be ridiculous, Luke. That's way too much."

"You're worth every cent. See you round, Louisa Belle." And I can see why Robbie likes YOU, she thought, as he walked out the door. And to think that only the other day she had been sighing to an elderly patron "Nothing ever happens in this hick town. I'm just about to keel over with boredom." She was rooting for Robbie and Luke. A love affair between two brothers – who ever heard of such a thing? The scandal would rock this little community to the core if anyone ever got to hear about it. But they wouldn't hear about it from her. Loubelle always kept her promises.

****

Luke pulled up outside his parents' house, and got out of the car. His mother came rushing outside to meet him, and Luke caught her in his arms.

"Luke, you've got to tell your father it's all just a terrible misunderstanding. I'm sure he didn't mean what he said to you yesterday. Grown men hug each other all the time. He got the wrong end of the stick as usual…" Luke realised his father had not told his mother what he had actually seen, and could hardly blame him.

"Where's Rob?"

"He ran off up into the woods before we could stop him. He had some crazy notion you'd be up there – where have you been, Luke? And Joe's gone after him. He's bound to find your brother soon, Rusty will pick up his scent, but I'm so worried …and you know your father has this heart condition…"

"All right. I'll catch him up." Luke set off at a run towards the mountain trail behind the bunkhouse. About half a mile up he heard Rusty barking excitedly, and seconds later came across his father, who was red in the face and breathing hard. He glared as Luke caught up with him.

"What are *you* doing here?"

"What do you think? I'll go get Robbie – I think I know where he is. Sit down and take it easy. You don't look so good." Luke tried to get his father to sit down on a fallen log, but Joe shook him off angrily.

"You've got some nerve."

"Yep. Must've inherited that from you." Joe wasn't actually all that surprised to see Luke, who'd always had a lot of gumption. The apple never fell very far from the tree.

Luke found Rob in the clearing by the creek head, where he knew he'd be. He was pounding a tree with his fists in frustration. He had expected to find Luke camping out in their old tree house, but his brother was nowhere to be seen. Hearing Rusty barking and thinking his father was right behind him, he yelled defiantly "You can't stop me from seeing my brother! He won't just go off and leave me. He'll come back. I know he will!"

"Damn straight" said Luke, grabbing him around the waist from behind and lifting him off the ground.

"I knew you'd come. Luke...what, what are you doing?" Luke had retrieved the coil of rope they kept underneath a boulder, and slung one end around a tree. Before Rob could protest, he had tied him securely to the tree and stood back to admire his handiwork. Rob still somehow managed to look like a million dollars wearing nothing but a torn T-shirt and faded jeans, his arms scratched by thorns, and his face smudged and tear-stained. Little darling, thought Luke. He had a sudden image of Rob clinging to him like a frightened child last night, when their father had unexpectedly shown up.

"Sorry, kiddo. I need to go check on Dad, and I can't trust you not to run off again. Not an ideal solution, but the best I could come up with at such short notice."

"Luke...come back!" Luke disappeared back down the trail, to where his father was resting. He was mopping his face with a handkerchief.

"You alright?" asked Luke, taking his arm. Joe stared at him as if he'd taken leave of his senses.

"Luke, what in the world…where's Robbie? Did you find him?"

"Don't worry, he's not going anywhere. I tied him to a tree to keep him out of trouble." Joe's mouth worked as though he were figuring out what response he should make, then without warning he suddenly chuckled.

"I'll be darned." Luke squared up to his father, feet apart, his right fist jammed into his front jeans pocket.

"We need to talk."

"About last night, the things I said to you…" began his father.

"You saw what you saw." said Luke. No point in pussyfooting around. "It's a helluva thing for any man to come to terms with. Most men would have reacted the same way you did."

"Your mother and I make allowances for Rob, because we know the boy is mentally unstable. He can't help a lot of the things he says and does. What's *your* excuse?" snapped Joe.

"I haven't got one" said Luke finally. What excuse was there for falling for someone's charms? There was no telling where or when Cupid's arrow might strike. Luke didn't think he was mortally wounded, and in time the madness would probably pass, as most things eventually did. His father shook his head, as if trying to clear it of a vision he found too disturbing to contemplate.

"But *why*, Luke? What in God's name got into you? I just cannot make head or tail of it." His father looked bewildered. Luke shrugged.

"They say Helen's face launched a thousand ships. But we can't blame Helen for that, can we. I've been thinking about it, and you were right. There are some impulses you shouldn't give into."

"Luke, I've been thinking too. I couldn't sleep all night. We don't want you to leave home. It would break your mother's heart. You don't want to break your mother's heart, do you?"

"No" said Luke slowly "No, I wouldn't want to do that." He didn't add that his father would not be able to prevent Rob from following him. That certainty remained unspoken between them. His parents would lose both their sons if he left. "You didn't tell her." It was a statement, not a question. His father shook his head. "Best if it stays that way" said Luke.

"You know, I should have tamed that wild streak in him years ago" said Joe. "I knew about it. When you were boys, even when I knew that he was in the wrong I always punished you, not him. I used the excuse that because you were older you should have known better."

"I'm none the worse for it" replied Luke.

"I could never raise my hand against that boy, even when he deserved it" went on Joe. "Maybe I'm to blame for this." When they had fought or misbehaved, Joe had chosen to beat Luke, saying "When I was a boy, my father used to break off a switch from a tree and thrash us. This hurts me more than it hurts you." As Luke had stood there stoically, just taking it, Rob would rush up to his father, yelling "That's not fair! Why are you hitting him? Luke didn't do anything. I started it." He would stand before his father, head bowed, waiting for a punishment that never came.

"He's always gone his own sweet way" Joe now said. "It's just the way he is." Luke gave his father a cool measured look. *You thought that because Rob had the face of a cherub when he was a kid he'd never get into trouble, that he didn't need parental guidance?* It was as if, very early on, Joe had determined that his eldest son was a true chip off the old block, the one who would eventually step into his shoes, whilst Rob was the cute baby of the family – cosseted and humoured – but never taken too seriously. But they had all been complicit in that, Luke reflected, his mother included.

"This whole business – Rob's mental condition - is putting an enormous strain on your mother" continued his father. "She shouldn't have to…"

"-Damned right she shouldn't have to! You're his father. He's got two parents, right?" Where were you, thought Luke, when I was in Vietnam and he was running amok, racing dragsters at insane speeds and Christ knows what else. It was a tribute to Rob's driving skills and his nerve behind the wheel that he'd actually made it through his teens in one piece. It had been Luke, not Joe, who had taught him how to drive and use a shotgun. As though echoing his thoughts Joe said "I know I should have been the one to teach him to handle a gun, but I left it to you because you know what you're doing."

"I can teach him how to fight properly and so on, but I'm not his father, you are. Reason I'm his number one hero is because you don't spend enough time with him."

"I've tried, Luke. God knows. But I'm no good with emotional stuff. Women understand these things better. And I'm busy out at the sawmill. That's why I hired this doctor, so Rob could get the professional help he needs."

"Fire him" said Luke. "You and I could do a better job than that wiseacre. He's come up with just about every harebrained notion under the sun apart from demonic possession and speaking in tongues." Joe chuckled. They both viewed psychiatrists as being little better than snake oil salesmen, peddling their dubious wares to a credulous public.

"The thing is, Luke, I *have* to keep paying this shrink. How do you think Rob's going to react if he's put in a war zone? He's not as tough as you. War messes with your head, and his head's messed up enough as it is. Even after the Japanese surrender in '45 many of us couldn't hear a Japanese voice without wanting to throw up or beat their heads in. It was years before I got back to being the person I was before I was shipped out, and I was one of the lucky ones. If the war in Vietnam carries on and Rob's declared mentally sound how can we keep him safe?"

"Point taken. I suggest we bring Rob into the business. Teach him some of the stuff you taught me." He meant woodwork and construction, using lumber and sawmill equipment. When Rob had once picked up a chainsaw and nearly lost control, instead of instructing him how to use it safely Joe had growled impatiently "Don't let that bubblehead anywhere near a chainsaw, will you." In Luke's experience most guys made a few mistakes on their first try, and there had been no need to make such a comment in Rob's hearing. On another occasion, his father had handed Rob a coil of fencing wire with only the most rudimentary instructions before disappearing. During a lull in the work, Luke had doubled back to check on him, and noticed the blood trail. He'd taken Rob back to the pickup where they kept a first-aid kit and bandaged up his shredded hands tenderly. Joe had merely been exasperated: "Didn't it occur to you to put on a pair of cowhide gloves?" Rob had just stared at the ground, biting his lip, and Luke had rounded on his father: "Didn't it occur to *you* to tell him to wear some gloves? He's never done this before." Because his eldest son happened to be bigger and stronger and picked things up faster, Joe hadn't bothered to put in the extra time and effort with his youngest son.

"I know. I should have done that years ago." Joe sighed. "I've left it too late...."

"No you haven't" said Luke. "He's still pretty young, and willing to learn. All he needs is a little encouragement. If we take him to work alongside us it'll keep him occupied, and that way we can keep an eye on him." Joe suddenly smiled.

"I guess between the two of us we're gonna lick him into shape."

"Something like that."

"Think I'd better go and untie him now" said Luke. They could hear Rob calling for his brother: "Sheriff, don't leave me like this." Joe raised his eyebrows. *"Sheriff?"* Luke laughed. "He thinks he's Billy the Kid and I'm Pat Garrett or Wyatt Earp. Just a game we sometimes play."

"Luke, this *cannot* go on" said Joe emphatically. "Whatever's going on between you and Rob, I cannot tolerate that kind of…" He struggled for words to define something he could not, and did not want, to comprehend "tomfoolery going on underneath my roof."

"I'm not asking you to." Luke wondered whether his father would have referred to the act of kissing his future wife whilst courting her as "tomfoolery." Probably not. What went on between a man and a woman was legitimate, that is to say it was sanctioned by society.

"Can you promise me that you won't ever…"

"No, I'm sorry, I can't promise you that." Luke possessed enough self-knowledge to realise that he could not make the promise his father was asking for, pleading for. He had begun to develop feelings for Rob, feelings which threatened to turn his world upside down. After last night, Luke had discovered he enjoyed kissing Rob. He liked the way Rob's full lower lip butted up against his own, the way his mouth parted and his eyes closed when Luke explored it with his tongue, the sweet warm pressure of Rob's body leaning into his when they slept in the same bed. At Rob's birthday party last night, he'd been aware of a growing attraction and desire for his brother, the electricity between them crackling like a live wire. He had not been able to keep his eyes off his brother. And he thought Rob was aware of this. Just as he'd been perfectly aware that Rob couldn't take his eyes off *him*. When Rob had asked if they could spend the night together Luke had made the only sensible answer he could in the circumstances, with all eyes on them. Luke had briefly glimpsed his brother's tears before Rob turned his head away, but had been unable to express the tenderness he felt, to reassure him that no rejection was implied or intended. At one point during the long endless night he had taken out Rob's note from the inside of his belt to re-read:

Dear Luke,

This is hard so I'll just come out and say it. I don't know how it happened and I wish it hadn't, but I think I'm in love with you. Maybe the doctor will be able to fix it, but I don't think so. I hope you won't feel disgusted when you read this, but it's not my fault and I've tried not to. Nothing is working. If you don't want to speak to me ever again I will understand but... Anyway, I can't think of anything else to say except I love you with all my heart. Rob.

He couldn't quite decipher the sentences that been crossed out, apart from the words *"...marry you..."* I love you too, baby, he thought, I'll take care of you. His brother had offered him everything he had to offer – his body, soul, and heart – and Luke considered it too precious a gift to throw away lightly. Luke chose his next words carefully. There wasn't any way he could sugar-coat this, make it more palatable in order to spare his father's sensibilities; nor was he going to offer up some half-assed apology and pretend that things would go on the same as they had before.

"What I can promise you" Luke now told his father "is that we'll keep it under *my* roof, and that I will never harm him. He's my brother, after all." He looked directly at his father. The unspoken implication was that his son was better off with Luke than with some other strange man who might damage him. Better the devil you know. Joe nodded slowly. He had no choice but to accept Luke's terms.

"And nobody else knows about this?" asked his father.

"It will go no further" Luke assured him.

"All right. We keep this thing in the family" his father said, having reached a decision. "Your mother need never know. Nobody need know."

"Agreed."

"And in the meantime?" asked Joe.

"We carry on protecting him" said Luke. "Like we've always done."

Rob glanced up at his brother reproachfully through his eyelashes. "I wasn't expecting to get tied up on our first date." Luke suppressed a smile.

"Any idea what trouble you've caused, huh? You little bundle of mischief." Rob widened his eyes innocently. His features had taken on that fresh-faced angelic look they sometimes did, making him look like a twelve-year-old.

"Sir?" Luke was careful to avoid looking into those beguiling blue eyes. Oh no you don't, Johnny Angel. It was a chilly autumnal day, and he could feel the goose bumps on his brother's bare arms as he untied him.

"Here, put this on." He took off his jacket, and put it around Rob's shoulders. "What happened to your forehead?" he asked in a more tender tone.

"I tripped over a root and hit it against a rock." Rob had a tendency to run through the woods at breakneck speed. When he was younger he had actually knocked himself out on two occasions, losing consciousness for a few moments. Luke fingered the bump. The cut had stopped bleeding but there was a little trail of dried blood by his right temple.

"Now what did I warn you would happen before the night was over?" Rob thought for a moment, and then it came to him.

"*It's my party and I'll cry if I want to.* That should have been Dad's signature tune:

*Nobody knows where my Robbie has gone
But Luke left the same time
Why was he holding his hand
When he's supposed to be mine?*

*It's my party and I'll cry if I want to, cry if I want to
You would cry too if it happened to you...*"

Luke was trying hard not to laugh. "You look sexy when you haven't shaved" said Rob. "I guess you didn't get much sleep either last night."

"Not much." Luke had spent an uncomfortable night with the front seat reclined as far as it would go, dozing fitfully and trying to ignore the constant flickering from the movie screen. "Oh, by the way, I never got a chance to give you your birthday present last night. Hunted high and low for a straitjacket but couldn't find one." Luke smiled at Rob and pulled a tiny gift box out of his pocket. "So I got you this instead." After Rob had left him on Main Street Luke had walked into the jewellery story and enquired, with some initial embarrassment, whether they could engrave a signet ring for him.

"Thank you" breathed Rob, when he could finally speak. "But I thought you already gave me my present." He was thinking about the way Luke had kissed him the other night. He had thought of little else since. It was the reason he had known Luke would come back, would never walk off without a backwards glance: *Frankly, my dear, I don't give a damn.* His brother did give a damn. He allowed Luke to slip the ring onto the ring finger of his right hand, recalling how Luke had taken his hand in his and examined it carefully: it was a perfect fit. The engraving was a very simple design - with their two initials L and R intertwined – but it meant the world to Rob, as Luke had known it would. "Does this mean…?"

"It means you're my sweetheart" Luke told him. "If I ever catch you with another man…" Rob didn't know whether he was kidding or whether he was serious, but didn't care. His brother was the only one for him, and always would be. He suddenly flung his arms around Luke, who held him against his chest, warming him with his body and tangling his fingers in his hair. Rob covered his throat with ardent kisses, his mouth coming up against the rough stubble beneath his jaw line. "Not here, Robbie" said Luke quietly. Rob's breath felt warm against his skin. "Dad's waiting for us." They came apart reluctantly.

"Wanna hear the rest of the song?" asked Rob.

Robbie and Luke just walked through the door
Like a queen with his king
Oh what a birthday surprise

Robbie is wearing his ring

It's my party and I'll cry if I want to…"

Luke started to laugh despite himself. "Hey, go easy on Dad, alright? He's had quite a shock."

"Sorry" murmured Rob, who had not meant to make light of what had happened last night, or of their father's reaction. "Sometimes I act the opposite of how I feel. It's like that time when I laughed all through Grandma's funeral even though I felt really sad inside, and Mom and Dad were furious at me." Luke nodded to signify that he understood; he'd been known to laugh himself in dire situations. In Vietnam some of the guys had been known to stand around cracking macabre jokes directly after a kill: their emotions were all strung out and it was one way of dissociating themselves from the immediate horror of their surroundings.

"It's been one helluva night. Take my arm if you like. So you don't trip over again."

"You're a true gent. But I only tripped because it was still dark outside then." They moved off down the trail together, Rob's arm linked through Luke's, not because he needed the balance but because he thought it was rather romantic. "Luke, about what you asked me last night just before Dad showed up."

"I haven't forgotten. They're still showing that Halloween double feature at the drive-in." Luke had spent some time thinking about where he could take his brother for a date without attracting public attention, and had come up with the unoriginal idea of returning to the drive-in movie theatre. It would be dark outside and if he parked up somewhere inconspicuous at the back of the lot, chances are they wouldn't be disturbed. Though he'd have to keep an eye out for those carhop waitresses, who had a tendency to glide right up to the window on their roller-skates, forgetting they were supposed to wait for the drivers to switch on their headlights - the signal they were ready to order: *"Good evening, sir. What I can get you?"* prompting lewd suggestions from certain male patrons, until they were slapped down by their dates.

"You know, most guys would just ask me out instead of saying *'I thought I'd stake my claim first'* continued Rob, giving his brother an oblique glance. "That would be the normal thing to say."

"I'm not most guys" replied Luke. "If we get too bored with the plot we can always get better acquainted in the backseat." The thrilling implications of this silenced Rob for a minute. "I'll swing by and pick you up tomorrow evening at about seven" he added, as if they didn't live a mere few hundred yards from each other.

"I'll have to check my diary to see whether I'm available" replied Rob in what he hoped was a normal tone. Luke had to smile at that. Perhaps Rob would eventually tire of all the flirtatious banter once the novelty wore off, thought Luke. But not too soon, he hoped. He rather enjoyed it.

"I look forward to our date" said Luke, who was still smiling. "Though I may have to subvert the order of Caesar's motto." As Rusty came bounding up to them, worrying a dead rabbit between his jaws, Rob struggled to work out his meaning: *I came, I saw, I conquered.* That was the right order. I conquered, I saw, I came, the reverse order. But Luke had said "subvert." There were times when he felt outmanoeuvred by his brother and totally out of his depth. This was one of those moments.

Connie was standing on the front porch when she saw her husband and sons walk up to the house, Rob cutting a much slighter figure between his father and brother, both of them strong, tall broad-shouldered men. They were conversing amongst themselves as though nothing out of the ordinary had happened. Rob was holding on to Luke's arm and looked positively radiant, though last night he had been inconsolable, sobbing as if his heart would break when Luke had driven off. The elaborate birthday cake had remained untouched, and she and Joe had been obliged to make their excuses to the assembled guests before taking him home. Close relatives were merely told that Rob had suffered an "asthma attack" due to over-stimulation, which had prompted more questions than it had answered from puzzled bystanders. As they approached the porch steps, Rob suddenly broke away from his father and brother, and started performing cartwheels across the yard, spinning like a Catherine wheel, while Luke turned to smile at his antics.

"I don't know where that boy gets his energy from" remarked Connie. "It's exhausts me just to look at him." A look passed between her husband and eldest son, a look she couldn't quite interpret. She would never understand men, she thought. But it was clear they had resolved their differences, and that Luke would not be leaving. Life would go on much the same as before. Everything would be all right.

****

The next morning, a large bouquet of flowers was delivered to the bakery. "A secret admirer?" grinned the delivery boy, who stood on the doorstep.

"Top secret" smiled Loubelle as she read the note inside:

"To Loubelle my dearest friend,

General, our campaign was successful! I owe you my life, my happiness, everything.

Love from Robbie"